Need punched at him from e

"Excuse me," Kalina said

"I have some checks that nee

tant wasn't at her desk."

Behind his desk, Rome s___, ___ ___ ___ ___

slowly over teeth that were suddenly too sharp to be

human. His nostrils flared as he inhaled and let her scent

permeate throughout his system.

It was her.

Inside, his cat roared, leaping at the surface as if it

knew her, too. It had been two years since he'd seen her.

He'd thought about her, too much to even contemplate

at this moment. Thought about her, dreamed about her,

fantasized about her. But he had no idea who she was or

where she went that night.

Now she was here.

TEMPTATION RISING

A. C. ARTHUR

St. Martin's Paperbacks

This is a work of fiction. All of the characters, organizations, and events portrayed in this novel are either products of the author's imagination or are used fictitiously.

TEMPTATION RISING

Copyright © 2012 by A. C. Arthur.
Excerpt from *Seduction's Shift* copyright © 2012 by A. C. Arthur.

All rights reserved.

For information address St. Martin's Press, 175 Fifth Avenue, New York, NY 10010.

ISBN: 978-0-312-54910-7

Printed in the United States of America

St. Martin's Paperbacks edition / April 2012

St. Martin's Paperbacks are published by St. Martin's Press, 175 Fifth Avenue, New York, NY 10010.

10 9 8 7 6 5 4 3 2 1

For Kathy Jenkens
Some people are only in your life for a season,
yet they have a lasting effect.

Glossary of Terms

Shadow Shifter Tribes

Topètenia - The jaguars
Croesteriia - The cheetahs

Acordado - The awakening; a Shadow Shifter's first shift

The Assembly - Three elders from each tribe that make up the governing council of shifters in the Gungi

Companheiro - Mate

Companheiro calor - The scent shared between mates

Curandero - The medicinal and spiritual healer of the tribes

Elders - Senior members of the tribe

Ètica - The Shadow Shifter Code of Ethics

Joining - The union of mated shifters

Rogues - Shadow Shifters who have turned from the tribes, refusing to follow the *Ètica*, in an effort to become their own distinct species

Prologue

He could smell her.

The scent was alluring, seductive, and mixed with something else. Fear.

It was the fear that pushed him forward. The knowledge that something was wrong. Quiet steps led him into the towering darkness between two buildings. The air was damp and thick from a day full of summer thunderstorms. The ground was slick with wetness, riddled with small puddles as he moved through the eerie blackness.

She tried to scream.

The sound was muffled, but he heard it. His entire body tensed; every muscle, every ligament stood perfectly still while the sound registered. A woman's scream. Rage boiled inside, rippling along his veins in heavy waves. Inside his cat roared, pushing to the surface with a ferocity that was almost unrecognizable.

He wasn't in the jungle where he could run free, hunt and be hunted. He wasn't beneath the deep green canopy of the rain forest with dense foliage and prickling sheets of cool rain pelting his body. No, he was on the streets of Washington, DC, in the city he'd called home all his adult life. The home of his human half.

This need to fight, to let the cat burst free, wasn't foreign, but it was strange for here and now. Yet as he pressed on, the cat stretched, muscles bunching, eyes focused, the fight inevitable.

Continuing forward, he needed all his strength to hold the animal inside. A warm breeze filtered past, massaging his face, bringing her scent closer. His nostrils flared as by his side fingers wiggled, tingled, burned with claws close to the surface.

His vision was acute. Even in the darkness the shadows ahead took form: a man, large, angry, intent. The woman—the one with the scent that reminded him of some other time, some other place—lay on the wet ground with the man hunched over her. The strange man was between her legs, her skirt pushed up, stockings and underwear ripped off so that she was bared for all to see. He held her hands atop her head, handcuffing both wrists with one powerful hand while his other violated her body. Each time he touched her she squirmed, tried to break free and scream, but something was stuffed into her mouth, muting the sound.

His cat clawed at the surface, scratching at the barrier he'd created to keep it back. It was against their laws, against everything they believed. He could not reveal himself to a human; it would surely begin the extermination of his kind. And yet he could not leave her here. He *would not* leave without helping her. That was also their law: Females were to be protected at any cost. It was that and the aching familiarity of this scene that had him moving forward, not entirely ignoring the doctrine of *Ètica,* but bending it to meet his will.

The beast ripped free with a roar that shook the surrounding buildings, echoing through the night. As if in response the skies opened, dumping sheets or icy rain down onto him. He relished the feel, the scent, the sound of the forest and leapt forward acutely aware of the man frozen in his movements over the woman.

The man didn't move, the idiot staying atop her like an animal protecting its prey. But that was not a problem. His jaguar was loose, hungry for a fight, and seeing an easy battle ahead. Bones stretched and molded as he stripped away his clothes, falling to his knees, muscles and sinew moving, shifting. If the woman was the man's prey, then he might as well kiss it good-bye. What a jaguar hunted, it killed.

Landing on the man's back, the jaguar opened its jaws, teeth sinking into the base of his skull and clamping down. Sound died in the man's throat, much the way the woman's cries for help had died in hers. Stepping back on its hind legs the jaguar pulled back, taking the body now growing limp off the woman. When there was no more movement, the carcass was tossed aside, hitting a wet cinder-block wall with a deafening *smack*.

Rage simmered as the beast recognized its kill. Its first kill here, in this place, since that time. That time when he should have been this strong, should have defended what was his, but hadn't. Guilt assailed him daily, rubbing along his skin like the fur that covered him now. It was second nature, a part of him that he despised but at the same time accepted. He would never be complete because of the past that he could neither change nor forget.

Lifting its rounded head, the cat released another roar of anguish as the scent of the human's blood seeped into its nostrils. Its chest heaved, eyes blurring for just a moment with uncertainty.

Then she moved. Behind him the woman was trying to escape, for he, too, appeared to be her enemy. Her fear was a tangy fragrance, mixed with courage, a stronger musk that struggled to overpower panic. It filled his senses, urged him to turn around, to face her.

This time he saw her through his cat's eyes. She looked back in disbelief, terror magnified a million times. Ripping the gag from her mouth, she let out an ear-piercing scream that had him stepping back.

The memory was quick and painful, slicing through both man and beast like a heated blade. The cat bared its teeth, took a step toward her, and swiped at her in shame. She jumped and it cringed, unable to find the right reaction in this form, almost unwilling to shift back.

Again and again he tried to relieve the ball of fire that racked his body, his senses. Her scent was the same, her fear was real and pure, but in her eyes he saw something else . . . recognition?

Impossible. The similarities were not possible. He was making it up. His beast mixing signals with the man who knew better. In addition to the inner turmoil, the secret was out. The jaguar that was also a man had revealed itself to her, a human.

But when he turned to face her again, to see the fear and disbelief in her eyes one more time, she was gone. He watched her running toward the only exit from the alley. He could have chased after her, would have definitely caught her. Probably should have to ensure her absolute safety. Or absolute silence about what she'd just witnessed.

But he did nothing.

Just like before.

Chapter 1

Two Years Later

It came again last night.

The dream, that is.

With its usual dismal terror it filled her night with an eerie darkness that was still holding on in the early-morning hours. It had taken her longer than usual to shake free of the hazy memory this time, a fact made clear by the late hour she'd stumbled into the shower.

Head tilted back, eyes closed, Kalina let the warm water run over her face. For just a second she was back in that alley, lying on the cold ground as rain began to fall. Those minutes seemed like hours, the fear of him hurting her, possibly killing her becoming a permanent part of her existence. Her heart hammered in her chest but she refused to open her eyes, refused the rescue she knew was there.

It was years ago; she should be over it by now. She'd tried to convince herself and everyone else around her that she was. But the dream just kept coming. The man who saved her life always appeared in the shadow of the night. And so did the beast. She could differentiate between the two, but didn't know for sure if she was supposed to. All she knew was that it was crazy to still have such a vivid memory of that night. She barely remembered the name of the jerk who had attacked her and later died for his efforts, yet she remembered the eyes of the beast.

The dream was always the same, the one she'd had countless times before with the huge black cat that scared the crap out of her.

Okay, to be fair, all cats, even the pudgy calico belonging to her next-door neighbor Mrs. Gilbert, made her nervous. She'd never liked cats, ever. As a little girl she'd crossed the street whenever one was in her direct path. The exact reason why, she'd never been able to pinpoint, just that she didn't like to look at them or hear them.

But in this dream she did both.

She heard its menacing growl as if they were in a cavern, its echo causing her body to tremble. She'd seen it, looked into the yellow-green eyes, felt as if it were speaking to her, and was always left with the same feeling—need. Aside from her terror of the deadly animal, the draw to it was undeniable. Its roar was like a broken cry, a ravaged request for something she didn't know she could give. That was silly, of course, and she usually brushed it off in favor of the scared-as-hell aspect of the dream. Or nightmare, she corrected. Still, there was something that kept the memory of that beast killing the asshole lower-level drug carrier—who'd gotten it into his mind that their deal should be sealed with sex instead of good clean American dollars—alive in her mind.

Six weeks of therapy during her medical leave from the Metropolitan Police Department, and what seemed like endless sessions at which she kept her real feelings inside, revealed she'd despised the drug dealer too much to really harbor any deep emotion about the attack. The fact that she'd managed to somehow break his neck and get away looked good on her employment record. So good that, two years later, she'd received this sweet undercover assignment that could expose an up-and-coming cartel in South America. She supposed she should thank the spineless drug-dealing bastard for something.

Then again, maybe she should have been thanking the beast she was positive had really been the killer. The one she purposely didn't mention to anyone after the attack, or ever. Nobody would believe her. Worse, she would have been demoted to a desk job for sure. Or even dismissed from duty for insanity. And everything she'd worked for, the life and the safety net she'd built for herself, would be destroyed. That wasn't an option for Kalina. So the big black cat with eerie eyes was her secret, one she would never reveal.

The warm water sluicing over her body as she stretched languorously in the shower almost seduced her to stay. The knowledge that she had an important job to do cut the shower short.

She'd just belted her robe and opened the bathroom door when she heard the doorbell. It was way too early for visitors so as she padded through the living room to answer it, she assumed it was Mrs. Gilbert coming to borrow something. The minute her hand touched the knob Kalina felt something. A trickling down her spine, like a warning, had her pausing. Turning the knob, she opened the door and was startled to see a man standing there instead of Mrs. Gilbert.

"Good morning, I have a delivery for a Kalina Harper. Is that you?"

His lips were moving and she heard him speaking but Kalina was more concerned with the growing heat of her body. The robe suddenly felt itchy against her skin; her nipples puckered and she shivered. It was the strangest thing, like a rush of arousal or sudden awareness that she was all female.

"Oh." She cleared her throat, pulled the lapels of her robe closer together. "Yes. I am. Thank you."

His extended arm held an envelope. Kalina reached for it. Their fingers touched and his gaze captured hers. He was tall and lean, his skin an olive tone, his eyes dark. Darker than any she'd ever seen.

"You're welcome," he said, a slow smile beginning to form.

Kalina pulled her hand away, took a step back, and closed the door. His eyes were different, and his smile was . . . she didn't quite know. The whole exchange had been strange.

"No, you're the strange one," she berated herself.

All this reminiscing about beasts in the night and cats across the hall had her jumping at shadows. She didn't have time for this; she was already running late. And that wasn't going to look good to her superiors.

Dressing quickly, Kalina was out of her apartment and on her way into the office half an hour later. This was her world, the one where she was an important officer of the law making a contribution to lives of others. It was her purpose, one she'd never felt she had before. She was no longer the orphan with no one to love and accept her, bouncing from one foster home to the next. No, this time she was exactly where she wanted to be. If lately there'd been a burning need for something more, that didn't matter. There was nothing more, at least not for her. Reaching for the impossible was a waste of time, a distraction she couldn't afford. Nothing besides her commitment to her job was important.

The envelope she'd received this morning, however, might be. So she pulled into the parking garage, parked her car, and opened it.

Something fell out into her lap. It was a photo. Flipping it over, Kalina felt her heart skip a beat then rapidly thump in her chest. It was a picture of her, the night she was attacked. Actually, she remembered as she continued to stare at the picture, it was just before the attack occurred.

Five minutes, that was all she was giving herself. Five minutes to feel concerned, even a little bit afraid. Resting her forehead on the steering wheel, she breathed in and out deeply. She wasn't doing this, fear was not going to dictate her actions. Not again.

Another fifteen minutes passed before Kalina walked through the double glass doors of Reynolds & Delgado, its name written in block letters just above the receptionist's desk. The decor was classy, rich but not overstated, professional but not stuffy. She walked across the glossed wood floor of the empty reception area through an archway; it gave way to a deep blue carpet that muffled the sound of her heels.

Accounting was down the hall and to the right on the fifth floor of the Reynolds Building in downtown DC. The sixth and seventh floors also housed members of the firm, while the first four floors were reserved for parking, and the remaining upper seven floors were occupied by tenants. Her desk was directly across from the office of the chief financial officer, as her position was accounts payable technician. This meant she processed all the outgoing moneys for the firm. It was exactly where she needed to be to trace the money going to South America. All those night courses she'd taken in economics, finance, and accounting had finally paid off.

Settling at her desk, she'd already started convincing herself that the photo was some kind of joke. Maybe from her co-workers at the precinct—they all had sick senses of humor in the narcotics division. Satisfied with that impromptu explanation, she put her purse in the drawer and booted up her computer.

As she waited for the computer to come to life, her throat felt dry. Actually it was more like her tongue felt too thick for her mouth, her back teeth aching a bit. This was something else that had been going on for a couple of weeks, another weird issue she refused to accept as important. Standing, she decided a cup of coffee would be good to get her started. Dan Mathison, the CFO and her immediate supervisor, wouldn't be in for another hour and the two remaining members of the department weren't in yet, so she still had time.

"He's got to be the sexiest man alive," Pam Winston, the fifth-floor receptionist, said with a sigh.

She hadn't been at her desk when Kalina first entered the office, and with a tinge of dread Kalina picked up her pace as she approached the reception desk now.

"At the very least the sexiest in DC," Pam continued.

"Yes, ma'am, I certainly agree." This was Ava Jackson, the paralegal from the estates and trusts department, which was on the other side of the floor.

But just about every time Kalina went to the kitchen these ladies were conversing at the receptionist's desk. She hated that she had to pass this area to get to the kitchen and her desired cup of coffee. Office gossip was another thing that made this particular assignment a headache. And just about every time she walked past these two they were talking about men. Today was no different.

"But he's so angry all the time," Ava was saying.

"I wouldn't say angry, maybe just grouchy." Pam contemplated for a second. "Still, he's the boss, so he can afford to act any way he pleases. And he still looks good. You see him yet this morning?"

"Uh-huh. What's he wearing today?" Ava asked with her contact-gray eyes growing larger.

"That navy-blue suit, the one with the stripes," Pam said, picking up a piece of the mail she was supposed to be opening and then distributing, using it instead to fan herself.

"And the ice-blue tie over the crisp white shirt. Girl, I see him in that every night in my dreams. Love when he wears that suit. Absolutely love it!"

They both laughed loudly as Kalina proceeded to walk by, wishing she'd had simple dreams about a man instead of a cat. This job wasn't permanent for her so making friends with the staff—these particular staff members—wasn't a requirement. Still, she tried to be as cordial as possible, even though their incessant gossiping made her want to poke their eyes out. "Good morning, ladies," she said with a smile that was as fake as the one each of the women was tossing her way.

Pam was a heavyset woman who paid a great deal of attention to her clothes, hair, nails, and makeup. Each day she was flawless, Kalina noted, everything matching right down to the fake tips on her fingernails. Today the color was orange, and it wouldn't have been bad if it weren't overdone, which was always the case with Pam. She twirled one jet-black curl between her fingers, orange rhinestone-encrusted nails clicking together as she did. "Good morning, Kalina."

That shouldn't have sounded snotty, but to Kalina's well-trained ears it did. She ignored it and attempted to keep walking.

"So what do you think about him?" Ava, dressed in a white linen pantsuit with turquoise stilettos that were meant more for the stripper pole than the office, asked her.

"Excuse me?"

Pam expounded, "Since you're new here, we were just wondering what you think about the boss."

"Which one?" she asked absently, as if she hadn't heard their previous conversation.

Ava nodded as if in agreement. "Mr. Delgado is fine, too. But we were talking about Mr. Reynolds."

"I think they're both fantastic lawyers."

Pam's peach-glossed lips turned up while Ava muttered, "Right. Okay."

Kalina didn't stand still long enough to hear the rest of the conversation, and she couldn't care less what they thought of her because of it. Or what they thought of Roman Reynolds. He might be their boss, but he was her suspect. End of story.

Back at her desk with a steaming-hot cup of coffee in hand, she chided herself for thinking about the tall, dark-skinned man with midnight-colored eyes and football-player build. As her fingers moved over the keyboard, she ignored the clench between her thighs while she envisioned his semi-thick lips, strong arms, and big hands.

She'd done a lot of background investigating on Roman Reynolds, age thirty-five, single and sinfully sexy. He was a reputed recluse, one with a hefty bank account and hundreds of women vying for his attention. He was a successful litigation attorney who lived in the Forest Hills District and drove a sleek black Mercedes GL550 SUV.

Finally, though, he was her suspect, not her lover. No matter how much she fantasized otherwise.

There were some people who were born to suffer. Right or wrong didn't matter much. Only the end result was important.

Roman Reynolds sighed, sitting in his high-backed leather office chair looking out the window to the streets of Washington, DC. He was wondering if this was where he was supposed to be.

It seemed he'd come so far in his thirty-five years of life. He'd been through so much and felt, deep within himself, that there was much more to come. More that he couldn't predict but needed to stop. Responsibility weighed on his shoulders heavily, starting with the death of his parents and leading up to the prospect of even more death. It was up to him to do something, to protect the people he cared about, to make the madness stop. Rome didn't take his responsibility lightly.

That was unfortunate for whoever made an enemy of him.

Work was his life, and his life was dedicated to the safety of his people. If he'd had a choice, the circumstances would be different. But he didn't and so it just was.

"You wanted to see me?"

The voice snapping him out of his reverie was that

of Dominick Delgado, his partner and best friend. Turning away from the window and looking up to see Nick peeking into his office, Rome nodded. "Come on in and lock the door."

What they were about to discuss wasn't law-firm business, and Rome didn't want any of the staff accidentally walking in and overhearing them.

"What's up?" Nick asked after walking confidently across the carpeted floor to take a seat in one of the guest chairs.

"Any more news about the attacks?"

Senator Mark Baines and his daughter had been murdered after leaving a fund-raiser three weeks ago. The bodies, found two days after they were reported missing, were mutilated. The report had made Rome uneasy and some of the other shifters suspicious.

"Rogues," Nick said simply. "I checked with the other Faction Leaders and they're reporting similar movement in their zones. They're definitely making a move."

Rome sighed. This news wasn't shocking. But it wasn't what he wanted to hear. They knew about the Rogues—every Faction Leader in every time zone knew about them. They were a group of shifters, defectors from every tribe, who instead of trying to live peacefully among the humans believed they were the superior species. They wanted money and power and had long since carried their rebellious movement against the Assembly and the tribes out of the forest.

"Do we have identification?"

Nick shrugged. "Supposition. Nothing definite. But it could be a problem."

"It could be a big problem. Any thoughts on how to cut it off as soon as possible?"

"Find them and kill them," Nick stated coldly.

"You make it sound so simple, killing people."

His friend shrugged. "Self-preservation. That's all it is. We need to either exist as one united front or not exist at all. I don't know about you but I'm partial to waking up each morning and breathing freely."

"It's that serious." It was a statement, not a question, because Rome knew that what his longtime friend was saying was absolutely true. "Our parents were putting things in place to deal with this. Maybe we should follow their lead."

Nick's parents were deceased, just like Rome's. They'd died in a car crash about five years ago. Nick didn't speak about it much and Rome understood why, so normally he didn't bring it up. They both had dark pasts, secrets that were probably better left alone. But if dredging up some of that old business could help in the here and now, they had no choice.

"I don't know that they were on the right track. I mean, trying to create some sort of democracy among the tribes, a penal system for a species that's not even supposed to exist? I don't see how that can work."

He couldn't see past the anger, was what Nick was basically saying. Rome knew the drill all too well. Nick's parents had disappointed him, angered him. That wasn't something Nick would forget, even in their death. Inhaling deeply, Rome considered how to proceed. He and Nick shared a lot; the depth of their pain was only one of the commonalities.

Although Rome wasn't angry with his parents, there were secrets they'd kept from him, things he would have liked to have known before they died. He couldn't bring them back, couldn't tap into some hereafter phone line and call them up. All he could do was move forward. Some days that was harder than others. Today he was trying to make it as easy as possible.

"It's time we had some sort of guidelines to live by," he said finally.

"We've got the *Ètica*" was Nick's response.

The shifter ethics code, traditionally called the *Ètica,* was their Bill of Rights, so to speak. It outlined everything they could and could not do as shifters. The code was mandated by the Assembly, three elders from each tribe equaling a fifteen-member council. The biggest problem was that they lived deep within the Brazilian rain forest in the secluded Gungi. The rules and limitations applied to forest living and were not really conducive to the mainstream life Rome and the other faction leaders were trying to achieve.

"I think we need more."

"So you want to pick up where our parents left off? Start trying to build some sort of government for us? We're not like them, Rome! We're not human!"

Nick's anger was apparent, and on another day Rome might have shared it with him. But today he was trying to stay focused, to not let his tumultuous emotions rule over good judgment. If the Rogues were planning something, only a cool head was going to keep them alive. A well-thought-out and perfectly executed plan would bring them the solidarity they desired. That was Rome's way, calm, cool, and overly collected. He could be dangerous, and crossing him usually was, but it was the smooth and precise way he handled his problems that earned him the title of the Lethal Litigator.

He didn't like the idea of rebel shifters any more than Nick did, but he didn't want a lot of bloodshed on their hands; that would only lead to what they desperately didn't want—for the shifters to be exposed and accused of being dangerous killers, animals that didn't deserve to walk among humans.

"Keep your voice down, the office isn't as well guarded as our homes. I feel your pain, Nick. You know I do. But we're not in the forest, we need to use our heads and not just our ability to fight and kill. Capturing these shifters is the better option. Find out what they're thinking, if there's some room for negotiation."

"How do you negotiate with someone who wants to take charge? They want to rule, Rome. They think they're the dominant species on earth. Can we really afford to invite them to lunch and try to talk this out?" Nick paused, then added, "Let's not forget they're responsible for your parents' deaths."

That was a deadly card to play. And Nick knew it. There was nothing—absolutely nothing—Rome wanted more than to find the Rogue who'd killed his parents.

Vance and Loren Reynolds had been brutally murdered, Rome suspected as a result of what they were trying to do among the shifters. Some of their old paperwork he'd found—notes from meetings with Elders and other Faction Leaders—led him to believe that his parents and their ideas for a democracy among the shifters were rubbing a few people the wrong way. He still had no real leads on their killers, just ideas. And he was still as pissed off today as he'd been twenty-five years ago when the murders had occurred in the bedroom his parents shared.

He'd remained hidden in a closet, prohibited from trying to save his parents' lives. A steady flow of rage simmered just beneath the surface of his cool lawyer exterior each and every day of his life. He would avenge his parents' killers—there was no doubt in his mind. That would be one time, one instance when he'd put aside the moral code he'd learned as a human, the justice he'd studied in law school, and become a hunter, the killer jaguars were perceived to be.

Revenge was a living and breathing source within Rome, but he couldn't let that dictate his every action.

"You know that's not what I'm suggesting. And make no mistake about it, when I find the Rogue responsible for the murder of my parents, his death will be slow and very painful. But that's my personal battle. That blood will be on my hands alone."

Nick shook his head. "It's ours," he replied. "You know we're in this together."

Rome nodded but didn't speak.

More death was coming, just as his gut instinct had warned. This battle of theirs was only beginning.

And . . . *Wait.* He inhaled deeply. Exhaled with a little more shakiness than he wanted to admit. Something else was coming, something or someone . . .

There was a knock at the door and before he'd uttered a word, before Nick had made it across the room to open it, Rome knew exactly who it was.

Chapter 2

Rome was hard instantly, need punching at him from every direction.

"Excuse me," she said the moment the door opened. "I have some checks that need a signature and your assistant wasn't at her desk."

Behind his desk Rome stiffened, his tongue rolling slowly over teeth that were suddenly too sharp to be human. His nostrils flared as he inhaled and let her scent permeate throughout his system.

It was her.

Inside his cat roared, leaping at the surface as if it knew her, too. It had been two years since he'd seen her. He'd thought about her, too much to even contemplate at this moment. Thought about her, dreamed about her, fantasized about her. But he had no idea who she was or where she'd gone that night.

Now she was here.

At his law firm, walking across the floor of his office heading in his direction. He watched her walk, long legs bringing her closer, curvy hips swaying with the motion. Her breasts were round, full, making his palms itch to touch them. The dress she wore wrapped around her body, tying at the side with some kind of sash, the material caressing each of her curves like a smooth jazz melody. Her hair, black mixed with a tawny brown color, was cut in a short spiky style that accented the exotic features of her face—the face that had haunted him for so long. Complexion the color of honey, high cheekbones, and full lips. Eyes the color of autumn leaves.

And she was handing him a stack of checks from his firm.

"You work here?" he asked and felt the amazing stupidity at the question. "When were you hired?" he rephrased.

She stopped abruptly just a foot or so away from his desk. Their gazes met, held. Then she cleared her throat.

"I was hired two weeks ago by Mr. Mathison. I work in accounting. If you could sign these I'll get out of your way," she said, casting a quick glance at Nick, who was staring at Rome.

Two weeks and he'd just caught her scent. Accounting was on the fifth floor, Rome's office was on the seventh. Still, she'd been *this close* to him for fourteen days and he hadn't known.

Why should he? She was nobody special, just a woman he'd helped out a long time ago. There shouldn't have been any warning signs that she was back in his life, or close to it. No announcement should have been made. He employed more than a hundred people, women included. This one wasn't any different.

She'd moved closer to the desk by now, extending her arm and holding the checks out to him. He reached for them, purposely let his fingers brush against hers, and gasped at the surge of heat that quickly spread from his arm through his body. Heat and lust so thick he could barely swallow, so potent his balls tightened with the thought of release. Against his zipper his thick length throbbed, aching for entrance inside her.

The arm she'd been extending quickly retreated, going first behind her back then down to her side in a motion that was meant to show control. Yet it was barely restrained control, Rome could see it in her eyes. There was heat there also, and confusion. With a deep breath he resigned himself to knowing exactly how she felt.

Grabbing a pen from the holder to his left, he began signing the checks. Looking at her was causing all sorts of things to go through his mind, feelings assailing his body. *Confusion* was an understatement.

"How do you like the job so far?" Nick asked, pausing to allude to the fact that they didn't know her name.

Her response was quick, her voice clear, almost melodic. "Kalina Harper. I really like it. I've never worked in a law firm before so it's a learning experience," she responded.

"Good. We'll have to do lunch sometime," Nick continued. "I make it a point to know all our employees. I can't believe I didn't know you were hired."

"The checks are done," Rome interrupted gruffly. Standing, he walked around the desk and stopped in front of her. The air crackled with the tension around them. She shifted from one foot to the next. Every nerve in his body pulsated, her scent filtering through his nostrils, dripping into his system like a powerful drug. But even that wasn't enough to mask the tendrils of pain that ebbed in the distance, the memory of suffering and fear. And something else.

"You like working in accounting?" he asked.

Her gaze met his almost defiantly as she reached for the checks in his hand. "Yes. I do."

Lie.

His kind could smell a lie or intended deceit just as easily as they could arousal. Then again, there was a large majority of employees who didn't like their jobs whether they worked for him or someone else. That was nothing new. Still, it alarmed him.

"May I have the checks?" she asked.

He smiled. Slow, seductive, convincing, he thought. Extending the checks to her, he kept his eyes focused solely on hers. There was something about this woman that intrigued him, turned him on, made him want her. Completely.

And what Rome wanted, Rome received.

"Here you go." Holding the papers with both hands, he made sure she had to touch him to retrieve them. The moment her hands were close he covered them, holding her still.

It was almost painful, this immediate and intense desire for her. But it was the way she looked at him that really caught his breath. In that moment her eyes were different, the amber color lightened, and he swore he saw flashes of yellow, remnants of knowledge.

Did she know who he was? What he was? Impossible.

"Nice meeting you," he said, smoothly releasing his grip on her.

She took a step back but didn't take her eyes off him. Her eyes seemed normal again, her composure slowly taking charge. "Same here" was her reply before she turned, smiled at Nick, then left the office.

"Well. Well. Well." Nick clapped his hands together and licked his lips.

"Back to work," Rome said, more than a little agitated now.

"Work? How can you think about work when that tasty little number just left?"

"How?" Rome asked when he was back behind his desk. He lifted a file into his hands. "My client is a cruel man who lies as easily as he smiles. And his soon-to-be-ex-wife isn't much better as she sleeps with any of his willing business partners."

Nick picked at a piece of imaginary lint on his dark suit. "Proving my point that marriage is an institution for the clinically insane."

Rome almost smiled even though he knew Nick was dead serious. Nick always said he'd never get married, no matter how much he liked women and loved sex. Thing was, to Rome and Nick the institution of marriage was drastically different than it was for Rome's clients. "They're both stubborn and selfish and self-righteous. Common sense says to just split everything and part ways, but that would be too easy."

"And nothing with women is easy," Nick added. "Did I tell you about the one I was seeing a couple of weeks ago?"

"Which one was that? I lose count." And he did. Nick loved women, and that was putting it mildly. And women loved him right back. As teenagers Rome would joke it was because of Nick's pretty-boy good looks. Nick's mother was from Panama, her family touring one of South America's many rain forests when she met Nick's African American father. So Nick has a golden complexion and wavy black hair. He paid more attention to his clothes and appearance than ten women, so he was always picture-perfect. And his bank account would make Donald Trump look like the designated home-less. Yet he didn't flaunt his wealth, didn't use it to gain what he wanted in life; he'd never had to.

They'd both been born in the Gungi rain forest in Brazil and relocated to the States with their parents at early ages. Rome and his parents to Florida and Nick, his parents, and his sister to Texas. The two of them were the same age, with only a two-month gap that made Rome the older. The decision to move to Washington, DC, had been made by their parents at the same time as well, when both boys were four years old.

What people usually didn't see at first glance with Nick was that he was a vicious opponent when crossed—deadly, to be precise.

Rome could claim the same about himself, but he didn't openly. Instead, his special breeding allowed him to be an astute attorney, winning cases because he had information that nobody else did. He used his other abilities to scent the lies, assess the damage, and strike quickly, efficiently. Nobody knew who or what he and Nick really were or what they were capable of. And they planned to keep it that way.

"Very funny. Speaking of which, when was the last time you had a date?"

"What's the point?"

"The point would be to relieve some of that tension you carry around like luggage. Damn, man, you're not that ugly." He chuckled. "Get out and get some for a change."

This was an old conversation between the two of them, and Rome could see exactly where Nick was coming from. They had great stamina. And their height-ened senses made the sexual experience much more intense than that of humans. He enjoyed sex, made sure the women he decided to lie with enjoyed it also. Still, Rome didn't partake as freely as Nick did. He couldn't afford to.

"It's not as important to me as it is to you."

Nick simply nodded. "Okay, so you won't mind if I go ask that sexy new employee out to dinner?"

Without a moment's hesitation Rome said, "Don't. Even. Think. About. It." Each word was enunciated and spoken in the deep low timbre that more resembled a cat's growl than a human voice.

Nick threw back his head and laughed. "Welcome back to the world of women, my friend."

"There's nothing here," Kalina whispered into her cell phone.

"What do you mean nothing?" the voice on the other end asked.

It was a little after five and almost everyone on her floor was gone for the day. Each day Agent Jack Ferrell, her immediate supervisor on this case, called for a status update. In the beginning she'd thought that was strange since the previous cases she'd worked hadn't involved Ferrell at all, even though he'd been at the MPD for almost thirty years. He was probably just nervous, watching her closely so that if she botched the investigation he could save face before the DEA brought down their entire unit. Besides, the DEA was really focusing on shutting down South American cartels. And if she could find the right information, she'd be a part of that resounding success. She would have done something extremely important, gaining a reason to be proud of herself in the process. She would be a part of something that changed the world, a huge accomplishment in her otherwise dismal life. Unfortunately, there was no one else in her life that could be proud of her as well.

"I've gone over all the records in QuickBooks dating back two years. I see the deductions, but the account they're wired to is the same one we've already had reports on. It's in the name of Roman Reynolds personally, and the deductions are written off the firm account as bonuses."

"So he's hiding additional income from the IRS?" Jack inquired.

"No." She sighed, pushing the buttons on her keyboard to shut down her computer. "It's all being reported. I have to tell you, Jack, he looks clean."

"But he's not!" he yelled into the phone.

For a second Kalina pulled the phone from her ear and stared at it. In all her years in law enforcement none of her superiors had ever used that tone with her; they'd never needed to. And she wasn't so sure she liked it.

"Look, I think being here's a bust," she told him finally. She wasn't quitting, she told herself, but the way she'd been feeling all afternoon since going to see Rome in his office bothered her. It wasn't just lust. That she could deal with. She had more than enough toys at home to get her off, if it was only about release. But when he'd touched her, the way he'd looked at her—the heat moving between the two of them as if they were the only people in that room—was disconcerting. The remnants of those weird feelings stuck with her the remainder of the day, pulling her mind in different directions, causing what felt like ripples of something beneath her skin.

For whatever reason, she wanted to get away from Roman Reynolds. Far, far away.

"No! You've got to find something. I know it's there. The account is located where?"

"Nova National Bank in Natal, Brazil."

"Any movement on the money from there?"

"Some debits but they're all made by him, for cash. There's no telling what he did with the money when he took it out." No ties to their known cartel contacts and no illegal dealings on record. Either Reynolds was super smart, or he was innocent. She didn't want to place too much confidence in the latter, especially after the dark vibes she'd gotten from him earlier.

"Maybe you're looking at the wrong records."

"What? We need to track his money. What other records would I look for besides bank accounts and financial files?"

"We need to track his movements, any movement that Reynolds makes. We need to know his contacts, who he calls on his office line, his private line, and his cell phone."

She could see where this was going, and it was info the DEA could have already secured themselves. Putting her in Reynolds's office didn't make her privy to his phone records. "Okay, pull his phone records," she suggested.

"Not enough. We need a personal connection, paperwork linking him to people in South America, specific people."

Like carriers, runners, buyers. She got that part. Still, she had a suspicion Ferrell was talking about much more. When this assignment was first presented to her, they'd said it was all about the movement of Reynolds's money. He had too much, most people in DC thought, to be just a lawyer. He was a good lawyer, a dynamic litigator with tons of high-profile clients. Still, he'd come from seemingly ordinary parents who were killed when he was just a young boy. There was no large inheritance, and no rich family member had stepped in to raise him. The only other logical explanation for his financial status was drug-related. Was this profiling on the DEA's part? Of course, but as bad as it seemed, Kalina felt compelled to do her job.

There was one thing she'd discovered in her investigation of Roman Reynolds, one small fact that stuck with her. After the death of his parents, Roman hadn't become a ward of the state. Even though he had no parents, he wasn't an orphan like her. Somebody had wanted him, loved him enough to keep him safe and to raise him into a successful man. Twinges of hurt pushed at her and Kalina pushed back, refusing to entertain another pity party.

"What do you want me to do?" she asked, because at the end of the day, the job was all she had.

"Get the information we need" was his simple reply.

"How?"

"You're the detective, Harper. Find it!"

The line went dead and Kalina restrained a string of curses that she could have gladly hurled at Ferrell. But she wanted more. Damn her, she wanted that promotion. This case would propel her in that direction.

Slamming the phone into her clutch purse, she stood from the desk. She was going to find him the information he wanted, turn in a kick-ass report that would lead to a warrant to arrest Roman Reynolds, then hopefully an indictment and conviction. Oh yeah, this was going to work out just fine, she convinced herself as she took the elevator up to the seventh floor. Pulling out her phone again she quickly dialed the office number, happy to receive the after-hours recording. Bypassing the nasal recorded voice, she punched in Rome's extension and was rewarded again with a recorded message.

He was gone for the day.

The seventh floor was just about vacant. If there was anyone working late, they were in an office and not out and paying attention to what she was about to do.

She was an officer of the law, she told herself the moment she approached Rome's office door. Taking a deep breath she vowed, "An officer of the law who needs this promotion." Testing the knob to see if the door was locked, she sighed, then reached into her pocket to find the bobby pin she'd stuck there. Picking a lock shouldn't be easy for a cop, but a few seconds later the click of the bolt sliding out of the way made her smile.

Rome's chest constricted, betrayal gripping him with indescribable strength. He didn't know her, and yet he did. So what she was doing scraped against his already raw emotions where she was concerned. He wanted to growl, to roar his displeasure as loud as he could, but knew that was not an option.

In addition to the sting of betrayal he felt the scorch of lust, the punch of desire that almost left him breathless the moment she slipped into his office. He'd gone into his private bathroom to freshen up before heading out to the meeting, but the moment he'd picked up her scent he'd stopped. Two seconds later she was closing the door to his office, moving toward his desk.

Curious what she was looking for, he'd stood in the

shadow of the partially opened bathroom door watching, waiting. She turned on the computer and tried to guess his security code to log in. He wasn't afraid; she'd never figure it out. It was everything else that gave him pause. Why was she here? What was she looking for? And who had sent her?

Taking a slow step forward, he vowed to get all the answers he needed, and the touch of her that he craved. No matter what the cost.

Kalina was on her fourth try, using every variation on his name, his initials, and the firm's initials that she could think of. "Dammit!" she whispered, then let her fingers rest on the keyboard while she considered.

Thoughts of passwords were interrupted by warmth against her neck, then the distinct sting of a bite against her shoulder. Jumping up out of the chair, she was already reaching behind her back for her gun, only to confront disappointment. She'd worn a dress today, not conducive to sticking a Glock in her waistband. Inside her purse was a .38, but that wasn't doing her any good at the moment since it was a few inches away on the desk.

As it stood she was cornered, her bottom pressing into the desk behind her since she'd turned to see who or what was biting her. It was him, and she wasn't surprised.

All her life she'd had a great sense of perception. Generally she could sense even when someone was simply staring at her. So she should have known someone was coming up behind her. Yet she hadn't heard a sound, hadn't been aware of any presence but her own. But here he stood, Roman Reynolds, not a foot away from her and moving closer.

"Looking for something?" His voice was deeper than it had been when she'd been in his office earlier.

And that wasn't the only difference. He seemed bigger, if that were possible. Taller, his shoulders broader, his face still handsome as sin, but now tinged with a lethally dangerous look that had her heart skipping.

"I forgot to send an email," she said, struggling to come up with a reason for being here at this time of day.

His arms moved and she reached back to grab her purse. Rome had a reputation for being dark, brooding, not necessarily dangerous, but not on the personable side, either. That's what she'd read about him. What she was feeling right at this very moment wasn't exactly a threat in the normal sense of the word.

The minute her hand was on her purse and she was struggling to get the zipper open with one hand, he touched her. Both his large hands cupped her cheeks, tilting her head up so that she was staring right into his face.

She swallowed. "I thought I could send it from your computer and head out for the day. That way I wouldn't have to go all the way back downstairs."

"Did you know that lies smell, Kalina?"

He leaned his face forward, inhaling deeply.

Her legs literally shook, knees knocking and all. And yet she wasn't afraid. She was aroused. So much so that her panties were already damp, nipples tingling as his broad chest just barely brushed over them.

"I'm not lying," she said in a voice that was much stronger than she was actually feeling. "Now if you'll get your hands off me, I won't have to file a harassment claim."

"But I could still file a breaking-and-entering charge," he said, his eyes lowering, falling to her lips.

She licked them instinctively and was answered by what could only be described as a deep rumbling growl rippling through his chest. Everything in her went on alert. She wasn't sure why but she felt it was imperative she fight him. So without another thought she lifted her knee, feeling a bit of glory when it brushed past his groin as he quickly avoided a stronger assault. Victory was short-lived as she attempted to push past him and make a run for the door. He grabbed her around the waist, pulling her to him effortlessly.

"Now, that was worse than you sneaking into my office and trying to break into my computer." His mouth was right up to her ear, and he nipped the lobe with teeth sharper than any needle she'd ever felt.

"Let me go," she said trying not to panic. She could see her purse on the desk, knew her only protection from him was in there. But he was holding her away from the desk, too far away for her to reach the purse without him knowing what she was doing. "Or I'll scream this building down. Every security officer in hearing distance will come running."

He licked her ear. Then pulled her closer to him, his thick erection poking into her bottom with persistence. Outrage should have been pouring through her at the audacity of this man. He didn't know her, had no idea if she was involved with someone or simply not interested in him. And yet he was rubbing on her as if there was a promise of more.

That was definitely not happening, Kalina didn't give a damn how much her center creamed for him right about now.

"I own this building. Therefore every security officer in here works for me. Just as you do, Ms. Harper."

He said her name with distinct sarcasm as he turned her abruptly to face him. "You work for this firm and yet you're in here trying to break into my computer. I want to know why."

"I wasn't," she started to say when he pushed his body up against hers. Her bottom pressed against the side of the desk and she struggled to remain upright.

"Don't lie to me," he snarled, showing just a hint of his teeth.

His body seemed to give off this intense heat that joined hers, mated with it until they were consumed by a dual desire that threatened both their sanity.

"I could fire you."

Slices of panic moved through her, but she refused to let it show. "And I'll definitely sue for harassment."

"I'm not harassing you."

"Oh really?" Beneath him she squirmed as if to confirm her point. That was a mistake. Every part of him was hard, right down to the dark glare he was giving her. His length pressed into her with such persistence she was about to simply throw her legs open and welcome him. Swallowing deeply, she tried to remain focused. "This is more than harassment, Mr. Reynolds. Do you treat all your staff like this?"

"None of my other staff makes my dick as hard as you do."

She should have been shocked, should have felt

embarrassed by his crude language; instead she was even more aroused. "Unfortunately, that's not a part of my job description."

"Funny, I don't think breaking and entering is, either."

"This is ridiculous," she said. "Let me go and we can talk like adults."

He shook his head. "I don't think I'm in the mood for talking now."

And if she was in the mood for talking, that stopped the second his lips touched hers. There was nothing soft about this kiss. No seduction or easy compliance. Instinct had warned her that there was nothing easy about this man. The kiss was hot and urgent, erotic and breath-stealing. She wanted to pull away, but her lips, his tongue, her moans, his hands, all of it melded into one scorching exchange.

Chapter 3

Her taste was sweet and primitive, stroking his cat while driving his erection to the point of pain. Sliding a hand down her arms to her thigh, Rome lifted the leg that had attempted to cause him great pain and tucked it around his back.

She was gasping, her breath coming in thick, heavy pants. Her mouth had ceased its argument, her body succumbing to the building inferno in each of them. Was this strange? Him about to fuck on his desk a woman he'd just met officially about five hours ago? Probably. Was it strange enough to make him stop? Hell no.

With her leg locked around him Rome moved so that his raging arousal was seated right at her center. If not for the barrier of their clothes he'd be planted deep inside her at this exact moment.

When he released her lips her head fell back, her fingers gripping his shoulders. She was beautiful, her face wearing lust and desire like designer makeup. Her back arched, breasts jutting forward, an invitation he could not refuse. He licked her then, his tongue creating a long path from the hollow of her neck down between the crevice of her breasts. The material of her dress wrapped around the succulent mounds but Rome didn't care. His tongue moved over it, teeth grabbing a nipple to suckle.

"Dammit." She breathed the word. "This can't happen."

"Oh, it can and it will," was his urgent response.

Rome was usually a patient lover, albeit an extremely thorough and voracious one. Right now he could think of only one thing. The scent of her arousal was a heavy haze around him, hypnotizing him so that she was all he could envision. There were consequences, he knew, and he thrust that thought to the back of his mind. There was also pleasure, a pleasure he was sure to find deep inside Kalina.

He was going for his zipper, deftly unleashing his thick shaft, when she pushed against his chest with a force he hadn't expected. He stumbled back and she used that moment to lift her legs, climb over his desk, feet landing on the opposite side.

"I said this wasn't happening." Her chest heaved as she spoke, lips swollen from his kisses.

If his erection weren't so painful, Rome might have laughed at the situation. Never before had he watched a woman literally run from him. And not for one minute did he think it was because she didn't want him. No, this was about something else. It was about why Kalina Harper was really here in his office.

"But you want it to happen?"

"No," she answered quickly. Too quickly.

Damn him for being so sexy, for having an appeal that any woman in her right mind would be drawn to. And damn herself for losing control of the situation. This wasn't like her. She'd never, ever gone this far with a man she'd just met. And on a desk in an office building no less. Okay, she'd berate herself about her momentary lapse of judgment later. For now, she needed to get out of this office and away from this man. Or everything she'd ever worked for would come crashing down around her.

"Are you sure?" His voice was low, deep as he stood on the other side of his desk, his hand gripping the most delectable arousal she'd ever seen.

Her gaze rested there, her mouth watering. Shaking her head, she focused once again on his face, on her job. Reaching over to the desk, she picked up her purse, felt safety in the weight of the gun she carried there. Unfortunately, Roman now had a weapon of his own. One he was currently stroking, fingers gliding over the smooth dark tip, enticing her, inviting her.

"What are you doing here if you don't want this?" he asked seductively. He knew she was watching him stroke himself, knew some part of her was enjoying it.

Damn him.

Kalina cleared her throat. "Like I told you, there was an email I wanted to send before leaving the office. I should have gone back to my desk but I was on this floor dropping off some other paperwork and I thought you were gone for the day. Coming in here seemed more convenient. I guess I was wrong."

He didn't speak, just kept his hot gaze fixed on hers, his hand still stroking his length. Her center clenched, dripped with essence, and practically begged her for release. She stood strong, or as strong as humanly possible under the circumstances.

"I'm leaving now."

"Are you sure?"

"I'm positive."

"It won't stop until you slake the need, Kalina." He was still watching her as he tucked himself back into his pants. "You're going to want me until you have me."

"You're an arrogant SOB!" She tossed the words at him on instinct. He was exactly that, but he was also technically her boss and the subject of her investigation.

She really needed to get out of here before she had no job on either front.

"I apologize for any inconvenience I may have caused by entering your office without permission," she said, turning to walk toward the door.

The minute her hand was on the knob he spoke again.

"I could still fire you."

She looked over her shoulder, bravado she didn't really feel sounding in her voice. "And I can bury your ass in the biggest sexual harassment suit of the year. Then where would you be, Mr. Lethal Litigator?"

He didn't answer. She knew he wouldn't. Roman Reynolds liked to play hard, he liked to assess his situation and then go in for the kill. She wasn't giving him the opportunity to do any of the above. At least not tonight.

He was right, he could fire her. And she was right, she could sue the pants off him—no pun intended—and his firm. But as she closed the office door behind her she had a feeling neither of them would take those actions.

Whatever it was that had just happened between them was too big for that.

Kalina had a love–hate relationship with the rain. And the dark. And being alone.

She sounded like a basket case moving to the window seat in her bedroom looking out into the night with a sigh. Her apartment was empty save for furniture and the few mementos she'd allowed herself to collect. There was no one there to welcome her home, no husband, no significant other. Not even a pet.

Every day it was the same.

No, tonight was different.

She'd gone to the precinct the moment she left the office. It was against protocol, she knew. Her routine needed to remain the same in case anybody was watching her. She should never go to the precinct unless called from undercover by her superior officer. But she needed it, her mind needed the one thing that remained constant in her life. The one thing that mattered. Work.

Roman Reynolds had touched her. He'd kissed her and she'd kissed him back, wantonly. The heat exchanged between them was unlike anything she'd ever experienced in her life and for the first time in a really long time Kalina was unnerved.

Her job was to investigate him, to find out what he was doing and bring him down. Not crawl all over his desk, getting hot and steamy with the man. Slapping a palm to her forehead, she allowed another moment of disgust. This wasn't a pity party she was indulging in this time, it was a reprimand. One she fully deserved from her superior but wouldn't get because she hadn't mentioned this new development to him. While she wanted the safety net of work, her mind really wasn't on the case she needed to build.

It was on the man.

He'd caught her trying to break into his computer and instead of tossing her ass out, firing her, and/or pressing charges, he'd kissed her.

And what a kiss it had been. Words could not

describe . . . it was beyond sensual, more than erotic, a step past intoxicating. She wanted more. Her body had practically begged for it. The strength with which he'd grabbed her leg, wrapping it around him, still had her center pulsating. The warm-shower-and-vibrator-assisted release she'd indulged in the moment she arrived home wasn't nearly enough.

How long had it been since she'd felt the touch of a man, welcomed it, in fact? A little more than two years. About a month before the attack. She'd told her shrink that she was okay with it, that the violation that piece of crap had imposed on her wasn't that big a deal. She'd survived. And yet, she really hadn't. Because as much as she enjoyed sexual release, the thought of another man touching her intimately had made her sick. The mere consideration over the past few months would send her into a panic attack that should have had her on medication. Had she dared to ever tell anyone about it.

Instead she'd stocked up on sexual toys and movies that would give her everything she needed without the physical presence of a man. The dark haunting of a memory.

Until tonight. Until Roman Reynolds.

Her apartment was minutes away from his office, on the top floor of a corner brownstone. The front entrance had a wrought-iron gate and matching screened door that wasn't locked. The mailbox showed her name and apartment number. The steps leading up to her were unguarded as he walked up slowly, predatorily.

A black door with a shiny gold number two on it was all that stood between him and her. Placing his palms on the door, Rome rested his forehead against it, inhaling deeply, painfully.

He wanted her.

There was no doubt about that and no real concern. Sex was sex and with Rome it was good sex. He'd been told that before, wore the honor like a soldier's Purple Heart. But this was different. He was smart enough to know and to admit that this wasn't just sex. It wasn't a normal urge. His blood heated, coursed through his veins like a raging stream at the proximity to her.

Not only had he picked up her scent the moment he'd crossed the threshold to the building, but he sensed her physically as if she now occupied a small space within him. She was here, just beyond this door. He could knock and she'd let him in. They would sleep together, no doubt about it. The sex would be wild, dangerous, alluring, just like their kiss. But what else?

There was definitely something else. Rome was wise enough to know that as well. It bothered him, this knowledge coupled with uncertainty. It was unusual for him not to know exactly what he wanted to do, when he wanted to do it. Taking precautions and planning was a natural part of him, the human him. Second-guessing wasn't.

Who was Kalina Harper and why did she have this effect on him? Why was he here, tonight, at her apartment? And why had he been there, that night two years ago, in the alley to save her?

His mother would say there were no coincidences in life, there was only fate. A destiny mapped out for each and every breathing being. Rome didn't believe that; he refused to believe in a plan that included someone's death. His mother's death. That wasn't fate. She wasn't meant to die and neither was his father. They weren't meant to go, but Rome had allowed it, because he hadn't been strong enough to stop it.

Turning away from the door but still standing utterly still in front of it, he vowed he'd never make that mistake again. He would never fail to act when he needed to, would never be caught off guard again.

He turned to walk away. Kalina Harper wasn't a part of the plan, she wasn't what he needed to focus on. Revenge was.

A hot tongue swiped over thick lips as eyes remained trained on the window. She was there, in a thin robe that did nothing to disguise the delectable body he craved. She sat in the windowsill—thank goodness for bay windows—knees pulled to her chest, the silk sliding down to her waist so that her calves and thighs were bared to him. Did she know he was there? Was she giving him a treat?

His pulse quickened, arousal lengthening along his thigh.

Her head fell back, resting against the wall, her breasts jutting forward. Her nipples were hard, kissable. He cursed, opened the car door, and stepped out. Rain sprinkled over his face, falling to his arms and hands as he stood paralyzed by her beauty, her sensuality.

He wanted like never before, craved the touch and taste that had been denied so long ago. At his sides his fists clenched. The time wasn't right. It wasn't now. There was more to it than just having her physically. There would be pain and suffering, long coming and well deserved. It was the way it had to be, the way it would be.

"Soon," he whispered, still looking up at the window to the second-floor apartment of the corner house.

Slowly stepping back into the car, water dripping all over the leather upholstery, he started the ignition and drove away. "Very soon."

Chapter 4

Today was a new day.

Kalina awakened on time, showered and dressed, and was in her car on her way to work before the first tingles of wariness itched along her spine. Stepping out of the vehicle she looked around, assured herself nobody was following her before stepping into the elevator.

She'd felt this way before, yet today was somehow different. Taking a deep breath, she reminded herself that this was a job. She was experienced in working undercover. There was no need to feel like something was about to happen that she wasn't prepared for.

Whenever she walked into a sting, garbed in her street clothes and black MPD jacket, gun in hand, target in sight, she felt something. Anxiousness. Pride. Adrenaline. She proceeded with caution, always. Knowing she had backup, knowing they were fighting a huge evil—drugs. She took down the bad guys without blinking an eye. She aimed her gun, gave orders, handcuffed and processed criminals for a living. It was an important job, a necessary one. And she was damn good at it.

So riding an elevator up to a law office shouldn't make her nervous or have her looking over her shoulder. And yet stepping off the elevator she did just that.

Focus.

Walking to her desk, the conversation with herself was like a pep talk of sorts. Despite what had happened yesterday she was back to finish up the job she was hired to do. Ferrell had been adamant yesterday when he called that she find something. And later when she'd stopped by the precinct, he'd been pacing in his office. She remembered thinking he'd looked like some kind of caged animal behind the glass doors moving intently back and forth, muttering to himself as if he were in his own little world. Of course she found that only minutely strange since Jack Ferrell wasn't exactly the sanest person she knew.

That could probably be said for a lot of law enforcement agents who'd been on the job for twenty, thirty, sometimes forty years. Something about working on the right side of the law tended to wear on people if they weren't careful. This job could become all-consuming, making any semblance of a normal life practically impossible. With a cringe she thought she was dangerously close to that very description and she hadn't even been on the force for ten years yet.

Still, Ferrell's behavior registered as strange, but not enough for her to forget the real priority. Dropping her purse into the desk drawer, she booted up her computer, all the while thinking of what else she'd discovered yesterday.

Roman Reynolds was one hell of a kisser.

That tidbit of information would not go into her report, but she remembered it just the same.

He was also hiding something, of that she was beyond sure. Catching her in his office the way he did called for more dire actions than tossing her on the desk for a little touchy-feely. Actually, the touchy-feely was out of line, but she wasn't going to argue that since she'd been breaking and entering.

But Roman hadn't called the police, and he hadn't fired her. Why?

Keying in a password to the company's financial database, she thought about more possibilities. He couldn't know who she was or why she was really at the firm. Her cover was airtight; Ferrell said his superiors made sure she was a normal working girl when they'd given her the résumé and references for the interview with the firm. She couldn't be traced back to the DEA, either, since she wasn't even on their official payroll. So why did Roman look at her as if he knew all her darkest secrets? And why did the look make her want to tell him anything he didn't know?

"Good morning!"

Kalina jumped at the sound of a cheery female voice.

"Oh," she said, fingers stilling on the keyboard as she looked up to see a woman she'd seen every day for the past two weeks. "Good morning,"

"Sorry I startled you," Melanie Keys said with her customary smile. In her hand she held a Tweety mug that spoke again of cheerfulness.

A forty-something woman, Melanie was about five foot three with riotous flaming red hair and creamy ivory skin with a parade of freckles across the bridge of her nose. She was a legal secretary. Roman's secretary.

There was a small kitchenette on each floor of the firm that housed coffeemakers, a small sink, and all the accoutrements to having a hot morning beverage. Kalina was generally a tea drinker, but each station had tea bags and hot chocolate packets as well. She was on the main floor with the large kitchen, which she assumed Melanie was headed to. Kalina just wasn't sure why.

"Coffee??" she said as if reading Kalina's mind and wiggled her mug.

The one thing Kalina had learned so far being at the firm was that the employees stuck together in clusters. Everybody seemed to migrate into one clique or another. She was sure that if she worked here on a permanent basis, she'd continue seeking the solitary confines of her cubicle. But since her main goal was to obtain as much information about Roman and his dealings as possible, getting coffee with his secretary was a prime opportunity.

"Sure," she said backing away from her desk. "I don't have my own mug."

"It's okay, they have firm mugs in the cabinets," Melanie said as they began walking side by side past empty cubicles of co-workers who hadn't yet made it into the office. "But I suggest you bring your own tomorrow. Just because they load the dishwasher in there doesn't mean they actually run it, or that it runs well, if you know what I mean."

Kalina nodded. "So why aren't you getting coffee on your floor?" That was a question she just had to get out of the way. She had a feeling that Melanie hadn't stopped by her desk by chance.

"Uck, somebody put three packs into the machine. It looks like motor oil and smells strong enough to have me walking in my sleep for the rest of the week. No, thank you."

"I see," Kalina chuckled. "I'm Kalina," she said since she and Melanie had never formally been introduced.

"I know. I'm Melanie, but you can call me Mel. Mr.

Reynolds had me pull the email we were sent when you started. Each time a new employee starts at the firm, human resources sends out an email introducing them to everyone. Mr. Reynolds said he must have overlooked the one about you. If you ask me he didn't see it at all, probably didn't even pull up his emails that day."

"Does he do that often? Not check his emails?"

"No. Normally he's on top of everything from emails to voicemails to mail that's come in and is going out. But these last couple of weeks . . ." Mel trailed off as they approached the front desk. The main reception area was located in the center of the floor, just across from where the elevator doors opened. The kitchen was on the other side so they had to walk through and pass gossip central to get there.

"Hey, Melanie," Pam said, giving Kalina a pointed look. "Good morning." Her head gave a nod to Kalina, but her eyes were saying something else.

This woman, Kalina noted, had a lot to say, all the time. If she weren't so loud and boisterous Kalina might have thought about pumping her for information, but something told her it was best just to steer clear of this one.

"Good morning."

"You ladies working on something together?" Pam asked.

"We're going to the kitchen for coffee, Pam. If anyone's looking for either of us that's where we'll be," Melanie said with a syrupy-sweet voice.

The minute they rounded the corner, leaving Pam and her nosiness behind at the receptionist desk, Mel made a gagging sound. "She's like nine-one-one central."

"Like her much?" Kalina asked.

"Yeah, like I want to poke needles in my eye while walking on hot coals."

Kalina was laughing as they stepped through the glass doors. She was beginning to like Melanie Keys.

"So you said Mr. Reynolds wanted to know when I was hired?" She had moved right to the counter, reaching up to open a cabinet to look for the mugs.

"Here, they're in this one," Mel said, opening another cabinet and taking down a cup. When she offered it to Kalina, she tilted her head as if studying her. "I've been here for ten years so I know my way around."

"This is my first law-firm job."

"Really? Where'd you work before now?"

Kalina didn't even blink before saying, "An accounting firm in Baltimore. I just moved to DC about six months ago. Needed a change of scenery, you know."

Mel nodded. "I understand. I wish I could get away. I've been here all my life, my family's here, my job. God, my mom would freak if I even mentioned moving to another state and taking the kids."

Now Kalina did falter. She could lie smoothly when it was a surface lie, something she'd memorized from the file the DEA had given her. But Mel's mention of family, of roots was something else altogether. She sort of had roots here in DC; the Department of Social Services downtown was the one that placed her with each of her foster parents. That meant she belonged here, right?

"That's nice you have a family." Clearing her throat, she tried again to focus. "You don't look old enough to have kids with an *s*," she said with a smile as she dipped the decaffeinated tea bag in and out of her hot water.

Mel had already poured her coffee and was holding the sugar dispenser over it while a steady stream of white emptied into her cup. Kalina liked her tea the same way. It made her smile to have something in common with someone.

"Twins, Matthew and Madison, eight years old, beautiful at birth, terrors as toddlers, and now more than a handful in elementary. Jonathan's thirteen—cell phone, Facebook, and girls, that's all he's thinking about right now. And Addy, a gorgeous sixteen-year-old, plays field hockey like a pro but can't grasp algebra to save her life." She stopped pouring, setting the sugar down with a clunk. "Pete and I've been married for twenty-two years, high school sweethearts. You? Kids? A man? I don't see a ring," she noted, lifting a dark eyebrow.

Kalina's chest clenched. Wasn't she supposed to be the one pumping Mel for information? This wasn't about her, not on a personal level. It couldn't be. Besides, the answer she had to this question, honestly, was dismal at best.

"No kids. No man." She shrugged. "No time."

"Well, you can't be dedicated to your work. Especially not here. Even though I hear Dan's brutal to work for." Mel seemed to go from one subject to another without much effort, which was a relief to Kalina.

After adding her own sugar to her tea, Kalina lifted her mug to take a test sip. The warm liquid filled her like an empty container. She blinked, trying not to think of how pitiful it was that a cup of hot tea and trivial conversation with a co-worker could make her feel just a little more complete.

"He's been okay so far. What's Mr. Reynolds like to

work for? He seems a bit rigid." As rigid and unyielding as a pit bull.

"Oh." Mel waved a hand, her silver charm bracelet dangling on her left arm. "He's all right once you get used to him and his moods. I've been with him long enough to know exactly how to deal with him. Today, for example, he has depositions all morning; they'll break for lunch and he'll close himself up in his office. Then, if the morning sessions haven't completed, he'll go back into the conference room and chew the other attorney's ass out a little more. Then he'll return to his office where he'll brood until about six, then he'll go home. Now, tomorrow—" Mel kept right on talking as they walked toward the door, mugs in hand.

"Tomorrow is Friday. He has this big gala to go to at the Linden Hotel. The cleaners already called about his tux being ready. I'll pick that up at lunch today."

"Does he like going to political parties?" It hadn't slipped Kalina's mind that Roman could be shielded by some higher-up in the US government, hence explaining why they hadn't been able to pin anything on him up to this point. Besides, that was the name of the game here in DC—I wash your back, you wash mine. It would be no surprise if there was a contact or two in government helping him. "Does he usually take a date?"

Mel stopped. Her head tilted again in that way that Kalina was beginning to realize meant she had questions coming. "Are you interested in him? Of course you are," she answered herself. "Every woman with eyes is hot for Rome. But let me give you a piece of advice, he doesn't like timid women. So if you want him, go for it. Don't dilly-dally around. Just make your move."

They were back at Kalina's cubicle by this time so she stopped, looked at Melanie Keys, and admitted she liked the woman. "I won't be making any move. He's not my type. I just remember seeing articles in the paper about his very active love life."

"Lies," Mel said quickly then sipped her coffee. "They print what they want, what they think'll sell papers. He's actually very discreet in who he dates and when. Hey, let's do lunch. There's a great sandwich place on Pennsylvania and it's near the dry cleaners."

Lunch with Mel. She'd probably talk about her kids, her latest PTA meeting, soccer practice, or something else . . . normal. Kalina warmed a bit but she wasn't sure if it was from the tea or the prospect. "Sure. Lunch sounds fine."

"Meet you at the elevator at one. I like to go later—makes the afternoon pass quicker."

Kalina nodded. "Me, too."

"Be good till then," Mel said, tossing her a smile and walking away.

Be good, Kalina thought, taking a seat. How could spying on a man and using the nicest woman she'd ever met be good?

The next afternoon, Rome felt like a stalker. Sort of, but not really. He was on his own property, doing something that wasn't totally out of the ordinary for an employer. There was no law stating he couldn't walk around his office, take a tour of what he'd created.

If he stopped in the accounting department, just a couple of feet away from the cubicle occupied by his firm's newest and sexiest employee, well, that was just coincidence.

He heard her voice just seconds after he picked up her scent. A scent he figured he might just be a little addicted to, even though he hadn't smelled it personally for a couple of years. He still remembered, as if it were yesterday, the first time she'd been close to him, close enough for him to feel a part of her reaching out to him.

"You could back up off me just a little, you know," she was saying, and Rome's protective instincts quickly kicked in. Surely no one in his employ was giving her a hard time. If so, he'd definitely deal with them. Despite their little encounter in his office the other night, or possibly because of it, he wanted to make sure he kept her in close proximity this time.

He took a step closer to the cubicle, ready to intervene and reprimand if necessary. But she continued.

"I'd be a lot better off if you'd stop calling every five minutes and let me do my job."

So she was on the phone, he surmised since the conversation seemed one-sided. He moved closer, the ammonia-like scent of hostility permeating his senses. Whoever she was talking to, she didn't much care for.

"Fine! Just don't call me back again."

Her words were terse, and she really meant them. As he turned the corner of the cubicle they were face-to-face and she wasn't happy to see him.

"Boyfriend problems?" he said without hesitation.

She didn't seem startled, only more agitated. "Creeping around the office after hours doesn't seem like your style," she quipped.

"No. That would be more your arena, right?" was his reply and her brow furrowed. He'd made her angrier, which really wasn't his intention. Hell, Rome had no idea what his intentions were where this woman was concerned. What he knew for certain was that he didn't want another confrontation. It was obvious they were attracted to each other, and from experience it was a lot easier to act on an attraction when you weren't biting each other's heads off every time you were together.

So he inhaled slowly, thought about the situation another second, then said, "Is everything okay?" He eyed the cell phone she was slipping in her purse as she stood.

"Fine," she said through clenched teeth. "Just dandy."

Lie. But he smiled anyway.

"Want to get a drink and talk about it?"

"No, thanks. I already have plans for tonight."

She made sure her computer was shut down then moved to pass him. Rome had plans as well, but didn't mind being a little late as long as it meant he could spend more time with her.

"Then at least let me walk you out," he continued, falling in step beside her.

She was tall for a woman—not as tall as him, but she could almost look him eye-to-eye. She walked with self-assuredness and purpose, her heeled shoes eating up the carpet as she moved. There was no problem keeping up with her as they rounded the corner to where the elevators were.

"You parked in the garage?"

"Yes," she said. Rome hit the DOWN button on the marbled panel.

"If there's a problem you're having, I can help," he said when she'd folded her arms over her chest. Today she wore slacks that covered her long legs the way he wished he could. Her blouse was a snug white material with just enough softness to have the insides of his palms tingling to touch. Her hair was slicked on the sides, spiked at the top, giving her eyes an exotic slant he wasn't sure he noticed the other day in his office.

Rome's body radiated heat, his dick so hard he bet he could push her against this wall and fuck her right here in the hallway. But that would be classless, something Rome was not. He didn't take his women in public places, not if he could help it. With Kalina Harper, he wasn't sure restraint was going to be his friend.

"I don't need a hero," she said as the elevator arrived and she stepped inside. Moving all the way to the back, she leaned against the wall and sighed. "Look, I'm sorry if I seem rude."

He let that comment linger a moment because she was straddling that fence to rude, but he sensed it was more of a defense mechanism than a purposeful snub.

"Guess I'm just having a rough day."

Rome nodded, pressed the GARAGE button, and stood beside her while the elevator began its smooth descent. "It's Friday, they're usually rough." She didn't respond. "But you said you have plans for this evening. So maybe your weekend will pick up."

She looked at him then; Rome knew because he couldn't keep his eyes off her. Again, he felt almost like a stalker staring at her every chance he could, even standing a little closer to her than was probably polite. But the way she was looking at him said she was more than a little intrigued herself.

"I hope so." Her tone was markedly lighter this time, the corners of her lips even going so far as to tilt upward in a slight smile.

As the elevator doors opened, Rome put his arm up to keep the doors ajar and nodded for her to walk out first. "Which way is your car?"

"I'm on this level at the end. But it's fine, I can manage alone."

Rome shook his head. "My mother would not be happy if I let a woman walk to her car alone in a deserted parking garage. Come on," he told her.

She walked beside him, stealing a glance at him every now and then, which only made his erection grow harder.

When they stopped in front of a dark blue Honda, he waited while she found her keys.

"Thanks," she said with that timid smile again. "For this, I mean, and for the other night."

He hadn't thought she'd mention it but was glad she had. Their little tryst on his desk had been one of the foremost thoughts in his mind today. "No problem. I should be thanking you actually."

"Me? For what?"

She'd found her key and moved in to slip it into the driver's-side lock. When she moved so did Rome, coming to stand directly behind her, so close that he could smell whatever products she'd used in her hair that morning. "For awakening something in me I thought was long buried." The words were more truthful than he'd intended, but she wouldn't know the real meaning behind them. *Hopefully,* he thought with only the slightest regret.

She didn't move, not even a flinch. But her body temperature spiked, mingling with his own. "That wasn't my intention," she said.

"Maybe not," he said, finally touching a hand to her

arm. "But there it is." He leaned forward, kissed the nape of her neck. "And here we are."

They were in a very public place. Even though the garage was empty, there were cameras everywhere per his own security specifications. Not to mention the fact that his guards were always close by. Even though he didn't see the two shifters assigned to his personal detail, they were around, no doubt about it.

But try as he might, Rome couldn't stay away from her. It both baffled and aroused him.

"This is so not a good idea," she said, slipping the key into the lock and clicking it. She had to back up to pull the door open. Rome moved with her, remaining close enough to keep both their body temperatures elevated.

"I thought that myself a couple of times with you being my employee and us barely knowing each other. But you cannot honestly tell me you don't feel what's between us."

She turned then, so that her back was to the open door and her front facing him.

"I feel the lust, Mr. Reynolds. I'm not a corpse and I'm not crazy enough to deny it. But acting on it's a whole other can of worms I'd rather not open."

Kalina lifted her palms to Rome's chest, the contact sending an electric charge through his system that almost had him gasping for breath. Then she pushed him back, far enough so that he was now a full arm's length away from her.

"I know a man whose mother trained him to be so chivalrous as to walk a lady to her car also knows how to take no for an answer."

She dropped her arms, sliding into the front seat without hesitation. Rome held the door to keep her from

closing it on him. Leaning forward, he got close enough
to touch his lips lightly to her ear.

"I didn't hear you say no, Kalina."

Her body tightened; the only movement was the rise
and fall of her chest. She thought he was going to kiss
her or at least try to. But he didn't. He simply stayed
right there, inhaling her scent, letting every nuance of
her filter through him. She hadn't said no and wasn't saying it now. He doubted she could any more than he.

Finally, she sighed. "Good night, Mr. Reynolds."

Rome pulled back, closed her door, and watched as
she pulled off. "A very good night to you, too, Ms.
Harper."

"Where'd you find this?" Nick asked the minute Rome
slipped into the backseat of the limousine.

Tapping the glass, Rome gave the signal for Eli to
drive. "The collar of my jacket."

"Tonight?"

He nodded tightly, remembering the moment he'd
slid his hands over the lapels and under the back collar.
The device was small, intricate, designed to be missed
upon inspection. For a minute he'd thought it was a pin
left in by the cleaners until tiny hairs on the back of his
neck had stood on end.

"It's tracking you. Why didn't you destroy it?" Nick
asked, still fingering the small diamond-like piece.

"Because whoever's bold enough to get close to my
clothes wants to get close to me. I figure it only makes
sense to oblige." Rome might be calm in his approach,
but when pushed he definitely pushed back. If somebody
wanted to know where he was, he wasn't going to make
it hard to find him.

"Let the games begin," Nick added, pushing the left side of his jacket back just enough to reveal the gun he had holstered there.

Rome rarely carried a weapon to functions like this, but Nick was always strapped. So there was no surprise seeing the gun and there was no doubt his friend would use it the minute he felt it was necessary. "We're keeping a low profile tonight. Ralph Kensington needs this fund-raiser to go well."

"And I know how much you like Ralph Kensington."

Rome hated the man, hated the stench of his lies and duplicity like a kid hated visits to the dentist. Still, it helped to keep up pretenses. Besides, Jace Maybon—the Pacific Faction Leader—had picked up a Rogue scent when Kensington visited LA last year. They were positive Kensington wasn't a shifter, but he'd obviously been in contact with one. Whether the well-known legislator knew that or not had yet to be proven. With that piece of information, Rome made a point to keep in close contact with the man who tonight would announce his run for the US Senate.

"Kensington's up to something. He knew Baines personally—they gave a dinner together earlier this year."

"You think he may know something about Baines's murder?" Nick's normally cultured tone was slipping, the wild edge to his voice revealing the animal within. It was a subtle change but one Rome knew well.

Rome shook his head, his fingers tapping on the door handle. "I'm not going on what I think right now. I know that Baines and his daughter had their skulls crushed then were ripped to pieces by something the medical examiner could only describe as a vicious, sharp weapon. That's not a normal murder technique. Jace picked up the Rogue scent on Kensington last summer. When I saw Kensington a few weeks ago, I picked it up as well."

Nick slammed a fist on the seat. "You should have said something then. We could have defused the situation sooner."

"I'm not killing Kensington. I want answers."

"If he's in cahoots with Rogues he's not likely to give you answers, Rome."

Rome's head snapped toward Nick, sharp canines pricking his lower lip. "He won't have a choice."

The Faction Leaders were scheduled to meet next weekend, the senator's murder bringing all of them here. The need to rein in whatever evil was brewing among the shifters was imperative. Their goal was to live quietly among the purebred humans, to not be discovered for fear of being considered natural-born killers. But every time Rome thought of the grueling way in which the senator and his innocent daughter were killed, he cringed. There was a small element of truth in calling them natural-born killers. He felt it rippling up his spine even now as he thought about it. If faced with the Rogue who did the killings, Rome wasn't 100 percent positive that he wouldn't snap the shifter's neck himself. But that was his animal half, the part of himself he tried to suppress as much as possible while living in this world. He was beginning to think the suppression approach wasn't going to last for long.

The Linden Hotel was midway to opulent. Pulling up in front, Eli—one of Rome's shifter guards—was out of the car first. His twin brother, Ezra, also a guard working under Rome's leadership, had parked the Tahoe he drove to the party and was already standing curbside waiting for them. As the Faction Leader and commanding officer, both Rome and Nick warranted guards whenever they traveled. Eli and Ezra were shifters who grew up in the Gungi but had come to the States as teenagers. Their large builds, death stares, and simple lethal aura cast them in the positions of bodyguards almost immediately. They'd been with Rome for almost ten years now. Besides Nick, Baxter, and his other shifter friend, Xavier, he didn't trust anyone with his life but the jaguar brothers.

Stepping out of the car, Rome immediately began scanning the area. People seemed to be everywhere, stepping out of limos, walking up the stone stairs to the front entry, coming out of the doors heading down the steps. It looked like a star-studded Hollywood event. The air was still, almost sticky, but not quite. Night air should have been cooler, but this was DC in the summertime. The fact that he wasn't sweating through his suit said it was probably as cool as it was going to get.

He'd lived in the city long enough to know that with the heat came trouble. Violence always seemed to escalate in the summer months, bringing the most notorious criminal element into an already volatile place infested with drugs and other unsavory addictions. Simply put, this was a breeding ground for the Rogues, a virtual cesspool of situations to exploit in their quest for dominance.

How they, the Shadow Shifters—as they were called by the human tribes living outside the Gungi—had gotten to this place, Rome still wondered. Even tribesmen did not know for sure that the shifters existed, which was why they called them shadows. All they knew was the report of glimpses of humans shifting into animals deep within the rain forest. But most of the tribesmen were afraid to venture into the rain forest, scared of unknown animals and eventual death. About half the humans believed the so-called myth; the other half strongly objected to the theory, and without any real proof the believers just looked more like weirdos to their people. So the secret was still safe. For now.

The Rogues would see that changed. They believed they were the superior species and were out to prove their point in any way necessary. That made them the public enemy number one to Rome and the stateside shifters.

Tonight, however, Rome thought he might have another enemy closing in.

As he moved into the large marble-floored foyer, his entire body tensed. Thick muscles bunched beneath the material of his clothes, causing the fabric to itch against his skin. High ceilings with large shimmering gold chandeliers opened to a huge space complete with ornate gold and cream furniture that looked as if it were inspired by the eighteenth-century decor. To the left was a large marble countertop where guests could check in to one of the five hundred rooms on the premises. To the right, where Rome and Nick were now headed, was another foyer. Men dressed in tuxedos, women in evening gowns and diamonds galore headed in that direction.

They were all going to the same function, one of the biggest political rallies of the year.

It had been rumored that Kensington was going to run for the Senate seat Baines's death left vacant, but most thought it was just rumor. Rome had been one of them. Ralph Kensington was a loudmouthed lobbyist.

He'd gotten his break after heading up the IT department of Slakeman Enterprises. The story was that Kensington found Bob Slakeman a buyer for his latest military-strength rifles, even though military officials had already declared the guns unsafe. The buyer had been foreign, and few details were given about the sale. Kensington suddenly became a richer man with aspirations in the direction of politics. Nothing had been proven and as far as Rome knew there was no ongoing investigation. That was a shame because he was sure there was more to the story.

Rome's second closest friend, Xavier "X" Santos-Markland, worked with the FBI. As a shifter himself, X kept an eye on the government's activities, especially in the area of suspicious beings. He reported directly to the Assembly, giving reports also to the Faction Leaders anytime there was activity or special investigations in their regions. He lived here in DC, but he traveled constantly in his role as special director at the Bureau. So far, X hadn't reported anything on the Kensington–Slakeman connection, although Rome had given him a heads-up about the situation almost a year ago. That just meant the government, as usual, would be the last to know when something went down in their own backyard.

Eli and Ezra were behind them, inconspicuously close, just as Rome suspected other bodyguards were to their employers throughout the massive ballroom they'd just entered. There would be some pretty powerful people in attendance tonight, powerful people with money. That seemed to be the name of the game lately. But Rome was here for a different reason. He was here to see Josef Bingham, his parents' attorney.

"How long do you figure this'll take?" Nick asked, flicking his wrist to look at his watch.

"Got another hot date?" Rome asked, looking around the room. He didn't want to be here any longer than he had to. The sooner he found Bingham and got what he needed from him, the sooner they could leave.

"Nah, not tonight. I just don't like the company we're in." Nick frowned as he looked around. "Too many bullshitters in one room for me."

Rome nodded. "I'm with you on that one. But it's a means to an end. Kensington wanted us here, sent a special invite, remember." One that Rome would have respectfully ignored had it not been for Bingham's follow-up message asking for this meeting.

"I remember. I didn't like it then and I don't like it now. Doesn't feel right." Nick was rubbing his chin, his fingers moving over the thin goatee he'd let grow in. Tension radiated from his body as his cat strained at the surface, ready for battle.

Rome had felt that, too, the edgy need to fight, to protect. Stateside shifters didn't fight often. They weren't in the jungle and strived to act more humane than their counterparts in the Gungi. But tonight, something was setting them off, irritating the beasts within until they were on edge.

"I know how it feels. Keep your eyes open. There's someone I have to see." Rome started to move away when Nick took his arm.

"Take Eli with you."

Rome nodded, turned to give a barely there signal to Eli, and walked away. Nick knew Rome was searching for his parents' killers. He knew that Rome wanted to search alone, so that if he found any information that might be sensitive to his parents' memory, he could keep it quiet. So both he and X tried to give Rome the space to deal with this situation. But by no means was Rome in this alone. He and X had Rome's back just as they knew he would have theirs if the tables were turned.

Nick knew there was a battle brewing, just as he knew that they would be right in the middle of it through no fault of their own. Reasons didn't matter to Nick; that sort of understanding-and-cooperation bull was for Rome. For him, it was what it was. If their parents had botched up something in their lifetime and it was now time for their children to deal with the repercussions, so be it. It was past time they dealt with this situation anyway.

As for Rome and his crusade, Nick supported him and would do whatever he could to protect Rome when the time came. Sometimes blood didn't have to be thicker than water.

Josef Bingham's law firm had been started forty years ago by old money and today was still thriving, making even more money. By normal standards Bingham should have retired about ten years back, but Rome had to admit that at seventy-six years old the man was still as feisty as ever.

Next to Baxter and Henrique Delgado, Nick's father, Bingham was the closest thing his father had to a friend. At least, that's what Baxter had told him. Trust didn't come easy for shifters, and came even harder when a shifter gave his trust to a human, but Bingham must have won his father over for the man to have some personal effect of Vance Reynolds's.

Rome found Bingham near the bar, exactly where he suspected he'd find him, drink already in hand.

"Mr. Bingham?" he said, clapping a hand on the man's shoulder before giving the bartender a nod to bring him a drink.

"Ah, Roman, my boy. Wasn't sure you'd show up tonight," he said, giving way to a cough that seemed to rattle the extra skin at his neck and probably most of his insides.

"I was invited," Rome replied. "And I rarely turn down invitations like this."

"Yes, I believe tonight promises to be a special night."

Over Bingham's shoulder Rome saw a young blonde with breasts that seemed hard-pressed to stay inside the bodice of her dress rubbing long-nailed fingers over the old man's shoulder. She could easily be Bingham's daughter, but Rome wasn't naive enough to believe that for a minute. "Really? Why is that?"

"Ralph's making his announcement, you know. People on the Hill might not like it. Gonna stir things up on the political scene, that one is."

Rome couldn't deny the truth of those words. But the kind of stirring-up he suspected Kensington was going to do wasn't what Bingham was referring to.

"I agree." Rome took a sip of his drink, let the warmth of the alcohol slide down his throat. What was Kensington up to really, and how did it involve the Rogues? Numerous questions mingled in his mind but it wasn't a problem. Rome knew how to multitask. "Did you bring it?"

"You don't beat around the bush, do you?" Bingham chuckled then gulped down the remaining contents of his glass. Lifting a blue-veined hand, he wiggled his fingers to signal for another drink.

Rome caught the bartender's eye just in time to mouth the word *no*. With a shrug the bartender moved on, and Rome looked at Bingham.

"You said you had something for me, something I needed to see."

Bingham nodded. "Right. I do." Reaching inside his jacket, he pulled out a disk. "Your father had a safe-deposit box."

"I thought all the safe-deposit boxes had been cleaned out after their deaths," Rome said looking at the disk, not yet willing to take it into his hands. Baxter, his parents' butler and the man who'd taken care of Rome after their deaths, had gone through all his parents' things. He'd told Rome he'd given him all their possessions. Now thoughts of what could possibly be stored on this disk ran through his mind, causing his heart to pound with both anticipation and dread. This might put him one step closer, one clue nearer to finding their killers.

"This one was in my name. I'd forgotten all about it until my assistant retired and the new girl they hired brought this invoice to me. I went there myself and cleaned it out."

"And that was the only thing in there?"

Bingham nodded. "And a note that I should make sure this got to you should anything happen to Vance."

And something had definitely happened to him. He'd been brutally murdered by one of his own kind. Rome only hoped this disk would tell him why.

This was insane, she thought for the billionth time tonight. Attending this function was dangerous for too many reasons. For one, Kalina deduced as she pulled her car to a stop, thumping her fingers on the steering wheel, she could blow her cover. Greer Culverson, the chief of police, would surely be here. His connections in the political arena were no secret; there were already whispers of him putting in a bid for mayor next term. Not to mention any number of suspects she may have come across, because despite what most thought, drugs and drug dealers existed even in the tallest office buildings and highest-priced houses in DC. The epidemic wasn't limited to the streets or what was called the lower class. Over the years she'd investigated and even arrested her share of businessmen and political wannabes for their roles in the drug game.

In addition, what if Roman saw her? What would she say? What would be her reason for attending this function? The decision to come here had been made quickly, just as the one to slip the tracking device onto the collar of his tuxedo had been, and the one to follow him to his house last night. She couldn't pass up the opportunity, she'd decided that when Mel invited her to lunch. The secretary had casually mentioned she'd have to pick Roman's tuxedo up from the dry cleaners and this plan was hatched. Hurrying back to her desk Kalina had called Ferrell, telling him what she wanted to do. Within the hour she was going down to the parking lot to meet Ferrell, who handed her the equipment.

"We'll work on getting you tickets to the event tomorrow. I want you to watch everybody he talks to and make note. He might be going to this thing for more than political reasons. It could be a transaction going down, and I don't want to miss it."

And yet he'd known nothing about Rome even attending tonight's ball until she told him. He'd been talking fast, his dark lips chapped from smoking too much. He wore a wool hat over his balding head but his eyes were astute, watching her like she was the one under investigation.

"Don't mess this up, Harper."

She snatched the plastic bag with the receiver in it from his hand. "I know how to do my job."

"Yeah, well, you're taking your own sweet time doing it."

She had wanted to punch him. Never before had there been a co-worker or commanding officer whom Kalina disliked as much as Ferrell. There was just something about his personality that made her want to puke, then wipe her mouth and kick his ass for making her go to all the trouble.

"I'll get the information. Just get me into that party."

"Right," he said, turning away from her as if she were the one who disgusted him.

Over chicken quesadillas and diet Cokes she and Mel had talked about Mel's family, her time at the firm, and how the woman enjoyed working for Rome. Kalina had been careful not to ask too many questions about the man. She didn't want to give Mel the wrong idea, even though she thought it was probably too late for that. While she didn't want Mel to think she was trying to snag the boss, she certainly didn't want her to know she was investigating him.

As soon as the device was activated, she'd switched on the transmitter and hidden it behind the monitor on her desk until the workday was over. When he'd been

there as she'd packed up to leave at five, she'd almost
been afraid he'd found out. Being busted by Rome again
was going to wreak holy hell on her confidence as a cop.

But as he'd stood there staring at her as if he could
literally eat her up on the spot, she suspected he'd stopped
by for another reason entirely. Walking her to her car
had been a shock. She hadn't pegged Reynolds for the
chivalrous type, and yet the kind gesture seemed to suit
him. The dominant aura that pushed his hard body
against hers had also seemed like second nature to him.
Roman Reynolds was definitely a man who got what he
wanted. Kalina just had to make sure that what he really wanted wasn't her.

Even though she'd pulled out of the garage before
him, she'd waited until his car had come out, then followed him to what she assumed was his home. It was a
large estate in one of the district's high-end neighborhoods near the Virginia state line. She only knew the
neighborhood from glimpses in the society pages but
now figured the newspapers didn't do the palatial estates
in this area justice. The house itself was huge, the grounds
seeming to go on forever, with the plushest, greenest
grass she'd ever seen. He'd stopped at a black iron gate,
punched in a code, and waited while the gates opened
for him. Of course they'd closed and she wasn't able to
drive up the winding driveway behind him. But that was
just as well. She didn't want to get too close.

Her body reacted strangely when in close proximity
to this man. Well, not exactly strangely . . . Kalina knew
sexual attraction when she felt it. She just didn't want to
feel it for Roman Reynolds. Still, as she'd watched him
walk to his car, briefcase and suit jacket in one hand
while the material of his dress shirt molded his abso-

lutely kick-ass upper body, her mouth had watered. Even now, just sitting in her car thinking about him had her nipples hardening, her center pulsating with need. A need that hadn't plagued her in years.

She tensed at the thought, heat moving in slow rivulets throughout her veins. Heat she hadn't felt in . . . heat she had never felt before in her life. That's what this attraction to him was, it was new and unwanted and she detested it. He was a criminal and deserved to be treated as such. How dare she want on her body the same hands that exchanged money with the cartels, which in turn shipped drugs to the streets that were killing kids? How could she sit here and wonder how it would feel to walk into that big house with him, to spend the night in his bed, beneath his muscled body, letting him do whatever he wanted to bring her pleasure? It was deplorable and ridiculously inappropriate to think of him that way.

And yet she couldn't stop.

So tonight she was at Ralph Kensington's first political banquet to support his run for the Senate. She didn't support him or the crooked people he had working for him—whom she couldn't actually connect him to. Kensington was in the drug game up to the crisp white collar of his expensive dress shirt, but he was good at covering up his less savory deals. Tonight, however, she couldn't afford to worry about all the corruption going on in the government. She was here to watch Rome and there was no turning back. Stepping out of her car, she handed the keys over to the valet, who looked young enough to still be in high school. He smiled at her as she walked by, that *I wanna get with you. Give me your number?* kind of smile. Kalina was flattered but not at all moved to try her hand as a cougar. Younger men were definitely not her style. As a matter of fact, no man—at least for the last couple of years—was her style. Funny she would think about that now—the fact that she didn't have and hadn't had a man in a long time.

Those thoughts cluttered her mind as she walked into the hotel, down the foyer, and right in the line of sight of one very sexy and angry-looking Roman Reynolds.

Thinking fast, she turned on her heels and moved in the opposite direction. Not out of the ballroom completely but toward the other side of the room. She didn't want Rome to see her, even though he had no idea she was following him. The quick glimpse of him had her heart thumping against her chest and some other vibration moving toward her center. Cursing as she moved through the ballroom, she hated the fact that he could arouse her on sight. Hated that her body felt drawn to him, like he sang a song for only her to dance to. It was crazy, she knew, but that's how she felt. Even now, as she moved farther away from him, that tug was still there, that urging inside her to go to him, to be with him in any way possible.

She ignored it, snagging a glass of champagne from a tray carried by a woman dressed in slacks, shirt, and jacket that made her look more like a man. She barely sipped, wanting to blend in but not sacrifice her good judgment. Champagne or any alcoholic beverage for that matter put her right over the top, and it didn't take much. So she'd learned long ago to keep her sips short and shallow.

She couldn't see Rome but she felt his presence, knew he was there and he was close. And wasn't it crazy that she was supposed to be here watching him, yet she was running in the opposite direction?

Get a grip, Harper. Her own words echoed in her head and she took another sip of champagne. Clutching her purse, she thought about her job at the MPD and how much she wanted the position with the DEA. She wasn't going to get it by running from Roman Reynolds. Whatever this physical thing was between them, she could handle it. She'd handled killers and drug-dealing scum for the last six years of her life; surely one sexy-ass man couldn't be that big a deal.

When her glass was empty she looked at it in surprise, then figured she was ready to face him. She turned and scanned the room but didn't see Rome.

But someone saw her. A trio of someones she noticed as her head turned in the opposite direction. Three men, all dressed in tuxedos, all looking as if their minds were on something other than this function. Something rolled beneath her skin—a warning, traipsing along the length of her arms.

Her gaze locked with the man in the middle, the biggest, meanest-looking one. He was dark, his skin like polished onyx, his lips thick, nose wide and flat. But it was his eyes that drew her, the eerie slant to them that made him seem more inhuman than he should. The other two beside him shared that different type of look—or she should probably say glare. And each of them was glaring at her.

Not even with all her training was Kalina prepared for the rush of anxiety pouring through her. They began to walk toward her, and everything around her seemed to slow so that only those three men moved. The wild thumping of her heart echoed in her ears, her skin itching with an awareness she'd never experienced before. Who were they and why were they coming for her?

When answers didn't come soon enough she turned, opting to get the hell out of Dodge, saving the analysis for later. But when she turned it wasn't toward an easy escape. Instead she rammed into an immovable strength, a force that might prove harder to deal with than the three strangers behind her.

"Don't move." His voice was deep and more sinister than any she'd ever heard.

It was also familiar.

Chapter 5

"What—" she started, but the hands that gripped her shoulders slid down her arms to stop at her waist. Heat speared through her body, halting her words.

He turned her so that she was at his side, his arms tightening around her, holding her there.

The party seemed to come back to life. She could hear the voices of those around her, the clinking of heels across the floor, the sound of murmured conversations. Searching the crowd, she quickly spotted the three men, who had stopped their approach but still glared at her menacingly.

"Making friends?" Rome asked from beside her.

"I don't know them," she answered trying desperately to hide how nervous she really was. Why three strange men scared her she had no idea. No, that was wrong. She knew exactly why they scared her, and the knowledge pissed her off. No matter how much time had passed or how many visits to the shrink she'd made, the events of that night still haunted her. On the streets she was a tough undercover narcotics detective, with her badge and her gun always nearby. She'd been trained to kill if need be, to bring justice at all costs. But one night none of that could help. She'd been alone, vulnerable, and afraid. And she'd hated it. Hated it even more when those emotions crept up, taking hold of her.

"You can let me go now," she said, bravado trying to win out.

"What if I said I like holding on to you?"

"I'd say I don't care. Let me go," she insisted, pushing against his side. He was a lot stronger than he looked garbed in his perfectly cut tuxedo—a tuxedo that just made him all the more attractive. Just one more reason she needed to get away.

"Not just yet," he whispered, but he wasn't looking at her this time. He was looking across the room.

Following his gaze, she wasn't surprised to see he was staring at the three stooges who had been taunting her with their eerie eyes and fullback builds.

"I don't know who they are." Why she admitted that, Kalina had no idea. It could be that she was still trying to figure out why they were watching her. This was so not the way her investigation was supposed to go. But suddenly she wasn't in the mood to investigate. He wasn't supposed to know she was here and now he did. Those men creeped her out—that wasn't supposed to happen, either, but it had. And now she'd rather go home and curse herself for being so stupid and so weak. How did she expect to get into the DEA if she couldn't handle following this one man and getting the goods on him?

His jaw clenched and she thought she heard a low growling sound. But Kalina was tired, her emotions were all out of whack, and she just wanted to go home. Coming here tonight had obviously been a bad idea. "Look, can I go now?"

He turned to her then, his expression quizzical. "I'll take you home."

She shook her head. "Don't bother, I drove."

"I'll have your car brought to your house," he said, turning away from the three goons and pulling her along as he stalked through the crowded ballroom.

"I don't need a ride," she said, finally yanking her arm free of his grasp. The action startled even her and she stumbled back a bit, only to feel another steel hardness behind her.

"We meet again, Ms. Harper."

His voice was smoother, his face just a touch softer than Rome's. She turned to stare up at Nick Delgado, his laughing hazel eyes looking back at her. He was a handsome man, there was no doubt. From the silky ink-black hair to the thick eyebrows and firm jaw. He had a great build, not bulky but toned. Sex appeal just about oozed from every one of his pores. And Kalina suspected he knew all his attributes without her running down a mental list. But he wasn't Rome.

And why the hell did she care anyway?

"Hello," she said tightly. "And good night," she finished, turning to look at a none-too-pleased Roman.

"Call Ezra." Rome looked over her shoulder to Nick. "Tell him to bring the car around back. We're leaving."

"Five minutes," she heard Nick say from behind.

"Let's go," he said as if just now remembering she was there.

"When hell freezes over," she snapped and moved from between them with a quickness she didn't know she possessed.

He followed behind her, giving Eli a nod as he did. The guard moved past him, getting closer to Kalina. Directly beside the huge open bar was a door, and through that door was a hallway and stairs that would take them to the lower-level parking garage and out into the hotel's side alley. It was Eli and Ezra's job to inspect any premises he went into beforehand. Knowing all entrances and the exits was imperative, especially in times like these.

They were shifters, the ones that had been coming for Kalina, just as he'd scented when he first came in. Rogues that carried the telltale stench of evil and corruption. It was a bitter tinge against the normal feline scent that enveloped the shifters, making them able to identify one another in this world of humans. All night Rome had wondered where they were and what they were up to. Even after he'd met with Bingham the sense that someone who didn't belong and was creeping about assailed him. He'd wanted to find out who, so instead of leaving right away he'd had Nick and Ezra cover one half of the ballroom while he and Eli took the other.

Rome had spotted them first. Or rather, he'd spotted their prey.

In the midst of a couple hundred of DC's most influential and attractive females, she stood out like a ripe apple in a barrel of rotten ones. For a minute he thought it was the smoky gray dress she wore that hugged her hips, thighs, and ass. Or was it the way that dress bared her back, cupping her breasts in the front so enticingly that his palms itched to touch her?

In the midst of desire he'd felt it, the clenching in his chest that had his protective instincts kicking in. His gaze wandered beyond her, resting on the three shifters stalking her. He didn't know them personally but he knew what they wanted. Hunger and lust filled their gazes as their bodies prepared to move in. They wouldn't care that it was three against one. They would use her together until one of them proved dominant. Then that one would take her alone, ravish her until she was useless, and kill her. It was their way, the no-boundaries way Rogues preferred to live. They preyed and they killed, it was as simple as that. And somehow, Kalina had been caught in their snare.

Possessiveness such as he'd never known washed over him and before Rome could think twice he was stalking across the floor determined to reach her before they did. It was close, the scent of Kalina's fear pushing him closer to the edge of insanity. If they'd managed to get to her, if one of them had put a finger on her . . . his temples throbbed, his heart thumping wildly. He had to get her out of here.

Finding out what she'd been doing here in the first place would have to wait until later.

She was just about to pass the bar when Eli moved in front of her, stopping her passage. She looked up at him and was probably ready to curse him into next week when Rome stepped up behind her, putting his hands firmly at her waist. Leaning over, he whispered in her ear, "If you scream or try to run you'll make a scene. They'll come after you. Your choice is simple, go with me or be taken by them."

Her body stiffened, the round globes of her ass rubbing against his own throbbing arousal. She was contemplating, her annoyance at him warring with her fear of them, the unknown. What she didn't know was that there was no way in hell he was going to let the Rogues get within feet of her, let alone take her.

"I won't hurt you," Rome said, his mouth watering at being so close to her skin. He wanted to lick her, to taste her once more so that he'd never forget such sweetness.

She gave the barest nod of her head. Eli led the way. They were slipping through the side door in seconds, Rome looking back only once to make sure the Rogues weren't on their trail. They did not give up easily, especially not when a female was involved. But they hadn't followed; they'd actually backed away the moment they saw him. He knew that wasn't due to any respect for his ranking among the shifters. They didn't give a shit what title he held; Rogues were supremacists with egos bigger than any human or shifter he'd ever met. The fact that they weren't coming after him gave him pause.

Eli headed down the stairs first with Kalina between the two of them.

"We're coming down," he spoke into the com link he, the guards, and Nick shared.

At the bottom of the stairs Eli pulled the door open. With a hand to the small of her back, Rome pushed Kalina through. Ezra pulled up first in the black Tahoe, the back door already swinging open. Eli grabbed it, stepping to the side with a swift nod to Rome. At the signal he grabbed Kalina by the waist, lifting her into the back of the vehicle. The door slammed behind them and they were moving before Rome was completely seated.

Eli would now drive the limo, which Nick had retained and pulled up right behind in the Tahoe. They would go in the opposite direction from Ezra and Rome just in case anyone decided to follow them.

Kalina slid all the way over, plastering her back against the opposite passenger door. "Take me home," she stated without hesitation.

"Your wish is my command," he answered, settling back in the seat. Taking out his cell phone, he keyed in her address, sending the text to Ezra in the front seat as well as Nick and Eli. Then he put the phone back into his pocket. "You can relax now, you're safe."

Folding her arms over her chest, she huffed. "How do I know that? You don't look any safer than those guys back there. Oh, and by the way, I'm no damsel in distress. I did not need rescuing, thank you very much."

No, she was no damsel in distress. More like a spitfire waiting to be ignited.

"You were in trouble. I simply arrived at the right time."

"Whatever," she said then turned, pushing her back against the seat. "Just take me home."

He scented her nervousness and agitation. Or maybe she was pissed he'd interrupted. Whichever, Rome wanted her to feel safe, and his gut told him that the threesome back there was anything but safe to her.

"What were you doing here?"

"What? I can't go to a political fund-raiser?"

"You don't look like the type to support Kensington in his race for the Senate."

"What's that supposed to mean? Is my political affiliation now scrawled on my forehead?"

"I thought you were a number cruncher. It just seems a bit out of place for you to be at a political function."

She looked at him like she wanted to hit him. His lips twitched at that thought. This woman had a lot of spunk and it aroused something in him.

"I'm well versed in politics as well as other things, Mr. Reynolds. Just because I work in accounting doesn't mean I can't think of anything else."

He held a law degree, was a Faction Leader to more than three thousand shifters on the East Coast, and stood to inherit a place in the Assembly should he ever return to the Gungi. Yet at this moment, instead of strategizing or analyzing what had just happened back there, he couldn't think of anything except getting her naked.

"Did you know those men? Was one of them the one you were speaking to on the phone to this afternoon?" The thought had crossed his mind that one of those stooges could have been the one giving her a hard time earlier today, and he wanted to know for sure if he was dealing with just a jealous boyfriend or something way more dangerous. Because they were definitely Rogues, and for reasons he wasn't quite ready to acknowledge Rome prayed it wasn't the jealous-boyfriend angle.

"I don't know who they were or why they were gawking at me that way. And you should try minding your own business. My phone call was private."

"It sounded more than private. Is someone harassing you?"

"Other than you?" she snapped, giving him an angry stare of her own.

"Let's try this another way. Just so you know, Kalina, I'm not going to let this go. Those guys were definitely gunning for you, and I want to know why. Either you're going to tell me or I'll find out on my own."

She exhaled deeply. "I don't know them."

"And the one you were talking to on the phone? Is he a problem?"

"He's my problem."

Rome's jaw clenched. This wasn't the answer he wanted, but like he said he'd deal with it in his own way. She didn't have to tell him anything else.

He also needed to deal with this painful erection before his mood became any more foul than it already was.

It seemed the hostility between them had only stoked the fire growing in the pit of his stomach.

Suddenly the truck's interior was a lot warmer than it had been before. In his haste to get her inside and out of sight, her dress had hiked up her legs so that it now showed an enticing amount of skin. The legs he remembered admiring as she'd walked into his office the other day were now displayed like a delicacy. Swallowing hard, he tried to adjust the burgeoning erection that threatened to drive him out of his mind. It had been that way since she'd walked into his office—each time he'd thought of her, remembered her voice, the feel of her writhing beneath him. He wanted her and *desperately* didn't quite seem to describe how bad.

"You're incredibly sexy when you're pissed off," he said, reaching out to brush his knuckles over her bare shoulder.

Normally he liked women with long hair, figuring it gave them a more feminine look. But the short, spiky cut of Kalina's hair did something for him, and it fit her feisty personality perfectly. When she turned her eyes narrowed, and she looked at him like a woman ready to fight. Behind his zipper his erection protested, straining to break free.

"We've had the discussion about sexual harassment before, Mr. Reynolds. And again, no means no."

"Call me Rome. It seems highly unusual to refer to a prospective lover so formally." He *would* be her lover—Rome knew this as surely as he knew his own name. There was something pushing them together; whether it was just circumstances or something more, he couldn't really tell. And didn't really care at the moment.

"What? You . . . we—" She stopped, took a deep breath, then released it in what could only be construed as a barely restrained manner. "You are the boss and I am the employee. We are not now, nor will we ever be lovers." She jerked away from him and heat soared through his body.

The challenge was clear, and the beast within acted quickly. He was across the seat in seconds, grasping her at the nape of her neck, pulling her to him until she was half sprawled over his lap. She glared at him, her lips parting in surprise just before he claimed them, swiping his tongue across them in one swift stroke.

"Tell me no, Kalina. Say no and I'll stop."

Her body shivered in his arms as he pulled her bottom lip into his mouth, suckling until her palms were pressing against his chest. His mouth opened over hers and he plunged into the kiss with all the fierce desire he had inside.

It had been months since he'd had a woman. Of course it had been his choice. Shifters were known for their insatiable and sometimes dark sexual desires. They were created to breed, and if it wasn't fighting for survival that occupied their minds it was most likely the sexual hunger that ate at them on a daily basis. Rome hadn't wanted anyone in particular for weeks, and so he hadn't taken anyone. Not until now, not until Kalina.

Everything about her appealed to him on a level he'd never ventured before. It was strange and yet it felt right. His mother would say fate. To be safe Rome was classifying it as opportunity. Her body was luscious, his hands slipping down her bare back to cup her plump bottom. She sighed, moaning into their kiss her pleasure at his touch. He lifted her leg, adjusted her until she straddled him completely, then let his palms knead her ass, his fingers grazing in between until the heat of her pussy tickled his fingertips.

"Say no," he whispered.

She should have kneed him in the nuts again. Her teeth could clamp down on his lips and draw blood. Memories of the night she was sexually assaulted sifted on the outskirts of her thoughts, reservations at being touched intimately by a man warring with the sweetest sensations he was arousing in her. She could give in to the fear, to the dark hatred she harbored for the one who'd dared to touch her without permission.

Or . . . she could just sink into this feeling—this foreign reaction to a man she barely knew. She could let the memories of the last time he'd touched her commingle with the heated dreams she'd had of him in the days since. And she could enjoy.

It wasn't something she did often, not normally having much in her personal life to enjoy. But this, his touch, the husky rumble of his voice in the dark interior of this truck, did something to her, pushed her to be what she'd never thought she could be again.

A woman.

In the moments since she'd been closed in with him Kalina had felt sexier than she had in her entire life. Her body hummed with anticipation. The way his eyes raked over her said *sex,* pure and simple lust that was now dripping from his every kiss, each touch of his hands along her bared skin. The tips of his fingers grazed her center through the thin material of her dress, and she sucked in a breath. That action lifted her breasts, had the tender nipples scraping along his chest. With erratic breathing and fingers that seemed to operate with their own intentions she gripped the lapels of his jacket, pulling him closer as she opened her mouth to his kiss.

Delving deeper she let her mind clear of all doubts, vowing to take, for once in her life to simply take. When his hands moved past the material of her dress to touch the bare skin of her bottom she hissed, arched her back, and sighed.

"You can't deny me, because that would be like denying yourself," he whispered, his lips fanning over the line of her neck as her head fell back. "Did you wear this hot little dress for me? Did you want me to see it and die from wanting to touch you?"

"No," she whispered.

"Do you want me to stop?" Sharp teeth nipped at her neck, sending spikes of desire straight to her core, now creaming at his silent command. As if he'd known that would be her reaction, his fingers slipped past the thin barrier of her thong, traveling along the dampened folds that opened to her desire. The second he plunged a finger inside Kalina's world changed. Everything she thought she'd known about pleasure, that she'd taught herself through mechanics and imagination, crumbled. What he was doing, this seemingly simple touch, proved all she'd known was drastically wrong.

"No," she panted.

"You want more?"

Her breath came quicker, her body inflamed by his touch. "Rome."

"Yes," he replied, his finger thrusting deeper, then pulling back.

She whimpered at the loss, pressing herself down on him immediately. "Don't stop."

His chuckle was hoarse, rumbling through his chest as he pushed back inside her. "You don't want me to stop. It's okay, I don't want to stop, either, baby. You're so wet and so ready for me. I want to feel you, taste you."

And she wanted whatever he had to give. Or at least she let herself believe she did. Right now it only mattered that he continued to give her pleasure, that his fingers continued to move inside her, pushing her to a pinnacle she'd longed to reach.

Her back arched further as she rode his hand with vehemence. It felt too good to stop, the journey toward that exciting edge too enticing to ignore. And so she traveled, with eyes closed, mouth opened to release each sound that tore from her instinctively. She held on to his shoulders, her breasts moving with the motion, tender and eager for his touch. He was saying something, murmuring words to her that sounded X-rated and highly inappropriate for two people who barely knew each other and who worked together, but aroused her just the same.

"That's good, baby. You want more?"

"Yes." She let the answer tumble from her lips without a second thought and moaned as he pulled out one finger and inserted two more.

It was tight and intense and her body shuddered with pleasure. She bit on her bottom lip, praying for sweet release before she drew her own blood.

"So hot and wet for me. I knew you would be."

"Please." She was begging, her heart hammering in her chest and the persistent need clawing at her.

If she could just get there, if her feet could finally fall from the edge where she'd tumble into ecstasy, she'd be okay. She'd regain her composure and get back to business. But until then, until that moment, she was lost. Purely and simply lost in Rome's touch.

Those sharp teeth of his tugged on a nipple and she screamed. He was driving her insane with need, heat engulfing her as if she'd walked through an inferno and unfortunately survived.

With persistent thrusts he milked her. She rode his hand, loving the feel of him filling her. And then she was there. Absolute weightlessness encircled her, bursts of light filling her as she tumbled free.

For endless seconds she seemed to float there, her head lolling forward to rest on his shoulder while she struggled to catch her breath.

The next thing she comprehended was his hands at her waist, smoothing down the material of her gown on her thighs.

"You're home," he whispered, kissing her temple.

She nodded, acknowledging that she'd heard him. He'd said she was home. The SUV had stopped moving, and distantly she heard the door opening, felt a tepid breeze entering the interior.

She was home.

But home suddenly felt very different.

Chapter 6

"Sabar's gonna kick your ass."

"Shut up, Chavez." Darel snarled, keeping his attention on the road as they drove through the city. They were headed back to headquarters, to check in, give the details of the night, and, yes, to get their nuts handed to them by Sabar.

There was no excuse for what happened tonight, none whatsoever. That's the way Sabar would see it. The man was an animal—literally and figuratively. He had no feelings, no reactions except angry and angrier, deadly and deadliest. He was the walking devil if you believed in such an entity.

Darel did. His mother had believed in Heaven and Hell, a Supreme Good and a Supreme Evil. She died when his father lost his temper and ripped her throat out. No wonder Darel was a little on the off side. Just the type of soldier Sabar had been looking for.

He'd worked for the leader of the Rogue shifters since he was sixteen, after he'd killed his father. *An eye for an eye* was Darel's claim to fame. Sabar said he'd liked that about him.

After tonight, there was no telling what Sabar would think of him. There was a semblance of hurt at that thought, if he was prone to take feelings seriously, which he was not. Or at least he tried not to be.

"You gotta laugh, though." From the backseat of the jeep Chi, a six-and-a-half-foot-tall Asian-looking shifter, chuckled. "You had her and you let her go."

"I wasn't the only one who had her," Darel corrected.

"Yeah, but you're the one in charge," Chavez pointed out.

It was true, he was Sabar's lead enforcer. It was his job to supervise all missions directly assigned by Sabar. This mission in particular was beyond special. Sabar had given specific orders. Find the woman named Kalina Harper and bring her to him—unharmed. Darel had no idea what Sabar wanted with her and didn't dare ask. He was told to do something, he'd had every intention of doing it—and then something happened.

Not something, someone.

"Where'd he come from and why didn't either of you warn me he was coming? We were so caught up in her, he could have snapped all our necks without us doing a damn thing," Darel yelled, jostling his passengers in their seats as he took a hard left turn doing eighty miles an hour.

Chavez shrugged. "We didn't scent him."

"And why was that?" They should have scented him. He was a high-level shifter, one of the shadows with a reputation that preceded him. Roman Reynolds might walk in this world as a human attorney, but in their world he was so much more. He was one of the shifter leaders, a strong one handpicked by the Assembly. He took his job seriously, hunting Rogues with a fierce calmness that scared even the most studious of Sabar's soldiers. Darel wasn't afraid, he just wanted to be prepared when the son of a bitch Faction Leader was on the prowl.

"Because we were all too busy scenting *her,*" Chi added, his usual laughing voice echoing throughout the interior of the jeep. "And damn, she smelled good."

None of them denied that. She had smelled good, aroused and primed. The scent had hit them each at the same time, drawing them to her like metal to magnets. Darel had instantly grown hard, his dick pressing painfully against his thigh each time he inhaled. They could take her together, he'd thought, before turning her over to Sabar. They'd done it before and it was so good. In fact, the three of them preferred it that way. Working together for the last few years had made them as close as brothers, bonding them in ways that weren't normal or acceptable in the eyes of humans. But they didn't live by human rules or moral codes. They didn't live by those of the Assembly, either. They were on their own, as Sabar told them often. They were the true leaders of this earth, so whatever they did had no consequences; it was their right to live above all other life-forms.

Darel had no problem adapting to that way of thinking. If he was hard for that little trick Sabar wanted, so be it. He'd have her. Then she'd go to Sabar.

"You get her address yet?" he asked Chavez, who was pushing buttons on the iPad he kept in the glove compartment.

Chavez was a computer geek, hacking his way into any and every system to get whatever the Rogues needed. That's why Sabar kept him around. Otherwise the beefy, slightly confused shifter had no real purpose.

"Got it!" He smiled at Darel.

"Fine. Put it in the GPS and let's go."

"Yeeee hawwwww!" Chi yelled from the backseat. "We're gonna party tonight!"

They were gonna party all right, Darel thought to himself. And Kalina Harper was going to be the main attraction.

There was something about Kalina Harper.

As Nick sat in the backseat of the limo parked at the top of her street, he watched Rome climbing out of the back of the truck, cradling the woman in his arms as if she were an infant and not a full-grown, exceptionally attractive woman.

He'd been surprised to see her at the function, even more surprised to see Rome shuttling her out of the ballroom with a look of pure rage on his face. From what he could surmise there'd been some kind of trouble. The stench of Rogues in the building gave him a partial indication of what that trouble was.

But Kalina Harper was an anomaly.

What was she doing there? And why was Rome hovering over her like she was to be protected at all costs?

Opening the door himself, he waved off Eli as he attempted to get out to see what he wanted. Nick didn't need the guard, he just wanted to stand here, to look at the building where Rome had taken Kalina inside. There was something going on here, something in the air that had him and his cat on instant alert.

Nick walked slowly, feeling the bunch of muscles just beneath his skin. He wanted to shift, to run through the night and find his prey. But he wasn't in the jungle, hadn't been there in far too long. Memories from his past picked at his brain, and he fought them back. Nick didn't go back. He'd promised himself a long time ago that there was nothing in the past worth traveling backward for.

But tonight, the sounds of the city street, the lingering danger and scent of female arousal in the air, had him wondering if that promise was really meant to be broken.

"How did you know where I lived?" she asked the moment she slipped her key into the door and he entered her apartment behind her.

"You work for me, remember?" He talked as if he hadn't just brought her to an amazing climax, his tone neutral—like they were just co-workers.

The simple fact was they were something more. He was the object of her investigation. This attraction wasn't going to work for them. In fact, it was probably going to make her job a hell of a lot harder. So maybe him acting as if nothing happened in the truck was a good plan. Hell, she didn't know what plan was good or bad at the moment. She'd messed up so royally tonight, she didn't know how she'd backtrack by Monday morning.

The one thing she did know without a doubt was that being in the same room with Rome right now was destroying any coherent thought she could muster. Taking a deep breath she put her purse and keys on the table then turned to bid him good night. But he wasn't there. Moving through her small living room, she entered the closet-like space that served as her dining area. He was at the window, looking out.

"What are you doing in here?"

"Shhhh." He turned to her, bringing a finger to his lips. "Maybe you should pack a few things and come stay with me."

It was eerily quiet, the dimness of her apartment cloaking them while slits of moonlight peeked through the open slats of her mini blinds.

"What? Are you crazy? Who's out there?" She was at the window instantly, looking out to what seemed to be the quiet street. "They didn't follow us." Assuming the "they" she was talking about were the three goons from the party.

Not that she could know for sure, since she was obviously preoccupied during the drive over here—another feather in her cap to make the DEA want desperately to hire her.

"Something's not right," he said, but he didn't look at her. Instead his gaze moved around her apartment like he was trying to find something. He didn't seem to miss a spot.

It was strange and not the nightcap she'd had in mind when she'd left for the evening, watching Roman Reynolds, the hotshot attorney and drop-dead-gorgeous bachelor of the year move about her apartment. But she did watch, did wonder what was going through his mind as he wandered around. He looked almost predatory the way he opened the hallway closet, moved to the bedroom, opening that door, the bathroom, the kitchen. He was thorough in his search, quiet and focused and scaring the hell out of her. "Look, everything is just as I left it. Maybe you should go, Rome." And maybe she should take a couple of those anti-depressants the therapist was convinced would help her recover. A nice dreamless sleep would probably do her a world of good, especially tonight when things hadn't happened the way she'd planned.

"Not until you're safe." He spoke as if that was a no-brainer.

He was in the living room now, looking around again. His broad body appeared strangely out of place in the modestly decorated space, her space. Kalina instantly felt claustrophobic. There wasn't enough air in here for both of them to breathe. He didn't belong here with her; she was used to being alone. Her temples throbbed as a headache made its debut. Dammit, at this rate she was going to have a real nervous breakdown, just like the one the therapist predicted.

"I'm fine and I definitely think you should leave. Now." He was making her edgier by the minute.

As if he hadn't heard a word she said, he kept moving and talking. "There's something . . ." His voice trailed off. "Lock the door behind me," he said suddenly, pushing past her.

She didn't move but looked at him, their gazes locking. For a second, just a split second, she would've sworn there was something different about his eyes. The color changed, the shape. Or did it?

"You sh . . . should go," she managed to say even while the look he was giving her had heat flowing instantly through her body, prickles of alertness creeping along her skin.

"Lock the goddamn door," he said, his voice low, deep, almost like a growl.

Then he was gone. For about two seconds Kalina just stared at the closed door, wondering what the hell

was going on. With her investigation. With her body.
With this man.

This wasn't how it was supposed to go down. She
was the one who needed to find information. He was
the target, not her.

Going to her closet, she reached up to the top shelf,
pulled down a metal box, and retrieved her nine milli-
meter. She was heading to the door, determined to follow Rome and find out what was going on.

Then she stopped.

Right there on the stand beside her door was an
envelope—a plain white mailing envelope that looked
strangely like the one that had been delivered to her a
few days ago. The one with the pictures.

With slow, precise movements Kalina walked to the
table, staring at the envelope as if by simple willpower
it would open and reveal its contents. It couldn't be
the one she'd had the other day. She'd burned that one
and the photo. There had been no delivery of another
one; she'd never have accepted it. And probably would
have shot the bastard trying to deliver it to her.

But here it was. Another envelope, with what inside
she didn't know, but she didn't think she could afford
not to find out.

So with gun in one hand she lifted the envelope with
the other. The flap wasn't closed, so as she held it up-
side down the contents fell to the floor.

More photos.

Kalina didn't want to look at them, didn't want to see
or accept that somebody had been watching her that
night two years ago and was most likely watching her
now. It was just a chance encounter, a drug deal gone
bad. It wasn't about her. It couldn't be about her.

But as she knelt down, picked up the first photo, and turned it so that she could see it, her heart plummeted. It was her. Today as she'd walked into Rome's building for work; this evening as she'd stepped out of the shower and reached for the gray gown she still wore.

Her gun slipped from her hand, clanking loudly against the hardwood floor. She picked up another photo and another until she was looking at different shots of herself, naked in the shower, standing near the closet, pulling on her dress, leaving her apartment, driving her car across town to the hotel, walking into the hotel, and finally standing in the middle of the ballroom floor with Rome.

Her chest heaved, her eyes blurring and refocusing on the pictures. The room seemed to close in around her. Eerie eyes appearing everywhere, blinking and staring, watching and waiting. She fought back tears, choked to keep from screaming. Kalina wasn't feeling crazy or on the brink of a breakdown any longer.

She felt hunted.

Chapter 7

Rome stepped out into the night air, his ears alive for sound. He'd picked up the scent as soon as he entered her apartment. Rogues had been inside, there wasn't a doubt in his mind about that. And it was probably the same ones who'd approached her at the party.

He wasn't surprised when Nick came up beside him, stealth-like, his body already bunched and ready to fight.

"I feel it, too," Nick whispered. "They're close."

"What do they want?" Rome asked but didn't necessarily expect Nick to answer.

"A fight. What else?"

Rome was shaking his head, refusing to believe that a fight was all this was about. Rogues didn't need to search for ways to unleash their violence, and they didn't normally single humans or shifters out. They were random with their viciousness, or at least they had been. Rome had a feeling the rules to the game were changing and he was a little late getting the memo.

But that didn't mean he couldn't still claim victory.

In a split second he heard a ferocious cry. It was a warning: Whatever shifter was in the area had scented them and wanted them gone. That wasn't going to happen.

He and Nick took the next steps simultaneously,

moving toward the sound, their bodies already alert, cats ready to pounce. There was already a cat out there, on the open streets hiding under the cloak of night. The *Ètica* prohibited them from revealing themselves to humans. It was the only way to preserve their species. Humans hated what they feared and they would definitely fear a part-man, part-jaguar shifter. Hate would lead to extermination and the end of the Shadow Shifters. They'd kept their secret for hundreds of years, the Assembly liked to believe they could go hundreds more. Rome didn't necessarily agree but he'd be damned if the exposure would come from his Zone.

The moment they stepped off the sidewalk there was another challenging roar.

"It's coming from the alley," Nick said.

"It figures."

Another male voice joined them and they both looked up to see X standing beside them, his cat already struggling to break free as they could see by the claws pressing through his fingernails.

"Whoa, X, hold on, we don't know what's down there."

"We know it's not good," X said with a growl of his own matching the one in the darkness calling out to them.

Rome thought of using caution, but the next roar seemed closer to the building. The building where Kalina lived. Caution was forgotten in that second as the change began to take over. His heart, his mind, everything was shifting to the cat.

Tearing the jacket off came next, fur already rippling along his skin. Toeing off his shoes, he caught a quick glance of Nick and X stripping out of their clothes as well. In seconds he was free, the cat bursting to the surface in a series of crackling bones that gave way to the sinewy skeletal build of a full-grown jaguar.

His paws hit the damp cement as the cat shook its large head, lips tearing back to reveal sharp canines. This time he was the one to roar first, the only warning the other cat would get that he was coming.

With slow, deliberate movements Rome moved deeper into the alley, not coming to a stop when the first eerie green eyes came into view. This jaguar was large, stepping to the edge of an old fire escape baring its teeth in challenge. It had been waiting, watching them from the moment they'd entered the alleyway, judging its prey, body tensed for action.

A different scent had Rome's attention moving to the other side: another cat. Another full-grown jaguar stepping from behind a Dumpster, its whiskers twitching to pick up the scent of Rome, Nick, and X.

From behind Rome heard a weaker growl, scented fear, and knew instinctively what would happen next.

X roared and Nick leapt into the air just as the jaguar from behind the Dumpster charged. Rome came up on his hind legs the second the jaguar from above pounced, their huge bodies meeting in midair as their bodies shifted in almost impossible positions. It was a brief battle, three on three, paws smacking against muscled flanks, canines nipping at fur-covered skin.

It was a gruesome sound, ferocious roars and grunts echoing off the buildings surrounding them, lifting into the city atmosphere with an eerie deranged resonance.

In the distance, but coming closer, was the sound of sirens.

Rome's ears lifted at the sound, his body bunching as the other jaguar took a swipe at him with a large paw. With his own paw Rome blocked just in time, hitting the other cat's body with a fierce swipe of his own. The other cat stumbled back and Rome turned to see Nick and X both overtaking their opponents. He gave a low roar, sending the warning, and watched as they both delivered dispatching blows.

They were first to exit the alley, preservation of the species more imperative than killing the cats that had dared attack them on a city street. The other cats stood together, growling and issuing warnings of their own on the other side of the alley.

It was like a gang fight dispersing unwillingly. Only these weren't normal humans. They were animals, deadly animals who had just seen the first acts of a war long coming.

As Rome, Nick, and X hit the mouth of the alley, they weren't surprised to see Ezra and Eli holding their clothes. The two men were half out of their tuxedos as well, most likely having been ready to shift themselves and join the battle until they heard the police sirens.

His mind registered the change back, his cat protesting while the man tried to focus on the here and now. They were on the streets, he was in charge. They needed to get away from this area, now. Slipping into his pants, Rome grabbed the rest of his clothes from Eli and yelled to the others, "Let's go. Take both vehicles and meet at my place."

Eli and Ezra nodded. Nick and X had donned their pants and were holding the remainder of their clothes as they moved quickly to the vehicles.

When Rome was in the car, the cool leather of the seats rubbing against his bare back, he breathed out a sigh.

This wasn't over. He would see those cats again, he was certain.

The war the Assembly had been trying to avoid for hundreds of years was just beginning.

Chapter 8

In the den of Rome's house three restless, angry jaguars paced. It probably made an interesting sight to see these particular three men with cats lurking just beneath the surface of their skin. Professional men with animalistic traits driving their thoughts and actions. The space was filled with tension as they moved within its small confines. In the wild, pure jaguars lived solitary lives; the only time they were together was as mother and cub for the first two years of a cub's life.

The Shadow Shifters were different in that they remained together. Each tribe created its own little community. This was both for protection and preservation. Even as they migrated to the States, most of the shifters lived in close proximity to at least two other shifters of the same tribe. There was safety in numbers to their way of thinking.

Tonight had been one shock after another. Rome knew that each piece was connected, from the bug in his tuxedo to the attack in the alley. They'd broken major *Ètica* rules tonight, but there'd been no other choice. The Rogues were coming at them with nothing but attack on their agenda.

"They weren't all Topètenia," Nick said finally.

After arriving at Rome's house, each of them had showered. Because Rome was the only one with a house and not an apartment or condo, they spent a lot of time here playing in his huge game room, watching sports, or running in the secluded wooded area behind the house. Both Nick and X kept clothes at his place for occasions like tonight.

Nick now wore sweats, tennis shoes, and a black shirt after his shower. He'd stopped pacing long enough to reach down to the coffee table and pick up one of the stress balls shaped like fruit from the large glass bowl to work vigorously in his left palm.

Rome stopped at the row of windows that made up almost the entire left wall of the room. His own loose-fitting jeans and T-shirt scraped against his skin as the cat inside pressed harder for release. He could see out over the vast lawn to the line of trees that were also his property about fifty feet away. The dark, desolate place called to him, beckoned the cat inside to break out once more, to come to the one place it could be free.

"How do you know?" he asked, his throat tight with the words. He'd sensed something different about the trio, but the one who'd been stupid enough to attack him was definitely a jaguar. One of the wilder ones, probably lost from its mother early in the forest and left to fend for itself. He wasn't built like the rest of them—he seemed to be bulkier, but naturally so. And he was sloppy in his fighting, probably hadn't been trained as precisely as the others had. No matter, he was still a killer at heart and some things were just instinct. "We were taken by surprise, running on adrenaline."

"At any time, in any circumstances, I know who I'm fighting, Rome. And you would have, too. It was a cheetah."

"No way," X said from the corner he'd boxed himself in after he'd finished pacing.

As if hearing his voice reminded Rome of his presence, he turned to the man. "Where did you come from? I thought you had some research to do tonight."

At his side X's fists clenched and unclenched. He didn't go for the stress ball, but holding on to his cat was a test as well. They all wanted to go back out, to find those Rogues and finish them off. The instinct to hunt and kill their enemy was strong, stroking along their humanity like a serrated-edge knife.

X was the largest of the trio, standing six foot four with broad shoulders, a bald head, and skin almost the same reddish brown tone he had in cat form.

It was no accident that their coloring stayed generally consistent in both forms. Nick's lighter shade coincided with the tawny brown jaguar he became, just as Rome's darker cocoa complexion melded perfectly into the black jaguar he was. As full-grown male cats they each had length and agility that made them the feral hunters they were reputed to be. Standing here in their human form, they were still magnificently built men, toned muscle and barely restrained strength. Only now they were using their intelligence to sort through this situation instead of violence, revealing the humanity they strived to retain.

"I arrived at the party just as you were leaving. When I saw the Tahoe and the limo I followed." X shrugged. "Good thing I did. Three against two."

"We've had worse odds," Nick stated. "Besides, Eli and Ezra were there."

They had fought together often, facing all sorts of

odds, years ago when all three of them were in the Gungi. Which is why all of them remained firm that even when living in the States, fighting wasn't a lifestyle they wanted on a daily basis. Tonight, however, there'd been no choice.

"The cops didn't see anything, Rome," X told him as if reading his mind.

"I know," he said, still not liking the fact that they'd all been in cat form as if it were the most natural thing on the streets of DC. "But they'll be back. Showing themselves tonight was like a preamble for what's to come."

Silence meant they all agreed.

"You think it's the three from the party? The ones that were gunning for Kalina? That was Kalina Harper, our new employee, correct?"

Nick was still working that stress ball, his brow furrowed, pupils now mere slits in the light of the room. Shifters had eyes that adapted to light and dark. In the alley where they'd relied on their night vision, their pupils were round and big, allowing them to see. In the light, smaller, dark slashes against the bright cornea showed. This was because the cat was still lurking, waiting. In the office or whenever they were completely human, with the cat resting inside, their eyes looked like any normal human's.

"It was Kalina," Rome said tightly. "They had her in their sights. I knew there were shifters in the building but didn't get a look at them until I noticed she was there." That knowledge was still scraping against his already raw nerves. Why were they aiming for her? Had they known she was going to be there?

"Who's Kalina Harper?" X asked, moving with quiet agility to sit on the leather couch.

"She's our new hot-ass accountant," Nick said with a bleak smile that withered only slightly when he caught Rome's glare.

It was bait, Rome knew, and he decided quickly to ignore it. "I don't know what she was doing there tonight," he said, still thinking of the way she looked caught in those Rogues' glare. Nothing could have stopped him from going to her at that moment, from taking her with him, showing the Rogues that she was under his protection.

"Maybe she just bought a ticket like most of the other people there," Nick offered.

"Maybe." But Rome wasn't convinced. There was still something about her that beckoned him. He remembered that night two years ago when he'd been heading home from a meeting. He never usually drove himself to meetings, especially not faction meetings. But he had that night. He'd been walking to the parking garage where he'd left his car when he took a detour. A scent he'd lifted had drawn him in the opposite direction. Toward that alley where the man was attacking her.

Tonight, he now realized, he'd been drawn to her again, this time before she'd been attacked.

As for what happened in the back of the truck, it was inevitable that it would continue. Rome was too strong-minded, too sure of himself to believe anything else.

"The bigger question is what we're going to do about those Rogues. Do you think they acted alone?" X asked.

"No way," Nick spoke up. "They weren't trained

fighters, or at least not trained well. It was a sloppy attack. I don't even think they expected us to be there."

X sat back on the couch. "Which means they were looking for the woman because you were just leaving her house, right, Rome?"

"Yes. I'd just come outside when I saw Nick. We picked up the scent at the same time."

"There wasn't time to do anything but react," Nick said then tossed the ball across the room, where it bounced off a bookshelf. "The fuckers snuck up on us."

"Retaliation," X said. "Rome took away their prize. You know how they are about females."

Rome nodded. "I know." And that's exactly why he'd been so intent on getting Kalina out of there. Now his concern was whether the Rogues were bold enough to go back to her apartment. "Put Ezra on her. I don't want her alone at any time."

Nick nodded. "The question's still: Why? What's her connection to them?"

"Rogues don't need a connection. If they want her they're going to keep going until they get her," X surmised.

"That's what they do in the Gungi. This is not the forest," Rome stated, hearing the hollowness of his words.

Nick interjected, "And the Rogues are no longer in the forest, as we now know. Just because we're acting civilized doesn't mean they will."

Rome reluctantly agreed. Tonight had proven that the rules had changed. The question was what they were going to do about it. "Get Baxter on the phone. I want a meeting first thing tomorrow morning," he told Nick. "Everybody is to be here at seven."

He was assembling his squad. Each Faction Leader

had a core squad they worked with to enforce the laws of *Ètica* in their zones. If the Rogues were stepping up their game in Rome's territory, he and his squad would be ready to do whatever was necessary to neutralize them.

Nick nodded. "Eli stays with you tonight. I'll send Ezra back to Ms. Harper."

"They weren't after me," Rome said.

X stood. "They are now. You're the Faction Leader, they know that. And you took something they wanted. They'll be after you just for the fun of it."

Rome went back to the window, looked out into the night. "Hunting me won't be fun for them. I can promise that."

Vicious claws sank into flesh with a sickening sound that mixed with the howl of a wounded cat. Rage spewed through each strike, filling the room with the acidic stench of blood and evil simultaneously.

They were in an old warehouse off Interstate 95 just outside DC in the northern Virginia area. The building had been abandoned long before they arrived but they'd taken over earlier this year. Slowly but surely, as money poured in, they were making it a more livable space. Soon it would be the headquarters of their empire. Just as soon they would rule, as their kind was meant to do.

This was Sabar's goal. He'd been born in the jungle, treated like an animal for the first years of his life, until he'd been taught differently. His eyes had been opened, his mind awakened to what was theirs for the taking. Now twenty years later he was here, in the United States, doing what was necessary for his species to survive. To rule.

His cat clawed at the surface, wanting to dominate the situation, to handle the reprobates itself. But that would end in death, and while he was no stranger to the act of killing, in this instance Sabar wasn't quite ready for these shifters to meet that end.

Still, they had to be punished. If there was one thing Sabar could not stomach, it was failure. These three should know this by now—they'd been with him long enough. Well, two of them had. The other one had only been with his group a few years, but he'd come highly recommended. Now Sabar wondered if that was a mistake.

"Get up!" he yelled, following the order with a kick to the shifter's stomach with the tip of his steel-toed boot. "Get your sniveling sissy ass up!"

He was a sissy because he wasn't a jaguar. In the forest the tribes were separated according to the feline family each cat was born into. That was the way of the Elders and the Assembly. Sabar had long since cursed their doctrine and their ways. So he'd accepted any and all members from any and all tribes. It didn't matter which tribe they were from, or even if their tribe didn't live in the Gungi; they were all shifters, all powerful in ways humans could never fathom being. But this one, this sniveling cheetah who'd been brought to him by one of the female shifters one night, could very well have been the weakest link tonight. The one that caused them to lose a key component to Sabar's success as a ruler.

"Tell me again why she's not here right now?"

He could hear the other two behind him, smell the relief that he'd backed off them for the time being.

"Sh . . . she got away," Chavez, the freckle-faced man, answered. With blood gushing from the wound at his neck where Sabar had first swiped at him, it was a bit hard to see the freckles that marred his face and neck. But Sabar didn't give a rat's ass about how he looked when this was over. He wanted answers.

"He came in and took her. We were going to get her but he took her," Chavez managed without stuttering this time.

"Who took her, Darel? And why didn't you stop them?"

From behind him Darel struggled to stand, then pushed out his chest, put his shoulders back, and spoke clearly. "Faction Leader Reynolds took her, sir. They disappeared in the crowd and probably left through some secret exit. We decided to go to her house hoping Reynolds would drop her off and we could get her when he left. But he didn't. When we approached he wasn't alone. They'd already shifted and were waiting for us. We were fighting them off when the cops arrived."

Sabar growled, blood dripping from his fingers where his claws tore the skin. "Where are Reynolds and his flunkies now? More important, where's the female?"

Sharpened teeth pricked at his lips. That's all he could allow of the change right now. Taking cat form at this moment would only cause the others to shift as well, and that would definitely lead to bloodshed and death. Beasts did not rationalize who they fought and why, they just fought to survive. In this Sabar reluctantly embraced the human half of himself, worked with the intelligence bred into human brains and adjusted accordingly.

"We all left before the cops could get to the alley to see us," Chi offered. He, too, was now standing at attention as Darel did.

Chavez was just pushing himself up, using the wall

for leverage. "They ran first," he stated, as if that made a difference.

"You should have run after them. Your kind's supposed to be faster, right?" To his own ears Sabar sounded prejudiced—against his own kind, at that. The thought didn't sit right in his mind, the human part. But the animal in him prowled close, ready to snap the other cat's neck at a moment's notice. He didn't trust this one, had thought about killing him just days ago. But as an old saying went, it was best to keep your enemies close.

"I don't care what you have to do, who you have to kill to get it done, but I want her and I want her now!" His words ended with a deafening roar that rattled the windows of the warehouse and shook each man/beast standing near him.

None of them spoke another word, but the trio filed out, walking along the cement floors to the back door they used to keep anyone riding on the highway from seeing them.

Rome ran as if his life depended on it. Through the forest that bordered a dense mountainous region in Virginia he ran and ran until his flanks were damp with sweat. Only then did he stop, realizing he was in a favored spot. Pacing around the two large trees, he padded along the softened foliage-covered ground. Lips drew back over large sharp teeth, and he panted air in and out. Through the slits of his gold-green eyes he saw the dark of the forest, loved the feel of the night air against his furred body. Leaping up he balanced on his hind legs, gripping the tree trunk with the paws of his front ones. With quick ragged strokes the cat scored the tree just as he had in the past.

This was his land—the human had purchased it and held the deed. But animal had marked it, claimed this territory so that any who dared walk on it knew. This tree in particular wore the claw marks of the cat that ran through this forest on a daily basis. Tonight's run was fueled by so much—anger, anticipation, hunger, lust. All these things ran through the human, pushing at Rome until he wasn't quite sure what needed to be done first. They clawed at the animal viciously, making him impatient and irritable.

Even in this form he couldn't outrun his demons. The dark parts of his past continued to haunt him years later. He was thirty-five and he was a successful attorney. He should be thinking of finding a wife, settling down to start a family—that's what his mother would have wanted him to do. His father, too, for that matter, was a man about family and heritage. Both his parents instilled a great love of their heritage in Rome so that now his loyalty to the shifters and their home in South America was as big a part of his life as his career. And with that came one of Rome's biggest burdens: finding out who murdered his parents.

The night of their murder was still fresh in his mind even though he'd been so young. He'd stayed in that closet because Baxter told him to and he'd been taught to listen to his elders. But he'd known something was wrong. Deep in his chest he'd felt a rising heat, then he heard the screams, his mother's screams. He'd stood then put his small palm on the knob of the door, ready to turn it.

"Sit tight, Mr. Roman. Do not move until I come back for you," Baxter had said.

Rome had already disobeyed because he'd moved

from the sitting position. What harm would it do if he left the closet? His mother needed him. But he didn't leave and with each sob he inhaled the tangy scent of blood. It consumed him until he sat in the closet close to vomiting. Then it was quiet for what seemed like forever, and Baxter did not come. He had to go to the bathroom and his stomach growled from hunger. But he stayed where he was told. And his parents had died at the hands of another shifter.

Opening his mouth the cat growled in pain, for the loss, for the memory, for the time he could not shift and protect those he loved.

But now he could. Rome was as powerful as a cat as he was in the human world. When he found his parents' killer he would most certainly make him pay.

And now there was another for him to protect. Kalina.

He hadn't known who she was two years ago, and even now he didn't know her all that well—or at least his human self didn't. Yet his cat felt a connection, yearned to break free each time he was with her. Of course he fought it, even wondered why the animal wanted to be free with her. He'd never felt that urge with another woman before. The attraction was strong, so much so that just thinking of her made Rome hard and the cat hunger for more.

When he'd touched her tonight, felt the clench of her inner muscles around his fingers, the man wanted to roar with pleasure. In her eyes he saw a banked fire, hidden for whatever reason. Beneath his touch she melted, her response as eager as if she'd known what to expect. But she wouldn't have, just as he hadn't known. Until he touched her. And now he wanted more.

Wanted her with a fierceness he'd never experienced before, which made this yet another issue for him to try and resolve. That was his job as Faction Leader—to resolve the issues of the stateside shifters. As an attorney he resolved the issues of his clients. Now the man had an issue. A woman who both perplexed and aroused him, and who also needed his protection.

Running again Rome remained still while the cat took what it needed, fed from the elements in the only possible way.

Moonlight could now easily be seen; that meant he was nearing the edge of his forest. Rome always made sure to unleash his cat only in the deepest depth of the forest so no human passerby could sneak a peek. Even though this was his own private land and the perimeter was gated, he left nothing to chance.

Just as the last line of trees displayed themselves the cat slowed, falling to its side still breathing quickly, sensitive nostrils flaring and lifting scents from the air. As the heart rate slowed, the beast calmed, opening itself to the man. In seconds the sinewy skeleton of the cat transformed into the male—six foot two and a half inches tall, 235 pounds of male muscle. Walking to the spot where he'd dropped his robe, Rome picked up the black silk, slipping it on as he walked through the last blanket of trees out into the night air. The grass was cool and just a little damp from the humidity as he walked barefoot back to the house.

Golden light spilled from the open patio door. When he stepped inside it was to a marble stand with a silver tray on top. And a glass of scotch. Baxter knew him too well.

Picking up the glass, Rome lifted the remote that

would close the door behind him and initiate the alarm system.

"Get some rest, tomorrow will be a busy day," Baxter said in his slow precise tone from the shadow of the doorway that led to the game room.

"Has the meeting been arranged?" he asked. He took his first swallow of the drink, let the burn soothe the ache deep inside his gut.

"Yes. Mr. Dominick took care of everything. Mr. Eli will stay in the house with us tonight."

"And Ezra?"

"He is with Ms. Harper. But you may consider bringing her here. It will not rest until it knows she is safe," Baxter whispered before disappearing in the darkness.

He'd thought of that already. Knew his cat was hungry to see her again, to scent her, touch her. The protective edge was growing, pushing at all his restraints in its effort to keep her safe. Inside the cat began to pace, growling every few seconds as Rome considered the options.

It wanted Kalina, there was no doubt about that. And right now Rome wasn't up for questioning the other part of himself. He was who he was because of his jaguar; they were partners, working together to make a whole. The cat wanted Kalina. The man craved her.

They both would have her.

Chapter 9

Tonight hadn't gone well for them, which usually meant it was going to go even worse for someone else.

Chavez was in a foul place, his beast ripping free as they walked down the dark street. It was close to dawn, the sky already shifting so that it looked like an angry storm of colors from deep indigo to rich fuchsia. They were still out prowling the streets after Sabar had finished with them.

What was still bothering them was not the missed opportunity to catch the woman Sabar had sent them for, but the heavy strain of unleashed lust that built up in a shifter, manifesting like a bitch of a hangover. Each of them felt it, maybe because their sexual exploits had been shared as of late. The animalistic desire mixing with the human sex drive rose to explosive levels among shifters. But in Rogues the feeling was absorbed, allowed to spread and anchor itself deep within until depraved sexual acts were a part of their natural state.

"You smell that?" Chi stretched out both his arms, stopping Chavez on one side and Darel on the other side of him.

The threesome inhaled simultaneously, then looked up at the building they were standing near.

There were females nearby, females in heat.

Without another word they entered the building,

followed the alluring scent up a dark, dirty stairwell. There was a door at the end of the hall. Actually there were three doors on this floor, but only one beckoned to them. Like trained animals they followed the scent, each of them growing harder with every step. Arriving at the door where the scent rested, Darel lifted his hand to knock. Chavez pushed it away, lifted his foot with the size eleven boot, and kicked the door in.

Two females who had been sitting on the couch hitting a blunt jumped up. One who wore only underwear, her large breasts all but falling out of her bra and a barely there thong, stood first, raising her arms as if she were under arrest.

Darel's mouth watered at the sight of those large mounds lifting with her motions.

The other one was too high to care. She rolled onto her stomach, peeking at them from the couch. Her ass was out, too; she didn't bother to wear a thong at all. She wore a bra but her breasts weren't visible because she was lying on them.

The three shifters stood there for only seconds letting the smell of weed and female desire fill their nostrils.

Then they pounced.

Through the open window came a stifling breeze. Kalina inhaled instinctively and the scent of rain permeated her senses, filled her with such longing she coughed in response. Rain and air and a fragrant scent filtered throughout the room, wrapping her body in a warm cocoon that she embraced wholeheartedly.

Kalina sighed, a lone tear traveling down her cheek. The breeze touched every pore of her naked body, and now she tingled all over. Standing, she walked to the window, pushing to the side the long sheer curtains now billowing in the breeze. When she looked out the window it wasn't to the scene she was used to seeing. Gone were the city street, the parked cars, sidewalks, and other houses. It had all been replaced by darkness. A darkness that was eerie and yet comforting at the same time.

Glaring outside felt like standing in the middle of nothing. No cops, no drugs, no competition. If serenity could be bottled and that bottle dropped and broken, this would be it. She couldn't see anything, but she could feel, and what she felt was like heaven.

"It's yours, baby. You just have to be brave enough to take it."

A deep voice sounded from behind, and the tingling against her skin instantly grew hotter.

He was there, again. Finally.

Her heart beat a little faster, her breasts rising and falling with her steady inhaling and exhaling. "I can't," she responded in the tiniest whisper.

Fingers that felt like feathers touched along her spine, moving downward until hands splayed across her bare bottom. She sucked in a breath as those same fingers slipped deftly into the seam, whispering softly over the tightened back entrance.

"You can."

She was shaking her head because his touch, there, in such a forbidden place, rendered her momentarily speechless.

"Tell me what you want and you can have it."

What she wanted, what she thought she wanted didn't seem half as important as this moment, this feeling. It was beyond intimacy, more than she'd ever thought could be a part of her. She knew him, had known him for a long time, and yet tonight his touch felt new, exciting, enticing.

She wanted to do what he said, to tell him what she wanted, to take what she needed. The urge to take had never been so strong before. And yet there was something else. Not too far in the distance was something that she feared, a being, a place—what was it that held her back?

Again she didn't speak.

But it didn't stop him. One hand slipped over her hip to brush past her clean-shaven mound. Thick fingers parted plumped dewy folds, touching the tender and tightened clit. She moaned, her head falling back to rest along his shoulders.

"You want me to touch you here? To fuck you this way," he continued in a voice that simply lulled her into a pleasurable abyss.

Kalina didn't know the answers. There was his other hand, behind her, pressing one finger slowly against the tight back entrance. Another finger moved through her wetness, finding her center then pressing inside. Sensations rippled through her and she sighed, moaned, welcomed.

Against her bottom was also the heated pressure of his arousal. Thick and hot it felt against her, and her nipples tingled with awareness.

She wanted him, desperately.

"Yes, that's what I want," she heard herself whisper.

Sharp teeth nipped at her shoulder, traced a pleasure–pain path along the nape of her neck, and ended at the other shoulder.

"Tell me," he urged. "Tell me what you want."

"I . . ." She could barely think of the words, much

less speak them. "I want you to . . . fuck me . . . like . . . this." They tumbled free, her mouth watering at the thought.

The hand that toyed with her anus retreated, as did the one drowning in her wetness, but he didn't leave her. Oh no. When she was just about to panic that he was gone again, she felt his palm at the base of her back, pressing her forward. Kalina gasped as her hands gripped the windowsill, the warm breeze still blowing over their naked bodies, the stillness of the night still her only view.

Strong hands parted her cheeks, and she whimpered at the feel of his heavy erection pressing closer. When the thick head of his dick brushed over her center, she bit her bottom lip. He pressed forward, slowly, and she wanted to scream. It wasn't going to fit. She couldn't see it, but she could feel and her heart hammered at the discovery. Tears of disappointment stung her eyes.

"It's for you, baby. Don't worry, it's all for you."

It was too much for her, that's what she thought. It, him, this moment—it was overwhelming and yet inevitable.

She was worried but she didn't speak, just let the breeze soothe her as he slipped more of himself inside her. The stretching should have been brutally painful, but instead it was pleasingly tight, pushing her to acceptance of what was more than just physical. She was opening, taking him in, taking in everything that was around her. The sultry breeze, the scent of rain and fresh air, the nothingness that seemed euphoric: It was all rippling around her even as his dick sank in to the hilt.

He began to move, slow, steady thrusts that milked her essence until it trickled down her inner thighs.

Pumping her bottom back against his ministrations was as natural as breathing. Feeling his hands holding her hips, guiding the depth of his thrusts anchored her somehow, kept her from soaring into the unknown.

"I told you it was for you." He moaned behind her, his pace increasing. "All for you."

Sweat poured from her body as his thrusts came quicker, went deeper. She was crying out now—his name, she thought, but she wasn't entirely sure. The sound of her voice was untamed and wild to her own ears.

"Yes! Fuck! Come for me, baby. Come so hard you can't stand any more. Come, damn you!"

His voice was a guttural growl, one she matched with a keening howl of her own as her release rushed through her like a raging waterfall.

It was a demand, not a request. Her thighs quivered in response to the sound of his voice—so familiar, so in tune with her. This felt like déjà vu, like this man had loved her this way before. Her entire body trembled at the thought. Maybe it was all for her. Maybe . . .

"Kalina! Kalina!" he repeated as he pumped into her fiercely, his thighs slapping against her moistened cheeks. His fingers dug deep into her skin, keeping her still while he pounded into her. Her release made her even slicker and his dick moved through that slickness like a professional violinist playing the symphony of its life. When he roared she should have been afraid, yet she was satisfied in a way she'd never thought existed. Every feminine part of her opened, bloomed like a flower at the sound of his pleasure, and as he emptied his seed into her she knew, without any doubt, she knew.

"You are for me, Kalina. Only for me," he said, his

voice rough against her ear as he bent forward over her, his erection still lodged inside her. "Only for me."

Only for me. Only for me.

It's for you, baby. All for you.

You are for me.

The words echoed in her head, dancing about as if begging her to memorize them, to make them mean something for all time. And as she awoke they stayed in her mind, playing and replaying.

Rome woke with sweat pouring from his body, his heart thumping wildly in his chest.

Pushing the covers from around his legs, he got out of bed and walked across the floor of his bedroom, trying valiantly to catch his breath. At the balcony doors he pushed the latch, and the glass accesses swung open. A cool night breeze flushed his damp skin. He inhaled deeply.

The scent filled his mind, seeped into his lungs, creating an acrid taste in the back of his mouth. Blood. Lust. Death.

Leaning forward, he planted both palms on the railing and stood naked on his balcony, closing his eyes to the memory of the dream.

It had begun with her, Kalina. The feel of her rounded backside beneath his palms still had his dick hard. She'd been so wet, so sweet, so open for him. They'd connected, linked, as if they'd always been meant to follow this path. Then he'd heard something in the distance. A scream or a cry. And the scent assailed him.

Blood. Lots of blood. And pain, so much pain he'd wanted to roar with the stinging feeling himself. He'd run, as fast as he could, shifted into jaguar form and run through the streets, searching for them, needing to find them, to stop this from happening. Again.

And he'd failed.

Again.

His chest heaved; he couldn't seem to inhale enough oxygen. He'd wanted to stop the pain his parents endured, wanted to prevent anyone from ever being murdered in such a vicious and senseless way again. The guilt hung on his shoulders like chains and his knees weakened.

They were still out there. The ones who'd killed his parents and possibly others that were after Kalina. They were killing for no reason but that they could. And Rome despised them, wanted to snap their necks and devour the carcasses the same way they did their victims. He wanted to hate as deeply as they did, to not give a damn about consequences or lives affected after the act.

But he couldn't.

His fingers gripped the railing until his knuckles felt as if they'd rip the flesh from his hands. His claws extended, pressing into the other side of his palms. Inside, a growl emanated as his cat threatened to surface.

He lifted his head, opened his eyes to the sky with the peach-and-pink color of dawn.

There was no other choice. As much as he wanted to remain diplomatic, he knew that before this was all over he would become what he despised. He'd kill like they expected an animal to do. He would lose his human morals and act as if he were trapped in the forest, hunting like a killer.

He would be their worst nightmare.

Chapter 10

Rome liked dark colors. He always had. That's why when he'd purchased this house he'd made a point of assisting the interior decorator himself. Of course he let Baxter have some say in his own sleeping quarters and the kitchen, but the rest of the house was Rome's. And the one thing he'd insisted upon was dark—or as the decorator had called them, warm—colors.

The conference room was on the first level, past the living and dining rooms. It was large enough to fit an eight-foot-long table with black leather-backed chairs. The walls were a deep cranberry color, with ash-gray carpeting. Along the walls were paintings of the rain forest, of his home. They'd belonged to his parents and he'd put them in here so that he'd feel close to them. Besides, it helped when he was having a meeting such as this one—it reminded them all of where they were from.

Baxter made sure the coffee carafe was full. Pitchers of iced water sat beside it on the presentation tables that lined the walls.

On one side of the table with dour expressions were the guards: Eli, Ezra, and two other guards who lived in the DC area. Sitting opposite them were officers under Rome's command, four jaguars who also blended into the community with jobs such as schoolteacher, store owner, and doctor. Rome took his seat at the head of the table, with his commanding officers, Nick and X, to his right and left. The other end of the table remained empty for whenever a member of the Assembly joined them for a meeting.

In the center of the table were two conference-call units. Each Faction Leader from each zone would be in on this meeting. What was happening concerned them all, and they needed to talk before next week's scheduled Assembly meeting. The Elders would want to know what was going on and how they planned to deal with it, because even though they were miles away in the forest, what was going on here would eventually affect them, too.

"They're gaining momentum," a voice said from the call unit. It was Jace Maybon, the Pacific Zone Leader. "There've been some incidents here in LA that reek of Rogue activity."

"It seems like they're getting bolder," Ezra commented. Eli and a couple other officers nodded in agreement.

"But what's their goal? Once we figure that out we'll know how to stop them," X added.

"I think that's simple—they want to rule. Just as they tried to do the forest, they want to rule in the States."

This statement was from Sebastian Perry, the Mountain Zone Leader. Rome was inclined to agree with him.

"They want to rule, think they're entitled to control." Rome nodded, sitting back in his chair and rubbing his neatly barbered goatee. "We're seeing movement here, there's movement in LA. How about the other zones, anything strange going on there?"

Cole Linden, Central Zone Leader, spoke up first.

"There's a definite rise in gang violence here. Brutal killings are becoming an everyday occurrence."

Sebastian chimed in. "We've had a few incidents that local authorities are baffled by. They don't seem to have a real connection—a corporate bigwig was murdered, a congressman is missing, and some government-funded lab was broken into. I've been keeping my eye on the news for developments but so far there's nothing connecting them to the Rogue activity."

"You said a government lab?" X asked. "Which one?"

"Comastaz Laboratories. It's in Sedona."

X nodded. "I know that one. I'll check it out and see what's what with that. But it sounds to me like they're gearing up for something. Getting everything in order for some grand play for power, and the United States is their battleground."

"So who's in control?" Rome asked. "One cat has to be leading them all. Find him and we deactivate the play."

It sounded simple, but Rome knew it wouldn't be. Finding the one Rogue that controlled possibly hundreds wasn't going to be easy.

"Kill the bastard and they'll all fall like dominoes," Nick added.

"I'm with you on that one," Jace said.

Ezra and the officers were nodding their agreement.

Rome was still hoping bloodshed could be kept to a minimum. "The ones we met up with last night seemed focused on one specific target."

"Kalina," Nick said, the sound of her name on his lips rubbing like an abrasive against Rome's skin.

"What does she have to do with any of this?" Eli asked.

Guards were an important part of the commanding hierarchy among stateside shifters. They were next in line after the commanding officers and Faction Leaders. Their job was important—they were like the shifter Secret Service. Therefore, if a battle strategy was being laid out, they were an active part of the discussion.

"I watched her place all night and left one of the other guards with her so I could attend the meeting this morning, but I've been trying to connect her to this all night. I'm coming up blank." Ezra shrugged.

And so was Rome. While he felt an extreme attraction to her, why the Rogues were hunting her he still had no idea. The fact that they were hunting her made his blood boil, so despite his hope for little bloodshed, he'd kill any one of them that dared to touch her.

"What do we know about her?" Eli asked.

"She started working for the firm a couple of weeks ago. Rome and I just met her a few days ago. I can check with HR get her file and see where she came from," Nick said.

X nodded, rubbing a hand over his bald head. "I'll run her name through the FBI database, see what I get, and report back to you," he told Rome.

"In the meantime, I want somebody on her at all times. She is not to be anywhere alone. Does everyone understand that?" Rome was speaking specifically to the guards and officers but knew that Nick and X were taking note of his orders as well. "Until we figure out who is running the Rogues we're all on alert. Exposure is still a priority. Rogues don't give a shit where they shift or who sees them. We do. Keep your eyes open and keep a low profile. They're out there and they're waiting for us to fall into whatever trap they're trying to lay. We're smarter and we know our territories better than they do. Capturing and interrogating is the better option," he said, looking from X to Nick. "But if the threat is too large, DTN." Do The Necessary.

The meeting ended with everyone in agreement. The other Faction Leaders disconnected from the conference call. Baxter, who had quietly moved from the room once the meeting began, was back, clearing water glasses and coffee mugs from the table in silence.

Baxter was like that. With his tall, lanky frame and leathery coffee-brown skin, he moved about in silence but always seemed to be there. He was more knowledgeable about the shifters and the Gungi than anyone Rome knew, and he could swing his prized machete with quick and efficient strokes when need be. In addition, he was an intricate part of Rome's life. He loved the man like a father.

"You think the leader may be here in DC?" Nick asked, coming to stand by Rome.

X came over to stand with them as the others filed out of the conference room.

"I don't know. But I'm betting Kensington does," he said.

"What makes you think that?" Nick asked.

"Jace said Kensington stank like a Rogue in LA earlier this year. Why would that be? He's human."

X nodded. "Unless he was in contact with them. Intimate contact."

"That's right," Rome said. When humans were intimate with a shifter, they carried that shifter's scent. In women it mingled with the scent of their lust, so it could be watered down a bit. But in human males, the female shifter's scent encompassed them, giving a whole new meaning to the word *whipped*. For the time the male was sexually involved with the female shifter, he was consumed by her; his thoughts, his actions, everything revolved around that shifter. Kensington could have easily been seduced by a female Rogue, making him a tool for their using.

"Find out what's going on in Kensington's camp," Rome told Nick. "I'll get Kalina's personnel file and I'll make sure she's properly protected."

"Ezra will make sure he coordinates the officers to put a net around her, Rome. We need to focus on finding the leader," Nick protested.

"You get us info on Kensington and that'll give us a clue. X, you find out what the connection is with that lab. The absolute last thing we need is for the US government to find out about us."

"Will do," X said, nodding.

Rome was already moving to the door. He'd waited long enough to see her. The urge to move faster was building inside him, pounding against him.

"Where are you going?" Nick asked.

"To make sure Kalina's safe," he said curtly and kept walking.

When he was gone, X gave Nick a questioning look.

"Yeah, I'm thinking the same thing. Why don't you do your digging on Ms. Harper, too? Find out everything you can on her. I've got a feeling she's connected to this situation in more ways than we know."

"And what about him?" X asked, referring to Rome.

"I'll keep my eye on him. Rome's not looking for a mate. He's never wanted one. But there's something about this woman that's eating at him. I noticed it that first day at the office."

X shrugged. "Could be lust. She's a beautiful woman and you know our appetites."

Nick nodded. "I know. She had my dick hard as stone the first day I met her, and her scent's beyond intoxicating. That's why I'm going to keep my eye on Rome. If she's reeling him in, I want to make sure she's on the level."

"Rome's too smart to fall for a setup, but I feel you. If he's getting pulled in by the lust he might not be thinking straight," X added. "I'll get to the office and get started."

"Hit me on my cell later with an update."

"You got it. And watch your back."

Nick grinned. "Always."

They didn't say it but both of them would be watching Rome's. They'd been friends for far too long to miss the warning signs. Rome was distracted, and that wasn't normal. More important, it wasn't safe for them or the woman he seemed hell-bent on protecting.

He'd said it was only for her. But that was a lie. Nothing in Kalina's life had been only for her. The parents she'd thought belonged to her had left her at an orphanage. The foster parents were only a loan and they gave her nothing but what the state required them to give. She had her job and her life but they weren't really hers. She worked for the city, doing good for the people of the city, but what was in it for her? It was a depressing thought and countered all the pleasurable sensations left over from her dream. But it was life—real, uncut, and uncensored. She'd learned long ago to just deal with it.

She opened her eyes slowly, praying the words in her head would disappear. Instead they moved around the room. No, not that she was seeing things, but they were in the air, like a litany of sorts. Something else was in the air.

Her window was closed and yet her body still felt a breeze. A warm summer's breeze that soothed the skin yet also flushed it with sweat. But she was sweaty and she was naked and between her legs was sticky.

It had been a dream.

A truly realistic, sexy-as-hell dream that had aroused her to painful proportions, she figured as she struggled to get out of bed.

Her body was as sore as if she'd really been fucked while standing at an open window. And the words in her head were now in his voice. The deep sexy voice that had seduced her into climax. The voice she recognized from her real-life sexcapade in a black Tahoe last night.

Rome's voice.

Dammit! Running her fingers through her short tresses, she wondered if she really wanted to be crazy. What if she really wanted to hear voices and have weird dreams for the rest of her life? What if on some deranged level this was the only way she'd ever be able to get off?

"Now, that is crazy," she mumbled, getting off the bed and staring at the clock on her nightstand. It was almost noon. She'd slept in, something she never usually did. Then again, she'd never screamed in pleasure from a long hard dick, either.

What the hell was going on with her? Everything she knew about herself had been changing lately.

The window was open, just a crack, not as wide as it was in her dream. Still, it freaked her out, so she padded bare feet across the floor to close it. Then she yawned and stretched, waiting until she heard at least one bone crack in relief as she did. Next it was a shower; then she had some research to do. She wanted to run the descriptions of those men she'd seen last night through the police database, see if anything came up.

They looked deadly, hungry for something, and almost criminal, although there was no real way to look at someone and say offhand that he was a criminal. She'd had that proven when she'd arrested a pastor of a local church for selling ecstasy. Looks could definitely be deceiving, but Kalina was betting those three were up to no good.

Speaking of which—what the hell had happened to Rome last night? She moved into the bathroom, thinking. One minute he'd been in her apartment acting all John Shaft, searching like he was the one with a badge and gun and not her. Of course he had no idea she was a cop but she doubted that his actions would have changed if he had known. Roman Reynolds was definitely a take-charge kind of guy. His very presence commanded attention, allegiance, fear in anyone who ever thought of deceiving him. He was, in her mind, everything a drug lord would be.

After she'd found those freaking pictures, she'd rushed outside to see if Rome's instincts had found something. Or if those three goons had followed her and he was macho enough to think he could take them on himself.

Gun in hand, she'd come out of her building last night and heard the horrific sounds.

Armed and ready to fight whatever had Rome running from her apartment, Kalina had been stopped cold on the front steps by what she could only describe as a series of roaring and chuffing sounds in the still night air.

Immediately she'd reverted to that night in her dreams. The one where the big-ass cat with the eerie eyes had roared over the body of a dead man.

Impossible. That's what it was and she knew it. They were in Washington, DC, not a jungle. There were no big cats roaming the streets killing bad guys. Yet her frozen feet didn't dare take her down those steps. While her mind warred over what was real and what was not, she didn't move. Going out farther into the night to investigate had not been a possibility.

In fact, when she swore she heard the sound again she'd run back into the building, not stopping until she was locked safely in her apartment and huddling in her bed. It had taken hours for her to finally drift asleep—and when she did, she dreamed.

Surprisingly not of the cat, but of a man.

Warm water sluiced over her skin and she hummed with the decadent feeling of relaxing muscles. She was tense, sexually frustrated, and driving herself crazy with thoughts of big cats and drug lords. She needed a vacation, she thought, picking up her sponge and lathering it with bottled vanilla-scented soap.

She'd just turned off the water and stepped out of the shower when she heard something. It sounded like a door closing. Her front door.

Instinct kicked in. Even though she was in the bathroom with nothing but a robe she could throw on and no firearm, her mind was already coming up with self-defense ideas. There were scissors in the drawer of the vanity. Kalina pulled it open and clasped them in her hand. Reaching for her robe on the back of the door she hurriedly pushed her arms into the sleeves and belted it at her waist. She was reaching for the doorknob when she heard another *thump*. Whoever was bold enough to break into her apartment early on a Saturday afternoon had better be bold enough to face her. She needed to get into the living room, or her bedroom, because she had a gun in both spots. But for now, the scissors would have to do.

Kalina had been attempting to pull the door open slowly when it was suddenly pushed in. She stumbled backward but quickly righted herself, raising her arm with the scissors in hand ready to strike.

The movement was like a blur of black it was so fast. She didn't see a face or register if it was man or woman; her wrist was caught in the tight grip of a hand as she was pushed up against the wall with a sickening *thump* that knocked most of the wind out of her.

She blinked, trying to inhale and exhale, her fingers still curled tightly around the handle of the scissors.

"What? Roman?" she said when she looked up into his dark eyes and furrowed brow.

He sighed, loosened his grip, then reached for the scissors. "Hello, Kalina."

She yanked her arm back, keeping the scissors in hand. "Hello? Is that all you have to say after you bust through my bathroom door and manhandle me?"

"I didn't manhandle you," he said in a tone that astonished her.

He was talking as casually as if it were okay to be here right now. As if she'd invited him in.

"How did you get into my apartment?"

"I opened the door and came in."

"With what key?"

"Why don't you have a security system? A young

woman living alone should protect herself better. You need an alarm system. Or a more secure building."

He was walking out of the bathroom now, having the audacity to look pissed off. Well, pissed off and exceptionally handsome in his jeans and fitted black T-shirt. As angry as she was becoming at his intrusion, she hadn't missed the chance to check him out one more time. The air sizzled with sexual dominance; when she gulped and swallowed, Kalina could taste it.

Rome exuded it. Just being in this room pressed up against his body for those brief moments had her center pulsating, her nipples hard.

Her wet feet slapped against the hardwood floors as she followed him out into the living room where he was toying with the door. "What are you doing?"

"This is a cheap-ass lock. I barely fiddled with it and it opened. You do realize you could be killed in your sleep for all the protection this provides?"

"I could also walk out the door and be gunned down or get on the subway and sit right next to a suicide bomber. Whatever is meant to happen will happen," she snapped.

His head jerked and he looked at her, a muscle in his jaw twitching. "You will protect yourself. That's not negotiable."

"And just who the hell do you think you are?" The macho I'm-king-of-the-forest thing was way over the top, even for an arrogant rich lawyer such as Rome. "I could call the cops on you for breaking and entering."

He stood and pushed the door until it clicked shut, the corner of his mouth lifting in a half smile. "Now, that would be ironic since I could make the same claim against you."

Oh yeah, she'd almost forgotten about that.

"What are you doing here, Rome?" she asked, deciding it was best to stay away from threatening him with the authorities—even if she was the authority here.

"I came to check on you."

"Do you check on all your employees like this over the weekend? Besides, I don't need to be checked on."

"All my employees don't incite the attention of unsavory characters at a party."

"You don't know that," she snipped and folded her arms over her chest. His gaze was roaming over her, touching the tips of her hair, coaxing a heated path down to her still-wet toes.

"Get dressed. I want to show you something."

She stared at him.

"You're not moving," he said, tightly pulling his cell phone from the holster on his hip.

"You didn't say 'Simon Says.'" This back-and-forth was interesting, probably proving that she was as stubborn as he was. She wondered if that surprised him. If he'd thought it would be simple to break into her apartment and order her around, after he'd made her come. She couldn't leave that part out.

"Kalina, I'm serious."

"So am I. You cannot just come in here and order me around. You may rule the office with your brooding looks and serious tone, but this is my place. You're on my territory now."

"I don't want to fight with you," he said slowly. "I'm just trying to protect you."

"Why?" she questioned. "Why are you so hell-bent on being in my life? I didn't ask for your protection and

I probably don't even need it. But you're still here. You're always here." She said the last quietly because it was true. Even when he wasn't physically in her presence, he was still there, inside.

She hated that realization, felt it gave her a weakness, one she didn't want to claim.

"I don't know," he answered, and she felt the honesty of that response ripple right through her. "I've always felt the need to protect. It's just a part of who I am."

Staring at him, she wondered, "And who exactly are you?" The question sounded strange but she really wanted an answer. "I know you're a successful attorney and that you've very active on the social scene around town. But I'm curious as to the real Roman Reynolds, the man behind the facade."

He rubbed a hand over his chin. "Don't believe everything you read," he replied.

"Then why don't you tell me. Tell me about you, about who you are and what you want."

"I want you," he said instantly. "I want you safe and I want to be inside you. I can't stop thinking of you, of touching you, tasting you. I want you." He took a step closer. "How does it feel to hear me say that, Kalina? How does your body react to those words?"

It felt different, that was for damn sure. She'd been attracted to him in his office and again in the confines of the truck last night. But right here, standing in the middle of her living room, with her naked body air-drying beneath the thin material of her robe and his words rippling through the air, the feelings spiraling through her were different. It was definitely sexual, these new sensations, there was no doubt about that.

Her nipples had started to ache as they scraped

against the silk material. Her skin felt sensitive, as if every particle of air touching her was bringing something alive inside.

"I'm not intimidated by your candor, if that's what you were aiming for," she said with only about half of that statement being true. "You're on my territory now, Rome."

"And what are the rules when I'm on your territory?" He folded one arm over his muscled chest, lifting the other to tap his cell phone on his chin. His legs were slightly spread and her gaze couldn't help but fall on the bulge between them.

He was aroused, highly. And apparently he wasn't ashamed. Hell, with the heated look he was giving her at this moment she half expected him to pull his dick out for her again. Her mouth watered at the thought.

"Rule number one, don't tell me what to do. You can ask and wait for my answer," she said in a voice that sounded strong, confident. Two things she'd always assumed she was.

"And?"

She swallowed because his biceps jumped as he spoke. His medium-size lips and chiseled jawline gave him the brooding look, she surmised. His skin was tones darker than hers, like a glass of root beer. His body was prime, excellent from what she could see. She wanted him, she thought with a start. Badly.

Holy hell she was in big trouble.

Rome wanted to fuck her right here, right now.

He knew she was naked beneath that robe, knew her body was still wet from the shower, her pussy wet from arousal. With every inhale he picked up the scent of her lust and wanted to bury himself deeper inside her by the minute. He had questions and yet couldn't focus on anything but the attraction between them.

"What were you doing in the shower?"

"What?" She cocked her head at him, her eyes narrowing as she stared quizzically. "What are you talking about?"

"While you were in the shower." He talked slowly, putting his cell phone back into its holster and taking a step toward her. "What did you do?"

She blinked, let her arms fall to her sides, and said, "I bathed. Isn't that what people normally do in the shower?"

"Did you touch yourself? Did you make yourself come?"

For a split second she looked as if she were about to admit truth in what he'd said. Then her lips thinned and fury flashed in her golden eyes. "Just who the hell do you think you are? This is beyond inappropriate. Everything you say to me is either offensive or downright crude. Since you found your way in you can just as easily find your way out!"

She turned away from him, preparing to stalk into her bedroom, he presumed. Big mistake.

Rome was on her in seconds, his arms wrapping around her waist, pulling her ass flush against his rigid arousal. Blood pumped fast and hot through his veins, thumping loudly in his ears.

"You came. Last night," he murmured, his lips right against her ear. He inhaled deeply. "And this morning. Don't try lying to me. Your scent's thick and heavy, lurking all over this apartment. It's driving me crazy."

An elbow slammed into his ribs as she tried to duck out of his grasp. "That's because you are crazy!"

Her struggle was futile. Rome wasn't letting her go. "You didn't come last night?" he asked, his hand flattening on her stomach, slipping slowly between the flap of her robe.

"I was drunk. Too much champagne."

He growled. "Liar. You were aroused. Just as you are now."

"You're a jerk!"

"You're addictive."

Rome licked her neck, let his fingers drift farther until he touched the moist heat of her mound.

Her breathing was ragged. "Why are you doing this to me?"

Nipping at the soft skin at the nape of her neck, Rome closed his eyes to the sensations washing over him, the need, the hunger. It was bigger than anything he'd ever felt, consuming him with every second he was near her. His dick ached to be inside her, to claim her.

No!

No. Rome did not claim any female. He did not believe in the joining—the Elders' philosophy of one true mate for every shifter. The desperate need and undying hunger they predicted when that mate was finally found were myths, something they'd made up to romanticize the dark sexual hunger of the shifter species.

Rome had that hunger. He had that darkness within him. It was living and breathing, coursing just beneath the surface every day of his life. His sexual cravings were tame compared with the majority of other shifters in the tribes. Still, they were darker than most humans were accustomed to. He felt that darkness swirling through him now, threatening to overtake him, to pour out onto this woman.

She moved slightly and his fingers slipped between her velvety folds.

"I don't know why this is happening," he admitted through clenched teeth. "It just won't stop."

He brushed over the tightened nub of her clit and she moaned, relaxing in his arms. Applying the slightest pressure, he toyed with the nub, loving the tiny sound of her muted cries in the otherwise silent room.

"I can't stop touching you. Wanting you."

"I don't want this," she whispered but parted her thighs ever so slightly in contradiction.

"You can't help but want it. Neither of us can."

"No."

"It's not going away." It wasn't, it was getting stronger.

Tracing his finger along the slickness of her vagina, he found her entrance, pressed one finger hungrily inside. She bucked, her head falling back onto his shoulder. Rome kissed the line of her neck, nipped her skin, pushed another finger inside her and moaned.

"I want you. Right here. Right now," he growled, pressing his thick arousal into the crease of her bottom.

"No," she sighed, her heart beating wildly. "No."

Her words drowned in the sound of someone knocking at her door and Rome cursed. She pulled away from him then, glaring at him as she pulled her robe closed tighter.

"I'm saying no, Rome. And I want you to go. Now!"

"This is not over," he whispered. "You can't just will it to go away. I know, I've tried."

"It is over! Despite what you've convinced yourself of I don't want you touching me that way. It's inappropriate. I want to keep my job."

Rome rubbed a hand down his face. "Your job's not

in jeopardy. But your life may be." The minute the words were out he regretted them. He hadn't wanted to scare her. Fear would most likely lead to carelessness, and he couldn't afford for her to be careless about her safety right now.

"What? Are you threatening me because I won't sleep with you?"

He grit his teeth so hard his jaw almost cracked. "No. That's not what I'm saying." Rome took a deep breath, cursed again at the persistent knock at the door.

"I have to get that."

"Who is it?"

She'd already walked past him toward the door. "If I said my boyfriend would that make you leave any quicker?" she said over her shoulder.

"Not at all. He'd be the one leaving," Rome spoke as his cell vibrated on his hip.

"You're an arrogant—" The rest of her remark was lost as he read the text message.

Rome looked up to see she'd opened the door. An older woman was standing there, holding a cat in her arms.

The cat spotted Rome and hissed, baring its teeth, arching its back in defense.

Kalina gasped, jumping back away from the door.

"Calm down, kitty," the old woman crooned. "Kalina, she's not going to bother you. I tell you that all the time. You're probably scaring her."

But Kalina wasn't listening. She was already moving deeper into the apartment, putting the couch between her, the door, and the woman with the cat.

"Mrs. Gilbert. Ah, what can I do for you?"

"Kitty and I heard yelling," the woman said, eyeing

Rome suspiciously. "We wanted to come over and make sure you were all right."

"I'm, ah," Kalina stammered and looked at Rome. "I'm fine."

Rome cleared his throat and took a step toward the door even though the cat was still hissing and narrowing green eyes at him. "Everything is just fine, ma'am. I was just leaving."

"You were, huh?" the woman said, still giving him the stink eye. "Well, you go on and leave. I'll just stay a few minutes."

Rome gave her a tight smile as she stepped into the apartment and he stepped out. On his way the cat took a swipe at him with its small paw. Rome only glared at it a second before the cat shrank back into its owner's arms.

"Oh my," the woman said holding her cat closer.

"Have a good day," he said. "I'll see you soon, Kalina." He looked at her one last time before turning and walking down the narrow hallway.

Again Kalina gasped. Not because of Mrs. Gilbert's cat, but because Rome's eyes didn't seem the same.

"You should watch who you let in here," Mrs. Gilbert was saying as she closed Kalina's door. That cat of hers was still making noises but didn't dare leave Mrs. Gilbert's arms. Kalina kept her distance, her chest filling with an unfamiliar feeling. Not quite fear, but definitely anxiety, like something was about to happen, something she wasn't sure was good or bad.

Chapter 11

"What's so urgent I had to drop everything and come over here?" Rome had left Kalina's apartment when all he'd wanted to do was drag her into that bedroom and drown himself in her for the next few hours, or days.

She'd definitely be safe in his arms. He wouldn't have to worry about the Rogues or why they were hunting her in the first place. As long as she was with him, she'd be all right. And the reason that was so important to him, well, he didn't have to think about that. Not right now.

They were in X's condo, which looked exactly as it had the first day he'd moved in here. The furniture was dark, contemporary, and sparse. X always said he didn't need anything but a bed, which he rarely used for reasons Rome still didn't understand.

High ceilings and crisp white walls made everything they said echo as if they were in a huge auditorium. The floor-to-ceiling windows were fitted with custom-made room-darkening blinds that always stayed closed. The entire place made Rome feel like he was in a hospital or a morgue, it was so still and sterile. Watching X's large body move through the place so mechanically only made the scene more dismal.

"I had a chance to scan that disk Bingham gave you at the party," X began in a dour tone.

He immediately had Rome's attention. Last night after their run-in with the Rogues and their recuperation at Rome's place, Rome had given X the disk to run through the FBI's virus program and spyware. He had most of the same technology on his home computers, but the FBI could also crack any encryption that may have been put on the disk. Besides, X had more experience with computers and such than Rome did. Whatever was on the disk, X would make sure it was clean and ready for Rome's perusal.

The investigation into his parents' murders had been a long-harbored vendetta for Rome. As his two closest friends, Nick and X had joined in the search a long time ago. The Assembly knew nothing about their quest. Dragging a hand down his face, Rome sighed. "What did you find?"

"Nothing traceable. It's old, mid-1980s I'd say. The information was encrypted with a fairly simple code."

"Did you break it?"

"You know he did," Nick said, coming from the kitchen with a bottled beer in one hand. "There's not a code in this world X can't break. Which is truly baffling considering how little attention he paid in school."

X didn't even spare Nick a glance. It was old banter between the two. Nick had been a straight-A student, Rome following right behind him with only a few B's sprinkled in for good measure. X, on the other hand, had never liked going to school, hated the confinement of the classrooms and stern teachers in their private school as well. It still amazed Rome that he'd entered law enforcement, landing solidly in the FBI, and seemed to enjoy it.

"I did, but I thought you'd like to be the first to go over the information. It looks like more journal entries from your father. I didn't feel right reading them before you." X moved to a wall that surprisingly held three photographs, black-and-whites of the mountains and oceans. They were crisp and simple, just like everything else in the apartment. But they were the only pieces that looked like they held some personal link to the man who lived here. Rome didn't bother to ask X why. Each of them—the three shifters who had long ago forged an unbreakable bond—had secrets and demons. The best part of their relationship was that they knew when to leave well enough alone; they didn't push one another, asking for answers the others couldn't or weren't willing to give. They simply accepted who they were and lived their lives accordingly. Not many could do that, especially not with the pasts they all shared.

Behind the middle portrait, the one with the huge plume of smoke spewing from a mountaintop, was a wall safe. X's large fingers moved nimbly over the dial until there was a clicking sound and the door popped open. Reaching inside, he retrieved the disk and handed it to Rome.

For quiet seconds Rome just held it. Then he spoke. "Baxter said my father kept lots of journals. He had them all over the house, each pertaining to a different subject. His work at the corporation, his thoughts on the forest, his childhood. Whatever was in his mind he put into words on paper." Looking down at the disk, he felt that a piece of his father was here, right in this room with them.

"This may give us more insight into what was going on with the meetings they were having," X said, moving to the fully stocked bar in the corner.

Nick swallowed a swig of beer. "We already know

what the meetings were about. They wanted to create some type of democracy, a government for shifters here in the States."

"A judicial system," Rome added.

Nick frowned, looking as if the paint on the walls held more appeal. "A system that wasn't going to work because Rogues don't give a shit about being democratic." It was no secret that while Nick was all about helping Rome find the killers, he didn't agree with what his parents as well as Rome's were fighting for. Nick knew they were a separate species; he'd grown up experiencing that separation in one way or another so he'd never forget it. And he'd never feel easy about trying to mix with the humans.

"We have to start thinking along those lines, Nick," Rome said, already knowing where this conversation would lead. But it didn't matter. He was Faction Leader and it was up to him and the other FLs to come up with ways the shifters could better co-exist in this land. In the jungle it was fine for the tribes to hide, to take shelter beneath the thick canopy of the rain forest. But here, in the city, it didn't make sense. If they wanted to live here, to build families and businesses, to prosper in this place, they needed to stand together. They weren't fully human and they weren't fully animal. They were different so it stood to reason that they needed a different type of government to protect their secret and ensure continuance of the race.

"I believe in creating our own government here, a hierarchy that will hear the differences and hopefully work them out without us fighting on the streets like animals."

Nick chuckled. "Look around, Rome. We're not the

only ones fighting in the streets. These so-called humans are killing one another without any help or instigation from us. They've been shooting and fighting and dying on these streets long before we showed up."

"But not by our kind. I know we can't change their world, their ways, or their government. But we can monitor our own."

"That's naive," Nick countered, finishing his beer and putting the bottle on the giant slab of marble that served as a coffee table.

"You sound like the Rogues," X said quietly, rubbing a hand down the back of his bald head. "They don't think we can act like anything but animals, either."

The last of Nick's semblance of control broke. It was a war within him. One side told him every day that they were different, tainted somehow. And the other— the one Rome and the other stateside shifters wanted him to see—insisted that even with their differences they could co-exist peacefully. It always saddened Rome to see his friend in this fight.

Nick stood quickly, glaring down at X as if he were ready to fight him. "Don't fucking compare me to those pussies!"

X didn't bother to stand but glared right back at Nick. "Then stop acting like a victim like them. Yeah, we're a different species, so what? It's time we move past that and make our mark on our own."

Tempers were rising—well, Nick's was. X was easily bated even though he and Nick had experienced their share of disagreements in the past. Rome, as always, was the peacekeeper.

"Nick will be fine. He knows this is the way to go,

it's just his nature to be rebellious." Rome prayed that was the truth.

"I need another beer," Nick murmured and stalked out.

"He's getting edgier about this by the minute," X said when they were alone.

Rome nodded. "I know. The appearance of the Rogues isn't making it any better. He's ready to kill first and ask questions later."

X shrugged. "It's our nature, Rome. I'm all for the government thing but we can't deny our animalistic heritage forever."

Rome knew that better than anyone. The slow prowling of his cat pressing against his human mind with daily persistence was proof. "I know. But there's a way to contain it when possible. I don't know that we'll always be able to deal with the Rogues this way, but we have to at least start thinking along those lines." He held the disk up. "Maybe there's some strategies on here we can use."

"Strategies? I thought we wanted clues to finding the killers. You still don't remember anything else about that night?" X asked.

"We . . . I do," he sighed. "I'm trying to do the right thing here, X."

"I know. And you know we've got your back however you want to play this."

"I want them dead."

X nodded. "As soon as we find them," he said solemnly.

And after they were dead, then what? A distant voice echoed in Rome's mind, making him think about the answer.

Taking a seat on the couch, Rome let the disk rest on his thigh, closing then reopening his eyes. "I can hear the sounds, feel the tightness of the closet walls around me. And then I can scent them. All of them. My parents, Baxter, the killers."

"So you'd remember if you scented them again?"

"Definitely."

X was the one to nod this time. "Then it's time we start lining up some suspects."

"Yeah." Rome glanced down at the disk again. "I believe you're right."

Kalina never thought she'd be happy to feel the slap of sticky humid air upon her cheeks, but as she stepped out of her car and began walking along the parking lot leading to the back entrance of the MPD, that's exactly what she felt. She hadn't even bothered to ask how her car had come to be parked in front of her building this afternoon when she'd come out. It hadn't been there last night. But she was sure it had arrived in the same manner as Roman Reynolds had with his breaking-and-entering, bossy-and-controlling self.

Mrs. Gilbert had stayed in her apartment after Rome left. She'd stayed about fifteen minutes past her usual quota of five minutes standing in the hallway, with that god-awful cat glaring and growling at Kalina. Normally Kalina's heart pounded the entire time she was in the vicinity of Ms. Kitty. Today she'd been so ticked off at Rome, she'd wanted to bare her own teeth and growl right back at the spotted cat.

As she walked across the asphalt, the low heels of her sandals clicked. She wasn't dressed in normal work attire; if she was seen, she could just as easily be viewed as a citizen visiting the police department for some reason or other. Besides, it was too hot for a lot of clothes. The summer dress with short capped sleeves and flowing bottom that flirted with her kneecaps was as cool as she could get without walking naked through the city streets.

Her goal was simple: pull the file on the Sheehan case—the one she'd been working two years ago.

The narcotics division was on the second floor of what looked like one of the city's plainest buildings. Stepping off the elevator, she heard the familiar buzz of interaction in what they called the bullpen. Departments were separated by glass-topped walls and double doors. On her way to the narc department she passed through homicide, nodding hellos to fellow officers but walking steadily forward. She wasn't there to converse. There was a reason she was getting these photos—someone connected to that case years ago was after her.

The pictures from last night were tucked in her bottom drawer beneath all her socks. Thinking back now, she figured she probably should have kept the first photo. But something had told her there would be more. Whoever this was wanted something from her. Looking past the fear that assailed her upon first seeing the photos, she'd found something else—anger. Whoever had taken the photos back then was here now, attempting to intimidate her, again.

That was so not happening, she thought, using her palms to push through the double doors leading to her department. It was kind of quiet, a Saturday afternoon; most of the detectives were probably working a sting or coasting the neighborhoods talking to informants. That was the tedious part of the job, but it was necessary.

Her desk was near one of the large dust-covered windows. She hadn't been there in weeks, so it was filled with files and mail and other paraphernalia her co-workers probably thought was funny to dump there. Sitting in her chair she pulled it close to the desk, being careful of the one wheel that usually stuck against the worn carpet on the floor.

She switched on her computer and while she waited for it to boot up pulled out her keys and opened the file cabinet beneath the desk to the left. Most files were kept on the computer now—vitals on all the suspects, details of the operation, official reports to be filed and copied to the court. But in her drawer Kalina kept her own personal file for each case she worked. The Sheehan case was a thick black folder worried from time and usage. She pulled it out, dropping it on her desk. Punching in her passwords, she pulled the computer file, browsing through the mug shots of all the suspects she'd investigated in the case.

None of them looked familiar or like the man who'd delivered the first picture. That man, she remembered, had a distinct look; he'd caused a memorable reaction she now thought was more strange than just a stirring of hormones. Something had happened when she saw that man, when he looked at her, said her name. Even now, thinking about him had her shivering, her skin itching. She sighed, sat back in the chair, and stared at the computer screen.

What am I missing?

Without any real motivation she pressed the arrow key, flipping steadily through photos. This time she wasn't only looking for one face, she was looking for three more.

The three stooges from last night who'd also evoked some weird reaction in her. After a few minutes she sighed.

Nothing.

No pictures to identify them. No connection and . . . nobody was bothering her.

There were easily a dozen people in her department right now. None of them said a word to her. That could be construed as a good thing, as she really wasn't in the mood for co-worker chitchat. Then again, it was still kind of odd.

If she took a moment to write down all the strange things going on in her life lately, she'd probably have a book by now. Things felt out of control. The goals she thought were so clear were wavering and she couldn't figure out why. All she had to do was investigate one man.

That wasn't going to be as easy as it seemed. Everything about him on paper profiled him as guilty. But his accounts were clean, his voice was mesmerizing, his touch downright sinful. He was right, she wanted him, craved him, and despised herself for it.

She wanted to work the case, find him guilty, move on. But he was a distraction. The photos she'd received were a distraction. Her mind whirled from one thing to the next and she took a deep breath to steady herself. Only for some reason the deep breath, the inhalation of familiar scents—warm paper from the printer, stale cigarettes from Kretzky's old tweed jacket that he kept hanging in his cubicle for days he was called to court, the musty aroma of thirty-year-old carpet that badly needed to be ripped up and burned—annoyed her, making her feel nauseous instead of nostalgic.

In the pit of her stomach something was brewing. It felt like a longing, but she dismissed it as hunger. Food hadn't been a priority by the time she'd awakened late this morning, and then her shower had been interrupted and Mrs. Gilbert arrived with that cat.

Cursing, she punched more keys on the keyboard. Something wasn't adding up, or maybe she just couldn't figure it out. Gingerly lifting the tattered file folder, she put it into her large purse. Shutting down her computer, she was grateful now for the lack of interest in her trip back to work. She left the narcotics division heading out of the building.

However, she was interrupted when she passed the meeting room midway between two departments. Double glass doors opened and people filed out. Detectives, plainclothes cops, and the chief of police walked by, all with sour looks on their faces. Something was up.

"Hey, Harper, what're you doing here? Thought I heard you were UC." Reed Sampson, a homicide detective with soft brown eyes and a killer smile, who'd asked her out too many times to remember, touched her elbow as he spoke.

"Hey, Sampson. Yeah, I was just there to see what else was going on and to follow a few leads I had on my case." That was a lie. There were no leads. She couldn't find anything on the guy, nothing except the feeling that he wasn't all that he appeared. But that had really just become more pronounced in their last two encounters, and she wasn't entirely sure if she was thinking along business or personal lines. "What's happening?" she asked, nodding toward the line of men dispersing among the cubicles and toward the elevators.

"You haven't heard? Probably not, since you're on

an assignment." Reed nodded his head, directing her to his cubicle on the other side of the conference room.

Kalina really didn't want to follow him, didn't want to be in the enclosed space with him, knowing he'd try to hit on her once again. But she did want to know what was so important the chief of police was sitting in on a meeting on a Saturday afternoon. So she followed.

Dropping his folder, notepad, and pen on his desk, Reed hiked up his dress pants and sat. Kalina sat on the stool wedged into a corner across from him. "So what's going on?"

"Two murders last night. SBFs, about your height and weight, sexually assaulted and ripped to shreds. Chief thinks there's a connection to the senator and his daughter, who were both torn apart a few weeks back."

Kalina remembered that case. Even if she hadn't been a cop, it had been on the news for the first two weeks after the senator and his young daughter had gone missing. Their bodies had been mauled to the point where they had to make ID through the dental records. "Still no suspects on that one?" she asked.

Reed shook his head. "I'm with the chief on this one, it's the same guy."

"You think it's a guy?" Kalina wasn't so sure. She didn't think it was a woman, but something about the pictures she'd seen of the senator and his daughter had made her think of something else. Something she'd sworn wasn't true.

"You think a chick would do something like this?"

Reed was a nice guy, a nice dresser, a permanent fixture in the department. He was probably just the kind of guy she should be looking at to settle down with. But . . . not.

She shrugged. "I don't know. I'm narcs, remember."

"That's right," he said, leaning back in his chair, flipping his tie over his shoulder as if that had some significant meaning. Other than to show her he was possibly partaking of too many donuts, she had no clue what that was. "You're big time now, working with the DEA."

The last was said with more than mild distaste. It was no secret that the local cops abhorred federal agents from any branch. Something about too much arrogance and too little street training. While federal agents—Kalina assumed—probably thought cops had too much time on their hands and didn't know their ass from a hole in the wall. How she could play both sides she wasn't sure, but it was a guess that made a lot of sense to her.

"I'm just working with them on this case."

"You're following that smooth criminal Roman Reynolds? Be careful of him," Reed warned.

This was a conversation she definitely did not want to have with Reed. "It's a job, Reed. Like all our others. So you have a list of possible suspects for these murders?" Changing the subject was the best course of action.

"Nah, these girls were nobodies. No family, no addresses, nothing."

Just like her, Kalina thought with a pang to her chest. If not for her job, these women could have been her.

"So that means it's not worth finding their killer?" Even to herself her tone sounded defensive. The surprised look on Reed's face confirmed it.

"I didn't say that. It just makes the pool of suspects that much deeper. If we had good background information, some type of friendships or connections, we'd have a starting point. At this stage all we know is that they were killed in the same manner."

Kalina rubbed her palms up and down her thighs, willing herself to calm down. Suddenly she felt very edgy. "I see what you mean. Maybe I could pull some of my contacts, see if they've heard anything on the streets."

Reed's smile was slow. "You'd do that for me, baby?" he asked, leaning forward, resting his elbows on his knees, and reaching for her hands.

With an easy movement she lifted her hands, putting one up to her head to smooth down the sides of her hair while the other rested on the desk. "I could ask around to help get a lead on the case."

"But aren't you working on something right now with the feds?"

Hearing about the brutal murders had turned her attention from that, even though she wasn't a homicide detective.

"Look, thanks for the offer," Reed said his eyes having a hard time staying focused on her face. Obviously the small hint of cleavage that showed in her dress was more appealing. "But I think I've got this under control."

She nodded. "Okay." Sure, he had this under control, just like the other twenty-something murder cases still unsolved on his desk. Reed was definitely not the top detective in the homicide department; something about him being lazy and more than a little disheartened by the crime he'd seen in his years on the force took away any chance of that title. Still, he kept his job, and they kept giving him new cases. No wonder crime was steadily on the rise.

"Hope you catch this guy," she said, standing and picking up her large purse with her own files and information inside.

Reed stood, too, this time grabbing her wrist. "We should really get together outside work. How about dinner?"

He was taller than her, but not taller than Rome. His slim build looked athletic and capable but didn't exude the strength and dominance that Rome's did. And she was losing her everlasting mind for thinking about a man who drove her absolutely crazy.

"Ah, that's probably not a good idea," she found herself saying. "We work together, remember?"

"Actually we don't," he said rubbing his fingers up her bare arm. The motion irritated her, scraped against something raw inside. "We're in different departments and you seem to be moving on to bigger and better things."

She sensed he was talking about the DEA again and wondered why he kept mentioning that. Probably jealousy. There was a lot of that in the department. But she was the last person anybody should feel jealous of.

Pulling her arm from his grasp, she gave a light chuckle. "I'll always be a cop at heart," she said. "I just think we should keep our relationship casual."

"Oh, I'm all for casual," he said, but his hands found their way to her hips, pulling her closer to him in the small confines of his cubicle. "No strings attached. You know what I mean?"

What Kalina knew for certain was that he was making her sick—literally. Her stomach roiled and she thought she was going to hurl right on his Pittsburgh Steelers tie—which wouldn't have been a crime at all since they were rivals to both the Baltimore Ravens and Washington Redskins.

"What I mean, Reed," she said, pushing away from him and pulling her purse onto her arm in a defensive manner, "is that we should stay co-workers. That's all. I'm not interested in anything more." There, that should be clear enough.

Reed nodded, dragging his tongue over his lower lip in a move that was probably meant to arouse. Instead it sort of provoked. Kalina took a step closer to him using the point of her finger to poke into his chest.

"Just co-workers. Got it?" Her last poke sent Reed stumbling back, and he looked at her strangely.

"Cool. Cool," he said, holding his hands up in the air as if she were about to arrest him. "I get it. Don't get all huffy. Actually, why don't you get moving to your big assignment with the feds? I'm sure they need you there," he said snidely.

Yeah, he was jealous and now scorned. She didn't care, she was tired of talking to him anyway. "It's the DEA and yes, they need me there."

Walking out of the precinct, she was racked by unsteady feelings both physical and emotionally. The DEA didn't need her; she was a nobody, remember? Just like those dead girls. Her stomach roiled again almost in rebellion against the words spoken in her mind.

In the safety of her car she cranked up the air-conditioning and set out for home, her mind tracing over the facts.

Four people had been killed. Mutilated.

The females sexually assaulted, then mutilated.

Connected?

Not to her case, Kalina thought as she drove back to

her apartment. It had nothing to do with her. While she was at the station she'd plugged in descriptions of the three goons she'd seen last night and come back with nothing. Something moved inside her, pushing past the nausea that had assailed her just moments ago. She rolled down the window, needing new air to breathe, and was greeted with a dry wind that filtered into the car's interior.

From the passenger seat her cell phone chirped. She activated her Bluetooth and answered, "Hello?"

"Hi. It's me, Mel. So we're having a cookout tomorrow and I thought about you. You know, being alone and everything, I figured you'd like to come over, have a couple burgers, and hang out."

Her co-worker, the chipper secretary with the envious home life. The word *no* was on the tip of Kalina's tongue. She did not want to be around people she didn't know, had too much work to think about socializing.

On the other hand, she'd never had a real friend. In all her years Kalina could count her personal acquaintanceships with males and females—outside of work—on one hand. She did not build relationships, didn't share any part of herself with anyone else, and had never experienced a giving of the same. Maybe it was time she opened the door just a little bit. Maybe this time would be different.

As more maybes rolled around in her head her mouth answered, "Sure. Sounds good."

Chapter 12

He called this room The Point. It was where he housed his shipments and distributed them to the dealers who would go out and make him and his growing establishment money to live on.

As rooms went it was large: twelve-foot ceilings with beams and wiring crawling overhead like veins. There were few windows, small and clouded with dirt and located high up on the wall so anyone looking in would most likely only see the old pipes and structure of the old warehouse.

On the floor nine-foot tables were lined as if a school of kids were expected for lunch, except there were no chairs. On each table at any given time a variety of items could be found, most often cocaine, since that was the drug he harvested and manufactured for himself. All the years he felt trapped and cheated being born in the bowels of the rain forest with all those other animals had finally paid off. Almost a hundred miles from where he was born in a dingy old hut at the base of the Gungi was where his empire had begun. Two years ago he'd found the land, or actually found the useless natives tirelessly working their callused hands to manufacture cocaine. The coke was being shipped to Raul Cortez in Peru then on to the United States, where Cortez had his army of dealers pushing it to those weak enough to become addicted.

After doing the useless minions a favor and ending their meager existence, he'd slept in the middle of what was nothing more than a huge tent. Sleeping and thinking, thinking and sleeping was what Sabar did for seven days. And in the same time that it had taken the God that humans worshiped to create this foul world, he had come up with a plan to control it.

Except instead of resting on the seventh day, Sabar killed. He hunted and devoured whatever crossed his path, letting the thrill of the hunt, the thirst for blood run gracefully through his veins. The idea had manifested over the weeks he stayed exiled in the forest, and eventually he'd gone out to find his own workers. Only these workers weren't filthy humans, they were shifters. Ones like him that the Shadow Shifters didn't want, felt like they didn't need. When, in essence, they were the better of the species, they were superior. He would show them, once and for all.

He could simply attack the tribes in the forest: take his growing group of Rogues and pillage their camp in the deep recesses of the night. But that wouldn't have the effect he wanted. It was too quick, too painless. What he had in mind for the Shadow Shifters was something much more drawn out and deadly. As the laws of revenge went, there were none.

Manufacturing his own product, shipping it to the States on security-cleared US military aircrafts, and having the humans he allowed himself to deal with push the product gave a much better profit than Raul Cortez had ever seen. The Cortez Cartel had nothing on Sabar and the Rogues.

Less frequently he worked in ammunition. One thing Sabar had learned from his military contacts was that the US government loved to fight, and they loved to have the upper hand in a fight. So they were always in the market for the latest and greatest in warfare. It just so happened that one of Sabar's newest associates had exactly what the government wanted—and more excitingly, what America's allies wanted.

So for the moment life was sweet.

But only for the moment. There were still some glitches in his plan, some issues that he needed to resolve.

The Kalina Harper thing, for instance. A chance encounter he'd never quite forgotten, one he'd finally realized was meant to be.

There were other issues, other legs of his plan he'd yet to reveal, but tonight was about taking the next step. Facilitating his plan was of utmost importance. If he wanted to rule he needed an army behind him. Drafting new Rogues wasn't difficult; there was a lot of unrest among the shifters, both the shadows in the forest and the ones stateside. The Shadow Shifters prided themselves on sticking together, following their rules, and living the life outlined for them—inside ridiculous parameters. They were loyal to one another, dedicated to their *Ètica* and their way of life. But there was division, an act Sabar had foreseen years ago. Now a shifter himself, he coddled the philosophy of breaking with tradition like a newborn baby.

Humans, on the other hand, loved three things: money, power, and respect.

All Sabar wanted from the spineless creatures was their money.

He already had the power, was blessed with it along with his inferior DNA. Being a shifter was his saving grace, being a step above the human race his reward. He loved the control and fear his cat evoked, loved the leader it had bred him to be. He'd waited a long time to step up and claim what was rightfully his, and now he was almost there.

As for respect, that would come or they would die. It was quite simple to his way of thinking.

"JC's ready," Darel said from behind.

Sabar rubbed a hand down the back of his close-shaved head, inhaling deeply before he turned. Darel wasn't afraid of him. Leery of what his next move might be, yes, but not afraid. This could be a good thing, Sabar noted, or it could be bad. He hadn't decided which yet. But he liked Darel, liked the kill-or-be-killed mentality the shifter possessed. Looking at the broad-shouldered beast with its green eyes glaring back at him almost made Sabar proud. He'd trained Darel, brought him under his wing when he was just a boy, raised him to be as vicious and cutthroat as he was. Yes, he was proud. But he wanted to be prouder.

"Did you check his receipts from the last time?"

Darel nodded. "I did. He was even."

"Good," Sabar said, taking a step so that he and Darel were now walking together toward the other side of The Point. There were four tables over there, filled with blocks of coke that JC was to pick up and distribute on the streets for quick sale. "Watch him, though. He stinks," he said, extending his long tongue to lick over his lips.

Beside him Darel grunted. "He's no fool, boss. He knows if he fucks up his ass is mincemeat."

Sabar nodded. "Make sure he doesn't forget that little tidbit of information."

"No problem."

Through heavy metal double doors a human walked. He was tall and built like a toothpick, his face sunken in and leathery like he'd seen too much sun and not enough sunscreen. Dark eyes darted around the room as he walked with a sure gait, his stench wreaking of fear. Sabar's stomach churned. If there was anything he hated more than the Shadow Shifters, it was a spineless human.

"Howdy," the man Darel called JC said.

Darel stepped in front of Sabar. "Here's the shipment. You've got a week to turn in the money and your receipts."

"Shit," JC hissed. "All this? You want me to move all this in a week?"

"If you can't," Darel said menacingly, "we'll find someone who can."

"Nah, that's . . . ," he stuttered. "That's . . . not necessary." Rubbing a hand through his greasy hair, he made a wide step around Darel to the first table. Long fingers moved along the silver-covered package as he blew out a low whistle. "I can do it."

"You'd better," Darel said with a growl that had JC jumping, almost falling over the merchandise.

"What the fuck are you guys?" JC mumbled as he looked up to see he was surrounded by the two of them.

"Your worst fucking nightmare!" Sabar snarled.

* * *

In the confines of his bedroom on Sunday Rome continued to stare at the computer screen. His back hurt, his legs were begging to be stretched, but his eyes remained fixated on the words, the letters, the feelings behind each sentence his father had written.

The last year in Vance Reynolds's life was a tumultuous one. Along with the Delgados he'd been trying to create a stateside alliance like the Assembly in the forest. They wanted a government in place for the Shadow Shifters who'd opted to live out in the open among the humans. In the forest there had already been whispers of an uprising, threats of rogue shifters staking a claim in the village they'd helped build. Vance figured it was only a matter of time before those rogues made their way to the States.

The stakes were much higher here in the land of the free. Shifters were living in the open instead of remaining hidden under the canopy of the rain forest, reported only as shadows or man–animal beasts. They could walk along the streets with their heads held high, make a living for themselves and their families, and still honor their heritage. But like any group living in unknown territory, they needed boundaries, rules, protocols to maintain their most protected secret.

In the last few months of his life, Vance had begun a preliminary outline for how they could make that happen. At that time there were no Faction Leaders in the Zones, no one to really keep tabs on what was going on all over the continent, and Vance could not do it alone. He trusted Henrique and Sofia Delgado, along with his wife, with all his plans and secrets. All but one.

As Rome stared at the screen, he knew without a doubt that neither his mother nor Nick's parents had known about Vance's latest plan. A plan that had shaken all Rome's ideals and beliefs in the man he looked up to.

Running tired hands over his face, Rome took a deep breath, wondering who else may have read these notes. Bingham said he'd just taken the disk out of the safe-deposit box. X said he'd simply broken the encryption. Rome believed X. He trusted his friend. He did not trust Bingham, which posed yet another problem.

"Find what you were looking for, Mr. Roman?" Baxter asked.

Rome thought he was alone, but he wasn't surprised at Baxter's quiet entrance. The man moved as if his feet barely touched the ground. Over the years Rome had grown used to it. Besides, this big house might seem lonely without Baxter. More often than not, he felt lonely anyway.

But it was the life he led, the life he had to lead.

"Found more than I was looking for," he answered finally. "Why didn't Dad tell me what he was doing?"

"Fathers protect their sons," Baxter said, moving through the room, no doubt looking for something to pick up. But Rome wasn't messy. To the contrary, he believed everything had a place and made sure it was there. His master bedroom was on the far left side of the house and looked as if three normal-size bedrooms could fit into it. His bed was a huge four-poster that sat in the middle of the floor directly across from a huge fireplace. Rich colors like mahogany and charcoal gray and sapphire blue decorated the space. Books lined the walls while thick duvets and plump pillows occupied the bed. The master bath was to one side; a small private exercise room, to the other. He could stay in his suite for days without needing to leave. But he didn't. The walls surrounding him would drive his cat crazy.

"Protect me from what? It wouldn't have done any harm to share what he was thinking. Maybe I could have helped."

"You were but a child, sir. Your father was doing what he thought was best."

"Was getting himself killed best?"

Baxter paused, his thin frame looking almost lost in the midst of the big room. "It was probably necessary. You would not have grown into your destiny otherwise."

There was that word again, *destiny.* His mother used it often, telling him there was a destiny for everyone, a life preordained for them. Rome thought it was all bullshit. He made his future. Yes, the job of Faction Leader, his allegiance to the tribes, that was probably planned. But his decisions led the way to what happened in the here and now.

"Some things are still hard for you to understand."

"That's because I get the feeling I still don't know everything. If there's more you can tell me, Baxter, please do."

"Timing is crucial," Baxter said, then moved to the bed, turning down the heavy gray duvet, removing the pillows that were simply for decoration.

He turned down Rome's bed every night, no matter how many times Rome told him it was unnecessary. The fact that Baxter still cooked, cleaned, and basically ran this household was probably unnecessary, but Rome couldn't imagine his life without him. He was the only family—besides Nick and X—that Rome had, pitiful as that was.

"The Rogues are plotting something now."

"You are correct. How do you plan to act?"

"I still believe in what my father wanted." Rome sat back in the chair and sighed. "Mostly." This new revelation wasn't what he'd expected. He hadn't figured out how he was going to deal with it yet.

"All the Faction Leaders seem to feel the same. Some sort of judicial system is in order."

Rome nodded. "I've got notes on that, suggestions for who should head up the Stateside Assembly."

"I think it should be you."

"Nah, not planning to nominate myself," Rome said. He stood, moving to his bookshelf where he had his law books.

"You will lead them better than anyone else, Mr. Roman."

"Not what I want to do with my future."

"Sometimes your future chooses you."

Rome didn't even want to ask what that meant. He wanted to check in with Ezra to make sure Kalina was safe. He hadn't seen her since yesterday when he'd stopped by her place. The emotions roiling through him when he'd been around her then had baffled him, made him feel like some distance might be necessary. Today he'd been closed up with his father's journals, trying to make sense of the betrayal he felt. But now she was on his mind. Truth be told, she'd never been far from it.

"You should go to her." Baxter's voice interrupted his thoughts.

"What?"

"The female who has haunted you for so long. You should not stay away from her. Trouble is brewing in that direction, too."

Baxter seemed to know everything. If Rome wasn't absolutely sure the man was human, he'd think he was some kind of tribal Seer or something. He always knew things before they happened, prophesying about the shifters as if he were one, or he'd been born in the forest himself. But that was not the case. From all Rome knew of the man, he'd always been in his father's employ; the where and why he didn't know, and never bothered to ask.

"I have that under control."

Baxter chuckled. "Then you are not as smart as I thought. You cannot control her until you understand everything and then—" He shrugged. "Control still may not be easy."

And that was supposed to mean what exactly? Rome was about to ask, his face probably showing the confusion he felt, but from the desk his cell phone rang, vibrating over the smooth cherrywood, effectively ending this conversation with Baxter.

Chapter 13

When was the last time she'd been to a cookout?

Checking her reflection in the full-length mirror behind her closet door, Kalina sighed. "Never."

She figured she looked okay in black capris and a gray T-shirt that could have been a size bigger if she cared anything about shopping, which she did not. Strappy sandals with a low heel completed her casual attire. She ran her fingers through her hair to give it an extra spike. It was growing out, so her two-toned tresses hung a little longer on the top than usual, but a trip to the beauty salon was another thing that wasn't on her agenda. Her short haircut was not for stylish reasons, but practical ones—she didn't like to do hair any more than she liked to shop. Maybe because growing up she didn't have the money to get into either habit. It would make sense that once she became a working adult she'd readily do all the things she'd been deprived of when she was young. Instead, Kalina shied away from them all. Especially the socializing part.

Today, however, was going to be different.

Last night she'd lain in her bed thinking of her life, of things she could possibly want in the future but would never have if she kept on the track she was on. She loved her job, wanted to excel at it more than anything else, but suddenly she realized that work might not be enough. It could have been the way Mel talked about her husband or her kids. Or maybe it was the invite to today's family function that kicked her mind into overdrive. Or maybe it was the way Rome kissed her, the way he looked at her like she was possibly the only woman in the world.

Now, that was a crock if ever she'd heard one. There was no happily ever after in her future; her life was what it was. Right?

Moving to the bed, she picked up her cell phone and grabbed the clutch purse she'd pulled out of the back of her closet to drop it in. It chirped, signaling that she had a text. Then she saw it was from Ferrell.

Need an update. Soon.

God, did he ever stop? It was Sunday afternoon, and the last thing she wanted to think about was how she didn't have enough information to convict Rome Reynolds.

Kalina ignored the message and the urge to spend the day trying like hell to find something on a man she was attracted to.

Forty-five minutes later she pulled up in front of a red-brick duplex with black shutters. She parked her car and just sat there. All the way over she'd been motivated and encouraged, listening to her favorite R&B station as she drove. Now that she was actually here, nervousness set in. Or was it anxiousness? Either way, her heart was beating a little faster than it should have been. Stepping out of the car, she inhaled the humid air. She should have started walking toward the house, instead she stopped, stood perfectly still, and waited.

Kalina wasn't sure what she was waiting for but there was something, somewhere; she could feel it. She just needed to wait for it to . . .

A car whizzed by and she turned quickly, her hand going to her clutch as if her gun were there. It wasn't. She'd convinced herself that today was about pleasure and not work. There was one in the glove compartment of her car, but she didn't have anything on her person.

Her gaze scanned up and down the street, but her body didn't move. Another car went by, this person obviously taking the thirty-five mph speed limit seriously. It was a regular car, a Toyota she thought as it passed her. She memorized the license plate and noted a driver and a front passenger. Ridiculous information, but it stuck in her mind regardless.

There was a snapping sound from behind and once again she jumped. Somebody stepped on something, and it broke. But when she turned there was no one there.

"Dammit!"

Taking a breath to steady herself, she swore she was losing her mind. Well, that would have to take place tomorrow. The nuthouse, where she was undoubtedly headed, could hold her bed one more day. She'd been invited to a cookout and dammit, she was going!

With sure steps she walked up the short walkway and took the steps one by one, all the while feeling the hairs at the back of her neck prickle. The air was still, yet something brushed along her skin. Lifting her hand to ring the doorbell, she looked back only once, to see nothing but parked cars, the street, normalcy. Shaking her head, Kalina turned just in time to see Mel pull the door open and smile at her.

"You made it! I'm so happy you came." Melanie was already reaching her long arms out to grasp Kalina in a hug.

They'd just seen each other at work two days ago and they hadn't even been acquainted that long. This type of reunion should have been reserved for a somewhat closer relationship.

Kalina hugged her back, letting the connection sink in. Then again, it didn't, not really. They were both women, yet it still felt like they were opposites.

Stepping inside the wood-paneled foyer gave Kalina a chance to shake the feeling of being watched or followed, or whatever had her jumping at shadows.

"I have such a surprise for you. Well, it's not a surprise for me, I actually think it's a cool idea. That's why I thought of it. But Pete's like, 'Don't interfere,' blah, blah, blah. But I'm like, 'I know what I'm doing.' So how are you? You look great. Wish I could look sexy in simply pants and a shirt."

All this was said in one breath as Mel walked Kalina from the foyer through a furniture- and knickknack-crowded living room and dining room, into a kitchen with counters overflowing with food.

"I'm fine. Thanks," Kalina said when they finally stopped.

Melanie went to the refrigerator to pull out yet another bowl of something. *Just how many people are coming to this little shindig?* she wondered.

"Ah, need help with anything?" she offered but honestly didn't know what she could do in here. Domestication was not one of Kalina's strong points. Sure, she could cook enough to keep herself from starving, and she cleaned house because living in a pigsty was not something she enjoyed. But that's where the Susie Home-maker bit ended.

"Sure, grab another twelve-pack out of that box. We can dump those in the cooler out back. I'm sure they're almost finished with the ones I put out earlier."

"No problem." Kalina moved to the corner of the kitchen, which looked like a liquor store with twelve-packs of beer stacked almost as tall as she was. Grabbing two, she turned and said, "Where to?"

"Here." Mel removed the top from a plastic bowl filled with fruit and stuck a big spoon inside. "Follow me," she said, carrying the bowl and her cheerful smile out the back door.

Kalina followed, stepping out onto a deck full of more furniture and now people as well.

With a nod of her red curls Mel signaled toward the cooler. Kalina walked to that side of the deck, pulled up the cover, and began unloading the beer bottles. A few seconds later Melanie was pulling on her arm again.

"Here, let me introduce you," she said. "Kalina Harper, my co-worker, this is Stephen Johnson and Eddie and Jamia Henderson. Stephen, Eddie, Jamia, this is Kalina."

Kalina smiled, reached out a hand, and shook those of the threesome staring at her with bright smiles. Eddie and Jamia were a couple, that was evident by the way Eddie's arm extended to shake her hand then hurriedly resumed its post around Jamia's waist. Stephen was alone, dateless . . . just like her. It only took about two seconds to see what was going on.

"And this is my hubby, Pete." Mel kept talking, leaving Kalina to stand alone while she went over to the grill and wrapped her arms around a tall, husky man with dark hair that was more than a touch too long.

"It's nice to meet you all," Kalina said, making sure her handshake with Stephen was the shortest of the greetings.

"Mel says you just started working at the firm, in accounting right?" Stephen Johnson with his tall athletic build and crystalline blue eyes asked. He looked like a superhero. Really? His hair was perfect, black and shiny, his eyes so bright they almost looked fake, his face chiseled with iconic perfection. He looked just like Superman, who just so happened to be her favorite superhero of all time.

Unfortunately, that was in the animated dream world of a teenager. Here and now, he was an eerily attractive guy.

"Yes, I did," she answered belatedly.

"How are you liking it so far?"

"It's a learning experience."

Jamia laughed. "That means she doesn't like it."

Kalina smiled. "Not really. Let's just say the jury's still out." That was true of a lot of things lately, including the boss she was determined not to like.

"I get it," Jamia said, then looked up at Eddie with what Kalina actually thought were stars in her eyes.

They were a cute couple. He was thick, not fat, but definitely on the positive side for the possibility. She was shorter, her head full of long bronze-colored braids that reached down her back, a good foot below his. They couldn't stop touching each other, couldn't resist the enigmatic pull between them.

Kalina wondered how that felt. How would it feel to

be that inextricably attached to someone? And how long did it last?

In the next hour Pete burned two hamburgers before finally giving Kalina one that wasn't going to leave charred flecks between her teeth. Eddie and Jamia thought it was funny, joking about how Pete was the worst on the grill but how Mel continued to have these get-togethers. Mel's kids came in and out, the older ones with plans of their own, just grabbing something to eat before they left; the twins had more attractive plans that consisted of sitting in front of the television in the basement watching some sort of cartoon marathon.

After Kalina had finished eating Stephen happily removed her trash and came back to sit beside her.

"Mel must really like you if she invited you to her house. She's usually a very private person when it comes to mixing business with pleasure," he said, his fingers wrapping around the neck of a bottle of beer.

"I think she's really nice," Kalina responded honestly. "I don't do a lot of socializing."

"Is that by choice?"

She nodded and he smiled.

"Maybe I could change that. Have dinner with me?"

He was a nice guy. She should feel something for him, or at least she thought she should. But beyond being cordial, she just didn't. "We just had dinner," she said trying to keep the mood light.

"You know what I mean. A date, you and me?"

Him and her. For a few seconds Kalina tried to let that idea take root. But try as she might, she couldn't see herself with Stephen. Or Reed from the precinct. All she could see was Rome.

"I don't think that's such a good idea," she said even

though she wasn't too pleased about her thoughts returning to the man who seemed determined to ruin every aspect of her life. Because not coming up with any goods on him to make her case just wasn't enough. No, he'd had to touch her, to kiss her, to make her want, need something she'd never thought to have before.

She did not do relationships—sex maybe, and not even that except solo for a very long time. She'd never imagined being the other half of a couple, wasn't even sure she'd know how to be with someone on a long-term basis.

And really, what the hell was going on with her? Two men hitting on her in two days was definitely out of the ordinary.

"I get it," he said with a contemplative look on his face. "You're already seeing someone."

"No," she answered quickly. "I'm not. I mean, I don't have anyone. I'm just not really into dating right now."

"You're not into dating me."

She sighed. "I'm really not seeing anyone."

"But you'd like to be. Does he know?" Stephen's voice was friendly, his eyes just a little pensive.

"Does who know what?"

"That you're interested in him."

"I'm not—" she started, then paused. She didn't know Stephen well. Hell, she didn't know anybody well thanks to her self-induced solitary status. She could talk to her therapist, but she despised him and would much rather stick toothpicks in her eyes and walk on hot coals then sit on that couch and open up to his sick, leery glare. She was a mess. Beyond a mess really, but Stephen seemed game for listening to her so she figured what the hell.

"I think he knows."

Still smiling, but not totally happy with her admission, Stephen added, "And? Is he interested?"

"I think, in a way." Admitting he wanted to sleep with her didn't really seem like the politically correct thing to say. Besides, how did she explain that she thought that was all Rome wanted to do?

Taking another swallow of his beer, Stephen leaned back in his chair. "He's an idiot if he isn't."

She couldn't help but smile at the serious way in which he'd said that, as if he really saw something in her he thought another man should appreciate. The thought warmed her, just like watching the other two couples together planted the smallest seed of hope inside her.

Maybe she could be relationship material after all. Drinking her soda she laughed off that idea, because it was ridiculously stupid. Stephen was talking off his fourth beer, he could say anything and not mean a thing. What Kalina knew definitely was that the orphan who was trying to make a difference didn't need the added stress of falling in love with the wrong man.

Instead she decided to enjoy the moment. She'd wanted badly to come to this cookout, to be included in the normalcy of friends on a Sunday afternoon, just this once.

As night settled over the deck, crowded with folding chairs and plastic-covered tables, a light breeze began to blow. Kalina sat at the table with Mel, Pete, and Stephen.

Lifting to her lips the soda she'd grabbed in exchange for the beer she couldn't quite stomach, she took a sip.

The cool liquid slid over her tongue and down her throat with a gentle motion. She let the taste of lime mingle in her mouth and was just about to say something when she heard it.

A moan, or a groan, or something akin to an animal sound. She looked around, but it didn't appear that anyone else had heard it. Maybe one of the neighbors had a big-ass dog that could growl that deeply. Somehow Kalina really didn't think that was the case.

Her body tensed as she sat up straighter in her chair. The sound came again, this time closer, and she wished she'd figured out a way to squeeze the 9mm in her glove compartment into her super-small purse. There was danger, that feeling she knew well as it gripped her insides, sending quick messages to her brain to be on alert. She'd always had this kind of intuition, these feelings that she knew were different from anything anyone around her felt. Right beside her the conversation between Melanie and her guests moved with casual ease, but Kalina's ears tuned that out, pushed it to the far recesses of her mind. In return she homed in on the sound of whatever was coming, waiting so she could react.

It was the strangest thing, a sense of déjà vu so strong she felt dizzy with it. She would have to fight; her fingers tingled with the notion. But who? She was at a cookout for crying out loud, who the hell was she gonna fight? The brother-in-law who came over thinking he'd been hooked up? The dad who burned her hamburger?

It didn't make sense.

But at the end of the yard where fat bushes lined the tall tiers of the privacy fence she saw a movement. Just a shadow, but definitely movement. Instinctively she stood, her eyes narrowing, focusing on that spot.

"Hey, you need something?" Stephen asked, already at her side.

"Ah, no. I um, I just need the bathroom," she replied. "Be right back."

And then she was gone, slipping through the back door into the kitchen. Walking swiftly through the rooms, Kalina searched for the basement door. It was there, along the foyer wall. She headed down the steps, hearing the blare of what she thought was the *Sponge-Bob SquarePants* theme music. At the bottom of the steps, she looked to her left into the room that was carpeted and paneled and again filled with furniture, including a big flat-screen television. Matthew was lounging on the couch and Madison sound asleep on the love seat across from him.

Tiptoeing past the doorway, she entered what was obviously the laundry room: cement floor, washer and dryer, clothes hanging or folded all about. But none of that mattered; the feeling that something was out there taunted her. There was another door and Kalina quickly opened it, grabbing a baseball bat she'd spied in the corner of the laundry room beforehand.

Slipping out into the night, she recognized that the adults were still talking and drinking just above her on the deck. She moved slowly, hoping their beer-muddled minds wouldn't see her creeping across the elongated length of the yard. Using the cloak of darkness and the dense line of bushes, Kalina moved deeper and deeper into the yard until a sound had her stopping.

It wasn't a groan this time, more like a chuffing she knew was animal-like because she'd heard it before. Last night and that night long ago. Still, Kalina prayed she was wrong. What she thought she'd seen didn't exist. Moving closer to the bushes, she let that thought play in her mind.

Through the bushes there was a flash of light. Green. Two orbs of green. Eyes?

Her heart pounded in her chest as recognition beat into her brain.

She paused, unable to move another inch.

Eyes in the bushes.

There was a sound behind her and she flinched, turning quickly with the raised bat in hand. What came at her was large and moved fast. But she was faster, swinging until the bat connected with a loud *thunk*. She would have hit it again or at the very least moved closer to verify what "it" was, but she was grabbed from behind.

A hand went over her mouth, another around her waist, pulling her into the bushes she'd thought were her shield.

Kalina struggled, but it was futile as whoever had grabbed her moved quickly. The privacy fence gave way, probably the opening where the trash cans were lined. But there was almost no sound—or maybe they were moving too fast. She felt wind whipping over her skin as if they were traveling at a high rate of speed.

The chuffing grew louder, into a sick-sounding mewl. But her captor kept moving and moving until she was being thrown into the back of a truck.

"Go!" a man's voice yelled.

The truck pulled off, wheels screeching along the asphalt.

Kalina rolled over on the leather-covered seat, turning

until she stared into eyes that freaked her out more than the green ones she'd seen in the bushes. They were gold, like flecks of the sun dropped into the face of a man with skin the color of night.

Now she really wished she had her gun.

Chapter 14

Umberto Alamar walked slowly off the private jet to the waiting black SUV. A different type of breeze hit his exposed skin, a scent of untamed and dangerous land tickling his nostrils. Approaching the open door of the vehicle, he unbuttoned the two buttons of the suit jacket and stepped inside.

Human clothes, he thought, itched like the devil.

The interior of the vehicle was dark and he was alone, as he was most of the time. As he had been most of his adult life. Save for the three years his jaguar mother had stayed with him, Umberto had been parentless, taken in by the females of the tribe, trained by the males to become the leader he was today. One would think at fifty-two years old he would have found some sort of solace in the life that had been chosen for him before he'd taken an initial breath.

But he hadn't.

He was where he was supposed to be, doing the job that was destined to be his. But it wasn't enough. He knew this just as he'd known three days ago that this trip to the States was imminent.

Things were changing, long-ago rules were proving deficient in this new battle that approached. And it was on foreign ground that the first spoils of this war would lie.

With a heavy sigh he sat back on the seat, wondering how they'd come to be in this position, knowing instinctively that it would not only be up to him to bring them out.

X greeted the Elder, holding open the door to the SUV that had brought him from the private landing strip in Virginia owned by the Shadow Shifters but titled to a couple of fake stockholders in Rome and Nick's law firm. With appropriate respect and honor he bowed and waited as the Elder stepped from the vehicle and stayed in that position until a heavy hand clapped onto his shoulder, granting permission for him to do otherwise.

He'd received word from the Assembly just an hour ago that Elder Alamar was arriving. He'd also been told to keep the arrival time and place a secret, until otherwise notified.

X did as he was told.

Usually.

Tonight was one of those off times that he listened to one of the Elders and kept his mouth shut about the arrival of Alamar. He did this for two reasons. First, he'd been instructed to take Alamar to Rome's house. This meant he wasn't keeping anything from his friend and Faction Leader. And two, it was either leave his apartment to pick up the Elder or sit there and let the walls close in around him, choking the last remnants of life out of him.

Normally X liked his solitude, enjoyed the quiet that calmed the darkness raging in his soul. Tonight he'd needed something else.

Driving the almost hundred miles to Rome's house from the airport gave him time to think, or more like not think, about the needs building inside. He was not a simple man, nor a simple beast, for that matter. No, it was not only X's genetic makeup that was different, out of the ordinary. It was so much more. Since first realizing that deep dark desires ran thickly through his blood, he'd been careful to keep it a secret. Only one kind of shifter craved the things X did, only one branch of their species took pleasure in the darker side of sexual exploitations.

The Rogues.

But he was not one of them. Every day he arose and with every breath he took, X convinced himself he was not like those betrayers, those killers. He was different. He always had been.

Pulling up in front of Rome's house, X got out of the truck, walked to the back, and opened the door.

"Where is Roman?" Elder Alamar asked pointedly.

"If he is not at home, I will find him, sir," he said.

Once they approached the front door, Baxter was there holding it open.

"Welcome, Elder Alamar. Come right in, sir."

Elder Alamar nodded and proceeded into the house. When X would have walked in behind him, Baxter put up a thin hand to stop him.

"You must go. Mr. Roman received a call and rushed out. I believe it is the woman."

The woman whom both X and Nick were very suspicious of and whose file had been blocked when X attempted to check on her. The woman who was beginning to play an integral part in whatever was going on. "Where and how long ago?"

"West Forty-first Street. About five minutes before you pulled up."

"Call Nick and make sure he knows."

Baxter nodded. "Yes, Mr. Xavier."

X headed back to the truck without any more questions. There was no need; all he needed to know was that Rome was out, possibly fighting in the night by himself for a woman they still knew nothing about.

She screamed, his name bouncing off the walls like high-pitched wails. Nick thrust his hips, pumped frantically until thick spurts of semen filled the condom he wore over his dick, which was buried deep inside her heated pussy.

His fingers were twisted in her long hair, pulling her head back as he fucked her from behind. The muscles in his arms and back bunched as he stroked, his body seeking release, his mind holding on to memories.

This was how he took his women, with fierce quick strokes, their backs turned and his eyes closed.

That way he couldn't see her.

Not the woman he was with.

But the one he couldn't have.

Even after all these years she still haunted him, filled his mind and his soul as if they'd never parted. As if they'd never been forced to separate.

An angry growl vibrated in his chest, pulling his lips over his teeth as he forced his body away from hers. She'd facilitated his release; that's all he'd wanted from this other woman. From the moment she'd rubbed her voluptuous body against his while he'd been sitting in the bar, he'd known they would end up like this. She wanted to have sex with him, he needed a diversion—it was a perfect match.

He hadn't kissed her, had applied no pretty words.

This hadn't been a seduction, more like a production of sorts. Get in and get out, that was his motto. It had to be or he'd lose more of himself than he had before.

And that was not an option.

But this woman whom he'd just met tonight hadn't brought his release. It was the other. The dream of the other female that aroused him continuously, pushed him toward that pleasurable precipice even though she was millions of miles away.

"Wow," the female voice said. "Let's get a shower, baby." She'd followed him, her hands roaming over his bare back.

His dick was still hard, his teeth clenching painfully, his mind at war with his soul. "No," Nick replied tightly. "You can leave."

The silence that followed said she was hurt. Nick couldn't care. His feelings had been held tightly in check for far too long to even venture down that route.

Instead he began walking into his bathroom, alone.

When he'd finished, the hot water from the shower all but scorching every dirty molecule of the sex he'd just had away, Nick came out to an empty apartment.

She was gone. The woman whose name he could barely remember and would no doubt never see again. And he was relieved.

His cell phone rang and he cursed.

"Delgado," he answered roughly.

A few seconds later he followed with, "I'll be there in ten."

Chapter 15

Rome drove like a madman, or his variation on the same, with his foot firmly planted on the gas, his nocturnal vision focused straight ahead.

Ezra's call had him acting without thinking for a change. The words "They tried to take her" still echoed in his head. He was talking about Kalina and no doubt the same Rogues that had been gunning for her at the party. At this moment the whys didn't matter, all that mattered was that Ezra had her and she was safe. For now.

He never should have left her, Rome berated himself as he turned down the secluded road where Ezra was to meet him. The guard wanted Rome to take Kalina while he went back to track the Rogues before the trail disappeared. It was a lot easier to track here in the city, where Rogues did not belong, than in the forest where all manner of species lived and breathed. So Rome drove and his heart pounded.

Why it was so important that she remain safe he didn't know. It was just a fact, one that was steadily becoming embedded in his mind. She was now his responsibility. Truth be told, she had been since that night in the alley, a night she didn't seem to remember, which was probably for the best. He hadn't realized then that their paths would cross again. Now he couldn't think of their lives not remaining intertwined.

Slamming on the brakes so he wouldn't pass the truck that was just slightly off the dirt road, lights turned off, Rome jumped out of his car almost before he'd shut the damn thing off.

The driver's-side door opened and Ezra jumped out. "Where is she?"

"In back. Sleeping. I had to give her something, she was hysterical."

"What?" Rome shouted. "What did you give her?"

"She's just asleep. She should be up by the time you get her home. But when she saw me she freaked the hell out. It was like trying to tame a wildcat for a while there."

Rome had wrenched open the back passenger-side door while Ezra talked. There she was, lying on the seat, her head tilted, fists still clenched at her side. He was lifting her out when he spoke again. "What the hell happened?"

"We were tailing her," Ezra said, skirting around Rome to open the back door of his Mercedes. "She went to this house and it looked like they were having some kind of party. I don't know, but as soon as we pulled into the back alley we picked up the Rogue scent. Peabo went around front to check the front of the house, and he reported Rogue scent as well. We decided to just watch and wait. The next thing I know she's off the deck coming out of another door in the house. She's looking for something in the yard so I get out of the truck.

"A while goes by, nothing big happening, then she

moves off the deck. The Rogue scent's getting thicker and I know it's a shifter. I'm trying to get a lock on him and watch her at the same time. I found them both simultaneously."

Rome pulled out of the car, slammed the door. "You what? Found who simultaneously?"

Ezra stood tall, his voice clear. "She was there. And the other shifter was, too. I think she might have seen him. It would explain why she was so crazy with fear when I got hold of her."

"She was probably crazy with fear because you abducted her."

Ezra was shaking his head. "No. She was looking at me weird, Rome. Like she couldn't believe what she was seeing. We may have to do some damage control here."

Damage control meant killing the witness. Shifters did not have some sort of memory-erasing power. In the end, to protect the secret they would have to erase the threat.

Rome saw red and once again reacted first.

His fingers twisted in Ezra's shirt as he pushed the guard back against the car and yelled in his face. "She does not die! Do you hear me?"

Ezra nodded, his hands remaining at his sides. He was a trained guard, he respected Rome and his position. And they were also friends.

Those facts had Rome backing off, his cat growling and scratching just beneath the surface. But the man pulled away. "She didn't see anything," he said tightly. "There's no need for damage control. I'll handle her."

Ezra nodded again. "I'm going back to look for the shifter."

"I want him alive," Rome said, moving to the driver's-side door. "Do you hear me, Ezra? Bring me that sonofabitch alive!"

"He's on his way back to the mansion. He's got the girl with him," Ezra told Nick and X when they both caught up with him. He'd already repeated the story he'd given Rome and watched as the two senior officers shared the same grim thoughts as he did.

"What if she knows?" Ezra asked.

"Rome said he'd handle it," X answered.

Nick looked skeptical. "Maybe we should head over there, make sure things are cool anyway."

"Yeah," X agreed.

"I know she saw that shifter. And she saw me," Ezra continued.

"You weren't shifted," Nick interjected.

"But I was close."

X was grim. The guard was probably right. Kalina had seen a shifter tonight.

What that meant for tomorrow, none of them was quite sure.

He watched her sleep. She lay on her back, her feet bare, her shirt lifted so that inches of her creamy skin were revealed.

For endless moments Rome just stared at her, wondering who she was, inside. He knew her name, her address; her personality said she was a fighter. She was beautiful and sexy and alluring.

And she was in his bed.

Because a shifter was hunting her.

At this moment none of that seemed to matter. All

he could focus on was the sight of her. She was in his space, a place no woman had ever been before. Everything in his mind rebelled against that thought, but his body, inch by inch, had warmed. From the moment he lifted her off the backseat of his car and carried her into the house, up the stairs to his room, his need for her had grown. Until now, standing here, it was all he could do to keep from stripping her, stripping himself, and taking what he so desperately desired.

She moaned, her brow furrowing as her head turned from side to side. He wondered what she dreamed, what thoughts went through her mind. Could she feel him? Did she want him?

He'd been wanted by a woman before, desired, lusted after. Somehow those feelings didn't amount to what he craved from this woman.

An arm lifted as she inhaled deeply. Rome watched as her chest rose with the effort, full breasts rising then falling gently as she exhaled. His mouth watered. Long fingers with neutral-colored nails went to the part of her stomach that was revealed to him and moved in slow circles near her navel.

His body tightened. The cat inside paced, hunger thumping wildly through them.

Her hand moved upward, pushing the T-shirt as it traveled. More of her lovely skin was revealed, a light moving in his line of vision. Up and up until a silky black bra came into view. She cupped her breast with one hand; the other arm had lifted and fallen so that it arched over her head. Through the slits of butter-toned fingers the black material of her bra showed in great contrast as she molded, squeezed, released her covered breast.

Rome's gut clenched, his dick harder than he'd ever felt it before, straining against the confines of his slacks.

Reluctantly he tore his gaze from her breasts to see if she was awake, if she was aware of how she was enticing him. But her eyes were still closed, her pert lips just barely parted to accommodate the quickening of her breath.

The arm that was above her head came down, that hand moving between legs that spread slowly. She cupped her juncture, fingers moving raptly over the material that covered her. With efficiency she undid the button and zipper, pushing her hand quickly inside. Her head thrashed from side to side as her breathing grew more labored.

Watching her aroused Rome, pushing his cat into a feral heat that scraped along his skin. They both wanted her, needed her on a level that was foreign, but still relevant. He undid the buckle of his belt, slipped the clasp of his slacks free, and pushed the zipper down. His dick throbbed, his own breathing increasing.

The scent of her lust permeated the air as he inhaled deeply, taking in every nuance that was her. Her moans grew louder as her fingers worked between her legs, the other hand pushing the cup of the bra aside and toying with a turgid nipple.

Rome gripped his shaft, stroking its length as he continued to watch her, pumping into his own hand as she was thrusting her fingers into herself. He wanted to see her, wanted her completely naked as he watched her pleasure herself. Then he wanted to get inside her, to plunge his length into the sweet depths of her core.

With those thoughts floating through his mind and with his hunger growing to the point of no return, he looked back to her face and groaned as he saw she was now watching him.

Hazel eyes flecked with golden highlights stared back at him. Their gazes locked, silent communication humming between them. Rome tore his shirt off, pushed his slacks and boxers down his legs, stepped out of his shoes, and stood before her naked. With a hand returning to his thick length he touched a finger to the weeping tip then extended his arm, tapping the damp fingertip to her lip. She moaned, her tongue quickly coming out to stroke the pad of his finger, to lick away his essence.

Rising up from the pillows, Kalina pulled her shirt over her head then reached behind her back and unsnapped her bra. When she looked up at him again it was with a hunger he'd always sensed in her. She looked different, her eyes glistening with need, her lips wet and parted as she panted with desire.

When she reached for him, he stepped closer to the bed. Her head lowered, nimble fingers wrapping around the base of his dick, applying the slightest amount of pressure. He thrust forward lightly and her tongue extended, licked the tiny bead of arousal at the tip of him. With small enticing circular motions, her tongue bathed the head.

His hands went to the sides of her face, thumbs rubbing along the smoothness of her skin.

"Take me deep," he whispered through clenched teeth, his entire body tensing with expectation.

This was what he craved, what he desired from her so desperately. Her touch, her mouth on him, her closeness, her need. The room grew hotter as her mouth opened wider, sliding slowly down the length of his dick.

"Fuck yes!" he roared, his head falling back as she sucked harder, pulled back so that only the tip rested against her tongue, then sank down again for another taste. "Suck me hard, baby. Suck me long and hard."

She obliged, with her fingers slipping back to massage his sack, her mouth working slowly, tortuously over his length. He gripped her head as he began slow movements, fucking her mouth slowly, deliciously.

"I've dreamed of this, of your mouth on my dick. Fuck, it feels so good. So damn good."

A little groan escaped her and Rome's cat roared. It craved, desired, needed, just as much as Rome did.

He looked down, saw her lips wrapped around the darker skin of his arousal, and almost came right in her mouth. Entrancing eyes looked up at him even as her tongue continued to stroke him.

"You like to arouse me. You want me hard and panting for you, don't you?"

She didn't answer but pulled him into the deep recesses of her mouth again, until his teeth clenched, his balls burned.

He rotated his hips, moved in correlation with the up–down motion of her mouth, his fingers gripping the short locks of her hair.

"Show me how hungry you are, baby. Suck me like you want me. Like you've always wanted me and nobody else."

She moaned over his length, her teeth scraping over the engorged crest. He watched her lips, watched her tongue, and felt himself sinking.

"More, more. Take all of me. Suck all of me."

Her lips were wet, her breathing ragged as she took

all his length in and out of her mouth, letting his tip rest at the base of her throat, her fingers rolling his tightened balls with erotic bliss.

"Harder. Deeper," he yelled, feeling the heated streams of his release bursting to the surface. "No going back," he said tightly. "No pulling out. Take me. Take . . . all . . . of . . . me."

There was a second's hesitation and he touched a finger right next to her lips. "All of me, baby. Just for you," he whispered as she looked up at him, something in her eyes relaying her uncertainty. "Trust me," he said.

He didn't know why he'd offered her his trust; he'd never done it before with any other woman. But she wasn't any other woman. She wasn't any other fuck he'd had in his life. This was why he had to protect her, would give his life to keep her safe. This was what she meant to him. Even though he couldn't find a word to describe it, Rome sensed it with every fiber of his being.

She deep-throated him again just as the first pulsating spurts were pulled from him. He watched her swallow without qualm, watched her take every drop of him while keeping her gaze locked with his.

"My turn," he growled seconds later, pushing her back onto the bed and stripping her pants and panties from her in one smooth motion.

He wanted to taste her, needed to feel the slick folds of her vagina beneath his tongue. Pushing her legs open wide, he moved between them, using his fingers to spread her open, his tongue to delve quickly inside.

A roar rumbled in his chest as the sweet honeyed flavor of her essence seeped into his mouth. He licked her long and slow, from the back to the front, loving the way her thighs trembled around him.

"Sweet," he whispered over her damp flesh. "So fucking sweet."

Kalina gripped the sheets beneath her, lifting her bottom, pressing her center toward him for deeper penetration. She licked her lips, still craving his taste, wanting more of him, more of this intense flavor.

His tongue moved along her center, touching every nerve, every sweet spot she ever knew she had then finding some of its own. When his tongue speared into her core while a finger pressed against her tightened rear entrance, she screamed.

A sound escaped she'd never known could come from her own lips, from deep within her soul. The pleasure was so intense she felt it in every limb of her body. He continued to thrust his tongue inside her, all the while his finger applying more pressure to her bottom. Her body shook and shivered, and she creamed into his mouth.

For a moment she was embarrassed by the quick intensity of her release, but then she reveled in the new sensations rippling through her body.

"I want you now!" he roared, rising above her, lifting her hips, and positioning her wetness against the head of his throbbing dick. Panic seared through her as she remembered his size, remembered the stretching of her lips over his girth.

"Wait," she whispered.

He shook his head. "Now!"

The tip was already pressing against her core, heat radiating from the contact.

She wanted him, felt empowered by the desire in his dark eyes, the ragged arousal she could hear in his voice. But it had been a long time for her, longer than she cared to admit and her heart thumped loudly at the prospect.

"I . . . ," she panted, trying to talk between his motions and her own rapid heartbeat. "It's . . . ah . . . it's been . . . I need—"

"I need you," he said, going still over her.

The way he looked down at her, his dark eyes seemed to say much more than the three words he'd just muttered. He was asking her, begging for permission to proceed because he'd ceased all movement.

She could attempt to deny that she needed him, too. As strange as all this seemed she could actually close her legs, get up, and walk out of here—and he would let her. That was the type of man he was. She sensed that about him.

Or she could continue, she could let her body rule for once, let her mind and the thoughts she'd been harboring take control. She wanted him, desperately. The pulsating in her center and the dampness of her folds could attest to that. Her nipples ached from need and when she swallowed, the taste of him massaged something on the inside, pushed and made room for his presence on a level she hadn't known existed.

"It's been a while for me," she finally admitted.

He leaned forward, whispered over her lips just before kissing her. "You're beautiful."

The kiss was sweet, his tongue delving deeper. She wrapped her arms around his neck, pulled him closer, and let her tongue duel with his. It was slow and desperate, vicious need enfolding in this simple act.

"I would never hurt you," he said, pulling back, his forehead resting against hers. "Never. Trust me?"

Kalina didn't know why, but she did. With everything swarming around inside her, she did trust him. "I do."

With her words he pressed gently into her, his tip pushing deeper into her core. She hissed, took a deep breath.

"Just relax. Take me as slow as you like."

She did as he told, relaxed her body into the firmness of the mattress, letting the feel of him inching inside her come slowly. He pushed a little, she accepted more. She shifted, opening her legs wider, lifting her bottom just a fraction.

"Just like that," he moaned, his warm breath whispering over the sensitive skin of her neck.

He felt big, his muscled body heavy but pleasant on top of her. He stretched her, with slow easy strokes, and pushed his way inside her body. And her soul.

There'd been something about him; she'd felt it from the day she'd met him in his office. The moment she'd walked out and let the office door close behind her she'd known it instinctively. They were connected, not by any criminal case or a fake job with his company. There was something more. There was this.

Her arms tightened around him as she buried her face in his shoulder, let her lips and tongue roam over the sensual taste of his skin. That alone was intoxicating, the way he tasted to her. She licked him again, remembered the taste of his arousal in her mouth, along her tongue. It was distinctive, a flavor unlike anything she'd ever known. It caressed something inside her, called to an inner feeling she'd long denied.

When he moved above her, pulling out slightly then sinking what felt like his entire length inside her, some foreign sound escaped her. He responded to that sound, or at least she believed he did, with a guttural groan and began to pump with intentional strokes.

Lifting her legs, she wrapped them around his waist. He reached behind them, locked her legs together at the ankles, then thrust deeper.

She felt him everywhere, in her center, in her legs, her arms, her mind. All sound ceased but for his words, his moans and groans. There was no scent but the musky male that was dominating her. No thoughts but that this was where she was meant to be, in his arms, giving him this part of herself.

It was just as Rome thought it would be, this all-consuming need for her. When her arms twined around his neck, pulling him closer, he felt her touch all over. Her tongue stroked over the heated skin of his shoulder and he trembled. Being inside her was bliss, a kind of sated pleasure he'd never imagined existed. They moved as one, her sugared walls clenching around his thick shaft. When she arched he thrust, when she sighed he moaned.

On and on the cycle went until her teeth suddenly replaced the smooth warm touch of her tongue and she clamped down on his shoulder. Something feral unfurled in him and he roared, his own sharp teeth surfacing, and he nipped her shoulder.

She locked her legs around his waist, using a strength he wasn't aware she had to flip them over so that he was now on his back. Above him she rose, like a sleek animal about to devour its prey. Her hazel eyes flashed gold, her tongue stroking her bottom lip just before her head fell back and she began to ride.

He lifted his hands to grip her hips, to guide her motions, but they were quickly smacked away. Rome lay back, let her have control, and watched in awe at the most beautiful sight he'd ever seen.

Kalina's body was golden, all sinewy lines and luscious curves. Her breasts were high, full, and he moaned when she lifted her hands to cup the gorgeous globes. As her hips undulated, her pussy clamping down with fervor over his dick, her fingers toyed with turgid nipples. It was Rome's turn to grip the sheets and mutter undecipherable words as she took him to higher heights.

"Take all you want, baby. Take it all," he groaned and lifted his hips to meet her thrusts.

Her movements picked up, becoming more frantic as her release soared through her. *Beauty* didn't quite seem to describe what he was seeing. She screamed his name, made some sound deep in her throat and moved over him in quick strokes that ended with a ragged cry torn from the deepest depths of her. When she arched and began to fall forward Rome caught her, wrapping his arms around her as she fought to collect her breath.

"My sexy little temptress," he whispered in her ear, his hands rubbing down her sweat-tracked back. "Sexy, hot little vixen." His palms found her buttocks, cupped the tender globes, and his dick thickened inside her, his balls full and ready for his own release.

When he figured she'd recouped, her thighs no longer shaking around his, Rome pulled out of her slowly. She whimpered as he shifted their bodies.

"Oh no, don't worry, baby. I'm not finished with you yet."

With a palm beneath her stomach he lifted her up

onto her knees then came between her thighs, one hand planted on the small of her back, the other guiding his length into her pussy with one quick thrust.

She arched back. "Roman!"

The sound of his name on her lips stroked him with the slickness of hot oil and Rome pulled out until the tip of his arousal hovered at the mouth of her entrance. He pushed back inside, deep and thorough, making every effort to fill her completely.

She gasped and he repeated the motion, once, twice, three times, and her thighs were once again shaking. He was beginning to like that reaction in her.

With both hands he smacked her ass as he continued to pound into her with all the desire he'd held since first seeing her. He'd dreamed of this, of being inside her this way.

He'd dreamed of other things with her, too, other, darker acts he wasn't sure she could withstand but hungered for just the same.

Staring down at the blush on her backside from his hand, he spotted another source of temptation. Her rear entrance was tight and virginal, he knew instinctively, and he felt desire raging through him once again. He would claim her there, take her and mark her for all time. It wasn't a question of if she allowed him, it was more like when.

Bringing a finger to his lips as he continued to work his length inside her, Rome licked the tip. Then he touched it to the tight ring, pressing slowly inside as his dick worked her to a delicious frenzy.

She was screaming his name now, a litany of praise that pushed him farther, stroked his cat until it wanted to roar its pleasure as well. In this position the cat was wilder, panting, eager for complete control. Rome slipped another finger into her tight backside, using his thumb to spread the dripping essence from her pussy to ease its entrance. Scissoring his fingers, he stretched her while his dick continued to move sinuously inside her tight walls.

"The dream," she panted. "Just . . . like . . . the . . . dream."

"I dreamed of this, too, baby. Of you, of me. Fuck, you're so tight. So deliciously tight."

"Please." Her breath came in quick pants now as she tried to speak. "Please, Roman. I can't take anymore. Please."

"You can take it. You can, vixen." He pumped into her with both his dick and his fingers, pushing her, pushing both of them to that precipice they'd both imagined. He'd wanted her hot for him, crazy with lust for his dick, but he hadn't counted on this.

Hadn't imagined what it would really feel like to be inside her, to feel her gripping him, accepting him, needing him.

It was as intense as it was frightening. But he couldn't pull out, he couldn't have stopped this pleasure if their lives depended on it.

When her release came her entire body trembled, her walls clenching his dick, pulling his own release right behind hers. He opened his mouth but no sound came. Inside the cat roared, hissed, pushed him farther. Coming down over her, he sank his teeth into her shoulder until he tasted the salty tang of her blood.

Chapter 16

In the morning Kalina was alone.

Rolling over in the large bed, she knew instinctively that he was gone.

Last night . . . her thoughts trailed off, assembling slowly like pieces to a puzzle. Last night she'd been attacked or something. There were eyes and roars and . . . there was Rome.

She was in his bed, her traitorous body telling the rest of the story. Aching thighs gave way to a center still pulsating with need and Kalina wanted to smack herself.

She'd slept with Rome. Her suspect.

Pulling one of the many pillows over with her arm, she dropped it on her head, screaming into it. "Idiot! Idiot! Idiot!"

How could she have been so stupid? She'd compromised her case by sleeping with the enemy.

More important, how had she been so naive as to think he'd be here in the morning?

It was his spot, yes, so a part of her figured he'd stay for that reason alone. But, not.

He was gone and she was here, alone. Just as she always seemed to end up.

It was ridiculous really, to have allowed herself to believe, to feel for even a fraction of a second . . . actually she'd believed from the moment she'd opened her eyes to see him watching her, the moment she realized he was enjoying the sight of her touching herself. She'd believed that he wanted her, that on some level he needed her. That want and that need had felt so good that she'd dropped all the pretenses, let the barriers she'd placed around herself all her life fall to the side. She'd welcomed him, giving him every part of her body he asked for.

And he still hadn't stayed.

The thought stung, burned like a fireball in the center of her chest. Tears stung her eyes. Then she shook her head, a defiance rising in her she'd never quite experienced before. Sitting up on the bed, she pressed her palms to her eyes and took a steadying breath.

To hell with him.

So they'd had sex. It didn't change a thing. He was still a suspect and she was still the cop who was going to bring his lying drug-dealing ass down!

Climbing down off the platform bed, she grabbed her clothes, which had been neatly laid on a leather recliner. Purposely she avoided checking out the room, experiencing his personal space. She didn't give a damn about the personal life of Roman Reynolds. How he lived, who he fucked, none of that was her concern. She had one agenda and some strange-ass events had veered her off that path momentarily, but now, as she stalked into the bathroom, slamming her hand on the wall pad to switch on the light, now she was about her business.

So Roman Reynolds had better watch his back!

"Finally, you grace us with your presence, Faction Leader Reynolds." Elder Alamar sat at the head of Rome's conference room table with all the regality of a king. His double-breasted brown-striped suit fit him well but was no match for the cool dominance of the head of the Topètenia Tribe.

Elder Alamar ruled the jaguars and served on the Assembly as their liaison. He was a man just reaching his midfifties, a powerful cat with cunning and killer instincts as fine and astute as the day he was born.

"Good morning, Elder," Rome said, nodding toward his two seconds-in-command, who'd called him on his cell phone only half an hour before to tell him about this meeting.

Later he'd ask why he hadn't known that Alamar was here—in his house, at that. Baxter had arrived just seconds after the call with Rome's suit and a dim expression on his face. There was no doubt the old man knew Kalina was in Rome's bed, just as there was no doubt he knew what had happened between them the night before. What Baxter thought about that situation Rome wasn't sure, and he wasn't going to find out right at this moment.

"There is movement in the forest," Alamar began without preamble. His dark hands flattened on the smooth surface of the table as his gaze pierced the three men. "Whispers of a revolt have reached the Assembly. Fear is mounting."

X nodded, sat back in his chair, and folded his hands. "There's something brewing here as well."

By the look on Alamar's face, he already knew that. "Supply shipments are being raided, most of the items not reaching the village. And there have been many killings."

Nick sat up, instantly alert. "Cats?"

Alamar shook his head. "No. Other forest residents, but their deaths are not normal. The brutality is obvious, like they are trying to send a message."

"Like the murders here," Rome added. "We've had a few brutal killings here. And just the other night we were approached by Rogues."

"You have seen them? Who are they? From what tribes?" Alamar asked.

"Jaguars," Rome said.

"And a cheetah."

"They do not fight together normally" was Alamar's reply.

"With all due respect, sir," Nick added, "this isn't a normal situation."

Rome interjected. "They're after something."

"No doubt about that," X added. "But what?"

They all looked to Alamar. "Power. It is what drives them. What they could not have in the forest is what they seek here. They will begin from the bottom and build their way up. Creating an army is what they are doing."

"And it's easier for them here because they perceive the humans to be the weaker species. They don't expect a fight—and even if there is one, the humans would never win," Rome stated.

"And once they have control?" X asked. "We're all shit out of luck."

"Well, if they want some," Nick said, his face drawing into a frown, "they can come and get it! I'm not going down without a fight."

Rome held up a hand to silence him. "None of us is

going down without a fight, Nick. But we're not going to fight like animals in the street. We have to be the smarter or our secret is out to everyone."

X nodded in agreement with Rome's words. But his face was grim; he was clearly thinking along warrior lines just like Nick. "We found the Rogue that was there last night," he offered.

That immediately had Rome's attention, almost shifting his calm and precise leadership into the beast within that craved a fight. "Who was it?"

X continued. "His name's Chavez. He's the cheetah we faced in the alley the other night."

"Who sent him?" Instinct told him the group had been sent by another Rogue. If the Rogues were building an army they'd need someone in charge, someone with the vision to create this legion of evil. The Croesteriia cheetahs were fast runners who hunted by vision instead of scent like the Topètenia. They were not from the Gungi; that there was a Croesteriia in the mix with the Rogues gave them all an idea of how volatile this situation was fast becoming.

"He's not real talkative right now. But that'll change," Nick said.

"He was at the party looking for the woman. And he was at that house last night trying to take her again. They want her bad," X said.

Nick looked at Rome. "You have to ask yourself why?"

"He is looking for a *companheiro*," Alamar stated slowly, his gaze narrowing on Rome.

"Who's looking for a mate? The Rogue?" Nick asked.

Alamar kept his eyes on Rome as he stood, moving closer to him. "I believe they both are. The joining is very strong, it links shifters for life, making the couple much stronger than either on its own. Joined shifters are almost undefeatable."

"This battle is not about a woman," Rome stated, even though thoughts of a woman occupied most of his time lately. Still, what Alamar was suggesting was more than Rome wanted to consider.

"No," Alamar said, stopping behind Rome. "Not just a female. A *companheiro*. The lifetime partner of a shifter, the one who will complete the joining." He put a hand on Rome's shoulder, closed his eyes, and nodded. "You have found your *companheiro*."

Hell no!

Rome stood to make the protest but watched as Alamar's nostrils flared, his head bending so that his face almost touched Rome's chest.

"Elder," Rome said as calmly and respectfully as he could. "You don't understand."

Alamar only shook his head as he rose, his body rigid as he stared at Rome. "You are the one who does not understand, Faction Leader."

"She's Rome's mate?" X asked, obviously not sure if this was what the Elder was getting at.

"As a leader of our people you know the legend," Alamar stated, stepping back only slightly from Rome.

It was Rome who cleared his throat, moving just a little farther from the Elder. "A *companheiro* is the lifetime partner of a shifter. The two are born to be together, to continue the species, and to build solidarity among the people. Once they complete the joining they cannot be separated unless by death. The scent of a *companheiro* is unique to each couple, a shared aroma that pulls them together in an urge to mate, to consummate the union. It is called the *companheiro calor*," Rome recited as if he were a schoolboy in front of the classroom.

"Holy shit," Nick sighed, sitting back in his chair to stare at Rome. "Kalina Harper is your mate."

"No!" Rome said, then clapped his lips shut. The denial was too strong, too loud, the sound rubbing raggedly against his skin. "I don't believe in this mating-for-life thing. It's just an old legend. Besides, Kalina would know if she were a shifter."

Alamar made an indistinguishable sound. "Do not blaspheme our traditions. It is those who came before us who made it possible for you to be where you are. They have seen much, know much. The legend is true. And she may not have had the *acordado* yet."

"The awakening," X whispered, still staring incredulously at Rome.

"In females it takes a little longer for the shift to take place. But if you are scenting her, if you have taken her into you, then her *acordado* is coming."

Rome attempted to deny that he'd been inhaling Kalina's scent like an addict would cocaine in the last week or so. But he kept that to himself. The thought of Kalina shifting into a cat was something he'd never considered and didn't want to entertain at this moment. This whole idea of *companheiros* and *calor,* joinings and awakenings—it was all ridiculous. He didn't believe a word of it, would not believe it. He could not.

"With all due respect, Elder, I decide if there's one person for me," Rome stated adamantly. "We are not in the forest."

"No, Faction Leader, the forest is in you."

Nick and X remained silent as Rome's temples began to throb.

"You cannot take out that which is a part of your soul, your blood, your heritage. You are a Shadow Shifter, one of the legendary men who are also beasts. Your entire existence is a legend to some, a truth to others." He nodded toward X and Nick. "You are also a leader of many. To deny what is your destiny is not an option."

"I have given my life to the Assembly, dedicated my time and my money to the care of the tribes. This," he said insistently, "I cannot give them. I am not looking for a mate, nor will I accept one on legend alone."

The fact that he was blatantly going against the word of an Elder was not lost on Rome. It was a serious offense, one that could cost him his role as Faction Leader. But he didn't care. He would not be linked to a woman just because their legend said so. It was yet another responsibility to him, one he was not willing to take on. Another life he would be responsible for protecting.

Besides, a *companheiro* had to also be a shifter. Which Kalina was not.

He left the room before anyone could speak another word, before the legend could begin to make any more sense given what was going on around them.

"Is she a shifter?" Nick asked X when they were leaving Rome's place later that morning.

"She has to be," X answered.

"But why wouldn't she just tell Rome what she was?"

"Maybe she doesn't know. Maybe she's a half-breed like us and was raised to believe she was human."

Nick sighed, approaching the driver's side of his Porsche. "So what does Chavez want with her? You can only be a lifetime mate to one cat. If Kalina is Rome's mate, why does Chavez want her?"

X shrugged. "You know some always want what others have."

"But nobody knows Rome has her. He just met her a few days ago."

"Are you sure about that?" X asked.

Nick looked contemplative. "No, I guess I'm not. So we need to find out who Kalina's parents were. Because if she's about to make her first shift and the Rogues have picked up her scent, we're looking at a much bigger problem than we first thought."

X nodded. "I'm on it. I'll check in with you later. What about Rome?"

Nick thought for a moment about the pensive look on his friend's face, about the fact that he knew Rome's hesitancy. A mate would be someone close to him— someone he could lose, the way he'd lost his parents. That type of loss would devastate Rome, most likely driving him to a deadly rage. It wasn't something Rome ever wanted in his life. He would fight it like a vicious attack were it to be true.

"Let's keep this quiet for now. We'll tell him what he needs to know when he needs to know it."

"You don't think he needs to know it now?" X asked.

"You want him killing every Rogue in this city without giving a damn who sees him or finds out about us? Because that's exactly what he'll do once he realizes they're out to take his mate." Nick took a deep breath, let it out slowly, and looked around to the clear summer's day. "I want to exterminate those bastards as much as anybody else, but I don't want all that blood on Rome's hands. He's dealt with enough. Let's find out what the threat is before we pull him in."

"He's not going to like us keeping shit from him," X said, opening the car door and sliding inside.

Nick followed, putting the key in the ignition. "True, but we're his friends. He's not going to snap our throats. He'll thank us later."

"Don't bet on it," X said as they pulled out of Rome's driveway. "And get yourself a full-size car or a truck, man. This tight-ass toy car makes my legs hurt."

"That's because your thick-ass body wasn't built for a sleek, smooth vehicle such as this. Me, on the other hand—" Nick slipped on dark Ray-Ban shades. "—I look damn good behind the wheel of this puppy."

Chapter 17

Kalina had just finished dressing and was on her way out the door headed for work. She was already going to be late, but at least she'd called.

She really needed to close this case and get on with her life. This attraction to Rome had been a source of conflict for far too long. And she wasn't about to let sex—even terrific mind-blowing sex—mess up her career aspirations. Roman Reynolds was a job and nothing else.

He'd sealed that deal the moment he climbed out of that bed, leaving her there to wake alone.

It was petty and probably a small thing to a more experienced woman. But to Kalina, who had taken only two lovers in her adult life, all before the incident two years ago, it was a big deal. Sleeping with a suspect was something she'd never imagine she'd do. But she had, because she'd felt something deep inside when Rome looked at her. She'd felt . . . like she belonged. To him, in his life, somewhere, finally.

But it was an illusion. No, it was a hit-and-run, a booty call that she'd answered like a wanton hussy. He'd probably kidnapped her—she was still fuzzy on exactly how she came to be in his house, in his bed. She remembered Mel and the cookout—which meant she'd have to face the cheerful woman this morning and explain why she'd gone AWOL on her last night. She remembered something else, too—eyes that glowed in the night. The thought sent a chill right down her spine.

Surely she was seeing things—again. No, that wasn't possible; crazy didn't go on hiatus for two years then resurface. On the short drive to work she thought about that over and over again. What had she seen, and was it real? Kalina also thought about Rome, about how she would react facing him again. That was an easy fix: She wouldn't go near him. She would stay in her department and find a link between Rome's money and that cartel in South America. In the several texts that she'd received from Ferrell yesterday after she'd ignored his first one, he'd mentioned the Cortez Cartel. Kalina would pore through financial records looking for the name Raul Cortez; once she found it Rome's ass would be toast.

"The minute she comes in I want to see her in my office," Rome said into the phone to Dan Mathison, his chief financial officer.

Rome had been furious when he'd left this morning's impromptu meeting. Kalina was not a shifter! She was a woman and she was soft and passionate and . . . something he'd never dared dream of in his life.

And she was his.

Not his *companheiro,* but his woman. He'd thought that each time he touched her last night, each time he'd stroked inside of her, each time she'd called his name as if he were the only man for her. He'd dreamed of her, longed for her for two years and she was finally here, finally a part of his life.

But she wasn't.

When he'd returned to his room she'd been gone.

Baxter, who normally had eyes in the back of his head, hadn't seen her go. Rome suspected that wasn't totally true. Ezra had bought her car back to Rome's house sometime during the night, which proved just too damn convenient for her getaway.

He'd made it into the office in time to find out she still wasn't here but had called in saying she was on her way. And the minute she arrived he wanted her here, in his office. He wasn't letting her get away from him that easily. He couldn't.

In the meantime, he had a phone call to make.

"Roman, my boy. It's good to hear from you again," Bingham said in his gravelly voice.

"I want to know who his contact was," Rome said without preamble. He'd pored over his father's notes on that disk and knew that there was a good chance Bingham knew what was there and who to contact about that information.

"I don't know what you're talking about."

"Don't lie to me, Bingham! I know what's on that disk and I know you do, too. Don't bullshit me. Tell me who my father was getting his information from."

Silence filled the line. Rome's patience grew thinner. "Look, he's gone. You gave his secrets to me. I have to handle this, and the sooner the better."

"He didn't tell me everything. There was so much I didn't know," Bingham insisted.

"Tell what you did know," he insisted. Bingham didn't know about the shifters, that was most likely true. The notes on the disk were just cryptic enough that if a person didn't already know about the tribes, they would simply assume Vance Reynolds was making a play for political office. The outlines for enforcement of a new government could have possibly been construed as treason or even a long-shot attempt at a terrorist uprising. Any of which was enough to plant his father's name firmly on Homeland Security's hit list, a thought that threw a few more suspects into the pool of killers. But Rome knew it wasn't a human who'd taken his parents' lives. The house had been invaded by shifters. He remembered their scent, remembered their laughter and the pure hatred that had flowed through them.

But Vance had known someone within the government was on to him, to what he was doing. Rome needed to find that person, he needed to know what they knew before he ordered them taken care of. He wouldn't kill needlessly, but he would protect their secret. That was a promise.

Kalina didn't want to be here, she didn't want to knock on this door or see the person on the other side. But her choices were limited. Dan had been adamant about her coming to see Rome immediately. Causing a fuss would have no doubt drawn unwanted attention to the reasons, so she'd simply clamped her lips shut and stalked all the way to the elevators. She'd staunchly ignored Ava's snide remarks about her being late and whatever else had come out of the woman's mouth.

Mel, thankfully, had not been at her desk, because that was another person Kalina wasn't up to facing. At least not before coming up with a convincing reason why she'd disappeared from the woman's house last night without saying a word. She should have never gone there, she thought now. Her resolve to keep to herself should have remained in place. Making connections and building relationships was just not in her. She was a loner and always would be. No matter how much that thought hurt.

So her knock on Rome's office door was rapid as emotions rippled through her body, making her temples throb. She braced herself, waiting to hear his deep voice telling her to come in, but the sound didn't come. Instead the door swung open and she was pulled inside and pressed against the wall as it slammed closed again. It happened so fast she lost her breath.

"What—" She tried to speak but words were lost by the crush of his lips against hers.

Kalina didn't want to kiss him. No, this was not how this meeting was supposed to go. There were things she had to say to this man, words that were meant to rip him a new one for the callous way he'd treated her. But damm if she could stop it.

His lips were like a drug and she sipped heartily, taking her fill of everything he offered at this moment. Her fists stayed clenched at her sides as she dared them to move. All he had was her lips and really, wasn't that enough? Her body responded to his instantly, heat pooling in her center, moisture dampening her folds already. She tilted her head, hoping maybe to end the connection, but it didn't work.

Rome plunged deeper, his tongue touching every recess of her mouth. She couldn't breathe, her chest heaving as her nipples tingled. She wanted to scream, to lift her hands to his handsome face and scratch until she'd given him just an inkling of the pain he'd inflicted on her. No, she wanted her gun, then she could shoot him right in the balls. But as his thick erection pressed against her she heard a moan escape and knew that was the last thing she wanted to do to that particular body part.

Damn her, she still wanted him.

He was the one to break the connection of their lips, but his mouth stayed hungrily on her as he scraped his teeth along the line of her jaw. She was so out of breath she let her head rest against the wall, panting, needing his touch and hating it just the same.

"Don't you ever leave me," he growled, moving down to ravage her neck with his mouth.

"What?" she asked through a mind blurred with arousal.

"When I returned you were gone." His hands moved to her arms, giving her a little shake as he spoke. "Don't ever do that again!"

Lifting her head Kalina blinked, then stared up into his eyes. "Are you serious? You're the one who left." A tiny remnant of her backbone reared up, and she lifted her palms to push at his chest. The action must have caught him off guard because he took a step back. And she took two steps away from him.

"I woke up and you were gone. All that was missing was the money on the table," she snapped. "If you wanted a cheap fuck you could have hired someone for that. Oh, I forgot"—she feigned innocence—"I do work for you, don't I? But sleeping with you wasn't in the job description." And that was no lie. Nowhere in the DEA's or the MPD's description of this assignment did it say fuck Roman Reynolds. She could attest to that.

"Wait a minute, you think I left you?" Rome said, moving to the door and switching the lock in place before turning to face her.

He wore a dark suit, or at least the pants were dark; his shirt was white with a coral-colored tie that was the perfect shade to offset his mocha skin. She assumed his suit jacket was somewhere in the office because he always wore a suit to work. His shoes shone like the gold watch at his wrist. He looked impeccably perfect, and her body ached for him.

"That's usually the conclusion people reach when they wake up in a bed alone where someone had once lain beside them."

He was shaking his head. "I went to a meeting."

"It wasn't even eight in the morning, Rome. You don't have to lie to me," she huffed, brushing her hands down the front of her clothes as if they were rumpled; she didn't know what else to do with them. "Look, if it was just meant to be a one-night thing, that's fine. I can deal with that. What I'd really like to know is how I ended up at your house in the first place? I went to a cookout at Melanie's. But then I wasn't there, I was . . ." Her voice trailed off as pieces began to click into place.

"What happened when you were at Melanie's?" Rome asked, taking a measured step toward her.

"I saw something, or I thought I saw something." She'd seen eyes in the bushes, eyes that weren't human. But something told her that telling Rome that wasn't going to end with the guy asking to spend another night with her. She cleared her throat. "I mean, I thought there was something in the yard. The neighbor's dog, I think. But then I was gone. This big guy grabbed me and threw me into a truck." She narrowed her eyes at him. "Into your truck? Why were they there? Did you have someone follow me, Rome?"

Rome didn't know what to say. How could he even begin to answer this question without revealing too much? Elder Alamar's accusation still rang in his mind, but as he watched Kalina, with her long legs clad only in nylons and a knee-length skirt that hugged her bottom and her hips to perfection, he didn't see a shifter. She was exactly as he thought she was, all woman.

"I told you I wanted to keep you safe."

"So you're having me followed? You don't even know me."

She might have a point there, one he badly wanted to remedy. "I asked you out for a drink, but you turned me down."

"Again," she said, giving him a bland stare. "So you have me followed and then kidnap me so you can sleep with me. That's a little over the top, even for a man like you."

"What do you mean 'a man like me'? Exactly what kind of man do you think I am, Kalina?" he asked, moving closer to her but not touching her. She was standing in front of one of the guest chairs and he sat down, right there, so he'd have to look up at her for a change. He loved the view from here, her luscious legs and full breasts at perfect touching range.

She crossed her arms over her chest. "I know you're an arrogant-ass attorney who thinks just because he has a good track record in court, he can't ever lose anything. I also know that you don't give a damn about the women you get involved with. They're all inconsequential to you, a notch on your bedpost so to speak. I cannot berate myself enough for falling into that trap."

Rome was standing before she could say another word,

and right up in her face. "Whatever you think you know about me and other women has nothing to do with what happened between us."

She leaned back slightly, tilting her head so she could stare up at him. "Really? Tell me, Mr. Reynolds, how am I so different?"

He didn't know what to say. How was she different from any of the other women he'd slept with? She was beautiful, sexy, attractive—all traits he'd thought the other women shared. But she was so much more. Something inside made her different, and whatever that was it called to him. Even now.

"All I know is that I can't stop wanting you."

She sighed and looked away. He cupped her chin pulled her back to face him.

"That's not all. I think about you all the time. When I thought those men were going to hurt you I was ready to kill. The thought of you being in danger rips me apart. That's never happened with another woman. Ever."

She didn't believe him.

Didn't want to but . . . his gaze locked with hers and it was no longer a choice. In his eyes she saw his honesty and his hunger and reciprocated with a measure of need of her own. "I wanted you to be different," she heard herself whispering. "From the very beginning I didn't want to believe the rumors. I don't know why. I just didn't."

"Don't believe the rumors. I'm not who they think I am."

"And you can't be who I think you are." He wasn't the man from her dreams, the hero who saved her from the loneliness she'd engulfed herself in. He wasn't the beast that aroused and yet scared her. He was just Roman, the man she was supposed to be investigating. "Why couldn't you be him? It would have been so much easier," she whispered.

"None of that matters now, Kalina. Only this matters," he said, wrapping his arms around her waist and pulling her so that her center pressed against the bulge of his arousal. "Only you and me."

He'd said something similar in her dream. Kalina fought to keep her thoughts in the here and now.

"I dream of you," he said hoarsely, his teeth nipping at the nape of her neck.

Strong hands moved upward, grabbing her breasts, palming them like melons, squeezing as if he fully expected to milk her. Her legs shivered as desire dampened the folds of her pussy.

He wasn't being gentle. To the contrary, his hands moved roughly. Her nipples were hard. His teeth bit into her skin and the tingle of pleasure/pain rippled through her body. Inside felt like the beginnings of a tornado, a small funnel of desire forming in the pit of her stomach and picking up speed with every touch, every word from him. Her mind clouded and filled with nothing except this man, this moment.

"I dreamed of you." With that breathy admission her head fell back onto his shoulders. "It was so hot. You were so hot."

"Was I hot for you, baby? Like I am now?"

He was unbuttoning her blouse, his fingers moving quickly over the small buttons. His palms spread the material to the side as he reached for her breasts again. Pushing down the cups of her bra, he freed the globes and kneaded them with hunger that sent sparks of lust directly to her pussy.

Kalina gasped, her own hands going up to cover his. She felt her turgid nipples and began to shake. Used to touching herself and gaining immense pleasure from the exploration, she was now drowning in the double sensation of both their hands on her body.

"Touch me, baby. I'm dying for you to touch me," his voice rasped. She dropped her hands.

Moving them behind her, she touched the hard bulge of his arousal. Lust ripped through her. She wanted him like she'd never wanted another before. Deep in the darkest recesses of her mind she wanted with a fierceness that almost frightened her. Instead of grasping the fear Kalina went with the lust, let the rising heat inside bombard any other feelings—even the ones that told her this would be a defining moment for them both.

"You want it, Kalina." His voice was raspy now, his hands tightening on her breasts until a scream scratched at the base of her throat. "It's yours, baby. Take it."

With her heart hammering wildly in her chest, Kalina shifted and turned until they were facing each other. Grabbing the back of his head, she was the one who took his lips this time. In a savage duel of lips, teeth, and tongue she poured into him all the heat that was ravaging her. His hands tightened on her hips, gripping her bottom then sliding down her thighs to push her skirt up.

Panting, she broke the kiss and let her palms drift down the muscled contours of his chest, his tight abs, to the belt buckle at his midsection. With trembling fingers she undid the belt, dislodged the snap of his pants, and heard the sleek slide of his zipper echo in her ears. It was an acute sound, one she'd never paid much attention to until this moment.

His hands framed her face now, his thumbs sliding over her swollen lips. She licked at them, eager, anticipating as her hands pushed his pants and boxers past his hips.

"I can't get you out of my head," she admitted, noting that the room seemed to fill with the same insufferable heat that inhabited her dream. "No matter how hard I try, you're always there."

"I'm always going to be here" was his reply.

His length filled her. She wrapped both hands around him, loving the heavy heated feel of his arousal and remembering the taste of his silken heat gliding along her tongue. Her mouth watered as she stroked him from the base to the bulbous tip.

Kalina remembered that night he'd caught her and they were in this very spot, her ass against his desk and his dominating presence surrounding her. He'd held himself out to her then, stroking his magnificent length as his eyes had devoured her. He'd told her she wanted him, wanted this, and he'd been absolutely right.

Sliding her body down along his she rested on her knees, tilting her chin so that his dick was in line with her lips. One pearl-size drop of desire eased from his tip. She extended her tongue and licked. Closing her mouth she let the taste of him once again fill her. This time was different from before. It wasn't an unexpected rush of excitement like a roller-coaster ride. No, this was anticipated, it was welcomed as if she'd known she would taste him again. Everything about him was welcome, as if something inside her was welcoming him home.

When she took him deep inside her mouth, he cradled her head, blowing out a rush of breath. Kalina worked her mouth over him, loving the slow rhythm they built—him thrusting his hips slowly, feeding her in measured strokes, and her twirling her tongue around his length, licking the underside like a treasured Popsicle. Her fingers massaged his sack, bringing ragged groans from his lips.

Everything about him seemed right; this time, this moment was where she belonged. For once in her life, she had a place and a purpose. He could bring her pleasure but Kalina realized in this instant that she could bring him release as well. He craved her, hungered for her touch, for the next stroke of her lips along his flesh.

To test her theory she pulled back, let his length slip past her lips until only the tip whispered near her mouth. His grip on her head tightened and he moaned, "More," before thrusting toward her lips again.

With a sly smile she peeked up at him. Her center pulsated as she caught his gaze. His eyes were bright and they were focused on her, emitting a sort of hazy spell that held her entranced. She opened her mouth, let him spear his erection inside as their gazes stayed connected. He fed her, she took him in, deeper, deeper until she thought she might choke. Rome pulled back at that moment, let her catch a breath, then sank deep inside her again. Her lips were wet, his length was soaked, her nipples ached. She wanted to be fucked. Right here, right this moment, by this man.

Grabbing the base of his arousal, Rome fed her his pre-pleasure release and watched with deep-seated desire as she licked every drop. Looking down at her gorgeous mouth wrapped around his length had pushed him so that his beast strained against him. There was a heat inside him waiting impatiently to burst free. But he couldn't move fast. He held on to his restraint as he'd been so used to doing in the past. But the more she milked his dick, the more he wanted to let go and give her everything he had inside.

He didn't know if she could take it, didn't know if he'd survive it, but feared it was coming anyway. Grabbing her shoulders, he lifted her up off her feet until her lips met his in a deep arousing kiss.

"I want to see you," he moaned against her lips. "I need to see you."

And he did. The need had been so heavy inside him he could barely breathe. He wanted to see her body, see her desire for him, needed it like he needed air.

He sat her on the desk, pushing her skirt up over her hips, cursing softly as he spied the garters and nylons she'd worn beneath. A wisp of lace covered her juncture, but he ripped it away. "Fuck! I'm dying here, Kalina. You're killing me," he groaned, rubbing his hands over the delicate buckles and smooth silk.

As if she knew exactly what to do, exactly what he needed, Kalina slid back farther on the desk, pushing back papers, pen holders—whatever paraphernalia was in her way—until she could lean back. Lifting her legs, she let the heels of her pumps clap down on the slick surface of the desk and dropped her knees.

Like a blooming flower she opened to him, her pussy bare and glistening with desire. Rome's mouth watered, his dick so hard his temples throbbed.

"Touch it for me," he said in a scratchy voice. "Touch my pussy."

She obliged, taking one hand and moving her slim

fingers over the damp folds. Clear nails moved over the smooth flesh, stopping at the tightened bud, working it until her breathing was labored.

"Just like that," he sighed, his hands going to his length, stroking as he watched her.

Rome loved this. He loved to watch her touching herself. Loved the look of her fingers in her sex, moving to bring pleasure. He could watch her forever, watch her body respond to her own ministrations and get off every fucking time.

"Two fingers," he groaned. "Two fingers deep."

Her head fell back as she thrust two fingers into her dripping center and worked them fiercely. Rome worked his length, thrusting as if he were right there inside her. He wasn't going to last long, his restraint was dwindling, the beast within was taking charge, he knew that with a certainty when his incisors pricked his lower lip.

Reaching for her, he pulled her hand from her center, brought her fingers to his lips, and suckled, licking them completely free of her sweet nectar. She lifted her head, her lust-filled gaze finding his.

"Please," she whispered. "Now."

He gave her what she wanted. Pulling her until her bottom was just at the edge of the desk, Rome thrust his length deep inside her. She arched her back and opened her mouth to scream, but he bent forward, catching the sound with his lips.

Pounding into her Rome could think of only one thing—she was his. Every part of her belonged to him. He would never let her go. Never.

She wrapped her legs around him, locked her ankles, and met him thrust for thrust. Her nails scored his back through the thin cotton of his shirt. Pulling out then sinking back inside her was addictive—it was enticing and mind numbing. His breathing was ragged as he stroked her, loving the feeling of her walls constricting around him, her arms holding him close like she was afraid to let him go.

The scent came slowly; like a light breeze, a soft musky aroma filtered through the air. Inside his cat roared and Rome's thrusts came faster. Kalina's thighs began to shake around him and he held her tighter as her release took over.

He stroked deeper, his entire length buried firmly inside her. The scent filled his nostrils, and his muscles bunched. He wanted to cry out, to roar with the power that surged through him; instead he opened his mouth, sinking his teeth into her shoulder until the tang of blood touched his throat. With his tongue now thick with anticipation he licked over the spot, licked and licked until her taste was embedded in his senses.

At that precise moment heat laced through his spine, shooting to his tightened balls, his release filling her in fierce spurts.

She was like jelly in his arms, relying on him to keep her from falling over the desk. And Rome held her there, loved the feel of her in his grasp. He was still inside her, his sex refusing to leave the pleasurable abyss. Her legs had unwrapped from him to fall at his sides. As he pulled back to look at her Rome received one final jolt to his system.

Her eyes.

They weren't the normal gold-flecked hazel they'd been when she'd walked in. They were all-gold with a tiny black dot in the center. They were cat's eyes and they were staring right at him.

* * *

"Have dinner with me tonight?" Rome asked, his voice still husky from the moaning and groaning of their tryst.

Kalina was stepping out of the bathroom, where she'd splashed soap and water on all the vital places, and straightening her clothes. "We should talk," she said. "I mean, really talk." She couldn't do this any longer. How did she investigate a man she thought she was dangerously close to falling in love with? How could she try to convict him when she knew he was innocent? She wouldn't find Cortez's name anywhere in Rome's financial records. For one thing, he was too damn smart to ever implicate himself in such a juvenile manner. And for another, he wouldn't do business with a cartel.

In the time she'd been looking over his records she'd seen that Rome was very generous in his contributions, selecting causes that she suspected meant something to him, the Every Child Needs Someone Foundation being one of the largest donations on behalf of the firm. She'd seen the receipts in the computerized ledgers and knew the foundation well because it was one she donated to regularly. While her donations in no way matched Rome's, it didn't matter to her; just the fact that he'd thought about those children endeared him to her.

But as they'd come together today, on his desk of all places, she'd realized that while she still didn't understand this attraction between them and she had more questions than answers, the connection between them was stronger than anything she'd ever encountered in her life. A connection she wanted desperately to hold on to. He hadn't left her this morning—that's what he'd said. He'd gone down the hall in his larger-than-life house to a meeting. Who does that, and what kind of meeting was he going to at the crack of dawn? See, more questions.

However, before she could demand the truth from him, she had to come clean about her own part in this charade. She also had to find out the truth about her assignment. All this time there'd been something bothering her about the way the DEA had come for her, of all the other cops in the narcs division. There were certainly some who had more experience than she did, more years on the force, and wanted to get out just as badly as she did. But they'd chosen her. Handpicked her, as her lieutenant had said. And they'd kept Ferrell in the loop. Why? Ferrell was a detective and had some years on her in the unit, but he didn't do fieldwork, hadn't in years. Still, he was the front-liner from the MPD, and she'd only met the DEA rep once. That just didn't seem right. She'd buried those facts in the glossy glow of being needed, wanted for something. But now she was seeing things clearer, as if this time with Rome had opened up some kind of locked door inside her. She felt invigorated and ready to unleash . . . what?

"I've been known to have a lasting effect on females, but this ignoring my question is a bit new for me."

She heard his voice, then her gaze snapped back to his. Kalina didn't know how long she'd stood there thinking, but he had obviously said something to her. "I'm sorry, daydreaming I guess. What did you say?"

He came to her then, wrapped his strong arms around her, and she felt that sensation once more, the one where something inside her reached for him. It was a yearning that came only when he was near, and when he touched her it pumped up a notch until she could barely think beyond him. She'd been afraid of this feeling before, but now she embraced its welcoming sensation.

"I asked about dinner and you said we should talk."

She nodded. "Right, we should."

"So we'll talk at dinner?"

"That's fine," she said accepting his kiss. "But I should really get back to work."

"I have to ask you this again. Are you sure you don't have any idea why those men would be following you?"

She shrugged. And wondered if she should mention what had happened to her two years ago, or even the pictures. Thoughts about those incidents being linked had lingered in her mind. But there was no telling Rome part of that story. Once she opened her mouth she'd have to tell him everything. That was her intention eventually, but there was more she needed to find out first.

"I don't know them or why they would follow me."

"Ezra, that's my man," he said matter-of-factly, "will be with you at all times."

She moved out of his grasp, not sure she liked that idea. A trip to the station was needed, and she certainly didn't want Rome's man going with her.

"I don't need a bodyguard, Rome. I'll be fine by myself."

He had moved behind his desk, was opening up his drawer and dropping something inside when she turned to him. "I appreciate your concern, but—"

"He's staying with you. Until I find out who they are and why they're interested in you, he's sticking close."

Kalina opened her mouth to argue, then thought better of it. He looked like he wasn't going to be talked out of it, and pushing the issue might make him suspicious. And well he should be; she'd been sent to find evidence to have him jailed for the rest of his life. He should probably have kept her locked up when his man had kidnapped her before.

"I'm going back to my desk before Dan starts looking for me."

"Wait," he said, then crossed the floor to where she stood. "Go this way."

Taking her by the elbow, he led her back into the bathroom to a door on the far side of the shower stall.

"You can take the stairs from here. That way no one will see you leaving my office."

As she looked into the stairwell, Kalina wondered just who Rome Reynolds really was. What kind of attorney needed a hidden exit?

"Use this often?" she asked almost casually.

"Only when needed" was his serious reply. "Keep your eyes open, Kalina. Something's going on that I'd rather you not be a part of."

He'd rather she not be a part of it but Kalina had the sinking suspicion she already was. "What's going on?"

Rome looked as if there were words he wanted to say, things he wanted to reveal. She knew that look because it matched the feeling brewing inside her.

He leaned forward, brushing his lips over hers. "Tonight," he whispered. "I'll pick you up at seven."

She accepted his kiss, let the warmth it exuded encase her for just a few minutes more, then slipped through the door.

Chapter 18

This was the last thing X had expected to uncover. He and Nick had already discussed checking out Kalina Harper. With the Elder's accusation that she was a shifter, he'd gone directly to his office to speed up the background check. He should have known there was a reason his original search attempts had been blocked. But once he'd gotten into the correct databases, forging clearance for some higher-level areas—it was really baffling as to why this seemingly average woman's file would be that buried—he'd hit the jackpot.

Leaning back in his chair with the sun setting through the window behind him, he cursed, long, slow, and fluent.

Rome was going to go ballistic when he found out.

And if Kalina was his *companheiro,* the shit was definitely going to hit the fan.

Dropping the reports onto his desk, X dragged a hand down his face, feeling tired and ragged. All sensations he was used to, but they tended to keep him going nevertheless. It was the desolate feeling, the creeping up of a hunger that worried him. He usually kept it at bay, going on with his life as normally as possible, but lately it had been gnawing at him, pressing for release in a world that frowned upon such actions.

From his hip the cell phone chirped and he hurriedly answered, welcoming the distraction of outside conversation. Trying to convince himself that he didn't need what his body craved was becoming monotonous.

"Is this line secure?" the voice on the other end asked before X could say anything.

"Hold on," he said. He walked to the door, locked it, and returned to his desk. There was a small radio in the corner near his computer; X switched it on and leaned forward so he was closer to its speaker. He worked for the FBI so he was well aware of how easy it was to place a bug in an office without anybody noticing. He normally swept his office every week to make sure it was clean, but he knew who this was on the phone and knew that if they were calling it was urgent. He didn't have time to do another check, but would use precaution instead.

"I'm here. What's going on?"

"I looked into that thing at the lab like you requested."

There was silence on the line.

"And?" X prodded.

"It's not good."

He let out a breath. Was this the day for bad fucking news or what? " 'Not good' means what?"

"It means we're probably about six months, give or take, away from being found out."

"How?"

"You should know. It's the ones you're working for that are on our backs. Somebody tipped them off so they're looking into the possibilities."

This was not what X wanted to hear, especially not after what he'd found out about Kalina. "The feds are looking into the possible existence of shifters?"

"You got it. They're asking questions so I gotta think somebody out there's giving up some answers."

Rubbing his free hand over his bald head, X ran scenarios through his mind as if there were a central computer planted inside his brain. None of them had a good outcome.

"And X?"

"What?"

"They're close. So close we need to be looking over our shoulders at every turn from this minute on. Tell the FL there and I'll let Sebastian know. They need to decide what to tell the Assembly and how to prepare the other shifters before the shit goes downhill."

As X disconnected the line, he figured it was probably too late for that.

He hadn't slept at all last night, his own demons picking that time to come out to haunt him. But Nick wasn't afraid of those demons, or any others, either. He wasn't afraid of anything, couldn't afford to be.

So what if he was at work? He'd been here since six this morning, with a sour attitude. It didn't matter because so far the only person he'd taken his bad mood out on had been the guy at the coffeehouse on the corner who had gotten his order wrong a record number of three times and had the audacity to catch an attitude with Nick when he called him on it and demanded his money back.

It was now just about closing time and he wasn't particularly looking forward to going home alone. He was sitting back in his office chair with one hand on his black address book and the other rubbing along his chin as he considered what type of company he was in the mood for tonight.

There was a knock on his door, an almost silent one that he probably would have missed if he didn't have the heightened senses of a shifter.

"Come in," he said wearily, hoping that whoever it was would state their business and get out in the quickest amount of time possible.

"Hi, Mr. Delgado. I just have a few letters that need to go out today, and Mr. Reynolds hasn't been in. I figured I'd bring them to you to sign."

Rome's assistant, Melanie something or other, came right in, bringing the letters up to his desk and dropping them down in front of him all while she spoke in that quick, efficient manner of hers.

Nick didn't even blink, just picked up his pen and began looking over the letters before signing.

"Mr. Reynolds wasn't in the office today," she said again. "I would usually have all the mail signed and out by now, but when he called this morning to say he wasn't coming in I had some appointments of his to reschedule and some other things to handle first. It's so unlike him to not come in, especially when he has things on his calendar."

How Rome put up with this woman's monologues Nick had no idea. He'd run screaming from the office every day if he had to listen to her ramble on and on like this. "Did you get everything rescheduled all right?" he asked, because he sensed she expected him to say something sooner or later.

"I did. Except Mr. Gwynn wasn't happy about moving this afternoon's deposition."

"Gwynn. That's the product liability lawsuit, right?"

"Yes, it is. And if you ask me he knew that glue wasn't meant to hold tempered glass together. That poor little boy who fell through the window suffered so much."

"Mr. Gwynn's our client, Melanie," Nick said slowly, moving on to another letter.

"Yes, I know and believe me I'm thankful for all our clients because without them I wouldn't have a job. But that doesn't mean he didn't put a faulty product into those new houses and didn't expect that those poor buyers would have problems at some point. The entire construction company should be sued if you ask me."

Nick shook his head. "I'm glad the plaintiffs aren't asking you."

"Anyway, you know who else was out today? Kalina Harper." The assistant stopped then, letting the question and anticipated follow-up answer linger in the air.

The implication was not lost on Nick.

"I was with her over the weekend, but she left my place so fast and without a word. I've tried calling her, but I don't get an answer. I'm kind of worried."

Rome had been in the office this morning and had left. He'd called Nick sounding a bit off, saying he had some things outside the office to take care of. Nick assumed he was still haunted by Elder Alamar's words from earlier that morning. As for Kalina, as far as Nick knew she was still at Rome's house. Now that Melanie was asking about them both, Nick had to wonder why.

She was clearly fishing for information. But what Nick found really interesting was that she'd mentioned being with Kalina over the weekend. He hadn't known the two were friends. It shouldn't matter to him who the woman saw on the weekends, but if this woman was Rome's mate, then it was up to Nick to be apprised of everything she did and who she did it with.

"Really? You and Ms. Harper spend a lot of time together?" he asked, looking up at her. She was a pretty enough woman with shoulder-length red hair and green eyes. Her smile was always ready and she was very efficient according to Rome, but she was definitely looking for some information from Nick. He just hadn't figured out what yet.

Melanie shrugged. "She's new, just thought I'd show her around a bit. Anyway, she left my place without saying a word so I was surprised not to see her this morning. And I keep calling her and calling her."

Nick nodded as he finished signing the letters and handed them to Melanie. "I'm sure she's just fine."

She took the letters from his hand but continued to stand there staring at him. "You're sure?" she asked.

Nick looked her right in those sea-green eyes. "I'm sure."

Later, after he'd received an urgent text message from X to meet him at Rome's place, Nick would think the entire exchange with Melanie was beyond strange and not coincidental. By then it would be too late.

He braced himself, held his shoulders squared in the fading sunlight of the afternoon. Rome left his suit jacket in the car as he walked through the solemn cemetery. Their burial plots were near the east entrance, right beside a biblical statue and a running fountain. The plots were just a front; his parents' bodies were not here. The *Ética* prevented formal burials, allowing only cremation for their kind.

It was peaceful here, the last resting place of loved ones. Even the birds above flew by in silence. Cars didn't seem to drive as fast when they passed the cemetery; the air around the entire place felt still.

But Rome heard thumping. It was loud and echoed with every footstep he took. Now that he was standing still the sound reverberated off every headstone in the vicinity. He didn't read the names, never read them as he walked through. He didn't know them and they didn't know him.

Only these two he knew.

He loved.

One three-foot-high stone marked the final resting place of Vance and Loren Reynolds. Just above the names was the tribal insignia of the Topètenia—a paw print with claws that dripped into a swirling circular collage. He saw that insignia every day—it hung in brass form in Rome's study. Looking at it made him straighten further, a sign of respect, allegiance to his lineage.

But as his gaze dropped to the names, rested on his father's, that allegiance wavered.

His father was a traitor. Rome still couldn't believe it, didn't want to begin to accept that the man he'd loved and respected had told their secret to a human. The journal entries on that disk outlined meetings, some here in DC, others across the States. He'd been meeting with a man who was promising to help regulate the shifters, to bring them into the fold with the human world.

His father had always wanted them to blend in, to be accepted among the humans. Rome, on the other hand, knew their differences and didn't argue them. He didn't flaunt them or begrudge the humans his personal DNA, but he knew that his kind would never be considered equal. That's why it was so imperative to govern themselves.

Vance thought differently. With the Rogues beginning their rebellion and the Assembly uncertain of what should be done, Vance had turned to someone he trusted, someone he thought could help.

Now it was up to Rome to find out if that trust was in vain. Everything inside him said it was. In the last days of his father's life he'd transferred large sums of money to an account in Cartagena. That account had long since been closed, but Bingham had finally given him a name—Raul Cortez.

Rome's chest constricted as he slipped his hands into his pockets. Words floated through his mind, questions he wanted answers to but from a man who could never provide them. He'd driven for hours after he'd left his office via the same secret exit he'd sent Kalina through.

Rome remembered this morning with a warmth through his body. He remembered her scent, her touch, her eyes. His forehead furrowed as he struggled with what was and what he didn't want to be.

Kalina was a shifter, and if this morning was any indication she was entering her *acordado*. In the next few days everything about her would change. Her senses would develop and magnify; her eyesight would sharpen, with night vision becoming acute; she would hear things from blocks away, scent lies as easily as she scented enemies. Her body would ripen, craving the touch of a male. Her scent would permeate the air, enticing any male in her proximity. His body hardened with the thought, while his mind warred with what all this meant for him.

It meant Alamar had been right. She was his *companheiro*. His mate.

His responsibility.

The question was, could he handle it? Could he handle what this would mean to him? More important, how would she react to finding out that everything she thought she'd known about herself had been a lie?

Questions formed a lingering line in his mind. His gaze stayed focused on the headstone just about a foot in front of him.

His cell phone rang and he reached to his hip to answer it.

"Reynolds," he said in a dour tone.

"We need to talk. Now."

X sounded serious. Rome knew not to question him. "Meet me at my house in half an hour."

"Later," X agreed and disconnected the line.

Rome put the phone back in its holster and inhaled deeply. The air was ripe with pollution, thick with the stench of death. It was all around him, coming on the stifling hot breeze, and soon it would knock on his door again. Rome knew this without a doubt.

But this time, he vowed to be ready.

Chapter 19

"Where's the Rogue?" Rome asked the moment he walked into his study and headed straight for the bar. Pulling a glass from the shelf, he poured himself a drink and gulped it down. He was carrying the weight of his world and then some on his shoulders. Liquor probably wasn't going to soothe it, but it would have to do for now.

X stood by the window. He turned when Rome entered the room and simply stared at him.

Nick was near the fireplace, standing right beneath the brass sculpture of the Topètenia insignia. The one that had Rome gripping his glass like a lifeline.

"He's locked down tight. Still not talking. Well, that's not true: He said that whoever he works for is going to feed us our nuts for breakfast. Then he shut up. Think his lip might have been too swollen to continue."

Rome frowned. "His boss isn't looking for him. Gotta wonder why."

X shrugged. "Collateral damage. There's always a percentage when you walk into a war."

"Then they'd better start keeping count, because if he doesn't talk soon his ass is a statistic," Nick quipped.

"But there's something bigger going on," X said.

Rome looked at him. "What's up?"

"It's about Kalina."

His already throbbing temples pulsated faster as Rome released the glass and flattened his palms on the cool surface of the bar. "What about her?"

"She's safe. Ezra's parked in front of her place as we speak," Nick said, knowing the worried look on Rome's face.

"She's a cop," X announced and was greeted by total silence throughout the room. He took a deep breath and continued. "She's been employed by the Metropolitan Police Department for eight years, becoming an integral part of the narcotics division. Working directly on the streets, she's nabbed a good number of criminals in her tenure.

"Three weeks ago she was given a new assignment, a task force being headed up by the DEA. Her target is Reynolds and Delgado LLC, specifically you," he said, looking at Rome.

"Fuck!" Nick cursed, rubbing a hand over his chin. "She's been at the firm spying on us? For what? What could they possibly think? That Rome's a drug dealer?"

"The assignment is to investigate Rome and his finances, figure out where his money's going. Specifically figure out which drug cartel in Brazil Rome's funding."

"What?" Nick roared. "Are you fucking serious?"

He was. Even without him answering the question Rome knew that every word X had just said was serious and most likely true. It explained so much, even as those same words traveled through his system like a burning infection. He didn't cringe outwardly; he refused to look as if this revelation bothered him on the level it really did. He was their leader. How would it look for him to crumble under this new development? He'd slept with the woman who was out to get him, so to speak. He'd thought he was falling in love with her . . . dammit!

"She was trying to get into my computer," he said aloud even though he'd thought the words were his alone.

"When?" X asked.

"Last week. The same day she came into the office with us, Nick. That evening I caught her trying to break into my computer."

"And you didn't have her arrested? You didn't think there was anything weird about that?"

Rome held up a hand. "Calm down, Nick. I did think something was going on. I questioned her and I believed she was lying to me. I didn't think it would be this, that's for sure. But I took precautions, reset passwords and made sure the firewalls and encryption devices were in place."

"You just neglected to tell me and to kick her sneaky ass out on the streets."

"No," Rome said with quiet insistence. "Kicking her out was never an option."

Nick and X stared at him for a second.

"Because you think she's your mate? You've thought that from the beginning, haven't you?"

This was X, the investigator, the one who was always full of questions. Nick was the action guy, ready to react.

Slowly Rome lifted the glass to his lips, taking a measured sip. He had to take it slow; gulping it would surely feel good, but getting pissy drunk wasn't going to make this day go any better.

"Whatever or whoever she is, she needs to be neutralized. Now, before it's too late!" Nick roared.

Rome was across the room in seconds, pouncing as if he'd scented his prey and caught it. "You are not to touch her! Ever!"

His fists had clenched in Nick's dress shirt, his friend's tie twining around his arms. Nick looked him right in the eye.

"She's going to find out what we are and she's going to tell. You of all of us should know how badly that's going to end. The only way she might keep quiet is if she's a shifter, too, but we don't know that for sure. Our situation is much bigger than her, Rome. Much more important."

"No!" Rome pushed his longtime friend away from him, hating that he'd put his hands on him in rage in the first place but bubbling with so many emotions he could barely think straight. "It's not bigger than her." He sighed and turned from both of them.

"It's about her," X stated quietly. "The Rogues want her and so do you. This fight is about a woman."

"It's about boundaries," Rome answered. "The Rogues don't want to accept them and we want to create them."

"Then where does Kalina fit in?" Nick asked.

"He wants her for himself," Baxter said in his even tone.

Again the man had entered the room without any of them hearing, and again he was as much in tune with the conversation as if he'd been here all along.

"What are you talking about?" Rome asked what the others were definitely thinking. "And how do you know about this?"

Moving to the bar, Baxter emptied the glass Rome had left and put away the bottle of brandy. With all eyes on him, the man moved as if he were simply a butler. Rome wanted to yell the roof off this house. He wanted answers, he wanted to change, he wanted things not to have gotten so far. But it seemed all he was going to get was more bad news.

"It is simple. The two strongest of the species, the leaders of the pack, so to speak, are fighting over a girl. I think that's quite poetic, don't you?"

"I think I want to know what the hell you're talking about. Who else wants Kalina?" Because it was painfully obvious that Rome did—even knowing she was a cop investigating him. A small part of him would wonder if everything she'd said and done had been a part of her job. Then he remembered her scent, the feel of being inside her, the look on her face when he was inside her, the look in her eyes when they'd both reached their pleasure. That wasn't faked. No matter how decorated a cop she may be, she wasn't that good.

"He is leading them but he needs her, he needs a mate to fulfill his own prophecy."

"Oh God, he's been talking to Alamar."

"And if you do not wish for the Elder to be in on this conversation, you should all keep your voices down. He's not happy that you walked out on him this morning and even less pleased that you, the Faction Leader, are doubting the legends."

Rubbing a hand down his face, Rome signaled just how impatient he was becoming with this situation. "Baxter, I'm going to ask a question and you're going to answer. It's that simple, ask and answer. Okay?"

Baxter raised one thick brow then nodded his compliance.

"Who is leading the Rogues?"

"Alamar believes it is Sabar, one of two jaguar brothers raised by Boden in the Gungi."

"Boden the sadistic cat that raped and butchered villagers and tribal females until he was finally beheaded fifteen years ago?" Nick asked.

Baxter looked at Nick and nodded. "That's the one." His gaze shifted back to Rome, whom he asked, "I am allowed to answer his questions as well?"

Rome decided to ignore the butler's sarcastic question and proceeded. "What does he want with Kalina?"

"Alamar thinks she may be of a pure bloodline, possibly a former Elder."

That wasn't necessarily the answer he expected to hear. "Why didn't he say that earlier?"

As if this were the last place he wanted to be and the imaginary speck of lint on the lapel of his black jacket was as important as the next presidential election, Baxter replied, "How would you have heard him? You stormed down the hall like a spoiled brat afraid to hear the truth."

Rome frowned at his words. "I'm not afraid of anything."

Baxter sighed, letting his arms fall to his sides and standing at complete attention. "That is correct, Mr. Roman. You are not afraid of anything. You are also not willing to accept everything that is. Since you were a young boy you've rebelled against what will be."

"Rebelled against what must be?" It was Rome's turn to roar now as he turned to his butler with an incredulous glare. "I've done nothing in these past years but work for this tribe, do what was best for this tribe! I don't have a life because I'm more focused on what's going on in the damn jungle then I am with what's happening right in my own firm. Hell, I didn't even know a cop was hired to investigate me!"

"She was meant for you. Take a minute and think about that. Accept that first and you will be able to continue with your duty."

"Right about now I don't give a damn about duty!" Rome yelled. "You're telling me she's trying to find information to have me sent to jail," he said to X. "And you"—he whirled to face Nick—"you want to kill her and everybody else who breathes the wrong way. Now you." He was back to Baxter again. "You want me to just man up and save the day for the shifters."

Silence fell over the room again. Rome felt like everything around him was spinning out of control.

"And what do you want, Mr. Roman?" Baxter asked.

"I want what I've always wanted," he answered.

"To find your parents' murderers and kill them?"

There were a couple of ways Rome could have answered these questions, but he just didn't feel like being politically correct at the moment. "That's exactly right."

"A good ruler must learn to act in the best interest of those he leads."

"My personal battle does not endanger any shifters but myself."

"Your split allegiance endangers us all," Baxter corrected.

X interrupted. "There's something else we need to consider here. In addition to finding out that Kalina is a cop, I got a call from my contact in Arizona. The Comastaz lab Sebastian mentioned at our last meeting is working on a new pet project, and it's top secret."

"What does that have to do with us?" Nick asked.

"Somebody out there, a human, knows about us."

Nick cursed again, but Rome and Baxter remained perfectly still.

"You already knew, didn't you?" X asked Rome. "You knew and you didn't tell us?"

"It didn't concern you—" Rome began.

"Bullshit! Rome, that's pure bullshit! If we're about to be ratted out to the world, it concerns all of us," Nick roared.

He was shaking his head. "No. It concerns me. It's my job, remember, to protect the secret, to protect the shifters."

"It's not your job alone, man," Nick said. "We've always been right beside you in everything. You can't think that would stop now."

"You don't understand."

"What is there to understand? You know we're about to be found out. For all we know this female might be out to expose us, too." X's tone was somber.

Rome walked away from all of them. He went to stand near the window, looking out into the sky. Day was turning into night; the sun was settling, casting the sky in an array of golds and deep oranges. Outside the world went on while inside, inside the world he'd known was being tested, everything he'd been taught and aspired to was being pushed to the brink.

"You don't understand what it's like to find out that someone you loved may have been responsible for leaking the secret. How do I punish a dead man for betraying us?" he asked in a soft tone. "How do I hold my own father accountable for the ultimate betrayal?"

"Your father? What?"

On the small table by the door the phone rang. Baxter stood quietly and answered in a hushed tone. "Mr. Roman. It is Ezra, sir."

Ezra?

Kalina?

Rome rushed to the phone. With all eyes on him, questions looming in the minds of his two best friends, he answered. "What is it?"

"Some guy just went into her apartment. He stinks like a shifter but I'm sure he's human. I've seen him before hanging around outside, but he just went in about five minutes ago. She's in there with him alone."

Not for long, Rome thought as he headed out of the room.

Chapter 20

Today was a day for revelations, Kalina thought as she slipped into black slacks. The gray silk blouse she wore fit her bodice like an alluring glove. The outfit was complete with three-and-a-half-inch black mules that gave just the amount of casual she aimed for tonight.

Technically, this was her first date with Roman Reynolds. Most likely the reason for the dancing butterflies in the pit of her stomach. All day long she'd managed not to think about the seriousness of this next step she was taking. The other things she was doing were good at keeping her mind off the man.

Dorian Wilson was the DEA agent in charge of this case. Kalina had called him twice today from her desk. When she hadn't reached him, she'd taken a chance and sent him an email. It was imperative she speak to him about this case, and she wanted to do so in person. That would be the only way she could get a true sense for what was going through the man's mind. She was willing to bet every penny she had in her savings that this case wasn't what they'd represented to her three weeks ago.

Ferrell had been texting her all day but she'd ignored him. He was an asshole and talking to him wasn't going to garner the information she wanted. She suspected he was just a cover for what was really going on and she was going to find out whether the MPD or the DEA wanted her to or not.

As a last-ditch effort that in her gut she knew was going to prove futile, she'd scanned all the financial records on the firm's database for the name Raul Cortez. Nothing. None of the wire transfers sent to Brazil had gone to the known cartel boss. Relief had washed through her at that knowledge while in the back of her mind the thought that the information could be on Rome's home computer nagged.

He wasn't a drug dealer, she told herself. He was just a man. A man with an enigmatic personality that had drawn her in instantly. A man with just the barest hint of sadness in his dark eyes. He had a past, just as she did. His life had been rough, just like hers. That was their connection, the link that had unwittingly drawn them together.

It wasn't this case. Kalina had to believe that. She had to believe that there was more between her and Rome than a case that was going to fall apart any minute now. Wanted desperately to believe there was more.

Did that make her an idiot? Probably. Did she care? Hell no. She'd waited a lifetime to feel what she did when she was with him. The intensity of their . . . what? Was it love? He hadn't said the word and neither had she. Could that be what she was feeling as her mind wrapped around thoughts of him and her body trembled in anticipation of his touch?

Insistent knocking at her door interrupted her thoughts. She looked down at her watch: It was half an hour before she expected Rome. Maybe he was as anxious as she was to get this date started. With one last look in the mirror she smoothed the sides of her hair, toyed with the longer tendrils at the top, and wondered briefly about letting it grow out to a softer, more feminine style.

As she made it through the threshold of her bedroom into the tiny hallway leading to the living room, an uneasy feeling replaced the happy little butterflies that had been mingling in the pit of her stomach a moment ago. Dread and apprehension swamped her with each step she took. The knocking at the door was loud thumping that almost sounded like it would splinter the wood.

It wasn't Rome.

The feeling she had was different. Whoever was on the other side of the door was bringing a shitload of tension and anger with him. Pausing at the table where her keys and her purse rested, Kalina slid the small drawer open and retrieved her gun, slipping it into the back band of her pants before approaching the door. She thought about asking who it was but figured the odds were slim she'd get the truth. Her gut said whoever this was wasn't here to wish her a happy evening.

So when she pulled the door open and saw Ferrell standing there she wasn't as surprised as she probably should have been. He pushed past her, moving quickly into her apartment.

"We need to talk," he said, moving to the window and looking out before turning to face her.

"Well, hello to you, too," she snapped, closing the door and turning to face him with all the agitation she was feeling at the way he'd knocked on her door and the fact that he was here at her home at all.

"Where are you with Reynolds? Did you get anything from his place last night?"

Kalina was about to answer him, about to share the

information about the Cortez Cartel, when she paused, tilted her head, and stared at Ferrell a little closer. He wore wrinkled khakis and an even more wrinkled white buttondown shirt with huge sweat rings beneath his arms. His forehead was beaded with moisture, his lips still so cracked she thought she could feel their pain.

"What the hell is wrong with you? And how did you know where I was last night?" she asked.

"You!" he yelled pointing a shaking finger in her direction. "You do not question me! I'm your superior! You answer my questions! Now, what did you find out?"

He was out of his damn mind, that's what he was. As much as Kalina wanted a promotion, she was sick and tired of his verbal abuse. She'd been taught, even if it was by her temporary parents, that to get respect you had to give it. Ferrell hadn't respected her from day one. And if she had to file a complaint against him she would, but she'd be damned if he was going to come into her home yelling like he'd lost the last bit of mind he had.

"You'll have my report soon," she said, keeping her eyes on the man because there was something about him that just wasn't right. Uneasiness swamped her and even though she stood perfectly still, inside she felt like she was pacing, watching, waiting for the right moment to . . .

"I want your report now! You tell me what you know about that animal before I . . ." His voice trailed off as he looked back, out the window again.

Kalina tried to look over his shoulder but all she could see was the crimson coloring of the fading afternoon. She could hear cars going by, but she wasn't close enough to the window to see if one had stopped outside, or was waiting for him, or what.

"Maybe we should call Wilson," she suggested, already reaching into her purse for her cell phone. This was the last straw; she had no intention of dealing with Ferrell and his unstable ass anymore. If that meant she was off the case, then so be it.

Kalina would have never given Ferrell credit for being alert enough to move so fast, but as her back slammed against the wall, his fingers gripping her wrist so tight she dropped her cell phone to the floor, she'd had second thoughts.

"You tell me what's going on right now! You fucked him, I know that much," he said before doing the most disgusting thing she could ever imagine: He lowered his head, sniffing down her neck, to the rim of her blouse just above her breasts. "Yeah, you fucked that animal. You let him touch you all over so now you stink just like him! Like them!"

"What the hell are you talking about?" The words came from her trembling lips because as Ferrell held her in his tight grasp Kalina battled with flashbacks of a night long ago. A night when she'd been grabbed just like this and thrown to the ground. When her clothes had been ripped from her and her body touched by vicious, vile hands she wished now she could cut off with a blunt-edged knife.

"Don't you lie to me, bitch! Don't you dare lie to me!"

His eyes were glazed as more sweat poured from his brow. He smelled awful and he was the one sniffing her. Her stomach roiled and she thought she was going to be sick. But the roiling continued, pushing at her as if begging her to do something, anything.

Ferrell's hands went to her neck. Instinctively she grabbed at his wrists, hoping to stop him before he could tighten his grip, but it was too late. He'd started choking her, all the while yelling in her face.

Her vision was getting blurry as she tried to lift a knee to his groin. The gun was at her back, she could reach for it, but her hands fought frantically at the hands squeezing the breath from her. He moved and yelled louder, choked her harder. She wanted to claw at him, to smack his hands away from her throat, but she couldn't. She couldn't think past wanting to breathe.

But she could see.

And it was familiar eyes that appeared in her line of sight.

It was the eyes of the beast that had been in the alley with her that night.

Rome had been furious when he'd left his house. Angry at himself for blowing up at the three men who were the closest to him, who had stuck by him all his life. He felt trapped in a situation he didn't know everything about yet and struggled to control. Panic gripped him as he drove through the city. He hadn't waited to see if Nick or X had followed him but he suspected one or both probably had.

Ezra had gone upstairs the moment he hung up with Rome and only heard voices as if they were simply talking, so he didn't go in. Instead he stood guard at the end of the hallway waiting until Rome arrived.

Kalina.

Her name was a litany in Rome's mind.

Who was she? What did she really want from him? And could he really handle the answers to those questions?

A cop. He would have never imagined it, but that

was probably because he couldn't see past the woman. The female who had enamored him from the first night he'd seen her. It wasn't a mistake, he knew instinctively. Meeting her two years ago wasn't a mistake and even though he hated to lend credence to it, he feared it was the destiny his mother had spoken of so frequently.

But if Kalina was his destiny, how would he deal with her connection to law enforcement, to the reason she was at his law firm in the first place?

Wasn't one traitor in his heart enough?

Jumping out of his car after he'd barely parked it in front of her house, he gave Ezra the signal to move in slowly, giving him a few minutes to get inside first. Then he took the steps to her apartment two at a time, trying to calm the rage simmering inside, the cat stalking just below the surface.

Who was she in there with? What were they doing? He'd kill any man who touched her, the thought casting darkness over his mind as his fingers flexed at his sides, willing his claws not to emerge. The cat wanted to break free, to burst through that door and . . .

She screamed and the sound pierced through the closed door, vibrating down the halls to echo in Rome's ears. His claws broke free at that moment, his cat roaring even as he lifted his foot and kicked down the door of her apartment. Through the mere slits of his eyes he saw the man with his hands on her, heard her screams and smelled her fear.

Just like before.

The animal in him strained to rip free, to clamp down on the man's neck until the cracking of his vertebrae signaled his death. Instead the warring human half of him reached out with clawed fingers, grabbing the man by his shoulder and lifting him off the ground with his animalistic strength.

Kalina fell to the floor gasping for breath as Rome stared down the man stupid enough to put his hands on her.

"Who . . . ," the man stammered then stared at Rome. "Fuck me! You're one of them. I knew it. I fucking knew it!" He was scrambling for the door, falling over something on the floor.

Rome hurried over, grabbing him by the collar of his shirt until his feet dangled in the air.

"You come near her again and I . . . will . . . kill . . . you."

"Get off me, you freak! Get the hell off me!"

"Gladly," Rome growled, tossing him the rest of the way to the door, knocking over a sofa table and all its contents at the same time.

The man hurriedly picked himself up off the floor this time, not daring to look back before running out the door.

Rome turned to Kalina then, fell to his knees, and reached out to touch her. He saw his claws and was about to pull them back when she reached out and grabbed his hands.

"What . . . who . . . ," she stuttered then dropped his hands and looked right into his eyes. "It's you." Her breaths were coming fast, her chest heaving as she looked from his hands to his face, her gaze imploring, questioning, knowing.

"From my dreams," she whispered. "You're the beast."

Chapter 21

If she'd said she had a contagious disease he probably wouldn't have jumped up as fast, turning his back on her.

Kalina's hands were shaking as she planted her palms on the floor then heaved herself up. Her place was a wreck but she really wasn't caring too much about that at the moment. With slow steps, keeping her eyes on his back, she reached behind her, slipping the gun from her pants. Removing the safety, she lifted it to him.

"Turn around," she said slowly.

His broad shoulders looked somehow broader. He seemed larger, like he was too big to be in this apartment with all this furniture, and her. He breathed in and out, slowly. Other than that he didn't move.

"I said turn around," she said in her best cop voice while trying to keep her hands from shaking.

"Now is not the time." He spoke in a low gruff voice.

It didn't sound like him. Like Rome. But then was he really Roman Reynolds or someone . . . some*thing* else?

"Now's the only time. Turn around so I can see you." She swallowed hard. "So I can see what you really are. Because I know it's not—"

He turned slowly and her words died in her throat. He looked . . . looked like Rome. His forehead was furrowed like he was extremely pissed off. But outside of that everything else looked—normal. He still wore the dark slacks and white dress shirt she'd seen him in earlier.

Her gaze instantly focused on his hands. She'd seen them, claws that ripped through the skin of his fingers. But they were gone. His hands looked normal with blunt-tipped nails and a gold watch at his wrist. Nothing abnormal, strange, unnatural.

But his eyes.

They weren't right. Not the color and not the shape.

"You were there, weren't you? Two years ago, it was you." The accusation sounded damn crazy to her own ears, but deep inside she felt there was some truth to it. There had to be. Part of her trembled but another part pushed to stand tall, to stay focused.

"Tell me the truth," she said, lifting the gun a little higher to aim right between his eyes. "Open your mouth and tell me who and what the hell you are or I swear I'm shooting your ass where you stand."

He didn't flinch or falter, but spoke in a calm rugged voice. "Grab some things and let's go. You can't stay here anymore."

She blinked. Had she heard him correctly? She was the one holding the gun but he was giving the orders.

"This is the last chance for questions and answers. In a minute I'm shooting and I shoot to kill."

He took a step toward her. "You won't kill me."

Kalina widened her stance, flexed her finger on the trigger. "You wanna bet?"

He continued walking toward her, lifting a hand to grab her wrist. "You. Won't. Shoot. Me."

His grip wasn't tight, even though she was positive he had the strength to squeeze the blood through her fingertips. But he didn't; his fingers just barely grazed her skin. She should have pulled the trigger, should have shot a hole right through his chest. But she couldn't. It was the unknown that held her still. The unknown that should be scaring the hell out of her, but had her dangerously curious instead.

"Put the gun down and pack some things. I'll answer your questions but we have to get out of here."

"I'm not leaving my apartment," she said, lowering the gun, taking her hand off the trigger, but leaving the safety off. Just in case.

"You don't have a choice. It's not safe."

"You don't tell me what to do." It didn't sound too convincing, but that could have been because she was still entranced by his eyes. They weren't Rome's normal brown color, but a vibrant green, like a slice in the center of dark orbs. He blinked and they didn't change. Something inside her moved—it was as if it turned over and stretched—and she wanted to touch him. At her sides her fingers wiggled with the urge.

"What are you?" she asked again.

"Here's the deal," he said, stepping closer, so close that when she inhaled his scent filled her nostrils. Not a cologne scent but something wild, untamed, enticing.

"I'll answer that question if you agree to get your things and come with me." He closed his eyes and looked as if he was enduring something immensely painful. She did lift her hand then, touched her fingertips to the line of his jaw.

It was hard, strong. She touched his chin, his nose, brushed her fingers softly over his closed lids. It all felt normal, but not. Heat speared through her body, starting at the pad of her fingers where she touched him, spinning a wicked web throughout her veins until she felt nothing but hunger. Need.

She pulled her hand away and swallowed again. "Answer me."

"They call us Shadow Shifters."

She'd turned her head from him and was staring down at the floor, because she was trying to decipher what was going on in her own body.

It was his turn to touch. His fingers lifting her chin, turning her back to face him.

"I am a shape shifter, Kalina. I can shift into—"

She backed out of his grasp, her breath coming in heavy pants. "A cat? You turn into a big black cat with weird green eyes."

A muscle in his jaw ticked. He nodded in agreement.

"Shit!" She looked down to see where she'd dropped her gun. "Oh my, shit . . . dammit, dammit." When she bent down to get it he was there, his hands encircling her wrists.

"Come with me," he whispered. "Now."

"Hellllooo? Hellllooo?" Mrs. Gilbert sang, peeking her head inside the open door. "Kalina, are you here? Are you okay?"

"Tell her you're fine and that we're leaving," Rome whispered. "Or you're going to witness a hell of a lot more than my claws coming out."

She looked at his hands that held hers, up to his face, then to the door where Mrs. Gilbert stood. She didn't have her cat with her. Thank goodness. The last thing Kalina thought she'd be able to take was another cat in the room.

Standing, she pulled her hands from his grip and turned to Mrs. Gilbert. "Hi, Mrs. Gilbert. I'm . . . ah, I'm sorry for the noise. I'm ah, I'm just trying to get some things together. Gonna be staying someplace else for a while."

"Staying someplace else? You sure?" the old woman asked, eyeing Rome suspiciously. "He going with you? You need some help?"

"No." Kalina was shaking her head as she walked toward her neighbor. "No. I'm fine. Just going to get some things and get going. I'll, um, I'll call you when I get settled in so you'll know I'm all right."

She'd never called the woman for anything, even though she had her number and Mrs. Gilbert had hers. Kalina had never been the one reaching out to her neighbor; it had always been the other way around. Realizing this made Kalina feel like an ass. The concern on Mrs. Gilbert's face was evident and she wanted to reassure the woman that things were okay, but really, how could she? The place was a mess, there was a strange man leering at both of them, and if the woman's hearing aid was worth a damn Kalina was sure she could hear the rapid heartbeat about to explode from her chest.

"Well, okay, if you say so." Mrs. Gilbert moved back to the door and out, but stood in the hallway still looking in. "But if you need anything."

"Right," Kalina said. "I know. I'll call you." Because she knew that even in the midst of all her self-imposed loneliness she could, and Mrs. Gilbert would answer.

With a little effort Kalina pushed the broken door until it just about closed. Then she turned back to face Rome.

"I'm only going because my door's a complete loss and it's a mess in here. Not because you said so."

He nodded. "Can you just hurry up?"

She was talking and asking questions and time was wasting. He'd smelled the stench the moment he touched the guy who was strangling Kalina. It was Rogue, but the man wasn't. Still, a Rogue had been here, in this apartment.

A Rogue he knew well.

A Rogue he'd vowed to kill.

And he'd been in Kalina's apartment. Death was definitely imminent now.

In the truck there was silence. She remembered being inside this vehicle before. Twice. Once with Rome and another time . . .

"I think somebody else has been following me," she said, because too many things were happening that she was second-guessing herself on. If sitting beside her was the beast she'd sworn wasn't real, then the person snapping pictures of her and leaving them at her apartment was a real threat, too.

He'd been quiet since she'd grabbed a bag and tossed another one at him before they left the apartment. She'd left with him, was in this truck with him, going she had no idea where. She had to ask why. The answer wasn't simple.

"What happened?"

"Pictures," she replied simply. "He keeps sending me pictures. Of the night of the party and of that night two years ago. Pictures of me."

"Do the cops know?" he asked without looking at her.

"No."

"Really?"

She glanced at him, wanting to see him again. Wanting desperately to see the cat.

It occurred to her that she should be afraid of him and what he'd told her he was, what she knew she'd seen. Maybe she should have killed him or at the very least arrested him, but for what? Saving her life yet again?

While there was a measure of fear of what would come next, she didn't instantly identify with that emotion. It was strange, coupled with all the other strange things that had been going on in her life. She wanted to go with him, wanted to hear what he had to say about who and what he was, why he was here. For a minute she felt like Lois Lane desperate for any answers she could get from Superman.

But this wasn't for an interview. For Kalina it was more. She wanted to know why she'd been attracted to someone such as Rome when she hadn't felt anything for a man in years. She wanted to understand what had drawn her to him and why.

"You were there that night in the alley when that dealer attacked me. You were there at the party when those thugs were coming for me. Last night there was something at Mel's house. I saw the eyes and heard noises from the bushes. Then I was knocked out and I woke up in your bedroom." She'd only remembered that as she'd packed in the last hour. The minute she'd seen this truck parked on the street in front of her house, it had all clicked neatly into place. "And you were there again today. Always there when—"

"When you need me," he finished. "I won't let anything happen to you, Kalina. Ever."

He spoke with controlled finality, as if it was a simple fact that she would have to accept. Well, despite him following her, he didn't know her at all.

"I didn't hire a bodyguard because I don't need one."

"Good. I'm not for hire."

He didn't look at her, just kept his gaze either on the back of the seat in front of him or out the tinted windows. That irritated her, too. She wanted to see his eyes, to look into the orbs that had haunted her for so many nights.

"Why didn't you tell the police about the pictures?"

"The same reason I don't need a bodyguard. I can handle it myself."

"I'll handle it."

"I don't recall asking you to."

"And I'm not offering. I'm telling you."

With those heated words he looked at her, his eyes now dark brown again but still smoldering.

"This is insane." She sighed. "All of it. You're following me. Someone else is following me. I don't even know who or what you are now."

He was quiet.

"Why won't you answer my questions?"

"I will but not here, not now."

"Oh that's right, I forgot. Everything in your time on your terms. Where are you taking me, or can't I ask that question, either?"

"I'll answer all your questions when we get there."

"When we get where?"

He sighed, then turned his head slowly to face her. "Do you ever stop asking questions? You're like Eyewitness News or something."

She almost smiled, almost sank back into the seat and rattled off a smart-ass answer. But his eyes stopped her. They were still brown human irises swirling with emotion.

"I'm just an ordinary woman trying to make sense of all this," she said quietly.

"No," he said seriously. "There's nothing ordinary about you, Kalina."

Below the city, through tunnels that used to belong to an old outdated line of the subway, the two of them walked.

"They've had him for hours now. What do you think they're going to do with him?"

"Kill him," Darel said without another thought.

"Shit. So what are we going to do about that?"

"Nothing to do."

"You're kidding, right? He's our partner. We can't just let him go down like this."

"He shouldn't have strayed from the plan. I told him how we were going to get her. He knows what Sabar's orders were."

"So? He was trying to get the job done. You're saying we should just let him die," Chi argued.

"I'm saying we don't have a choice," Darel told Chi seriously. "Look, you don't know what screwing Sabar over will get you. Those shadows are probably going to be a lot more merciful with him than Sabar would have been. So count his stupid ass as being lucky."

"Dying's not lucky. And leaving your partner down is just foul."

"I'm not discussing this," Darel said finally. "We've got other shit to do. Sabar's not pleased with our botched attempts to get that bitch. We need to tread lightly with him right now or we'll be just as dead as Chavez."

She'd risen in status from trick to bitch, only because he'd watched her shower again this morning. Darel hadn't seen her naked in weeks, and only on the days that Sabar allowed him to keep watch. Usually it was the head Rogue who liked to watch her, got his rocks off in his car by doing so.

This morning it had been Darel, in his car all alone. The bugs and cameras were now in place inside her apartment, giving Sabar some info to use when he finally captured her. Even though Darel had no idea how that info was going to help in what Sabar had planned.

At any rate he'd watched her lather up a sponge and drag it over every crevice of her body. His beast had roared for release until he'd had no choice but to free his own burgeoning erection, rubbing and stroking to the sight of her. The release had been powerful and painful, an urge he'd slaked just because it was there. One he didn't want to have, but would act on regardless. He wasn't happy about Chavez being caught and he was even less happy that it was this bitch who'd put him in that position to start with. So no, he shouldn't want to fuck her senseless, but he did. He wanted to pound inside her until he hurt her, until she bled and cried out for help.

Just like those two the night before.

That had been delicious, the drum of arousal in his ears, the feel of their hot flesh beneath his hands, the scent of their horrific fear in his nostrils. They'd all been aroused and angry and feasted on the two hookers without qualm. The killing may have gone over the top, but even that had felt good. To each of them.

Now it was just two of them, but they would have a chance at a feast like that again. Soon. And when he and Chi took Kalina Harper, they'd make her sorry that her worthless lover and his goons had killed their friend.

"Where are we going now?"

"To collect Sabar's money."

"We're in the freakin' sewers, man. Who collects like this? We aren't dime store dealers."

"No, we're not," Darel answered. "But those shadows are looking for us. We'd be fools to go walking right out in front of them. We need to get in here and get out."

"What if he doesn't have the money?" Chi asked as they came upon a rickety stairwell he knew led to another manhole that opened into an alley right beside a parking garage in downtown DC.

"Then we take it from him and shut his dumb lying-ass mouth for good. Just like we did the good senator," he said.

Chi smiled, climbing the stairs behind him. "Yeah, that was sweet the way you ripped that guy's throat out."

Lifting up a hand to reach the manhole, Darel looked back. "He's not threatening to talk anymore, now is he?"

He pushed the manhole open and streams of sunlight filled the dark shaft as Chi laughed.

Hell no, Senator Baines wasn't talking anymore, and neither was his daughter who'd made the mistake of calling Chi an animal as he'd fucked her. They'd both grown quiet as they choked on their own blood. A sound Chi would never grow tired of hearing.

Chapter 22

This time Kalina was helped out of the truck by another man. He was as tall as Rome with an even bigger build. His skin was dark and his eyes even darker as he reached for her hand while she stepped down. The minute she was on the ground Rome was beside her and the other man dropped her hand like a hot coal. Rome nodded and the other man moved around to the back of the truck—getting her bags, she presumed. Rome's hand slid to her elbow as he guided her toward the front doors.

She felt like royalty, but not. Every man around her seemed to cater to her but didn't say a word, as if these commands were simply known. It wasn't a world she understood and didn't know if she really wanted to. What was absolutely clear to her was that Rome was no ordinary lawyer or citizen, and neither were the people around him.

It was a massive estate and looked even more palatial than it had when she was here before. Kalina hadn't taken a good look last night, but today she absorbed every detail. From the plump shrubs crowding the five steps she walked up, to the large, glossy double doors that opened slowly as they approached.

Another man, tall with leathery skin and keen eyes, looked at her this time.

"Ms. Harper, what a pleasure to finally meet you," he said, extending his hand to her. For a minute she thought he'd looked to Rome for permission, but instead it was Rome's hand that fell from her side. She reached out and shook the older man's hand, muttering a timid "Hello."

He knew who she was, that was obvious, but she had no idea what Rome had told the man about her. Or why he'd talk about her in the first place. This all seemed surreal, her here with her prime suspect, on his personal turf. The DEA couldn't have planned a better sting.

"Call me Baxter," the older man said as he escorted her through the foyer. "Whatever you need I will take care of. You will be most comfortable here."

"Thank you, Baxter," she said, but she wasn't sure how long he thought she'd be staying.

"Take her bags to my room," she heard Rome say from behind.

"I don't get a choice of where I sleep?" she asked. She was treated to all three men staring at her in response.

No one answered. Rome simply nodded again and the man moved on with the bags. What was it with him and the nodding commands? And why did they all obey him so easily?

"Are you hungry?" Baxter asked, interrupting her thoughts.

"No, thank you," she responded.

"Then I'll get you a drink. Mr. Roman, she looks tired. She should rest." Baxter spoke and then he was gone.

Just like that, she thought. The feel of this place was one of quiet authority, which she figured she'd be subject to for as long as she was here.

"He didn't even ask what kind of drink I liked," she said when it appeared she and Rome were alone.

They were still in the foyer with its glossy dark marbled floors and cranberry-painted walls. There were no pictures or paintings on these walls but every couple of feet along the one wall were podiums with marble statues on top. She walked closer to one, touching the rounded head of a black cat.

"He already knows what you would like to drink," she heard Rome's deep voice say from behind.

Her fingers trailed over the cool object, along the line of its back, around the muzzle of its face. "He doesn't know me."

"Baxter knows things about everyone."

She turned at those words. "What is he?"

"He is not a shifter," Rome answered.

"Is he like a psychic?"

"I don't really know. He's always been here with me, so I've gotten used to his sixth sense. You'll get used to it as well."

"Don't count on it," she mumbled but had turned to the statue again. "I have more questions."

Rome hadn't doubted that. All the way out here he'd chastised himself for telling her, but there'd been no other choice. He hadn't been able to hold back every part of his cat when he'd seen the man attempting to hurt her. Just like that night in the alley. He'd revealed himself to her once again. And even though it would jeopardize their entire people, he knew he would tell her even more.

"Let's go upstairs."

She paused. Going upstairs with him meant something. It meant that she was not only agreeing to stay here with him, she was agreeing to *stay* with him.

Was that what she wanted? To be Roman Reynolds's woman?

If she'd been asked that question this morning or even earlier this afternoon, she would have probably said yes instantly. Right now, after seeing what she'd seen an hour ago, she wasn't sure.

"You knew who I was all along, didn't you?" she asked.

He approached her and Kalina stood her ground. He moved with a fluidness she'd thought was simply confidence before. Now it appeared to be something else, like carefully measured steps bringing not only his physical form but everything that lingered inside him closer to her.

"It feels like I've known you forever."

Inside she sighed. Outside it was important that her resolve stay in place.

"Why?" He was close enough that her body was having its usual drop-everything-and-get-naked spasms. "Why me? And why didn't you tell me that first day in your office?"

"It's complicated" was his reply.

"Life usually is," she quipped.

"That night, two years ago, I just happened to be there. I wasn't following you then."

That could be true, she surmised. But what were the odds that two years later he'd end up being the subject of her investigation? Considering where she was at this very moment, the odds were pretty damn good.

"You saved my life."

He cupped her cheek with one hand. "I'm glad I did."

The instant response to his touch sealed the deal for her. Not the intense heat that was steadily building, but the tender acceptance that seemed to uncurl inside her. The feeling that made her want to say *Finally*.

She pulled away, turned from him, and headed toward the stairs. As she took the first ones she berated herself for remembering part of the layout of this house. For knowing that his room would be to the left as soon as she got to the top; down the hallway at the very end would be the door. But as she walked and knew he was close by, she felt desired, needed, empowered.

Rome walked behind her, his slow steps quiet. But he was there, he was with her, his essence accompanying her as she moved. Kalina let that feeling mingle inside, finding there was a part of her that enjoyed it, relished this procession, like a duo finally joined.

Inside, she looked around again, taking measured steps around this room that belonged to him. She'd studied him for so long, read every article, every work-up the department had done on this man—and yet right now felt like she was just meeting the real Roman Reynolds.

These walls were dark, like the interior of the house seemed to be. He had lots of books, everything from Shakespeare to Carl Weber. There were law manuals and research guides. She smiled as her fingers traced the spine of the *Idiot's Guide to Meditation*. She could certainly see the reserved and brooding Rome meditating in here.

The feeling was that of a sanctuary, a solitary place where he could be exactly what he wanted to be. A huge bed on a platform sat in the center of the room. She remembered that bed and what had happened between them in it. Walking past she stayed on the lower level of the room and passed his desk on her way to the patio doors. There was heavy brocade drapery that when closed she suspected kept all sunlight out. It was late afternoon and the drapes were partially open. She pushed them open all the way and sucked in her breath at the view.

It felt like she should be in a country house with all the lush greenery and the tips of full-grown trees she could see. It was open space then woods, a place where a big cat would like to run.

She turned and wasn't surprised to see him standing a few feet behind her, his stance casual, hands slipped into the pockets of his slacks, chest moving evenly with every breath he took. He looked like some kind of god with his chiseled mocha-toned face and probing eyes. Lust slid through her as if she'd had that drink Baxter promised her and it was something of the alcohol family. Only she didn't want anything about this moment impaired. She wanted the entire truth from him, because maybe, just maybe she hadn't been crazy for the last two years. Maybe there really was a big cat protecting her. And if so, her next question would be why.

"Why are you here? Or should I say, always there when I need help?" She'd almost said *need you* but didn't feel entirely comfortable admitting that just yet.

"Our kind come from the Gungi rain forest in Brazil. We're born and most often raised there."

"In the jungle?" she asked incredulously even though she knew there were human tribes living around the rain forests.

"We are a species that has been around for a couple

of hundred years, a complex blend of human and animal. As you can understand, I'm sure, this is not common knowledge."

"Who else knows about your kind?"

"Nobody, or at least no humans. And we'd like to keep it that way."

"I want to see," she said without hesitation. "I want to see what you are. Right here, right now."

He frowned, and she knew he was preparing to say no. Taking a deep breath, she licked her lips and continued, "I've dreamed of you. Ever since that night two years ago, I've seen you in my dreams. Your eyes, your body. The muscled body of a cat. I've carried you with me all this time and I . . ." Her voice wavered for just an instant. "I'd like to see right here in the light of day while I'm fully awake that I'm not cr . . . crazy."

A tiny smile tilted his lips and Kalina wanted to groan with the instant punch of arousal that speared through her. This had to be insanity as well, the way she continuously wanted him as if the two times before hadn't been enough. Knowing what she now thought she knew about him, it was even stranger.

"You're not crazy," he said, taking steps to close the distance between them.

She laughed nervously. "I can't tell. I mean really, first I'm in an alley being attacked, then here comes this . . . I don't know. I hear roaring. Can you imagine that? Roaring like I'm in the jungle or something. Then I see—no I don't really see it—" She felt like she was back in the therapist's office, sitting on that fake-suede coach trying to dig deep enough into herself to tell the old bearded man what really happened. But she couldn't. Yet now, she could.

"I saw you over me, grabbing him by his neck." Rome was standing right in front of her now, his height towering inches over her own. Another time she might have felt like he was crowding her, but today she didn't. His presence, this close, felt just right.

"Huge teeth and jaws and the man's face went from shock to stark fear. When I saw your eyes, I closed mine." Her voice was getting lower as the words came faster, her heart thumping. "I could hear the sounds and I felt the rain, splattering my face and my arms. My blouse was ripped so I felt cold all over. I wanted to get up, to run as fast as I could, but my body wasn't working at first. There were these other sounds, like little growls, and I opened my eyes again." Telling the story again after all this time had her trembling. Rome took her in his arms, rubbing his hands up and down her back. Tilting her head just slightly, she looked right into Rome's face. "It was you. You were there, pacing, making those noises. Almost like you wanted to run, too, to leave that alley and just run."

"I frightened you," he whispered, lifting one of her hands to his lips and kissing her fingers.

"No," she replied. "I don't think I was afraid of you. Of a feeling, I think." A feeling that had started from someplace deep inside her the moment she looked into the eyes of the cat.

"I'm sorry," he said.

She was shaking her head. "No. It wasn't your fault. I mean, you saved my life."

He still held her hand and with his other his fingers

feathered over her jaw. "I will always protect you, Kalina. Always."

Kalina felt dizzy, like everything around her was spinning. Inside her body was on fire with need. But her mind craved more. She needed this confrontation, needed to end the speculation once and for all. "Please," she whispered, turning her face slightly so that her lips brushed along his fingers.

He didn't speak, just moved from her, showing her his back as he walked away. When he was close to the platform of the bed he stopped. She held her breath in anticipation. His shirt fell from his shoulders first, and she watched the muscles of his back bunch and contract as he bent over to remove his shoes and socks. Her nipples tightened when his slacks drifted past his hips, down his thighs, along with his underwear. If she thought he was a gorgeous specimen in clothes, out of them he was beyond words. Even a full back view was enticing enough to have her nipples puckering. Tight buttocks dimpled as strong thighs moved to kick the clothes farther away from him.

Then it happened. Right in front of her eyes, the six-foot-two-and-a-half-inch man dropped to the floor and shifted to a large cat.

The transition was swift, an elongating of bones she barely heard cracking. Dark fur rippled along the surface that was seconds ago smooth skin. The cat was as long as Rome was tall with a hulking body that gave the impression of being very heavy. But that was just the physical.

Even though her heart beat so loud she was sure Baxter could hear it from wherever he was in this house,

Kalina walked toward the cat that now swished its long tail and turned to her.

She kept going until she was standing not even a foot away from it and could do nothing but sigh. Her shoulders sagged as she felt a tremendous weight being lifted. Going to her knees and letting her bottom fall back on the heels of her feet, she simply stared.

He was beautiful. Majestic. Regal. Powerful.

She reached out a hand and touched the huge circumference of his face, her fingers shaking only slightly as the softness of the fur tickled her skin. It was like onyx, this dark, smooth, thick fur that covered him, and yet she could see darker spots here and there. He made a grunting sound and the warmth of his breath from flaring nostrils drifted over her skin.

Kalina had always been afraid of cats. If she'd see a cat walking on her side of the street she'd quickly cross to the other. Mrs. Gilbert's pudgy feline scared her on a daily basis, and yet here she was, with the head of what she presumed was a black jaguar in the palm of her hand.

Rubbing past his head, her small hands trembled along his back and down his sides. The pattern of rosettes was visible, giving him a distinct exotic look. To say she was amazed would have been an understatement.

Everything about him said strength and control and— she realized with a jolt piercing throughout her body with only a small amount of confusion—lust. Something, somewhere deep inside her rose, standing at attention. Her gaze found that of the cat once more and held. They were the eyes she'd seen in her dream, the ones she knew so well, and they were staring back at her. He made a chuffing sound, rubbing his head along the palm of her hand, and her heart raced. The flattened nostrils of his nose flared as he sniffed. Then the head moved closer, pushing past her hand and rubbing along the inside of her arm. The fur was so soft it sent shivers up her arm to trickle down her spine.

He sniffed again, this time closer to her breasts, and Kalina swore her own nostrils moved as well, searching for a scent she could recognize. And it was there, not completely to her surprise. A faint scent filtered in the air around them, a sweet sort of musk that once it reached inside her body had everything growing warm. That part of her that seemed to have risen to meet this animal part of him was at full attention now, pushing against the barriers of her human skin with an urgency that Kalina could not contain.

She dropped her arms to her sides as his head continued to move over her chest and down her torso. At her midsection he gave a little push and she instinctively opened her legs. He came closer, that chuffing sound muffled against the inside of her thigh. When his head settled between her legs, his nose at her center, Kalina shivered, her breath catching, nipples tightening. The scent permeating the air melted inside her like some liquid drug and she felt her body going limp against the floor.

She'd stretched out, watching as the big cat stood over her, stalking around her in slow languid movements. His eyes were intense as they raked over her body. When he paused at her feet Kalina wondered what would happen next. She struggled to differentiate between the sound thoughts of a human female and the rising sensations of another.

As quickly as he'd transformed from the man to the cat, the man returned in all his naked splendor. Above

her Rome stood with one strong hand cupping his elongated arousal. She licked her lips, her tongue eager to
touch the engorged tip, to lick its thick length.

He went to his knees, stretched his body along the
length of hers, keeping the bulk of his weight off her by
propping up on his elbows. Her arms were flat at her
sides but she lifted her head, anticipating his kiss.

"This is what I am," he whispered, staring down at
her as the words tumbled from his lips.

He was the handsome attorney with the sharp suits
and keen wit. He was the dominant yet considerate
lover who had made her come with just the touch of his
hand. He was the beast who'd haunted her dreams. And
he was exactly who she wanted.

Shifting to bring a hand up, she touched her fingers
over his jaw, let them trail until they feathered over his
lips. "This is who I want," she replied.

His head lowered and their lips collided in a hungry
kiss. She gripped the back of his head, pulling him closer,
trying to get deeper. She craved his taste, wanted every
bit of his tongue in an attempt to quench this persistent
thirst.

He gave her everything: lips, tongue, moans, nipping
teeth that had her hissing at their contact. Her body
trembled, aching to be touched, taken. As if he'd read
her mind his hands began to move frantically over her
body, severing their kiss while he worked. Her pants
and panties were stripped quickly from her bottom; she
toed off her shoes during the process. He grabbed the
hem of her shirt, pulling it roughly over her head. His
teeth found the sensitive skin of her neck and traced a
stinging path of heat down to the crevice between her
breasts. With her chest heaving, her back arching to

meet his assault, she heard a snap and felt her bra slip from her body.

Rome took a bare breast into his mouth, suckling so deeply the turgid nipple burned. Simultaneously he cupped the other breast, squeezing just as tightly. Kalina's thighs shook, her pussy creaming with expectancy. She gasped and clamped her hands onto his shoulders as he continued his assault.

"Mine," she thought she heard him mumble as his lips moved from her breast down her torso to where his tongue stroked longingly over her navel.

His palms still held her breasts, and she lifted her hands to his wrists to keep them there. With each stroke of his tongue over her skin, she felt a new layer of herself being peeled away. Nothing was the same, not the sound of his voice, the feel of his kisses, the sensations rippling through her body. It was all different, new, vibrant in a way she'd never imagined.

When he nipped along the line of her juncture she cried out his name and realized her throat felt hoarse, like she'd been yelling and yelling for hours. She moved her head from side to side, seeming to go in slow motion as flashes of scenes filtered through her mind.

A picturesque jungle. Majestic cats standing together in unity. A colony. A whole new world.

His hands left her breasts to spread the plump folds of her pussy until cool air whispered over the tightened bud at her center. When the flat of his tongue covered that nub everything inside Kalina rushed forward, raging as the sound of a vicious waterfall rumbled in her ears. He licked again and again, using the full length of his tongue. She arched from the floor panting and screaming as each stroke pushed her closer and closer, until she was finally freefalling over the edge. Falling and falling only to land with swift efficiency on her feet.

The landing was like an awakening and Kalina's body fully responded.

Grasping his head she worked her hips over his mouth, directing his strokes and begging for more.

Chapter 23

Rome felt the shift, felt the exact moment Kalina's cat had taken charge inside her. It was a silent challenge, a hello-baby-I'm-home. And he was there, completely game for their meeting.

Thrusting two fingers inside her, he continued to work the nub at the hood of her center. She was pumping against him, giving him every angle, taking the pleasure she'd so longed for. With his other hand he found her rear, touching the tight entrance timidly at first, waiting to hear her response, then pressing farther when her breathing hitched.

He slid one finger inside her rear while the other hand worked her core until her essence was dripping. He wanted to lap at the thick honey flowing from her, but wanted to prepare her for his taking even more. So instead he pressed another finger into her rear, scissoring them to stretch her farther.

"I need you now," a voice deeper than hers whispered. She moaned and it was a guttural sound, a rasping sound that rubbed over his body like a silken cloth.

"Not yet, baby. I'm hungry for you, too, but dammit, not yet," he said through clenched teeth, wanting to sink his dick deep inside her warmth with an urgency that threatened his sanity.

But there was something else, some part of him that

knew this was a defining moment, that what he did to her, what she did to him at this time would take them both to a place foreign to them. He couldn't stop it but that didn't mean he knew how to handle it, how Kalina would handle it. They'd known each other officially for about a week now, but unofficially it seemed like forever.

Unknowingly his cat had been in search of hers—the man in search of the perfect female. He'd never had admitted it, not to anyone. Except at this very moment there was no room for denial. He couldn't—not that he'd ever considered this an option in any facet of his life—run from the inevitable.

She bucked beneath him and his body tensed, his balls drawing so tight he could barely swallow. The tip of his dick dripped with pleasure as his fingers moved through her silken heat. Her scent permeated the air, mixing with his, combining to form the *calor*. Together it was intoxicating, this scent that sealed their mating.

From this moment on Rome would not be able to keep his hands off her. She was in his blood now, her cat mingling with his, the female joining with the male. No other males could touch her now even though they'd pick up her scent and translate it as her being in heat. They'd want her, crave her, but die a quick death if they dared touch her.

For her, she would ache for him, her body would forever be ready for his touch, his taking, almost to the point of pain whenever they were near. And when they were apart her scent would thicken, sending out a message for him to come to her. Another male venturing near her would get an extreme reaction—either her intense arousal or rabid anger. Both would be dangerous to anyone other than her mate.

That was the way of their mating. Shadow Shifters mated for life.

And as Kalina arched up off the floor, her hazel eyes turning golden, touching their heat to him wherever their gaze landed, he knew he'd have it no other way. This was his *companheiro* and nobody was going to take her away from him. He'd protect her with everything he was, that was a promise.

"Rome, please," she panted, his name a sweet whisper to Rome's ears.

"Yes, baby," he crooned, slipping his fingers from her then lifting her to carry her to his bed.

With the utmost care Rome lay her on the bed, but the she-cat would not have it easy. She rolled over, coming up on her knees, offering her luscious bottom to him. Then looking over her shoulder with eyes glossed with lust and hunger, she said, "Take me, now!"

He wouldn't deny her, couldn't even if he wanted to and he definitely did not want to. There was nothing in all this world—Rome was absolutely positive—more beautiful than the sight of his woman's ass poised and waiting for him.

Inside his beast thrashed, slashing him with stinging lashes of hunger, need. He almost roared but bared his teeth instead, feeling the prick of their sharpness against his bottom lip. Stepping closer to the bed, he grabbed the soft cheeks of her behind, pulling them apart so he could see the slightly stretched rear entrance. His mouth watered with anticipation, his dick straining for admittance.

Rome wanted to go slow, to be easy with her, gentle even, but wasn't sure he could. Need tore through him, and the second his tip touched the tight entrance his entire body heated. He pushed slowly, holding her hips still while he made the first attempts at entry. Her tightness gripped him, sucking him in the moment she had a small taste.

Kalina pushed back and he slipped deeper inside.

"Damn, so tight, so deliciously tight," he whispered.

"More," she demanded.

Rome thrust his hips a little, still holding back, not wanting to rush her acceptance of him. Spreading her wider, he glanced down and almost lost the last remnants of his control at the sight of his thickness stretching her, filling her. Her body welcomed him, like a hungry mouth, opening wider to take him completely.

His legs trembled, his mouth watering as he leaned forward and licked a heated line up her spine. She arched and moaned. He continued licking over her, loving the musky-and-sweet blended taste of her skin. She was smooth and hot and eager for him to take her completely as she rotated her ass over his dick. He pushed farther, planting his length deeper into her rear. His teeth nipped her shoulder blade and she screamed his name.

"Please, if you don't take me now, I'm going to die." She was panting, her body bucking back against him. "Now, dammit!"

"Gato inferno," he mumbled against her skin, bracing his feet, planting his stance, preparing to thrust deep one final time. "My little hellcat," he repeated in English, the Portuguese rolling from his tongue as if he spoke the traditional shifter language every day of his life.

"Yes!" she murmured, her fingers clenching in the sheets, her back arching upward.

Rome licked her again and again, absorbing her taste and scent at the same time. He thrust deep inside her and was rewarded when her head snapped back and a long slow moan escaped her lips. He couldn't hold back another second, pumping fast and deep inside her; every muscle in his body bunched and contracted with the motion.

Kalina moved with him, hungrily matching his thrusts with her own. She was wild and hot and everything he'd seen in her eyes. He'd known this passion was in her, waiting to be unleashed. And now he'd unleashed it, he'd captured the hellcat and was marking her, making her his.

Reaching an arm around her waist, he slipped downward, finding her moistened center, brushing past plump lips to find her drenched with arousal. Pushing two fingers inside her pussy, Rome grit his teeth as her rear gripped him tighter. He pumped her fiercely now from both directions, loving the feel of power, of dominance pouring through him.

But Kalina would not be taken, she was determined to give back all that she received. With Rome filling her both ways she wanted to scream with pleasure as spiky tendrils of desire ripped through her. She pumped his fingers and his dick, loving the fullness and completeness he brought her. Her head thrashed and she was making sounds that didn't sound entirely human to her ears but she didn't care.

Nothing mattered, nothing but this man, at this time. She was completely open to him, taking all that he gave. At the same time she was giving him something, a part of her she hadn't even known existed. Sure there was a sexual craving, but Kalina sensed this was so much more. Her body responded to his every touch, her nostrils flaring at his scent, longing for him even more.

It was a sweet salty aroma that permeated the room now and it fed her, pushing her to go farther, to break past barriers she'd erected in her mind.

He wasn't what he seemed—not from the first time she'd met him. And yet she felt instinctively that neither was she. At least not this way. Kalina had never imagined herself loving like this, needing like this. She'd never imagined Roman Reynolds.

Now, with him planted so firmly inside her, steadily stroking the heat in her until she threatened to implode, she could not imagine being without him.

His fingers ministered to her, thrusting deep inside her pussy until her thighs shook with longing. In her rear he stroked her long and deep, with measured thrusts that swept her up into mindless pleasure.

Her release came quickly, ripping through her body like an unexpected storm. She screamed with its intensity, letting every nuance of pleasure rack through her entirely. Rome leaned over her, thrusting even faster.

"That's right, my little hellcat. Feel that. Feel us."

Oh she did, she felt it everywhere, from the spikes of her hair to the tips of her toes. Her body trembled in response as he continued to work her.

"Feel me and no other," he murmured, his lips close to her ear. "No other. Ever!"

His words were dominant and insistent. She heard them with different ears, not of the woman, but of something else, and she roared, turning her head slightly to nip at his lips.

He took her mouth, thrusting his tongue as deep as his dick and fingers still were in her. She returned his fervor, their tongues dueling even as he worked her sex until she threatened to come again.

When he tore his lips from hers she made a sound of protest and thought she saw him bare his teeth—sharp teeth that then sank into her shoulder. The contact was instantly painful, mixing beautifully with the pleasure soaring through her from her sexual release.

He pumped harder, faster, then roared himself, his tongue licking over the spot where he'd bit her.

"My *companheiro,*" she thought she heard him whisper before pulling them both down onto the bed.

Kalina didn't know what that meant but it couldn't be bad because Rome wrapped her in his arms, holding her tightly against him. And she lay there, not wanting to move or question or even think about what sleeping with a half man, half cat would do to her.

Chapter 24

"Tell me something," he asked when they'd lain in silence for too long.

"Hmm," she murmured, her cheek against his naked chest, her bare legs entangled with his.

"Is this a part of your investigation?"

She stiffened.

"What do you mean?"

"I mean the investigation the DEA has you conducting on me. Is sleeping with me going into the reports?"

She tried to get up, to move away in lieu of answering, but Rome held her tight. His arms had been wrapped around her. She'd cooed as he pulled her closer after their mutual release. Now she wanted to bolt. Well, that was just too damn bad.

"Was sleeping with me the next step since you couldn't break into my computer?"

Kalina remained silent, her heartbeat thumping wildly against his chest. She was thinking of a response. It wouldn't be a lie; he didn't pick up that rancid stench. She would tell the truth, but he sensed she wasn't going to enjoy doing so.

"This wasn't how it was supposed to turn out," she said, her voice almost too quiet for him to hear.

"What was your plan? Find the incriminating evidence on my computer then have me arrested? You'd receive accolades, maybe a promotion, be the biggest, baddest female cop on the force because you'd brought down the infamous Roman Reynolds." He couldn't help the edge his voice had taken on. Since learning of her betrayal, he'd been on a roller coaster of emotions trying to figure out what his reaction should and would be.

On the ride over to her place, he was unable to think of anything but the possible danger she might be in. Once he had her safely in his grasp, he couldn't think past fucking her. Now, sated and secure in her safety, he was pissed the hell off.

She tried to break free of his hold again and this time he let her. Running wasn't going to help, he could guarantee that.

Pulling some of the sheet with her, she wrapped her naked body and slid a few inches away from him. The fact that she didn't get off the bed and head for the door instantly told him a lot about her. That spunk he'd seen in her that night in his office was full-blown confidence now. The way she lifted her head and squared her chin said she had no regrets and he'd probably not be hearing an apology fall from her still-kiss-swollen lips.

"The DEA planted me at your firm to find out who you're sending money to in Brazil."

"Who do they think I'm sending it to?"

"A drug cartel. They don't know which one."

"Did you find the evidence you needed?"

She sighed, smoothing a hand over the back of her hair. "No."

"Really? I would have thought that sleeping with me and doing as good a job of it as you did, you'd have the keys to my safe and personal access to all my accounts by now. Tell me, did how many times I made you come make it into your report?"

"Don't be crass. It's so beneath you," she said, turning to toss him a cold glare over her shoulder. "To answer your question, even though I don't know why I should since I clearly was not the only one lying in this . . . whatever you call what we're doing. Anyway, I did not plan this. Sleeping with you was not on my agenda."

Rome didn't even breathe a sigh of relief, because he'd known that all along. Kalina was not the type of woman who would do anything she didn't absolutely want to. And judging by all the sex toys he'd spied in the bedroom at her apartment, she wasn't missing any sexual fulfillment by not being with a man. No, Rome was positive she'd wanted him, right from the start. She hadn't liked that idea, not one bit. Now he knew she had reason to be resistant. Still, the idea that the feds were attempting to investigate him for something as ridiculous as drug trafficking still grated on his nerves.

"Why didn't you just tell me when I caught you trying to break into my computer?"

"Oh I don't know, probably the same reason you didn't rush to tell me you were a human shape shifter."

"Not the same," he replied, quickly folding his arms behind his head as he watched her. "So if you don't close this case, you don't get the big promotion?"

"How did you know about the promotion? How did you find out I'm a cop? Or used to be one. After this, who knows what I'll end up doing. Maybe flipping burgers right beside the high school kids."

"You graduated from high school and went right into the academy. From there you started out as a beat cop, tumbled onto a few dealers who turned state's evidence and gave you their big boss. Moved up to narcotics about five years ago. You were working a case to bring down one of the Cortez Cartel's biggest street hustlers when the sting went bad and you were attacked in that alley."

Somewhere around his second sentence she'd turned and looked at him. "Thorough background check your firm does on its employees, huh."

Rome shook his head. "I'm a Faction Leader for the shifters."

"What does that mean?"

"I guess you could say I'm the leader of all the stateside shifters on the East Coast. That means I'm privy to a lot of classified information, especially when it threatens us."

"I'm not a threat to you," she said. "Not anymore. I mean—" Taking a deep breath, she let it out in a quick whoosh. "I don't have any evidence to convict you. My report will say that. I'll go back to the MPD and you can go back to whatever it is you really are doing in South America."

"I help support my people in the rain forest. The money I send buys supplies and food and weapons so they can defend themselves and our secret."

"Then why do they think you're supporting a drug cartel instead?"

Rome figured it might have something to do with the meetings his father had with an associate of Raul Cortez. But even Rome didn't know what had transpired at that meeting. He didn't know what his father had told that man or what was supposed to come of the meeting. Bingham had only given him Cortez's name, nothing more. The old man simply didn't know any more, and Rome accepted that. If his father didn't tell him, Baxter, or even his mother what he was doing, the odds that he'd tell his lawyer were slim. So it looked like whatever had transpired years ago was about to come to light and the shifters would be the ones dealing with the repercussions. Not if he could help it.

"I don't know" was his reply, because until he had more to go on than a name and an appointment in a journal he wasn't talking about this situation, especially not with a cop.

Kalina waited a beat and figured she'd just been lied to. But that was fair, she figured; she was now the enemy. Which made the feelings she now knew she had for him even more difficult to deal with. So without another word she slid off the bed, taking the sheet with her as she moved closer to her clothes.

"Look, I can get a uniform to sit outside my apartment and keep watch. I'll report the pictures and Ferrell's weirdo act this afternoon and all will be well. I don't have to stay here." Bending over, she began picking up her clothes that were strewn about the floor.

She gasped when a strong arm came around her waist, pulling her upright against the hardness of his body.

"You're not going back there alone."

"This is ridiculous," she said even though her body was saying something totally different. This desire for him was getting worse, like a craving that just wouldn't go away. And she wanted it to, oh how she wanted it to. Because despite what she was feeling physically, this thing between them would never work. "I have to get out of here."

Her voice sounded desperate and almost frantic to her ears. She couldn't stand it.

"I won't hurt you."

Oh, but he already had, she wanted to say. His accusations, although basically true and brought on by her own dishonesty, had hurt. The fact that he thought she could sleep with him as a part of her job hurt. The fact that she ended up sleeping with him as a result of her job was embarrassing and painful. And the mere thought that he wouldn't want her anymore because of everything he'd learned about her was going to make her physically sick in just a few minutes.

"It doesn't matter," she said, trying to pull away from him.

"It does." He loosened his grip on her only slightly, so that she could breathe but she still couldn't break free. "I asked you to trust me before, I'm going to ask you to do it again."

She was shaking her head. "I can't. And you don't trust me. So we're even."

"I trust you," he said solemnly. Then as if to show the truth to his words, he let her go.

Kalina spun around and looked at him in all his naked splendor. She simply stared, wondering what was about to come out of his mouth, seeing in flashes the beast he'd turned into, remembering with startling clarity the compassionate lover he'd been. "Why?"

"Because I can scent a lie miles away. Because I knew from that moment I saw you in the alley there was something special about you. Because like it or not somebody is after you and I think that somebody is a shifter."

"What? Why would a shifter be after me? It's probably one of the dealers from that night. One who didn't get busted."

"Then what does he want with you now?"

"Revenge."

Rome shook his head. "No. They wouldn't wait two years to get back at you. He would have struck sooner. This is about something else. When did you get the first pictures?"

Thinking, Kalina tilted her head as she looked up at him. "The day I met you in your office."

"Whatever they want from you is personal. Ticked anybody off lately?" he asked, his lips lifting into a small smile she suspected was meant to lighten the mood.

As far as after sex banter went—this was rating a low three at best.

With a heavy sigh, she admitted, "I don't know anybody to tick off."

"What does that mean? You have to have friends, family. Somebody who'd get angry with you at some point."

It was Kalina's turn to shake her head. "I thought you did your research," she said, but it was spoken so low it lost any biting sarcasm she might have attempted. "I have no family and the only person I know is Mrs. Gilbert, my neighbor. I don't socialize much."

"Why?"

This had turned into a question-and-answer session, but she really hadn't expected him to ask her that. "I don't know. I just don't do well with people or relationships or something like that." Why couldn't she just say she was afraid to give herself to anyone in any capacity, in case they left her just like her parents did?

For a few seconds Rome was utterly silent.

"I can relate to that."

"No, you can't. You're *the* Roman Reynolds, playboy attorney, richer than most and on every woman's to-do list. I'm sure you have no problem with relationships."

"Relationships that count," he said solemnly. "You're quoting the tabloids and making assumptions. I have very few relationships that count, Kalina."

"Why? You have everything. What reason could you possibly have for being as reserved as I am?"

"No amount of money or success can block out the pain. If something has hurt you, odds are you're never really going to get over that hurt." He shrugged. "I've resigned myself to that fact and I function accordingly."

"And does 'function accordingly' mean sleeping with women then moving on?" Her lips snapped shut. That question had just sort of rolled out. She'd been thinking it and there it was. To his credit Rome didn't look too affected by her words.

"That's been my past experience."

"And now? What's this for you now, Rome?" Because she really needed to know. For her, it was getting too deep. What she'd been feeling as she'd lay in his arms, the thoughts growing steadily in her mind, were so much more than she'd ever anticipated in her life. Much more than she'd ever been willing to risk. The least she could do was get a direct answer before suffering the disappointment.

He looked as if he were contemplating his words. "It's more than I ever thought would happen to me."

She didn't know what to say, how to respond. "Oh," she finally managed. She wanted to kick herself, it sounded so lame.

"I didn't intend for this to happen," she told him honestly. "I was just trying to do my job."

"And you love your job?"

"It's all I have." Damn, again with the slipping of the tongue. She was telling this man too much, giving him even more. It was a dangerous situation, she knew.

"Now you have me."

His words were somber, serious, and she wanted to grab hold of them, wrap herself in them, and believe that maybe, just maybe, they were true.

"I've never had anyone. My parents didn't want me and neither did most of the foster parents I lived with."

He was moving closer and she knew she should retreat, protect herself from this bad situation growing worse. But she didn't. Couldn't. His gaze, his simple presence held her still.

"My parents died when I was young," he said, coming to stand right in front of her, reaching down to take her hands in his.

"I know," she said softly.

"I was so angry when they died and I felt so alone."

Kalina shook her head. "But you weren't alone. Your housekeeper took care of you." When he looked a little stunned at her words, she shrugged. "I did a lot of research on you."

He smiled. "We're some pair, huh? You investigating me and me following you."

"Not really a match made in heaven," she added with a tentative smile of her own.

"But we're a match," Rome said, his warm breath whispering over her face as he moved in. "We belong together, Kalina. Without knowing the why or how, we belong together. I believe that."

And God help her, so did she.

Closing her eyes as his lips touched hers, Kalina thought, *We belong together.*

Kalina's cover was officially blown.

Rome didn't want her back in the office, which was fine. She'd found about all she was going to find there. But she wasn't finished investigating. There was still a reason why the DEA was looking at Rome in the first place and she wanted to know what it was. Pulling out her cell phone, she called Agent Dorian Wilson again, this time leaving him a message letting him know it was about the case and she had a new development. Then she'd tried to call her commanding officer at the precinct, only to be told that he was out investigating a new murder.

She was still at Rome's house, in his room. He'd gone downstairs—to another meeting, he said. He seemed to have a lot of those. On the desk was a laptop, so she made her way over to turn it on. If she were at home she would have turned on her police scanner to find out what was going on that the top brass wasn't in the precinct at near ten in the morning.

While she waited for the computer to boot up, she thought about last night. Of all the things she'd discovered and how they made her feel in the light of day. She felt rejuvenated, actually, like a new person in her old body. It was weird and almost too good to be true. But Rome wasn't angry with her for betraying him, he still wanted her—a fact that thoroughly baffled her. She'd never been wanted before, never felt the completeness of a union of any kind. This morning she was thinking that maybe, just maybe, that was all changing.

Parts of her future were still uncertain—what she

was going to do about her job for one. The fact that she hadn't found anything incriminating against Rome—and not for lack of trying—was enough to raise a few eyebrows. That was one of the reasons she was so desperate to talk to Agent Wilson. The other was to report Ferrell and his strange and unprofessional behavior. Kalina was sure he'd been high on something yesterday when he'd come to see her. And just before Rome had come in, she'd thought she smelled a familiar scent. Which was strange in and of itself; scents weren't usually what she remembered about people. Eye color, voice tone, a strange birthmark, and even an accent were usually the traits that stuck in her memory. Yet she was almost certain it was Ferrell's scent that was ringing a bell in her head.

Noises from the laptop jolted her from her thoughts. She moved closer to the desk, fingers hovering over the keyboard in hopes of at least accessing the Internet.

She found the link to the local paper and read today's headlines.

SAVAGE KILLINGS CONTINUE IN THE DC METRO AREA

She read down farther. The article cited the brutal slayings of Senator Baines and his daughter a few weeks ago. Ralph Kensington was being linked to Baines through their mutual political ties. Yet another murder—this must be the double homicide Reed was talking about the other day—involved two suspected prostitutes, brutally killed in the same vicious manner. What did all these killings mean? The press alleged a serial killer. The police declined comment. Words like *Mafia, cartels, drug lords, retaliation, gang recruiting* all circulated through the two-page article.

A feeling of dread washed over Kalina. She kept clicking to find more information. The screen blinked furiously with her clicking as her mind seemed to move faster than the speed of the Internet connection. Then she must have hit a wrong button with all her clicking, because the screen went black, then blinked on and off. When it came back on the background was black with white pages. The pages looked like they'd been scanned and had handwriting scrawled over them. Instinctively she began to read:

Joining forces . . . governing accordingly . . . accountability . . . discretion . . . and finally a name that stuck out as if it were printed in bold block letters, Cortez.

Kalina's heart pounded as she read further. A lot of the writing she didn't understand, or rather she couldn't figure out what the writer was referring to. There were names she didn't know, only Cortez striking a chord with her. But it sounded like the writer was planning something and that maybe he needed Cortez's help.

Then a particular passage caught her attention. "My work is so that my son and those after him will know what it means to be a Shadow Shifter and to live freely with dignity among the humans. Roman will one day lead the shifters. The relationships that I form now will assist him. These human men are powerful and will be an asset to our cause."

The writer was Rome's father. Rome's father knew Cortez.

Flipping through her mental database, she pulled up

what she knew about Raul Cortez. He was only thirty-five years old, having just come into leadership of his father's organization. These documents were written when Cortez would have been only eight years old. It didn't make sense, unless . . . the writer was talking about Julio Cortez, the father of the Cortez Cartel.

She heard voices in the distance and hurriedly pushed buttons to clear the screen. The computer was still acting wacky, the screen changing colors then going back to the Internet page she'd been searching in the first place. When the voices grew closer, she simply hit ESCAPE and watched as the power died before closing the laptop.

Just as the door opened she stood. Rome walked in with two other men behind him, one his partner from the firm, Nick Delgado. She didn't know the other man and felt wary because of that fact.

Rome's gaze found hers. No matter where they were or who else was in the room with them, they found each other instantly. Moving from behind the desk, she tried for a smile but didn't really know if it worked. Her mind was tossing with all the new information she had and she wasn't quite sure how to act around Rome and his friends. Were they shifters, too?

"X thought it might be good to go over everything you know about the DEA's investigation of me and the firm," Rome said, still staring at her strangely but talking as if nothing was wrong.

She shrugged, not really comfortable telling them all she knew. Even though she didn't think Rome was guilty, there was definitely a reason he was being investigated. Seeing the name Cortez in that file sealed that deal for her. "I don't know much really. They just pulled me in, told me to trace the money and find out who he was dealing with." She wondered if she'd said enough to get herself fired. Technically her job was already on the line if her superiors found out she was telling them anything.

"Who hired you?" the one who looked like a full-back said. He was a few inches taller than Rome with a much thicker build, bald head, and fierce-looking eyes.

"I work for the MPD," she said straightening her back. No way was she letting them intimidate her.

"But the MPD aren't the ones looking at us, are they?" This was from Nick, the too-handsome playboy with smiling eyes that held a hint of danger.

"The MPD and the DEA," she offered. "I should be the one asking why. I mean, here I am trying to do my job and you turn the tables by doing an investigation on me. Who are you people?" she asked and received the pleasure of three intense gazes drilling her at once. She felt like she was displayed for sale—and that really shouldn't have made her hot.

"Nick and X are shifters, like me," Rome said.

She swallowed and looked at each man, somehow knowing Rome's words were true. They were all shifters, a species unlike any she'd ever known or read about. Now the differences were clear. The muscular builds didn't look gym-made but naturally acquired. And their stance—it was predatory. They were ready for anything, always watching, always waiting. Suddenly Rome's master suite felt just a little smaller.

"How many of you are here? In the States, I mean?"

"More than you can imagine" was Nick's reply.

"But we don't mean anybody any harm," Rome added, quickly tossing Nick an annoyed glance.

And then as if what they were saying just clicked in her head, Kalina gasped.

"What is it?" Rome asked moving closer to her.

"The murders," she said slowly. "Brutal murders, now four of them. It's all over the news."

Every step she took back he took one forward, coming closer to her until her back hit the wall.

"It's not us, Kalina. We do not kill."

"But you did," she whispered. "That night in the alley you did. You killed that man. They thought I did it. I let them think that because I didn't want to . . . to . . ."

"To what? Admit that you'd seen a man change into a cat? That's what you saw that night. A man shifting into a cat and that cat protecting the woman that was being hurt. To protect you, Kalina, I'd kill any man or cat. Believe me when I say that."

Oh, she did believe him. She looked into his eyes, saw the bunch of his shoulders, and knew he was perfectly capable of killing.

"Shadow Shifters do not kill needlessly. We are a peaceful species."

Nick smirked. "Until you piss us off."

"Think about it, Kalina," Rome said, ignoring Nick's comment and keeping his eyes on her. "Think about who I am, all that I've told you, and all that you've learned about me. Do you think I'm a killer?"

She didn't know what to think. Her brain was on information overload and her stomach was twisting and churning at the sight of three live shifters in the room with her. What if they all shifted at this very moment? Would they attack her? Would they kill her?

Then Rome touched her. His hand lightly cupping her cheek.

"Trust me, Kalina," Rome said.

He kept saying that, kept asking that of her. Why? How could she trust a man she barely knew? But she did know him, knew him in a way that wasn't conventional, wasn't scripted, and wasn't actually explainable. But did she trust him?

"The police are linking the murders by the method of the killings. They believe the brutality spells serial killer. What do you know about them?" she asked Rome, searching his eyes, his facial features, for any semblance of untruth. There was none. And she was relieved.

"I know who might be responsible."

"Like X said, Rogues," Nick put in, reminding Kalina they weren't alone, although Rome was still cupping her cheek and staring into her eyes as if they were.

A muscle clenched in his jaw and he turned from her. The loss of contact had her gasping again, and before she could stop herself she was leaning into him, her front touching his back.

"We need to pull everyone together while Elder Alamar is still here," Rome said. "Nick, you call the Faction Leaders, see what their availability is. X, you find out from that bastard Rogue you've got locked up who his boss is, tell him I'm not bullshitting with him on this. He can talk or he can . . ." Rome's words trailed off.

She heard him speaking, felt the rise in his body temperature, but couldn't tell if it was because she was touching him or if it was a reaction to his own words.

"Right," X said. "I'll take care of it."

"What about her?" Nick asked.

Kalina knew exactly what "her" he was talking about. Reluctantly breaking her contact with Rome, she stepped from behind him. "I have to go back to work."

"No."

All the men echoed in unison.

"I'm not just going to sit around here twiddling my thumbs. I still have a job." At least she hoped she did.

"You cannot go back to the station. Your investigation is over."

"Excuse me, but that's not your decision to make," she argued with Rome.

"Kalina," he said, turning to look at her. "Do you think I'm funding a drug cartel?"

"No," she answered without qualm. "But that's not the point. There are drug cartels out there and if the FBI thought you were funding them, then somebody's putting your name in the mix. Wouldn't you rather I be the one to find that information?"

"She's got a point, Rome," X said.

Rome's head snapped in the other man's direction so fast Kalina thought he was going to attack him. "She's not going to that office."

"She doesn't have to. She can set up an office and work from here," X offered.

"That's ridiculous. I need to get out into the field," Kalina argued.

"You cannot take what you know now into the field," Rome told her.

"I wasn't planning to. I mean, I'm not going to talk about you and the others. I just want to find out who's trying to frame you."

"You think it's someone other than Rogues?" Nick asked.

"Everything can't be blamed on the Rogues, Nick," Rome replied brusquely.

Kalina thought the connection was with Raul Cortez

and now the papers she'd seen on Rome's computer, but she wasn't about to tell him that. Not yet.

He wanted her to trust him, and to an extent she did. But there was something else going on here, something she wasn't even sure Rome and his cohorts knew about. So until then she would keep it under wraps.

"Who are the Rogues?" she asked, hoping to gain more info and steer them away from the part of the conversation that involved her staying in this house.

"Bad-ass shifters who think they're taking over," Nick said then cleared his throat. "They were born Shadow Shifters, but somewhere along the line thought they could do better on their own."

X intervened. "We're thinking they might be starting to make their move here in the States."

"The three that approached you at that party were Rogues. They knew who you were and followed you home. When I was at your place yesterday, I picked up their scent. They'd been there."

Putting a hand to her throat, Kalina refused to show the fear coursing through her body. "In my house? Why?" Then she remembered the pictures she'd found the night of Kensington's banquet. The pictures that were in her house and she'd wondered how they got there.

"That's what we'd like to know," X stated.

They all looked at her now, but she had to admit that they weren't looking at her like she was the enemy. More like she was the point of interest and they had to keep an eye on her if they wanted to get to the bottom of whatever was going on.

"I told Rome I didn't know those guys."

"Have you ever seen them before?"

She shook her head. Then paused, remembering the

guy who'd delivered the pictures to her apartment. No, she would know that guy anywhere. At the memory a sliver of heat eased down her spine. "No. Never," she said, clearing her throat.

"Get everyone together," Rome told X. "Tell Eli I want him to stay here with Kalina."

"Where are you going?" Nick asked Rome before Kalina could get the question out herself.

"I have something I want to check on myself."

Something, Kalina thought, that she was thinking of checking on herself. She didn't say anything, but her plan was simple. Wait until Rome left then follow him.

Chapter 25

Three hours later Kalina found out that plan was a lot easier thought than done.

The man named Eli—or should she say the guard from Hell—kept so close an eye on her, all she could do was go to the bathroom alone. He sat right outside Rome's bedroom door, but every time she moved he knocked and came in, like he was expecting to see her hanging over the balcony trying to escape. Which she'd thought of doing a couple times.

Ferrell was calling her cell phone like there was no other number in his phone's memory, but she refused to answer. Whatever he wanted with her Kalina was going to feel a lot better if he went through Agent Wilson and the DEA to get. She didn't want to deal with Ferrell on her own ever again.

But the next call that came in was one that startled and cheered her.

"Hey Mel," she answered.

"Hi, Kalina! It's so great to hear your voice. I've been trying to get in touch with you for days."

Kalina sighed, guilt relaxing on her shoulders. "Yeah, I've been meaning to call you about the other night."

"Oh, don't worry about that. I just figured you'd had enough of Stephen. Anyway, it's been a while since we've chatted. Want to have lunch?"

Kalina looked around the room. She didn't actually want to have lunch with Mel, but she did want to get the hell out of here. She'd felt caged, trapped for the better part of the day.

"Ah, sure, that sounds like a good idea."

"Great. I'm off today so I can pick you up in about an hour. I have one quick errand to run. Then we can get a bite to eat, do some shopping. You know, have a girls' day."

Mel sounded so excited, a little too excited for Kalina's taste, but it was the excuse she was looking for to go against Rome's wishes.

"Good plan," she said then rattled off the address and disconnected the call.

It took Kalina about ten minutes after the call to realize she probably shouldn't have told Mel to pick her up from Rome's house. That would certainly generate more questions about her relationship with Rome, questions she definitely did not want to answer. But it seemed like her only way out and right now, getting out to learn what was going on with Rome was much more important than trying to figure out how to handle Mel's inevitable questions about her love life.

Rome had asked her to trust him. She did. But he also needed to trust her. She still had a job to do, even if it had shifted focus in the last couple of days. Besides, did he really expect to keep her locked up in his bedroom until he returned? Well, if he did then he didn't know her well at all.

Kalina went into the bathroom and switched on the water in the jet pump tub. Eli wouldn't dare come into the bathroom to check on her. At least she hoped he wouldn't. Sitting on the side of the tub, Kalina thought about all that had happened to her in the past few weeks: the job promotion, seeing Rome again, falling in love. With a heavy sigh she tried not to think about the last too deeply. Rome hadn't said he loved her, just that he wanted her, needed her. That should be enough since Kalina had never heard that from anyone before. But somehow it wasn't.

She hadn't told him she loved him, either. No matter how strong a woman she considered herself to be, that sort of rejection wasn't high on her to-do list. Besides, how did one go about loving a shape shifter? That was a world she knew nothing about, but she admitted it intrigued her.

When about ten minutes had passed and the tub threatened to overflow she turned off the water and went back out into the bedroom, making a big show out of going to take a bath. Then she returned to the bathroom, pulling the door closed loudly. She waited a beat and when she didn't hear Eli attempting to come in, she moved to the double glass doors. Quietly she undid the lock and slid the glass door open just enough so that her body could slip through the opening. On the balcony she eased over the railing and prayed she didn't break a bone on the one-story drop down. An army of soft blue hydrangea bushes broke her fall as she landed steadily on her feet.

She had no idea if Rome had cameras that scanned his property or not, but figured with the secret he was guarding he probably did. So crouching low, she moved beside the line of trees that ran along the back of the house. When they abruptly stopped, giving way to the front lawn, the winding driveway, and a small fountain, she tried to figure the best way to get to the gate without being spotted.

It was a hot sticky day, the sun beaming down with a vengeance. A light sheen of perspiration had already begun to line her back when she finally decided it was do or die. Kalina broke out into a run, her legs moving swiftly, smoothly beneath her as she covered the length of the front yard with extreme ease. Larger, fuller trees lined the iron gate that circled the perimeter of Rome's house. She slipped through a section of them to a narrow space between gate and trees then waited. She was close enough to the front entrance that she could make herself visible as soon as Mel pulled up but still guarded enough by the trees that she was positive any cameras in the house couldn't see her.

The trees also provided some shade as she stood waiting for Mel to arrive. All the while thoughts of Rome and how upset he would be when he found her gone filtered through her mind. Her heart ached a little because she didn't want to hurt him in any way. He'd asked her never to leave him, but she hadn't promised that she wouldn't.

This was helping them, Kalina thought, resigning herself to her mission. Finding out what exactly her assignment had been would help when she attempted to clear Rome's name. Figuring out what his father had to do with Raul Cortez would go a long way to helping Rome let some of his guilt about his parents' death rest. He hadn't told her much about his past, but she sensed that pain in him, that sense of loss that only another person who'd lost loved ones could relate to. Knowing he'd seen those papers on his computer, she could only imagine the sense of betrayal he would have felt reading them. So she was helping Rome, helping the man she loved by sneaking out and going against his wishes.

That didn't really make her feel better.

With an excited gleam, she raked her nails down his back. Once. Twice. Third time being the charm, streams of crimson blood bubbled from the broken skin. Below her he moaned and she shifted her hips, let her naked clit rub over the base of his back. He said something but she didn't understand him, didn't really care.

She'd been doing this guy for almost a year, giving him whatever he craved, taking what she needed and getting everything Sabar wanted as well.

"Harder!" he yelled this time, and she dragged her claws down his back once more. He got off on this, the pain. Each time she was with him it was all about causing him more pain.

Truth be told, she got off on it, too. Something about the smell of blood, the feel of power rushing through her each time she made him scream, had her coming all over the place. Take now for instance; she was creaming all over his lower back as she watched the blood from the fresh wounds trickling off the side of his torso to land on the white hotel bedsheets.

"Your friend didn't pay up. Sabar's not happy about that," she said then rubbed her clit over his rough skin, loving the friction the movement created. "You'd better talk to him or he'll end up just like Baines."

"Come here, baby," he grumbled and turned so that he was now lying on his bloodied back.

She adjusted herself, lowered her body until his short, fat dick managed to slide inside her wet pussy. He moaned, his dull gray eyes rolling back into his head.

With pudgy hands he gripped her hips, holding her still as he pushed upward, believing he was driving deep inside her.

There was no real feeling, that's why she had to get off in other ways when she was with him. Leaning forward slightly, she clawed his chest with deep angry strokes. His eyes opened wide just like his mouth, and the scream that ripped free made her come instantly. Then she began to ride him, being careful not to pull up too much or his puny length would slip right out of her. He was breathing heavily, the flab from his second chin vibrating as she worked him.

"You gonna get your people to pay up?" she asked, flattening her hands on his chest to feel the blood on her palms.

"Shit . . . shi . . . yes . . . yesss. I'll tel . . . yeah . . . I'll call him. Fuck!"

"That's right, if you wanna keep being fucked by me and keep breathing long enough to make that run for the Senate you just announced, you'd better make sure all of them pay up when they're supposed to."

"Yeah, yeah, I'll do it. I'll do it," he panted, his fingers pinching her hips. "Just fuck me harder. Harder! Harder!"

She moved quicker, knowing he was only good for another minute or so. Watching his face contort she leaned forward, felt her canines extend, and bit him, right on his nipple. He yelled and came at the same time. She slid off his sweaty, bloody body and went to the table where her cell phone was. Punching in a familiar number, she said, "I'm done."

"Good. Now go get my mate," Sabar's gruff voice replied from the other end.

After grabbing a quick shower and slipping back into her business attire Melanie was on her way out when a half-dressed Ralph Kensington puffed on a cigarette and glared at her through the ring of smoke he'd just released. "You're a wild one. But I can tame you," he said.

She slipped her purse on her shoulder and chuckled. "Not in your wildest dreams, old man."

"Marry me?" he asked.

"Can't, I'm already mated." She opened the door and stood there a moment. "Besides, you're not my type." Closing the door behind her, she missed his ending comment.

"You're right," he chuckled, scratching his protruding belly. "I'm not a cat."

The second she approached the gate Kalina knew she'd made a colossal mistake.

Mel stepped out of a black car looking absolutely nothing like the woman Kalina had spent a Sunday afternoon with. Gone was the supermom, the housewife, the dedicated employee.

What was before her now was like a total transformation—and not like those Oprah makeovers, either. This was deeper. Mel looked at her with eyes slanted just slightly and lips poised, shoulders squared and hips that swayed with the wind. She wore a shorter-than-short skirt tight enough to choke a dog and halter top that put her breasts on display through its sheer material and sky-high heels. Her red hair seemed brighter and was pulled up so that her long neck was bare.

"So nice to see you again, Kalina," she purred.

That's right, her voice, her movements, everything

about her said *cat.* Okay, so maybe Kalina was overreacting. Just because Rome admitted to being a cat shifter didn't mean that everyone she saw was one now. Still, this was a different Melanie.

"Hey, Mel. What's up? You sounded like it was urgent." Kalina talked and measured the distance between her and the house. Mel was on the other side of the gate in a car with tinted windows, which told Kalina she was probably not alone. Besides that, it was a luxury car worth much more than the meager salary Mel was making at the law firm. This entire situation was off, and when Kalina inhaled she could swear she smelled a setup.

"Just wanted to see you again. You haven't really been in the office. I asked Nick about you." She was walking, touching her fingers along the gate and looking at Kalina with a sultry sort of smirk. "He seemed convinced you were all right. I guess if you're staying at the boss's place, you would be considered all right."

Kalina shrugged, trying to remain calm. She didn't have a gun on her—nothing that vaguely resembled a weapon. Still, her fingers flexed at her sides as if preparing for a fight. "It's a temporary situation. Why did you call me?" Kalina decided to just cut to the chase.

"I said I wanted to see you again."

"Why? We just met."

Mel stopped walking. "Well, I thought we'd made a connection. You know, like you connected with Rome and with his . . . kind."

"I don't know what you're talking about."

Mel tilted her head, thin wisps of hair circling her face. Her eyes did something funny, changed color. *No, it's the sun,* Kalina told herself, but she knew better.

"I think you know, Kalina. You know a whole lot,"

Mel said, coming to stand by the section of the gate where Kalina was.

"Listen, maybe we should have this girls' day another time," Kalina said. She was about to turn and leave when something behind her made her freeze. She couldn't see but she knew there was something there, something that wasn't human. She could feel the slow movement, knew the eerie eyes that would be watching her back.

Looking to Mel she asked simply, "Why?"

The she-cat tossed back her head and laughed. "So naive, little cat. So fucking naive. Well, that'll all change in time."

Before Kalina could say another word Mel had reached a hand inside the gate, grabbing her arm and pulling it until her shoulder slammed painfully into the iron. Next there was a stinging sensation in her upper arm and then there was blackness.

Chapter 26

Sabar needed a mate, one who would stand by him in this battle, who would watch his back and bear his children. Rogue children that would grow up to rule when he was gone. There were other things on Sabar's need list, but this was by far first and foremost. It was so important that he was beginning to doubt his own logic in sending Mel to get her.

He should have done it himself. He'd been in close contact with her before; surely she wouldn't be alarmed to see him again. Darel and Chi had redeemed themselves by taking care of that lying bastard congressman who thought he could cheat him out of his money. These humans were so fucking stupid. Just because they had titles and money, they believed they also had power.

Until they met him.

Sabar relished the fear he was spreading among Washington's elite. Soon everybody in this stinking town would know that if they wanted to play, they'd have to pay. He was taking over the drug game here, slowly but surely, knocking off the lower-level dealers until he could get the big ones out of his way as well. Drugs and guns were a multibillion-dollar industry and Sabar wanted his piece of the American dream.

And he was willing to kill to get it.

It was dark. Late night had come upon him quickly

as he'd gone about some business waiting for his enforcers to do their jobs. They'd been told to be here tonight with his goods and his money. As Sabar entered the back door of the abandoned row house he'd claimed as the enforcer headquarters, he inhaled deeply.

His dick hardened instantly as her scent sifted through the humid air.

She was here.

His mate was here and his mouth watered to touch her, taste her. Finally.

Kalina felt sick, bile forming in the back of her throat as she tried to look away.

She should have stayed in Rome's room, locked behind that door. Leaving had been a mistake, one she'd realized too late. Now she was in what looked like a room inside an old dilapidated house. She'd been blindfolded when they bought her in, but she'd smelled wood and mold. The extra-sensitive senses she'd had all her life had her smelling and hearing things much more specifically since her eyes were covered.

They'd taken her from the car, one carrying her and two others walking with them. They'd traveled up two flights of stairs and into this room, which she suspected was in the back of the house judging how many steps they took from the stairway. Then she'd been plopped down into a chair that squeaked under her weight.

Knowing that plotting any kind of escape would work better if she could see her surroundings, she'd prayed they would remove the blindfold. Now, though, she almost wished she couldn't see at all.

Standing in front of her was the man who'd delivered the first envelope of pictures to her. Or at least it seemed to be. Tonight, in this dank old house, he looked different—almost deranged. Now he was in her face, his hand cupping her chin roughly as he leaned in closer.

"I've waited a long time for this moment," he said, his hot breath fanning over her face.

His eyes were an eerie shade of orange, darting around like those of the people she used to find high on cocaine or some other drug. His voice was deep, much deeper than the day he'd showed up at her door. But as she looked into his eyes, she remembered him clearly. His eyes hadn't been this orange color on that day, but they'd been strange. She remembered thinking how odd they looked. So this was the man who'd been watching her, taking pictures of her. This was her stalker. She wanted to spit on him, to kick him in the balls, then in the face as she watched him squirm. What she really wanted was to cause him some kind of damage for all the worry and fear he'd brought to her life these last few days. But they'd gagged her so she couldn't say anything.

"This is going to be monumental," he said, licking his lips, leaving a glistening sheen over the fatter bottom lip that made Kalina gag. "We're going to rule together, baby. Me and you, together," he said, letting his fingers slide from her chin to touch along her neck then down to grab her breast.

She didn't care that they'd tied her hands together behind her back—her ankles as well—didn't care if she was gagged. Kalina was determined this filthy man was not going to touch her. She kicked out, both her feet flailing in the air toward his groin while her bottom held her firm on the ground. When she wobbled a bit, he just held on to her breast, squeezing until tears pooled in her eyes.

"Yeah, you're gonna be so hot."

"That's the same thing I said," the one called Chi murmured.

Of the three in this room Kalina knew just who to be afraid of, and it wasn't Chi. He took his orders from Darel, who obviously took his orders from this new one, named Sabar. Mel was off in a corner, her golden gaze locked on Kalina's in what looked like a feral challenge. They were all idiots in Kalina's mind, stupid, selfish idiots to think they were going to get any cooperation from her.

They'd brought her here after drugging her. She knew this because when she'd awakened she'd felt the hazy effects of whatever had been in that needle. At first she'd only been tied and seated in this chair in the middle of the room, like she was on display or in an interrogation—whichever didn't creep her out the most. The three of them circled her, looking at her with equally disturbing glares.

They were all shifters, she knew now. The two men who'd been at that party had watched her with the same evil glare. Then they'd begun talking, or rather arguing over who would get her first.

"If either of you dirty street cats touches me you'll be damn sorry," she'd snapped at them.

Mel had stepped right up, slapping Kalina across the face. Kalina had returned the assault by spitting on the cheap-looking bitch and daring her to do it again.

"Don't hurt her," the bigger one had said. "Sabar won't like it if she's hurt."

"Shut the hell up, Darel!" Mel had yelled. "You're always talking about what Sabar likes and what he doesn't like. Always up his ass!"

The one called Darel had grabbed Mel by her neck, pushing back until her head slammed into the wall. "I'm the one in charge here, bitch. Don't forget that."

"Chill," the other one said. He hadn't stopped glaring at her, licking his thick lips as he did. He was aroused, she could see, and if he got even an inch closer she was going to kick him right in his burgeoning erection.

"There's enough of her to go around," he'd said, and Kalina's stomach had roiled in disgust. "Besides, she needs to tell us where her little boyfriend hid Chavez. I'm gonna kill that cat when I see him again."

She'd known they were talking about Rome. They'd been asking about him and the Shadow Shifters from the moment she'd awakened. They wanted to know where they were all located, what they planned to do, how much money they had, how much power. All questions Kalina really didn't know the answers to but wouldn't have told them if she had.

They'd finally slapped a piece of duct tape on her mouth after she'd cursed them all until she was hoarse.

Now she looked at the four of them, hating each and every one of them equally. She should have listened to Rome, should have done what he said. But it was too late for regrets now.

The only thing she could do now was survive.

She screeched when the one called Sabar, the one who'd come to her house, ripped the tape from her lips.

"Bastard!" she cursed and licked her dry lips.

"Pretty mouth," he said, leaning in closer. "I want to kiss that pretty mouth."

Kalina remained perfectly still, waiting, hating the stench that burned her nose. The minute his lips touched hers she struck out, biting his lips with teeth sharper than she'd thought: As he yelled, pulling back from her, she saw the steady stream of blood dripping from them and felt a measure of satisfaction.

"Yeah, you're for me," he said wiping the back of his hand over his mouth. "An evil ruthless bitch just like me. We're gonna rule this world together."

"Go to hell!" she spat.

Sabar threw his head back and laughed. "Only with you right beside me."

He reached for the buckle of his pants and began undoing them, all the while keeping his gaze on her.

Kalina felt sick, then she felt hot, and then . . . she felt something else.

It moved inside her, slinking around as if it had been just awakened. Rising slowly it filled her; from her feet to her fingertips it was being reborn inside her. The feeling was eerie, and she thought instinctively she should have rejected it. Then she paused, recognized this other part of her, and welcomed the reunion. It had been there all along, revealing itself in the extra-sensitive senses she possessed, in the instincts she'd called on following her gut. Suddenly the memories came flooding back: the way she always felt as if she didn't belong, no matter how hard she tried; the feeling of something itching just beneath her skin. It all made sense now, illogical and unheard-of sense.

Now whatever had loomed just beneath the surface all her life was standing tall, making its grand entrance. And it was mad as hell.

The meeting place wasn't what Rome or the other shifters had expected, but then this entire situation was way beyond the norm. Rogues didn't give a shit who they killed, or when, or where, so calling them to an abandoned house on the end of one of the dirtiest streets in the city—literally and figuratively—was not their MO.

Eli had driven the Tahoe, with Rome, Nick, and X riding in the back. Ezra was parked right around the corner in the Hummer with three more guards, should reinforcements be necessary. The message said for Rome to arrive alone. Yeah, like hell was that happening. Not only were Nick and X never going to allow it, Rome didn't take orders from anybody, especially not a group of backstabbing Rogues.

There were no words to describe the rage that ripped through him the moment he found out Kalina was gone. Eli looked as if he were about ready to shoot himself when Rome walked into the house and he had to deliver the news. At that exact moment Rome wanted to kill. Not Eli, because he was a friend and Rome knew he'd done his best. Although when this was all said and done the guard was definitely going to feel Rome's wrath.

But right now, at this second, Rome knew Kalina was in trouble. If she wasn't here with him, she was in danger, and that was unacceptable. It had only taken about fifteen minutes for his house to fill with Shadow Shifters ready to comb the DC streets in search of her.

"He will not hurt her," Alamar said, coming into the hallway where they'd all aligned like an army about to move out.

"How do you know that for sure?" X asked, probably because he knew words weren't coming easily for Rome.

Alamar held up a note. "He believes she is his *companheiro*. He will not hurt her."

Rome snatched the note, read it, and wanted to roar

his fury. Instead Nick took the paper from Rome's hands. "So he wants Rome to know he has her. To know he's taken her away from him. Dumb fuck!"

"Let's go," Rome said through clenched teeth.

"Remember the *Ètica*," Alamar said as they began to move out.

Rome was already shaking his head. "No. Not this time. This time I've got my own code to go by."

As they filed out of the house, Nick and X right behind Rome, the Elder looked to Baxter.

"He will do the right thing," Baxter said.

The Elder nodded glumly. "For all our sakes I hope that you are right."

Now, half an hour later, they were here. And Rome's cat was ready to break free, to rip the throat from the Rogue who threatened what was his.

Again.

It was the same one, Rome thought with disgust. He'd recognized the scent at Kalina's apartment. Remembered it from years ago when he'd been just a little boy. It had been mixed with another Rogue scent, but Rome knew that specific one and as he stepped out of the truck walking toward the corner house he smelled it again.

Rage rippled, his cat roared inside clawing at the surface to be set free, but Rome, the man, walked purposely up the steps.

"What's the plan?" X said from behind him.

"I'm going to get Kalina. When she's safe I'm killing every sonofabitch Rogue in there then burning this fucking house down," Rome said, reaching for the doorknob.

Nick shrugged. "Sounds like a plan to me."

* * *

A plain unmarked slate-gray Buick pulled onto the street about five minutes after Rome, Nick, and X walked into the row house. Pulling into an open parking space about five houses up from the end unit, which was his target, he stopped the car. Switching off the engine, Special Agent Dorian Wilson sat back against the leather seat, his eyes examining the SUV not too far in front of him. All the windows were tinted—and even if they weren't, it was well after midnight. This street had obviously not been on the city's cleanup list in a long while, because in addition to the majority of the windows on these houses being broken out, the lampposts had suffered the same fate. Saying it was dark as shit was an understatement.

But Dorian knew it didn't matter who drove the Tahoe. He knew who it was registered to. Roman Reynolds. He did wonder which one of Reynolds's bodyguards was driving it tonight. The man never traveled alone. That was part of the reason Dorian and his team had begun looking at Reynolds and his law firm in the first place. The other part was still on a disk carefully hidden in a safe in Dorian's apartment.

Jack "JC" Ferrell of the MPD took a long swig from the bottle of vodka he'd lifted from the liquor store around the corner. All he'd had to do was flash his police badge and the tiny little Asian woman minding the cash register had looked the other way. They knew him around here, knew what he liked and what he wouldn't tolerate. After tonight they might know things JC didn't want them to know.

He was meeting with Sabar and his henchmen tonight, supposedly to give them the money from the stash he was assigned to sell. But JC didn't have their money. He'd smoked half of it then put the other half in an account for his two sons. That's the least he could do for them, since being Father of the Year wasn't in the cards for him. But he wasn't running; that wasn't something he'd ever done in his life. After thirty-two years on the police force, two wives with dollar signs in their eyes and other cops' cocks in their mouths, he'd given up the scared-and-begging sort of lifestyle he'd once lived. Now it was all about him. He lived for the moment, didn't answer to anybody, and didn't give a damn what anybody thought of him. Especially not now. Not tonight.

This business with these crazy-ass animal people was coming to an end. JC had done a lot of shady crap in the past ten years of his life, but working alongside some half-breed animals was not going to be listed in his obituary. They were crass motherfuckers that didn't care about anything or anybody; whatever they wanted they got, and it didn't do any good to try to stop them. Living like that, JC figured, was sure to get those weirdos sliced and diced fast, and that he wasn't willing to be a part of. He'd figured out a long time ago that with all the death and self-destruction he'd seen, his demise would probably come about the same way. But again, he wasn't scared.

He was shit-tired, though, ready to go someplace and lay the hell down for a while. A long while, he thought, as he entered the house and took the first steps to the upper rooms where the lead hairy bastard liked to stay. But as he took those steps a sound unlike any he'd ever heard stopped him.

Chapter 27

As the three of them took the steps, Rome scented Kalina and his chest constricted. Not only was she here, she was in full *acordado*.

Her scent was different, heavier, tinged with a sultry floral aroma that permeated his senses, putting every muscle in his body on full alert.

"Let me go first," he whispered to Nick and X, who nodded behind him.

They climbed two flights of stairs, each of them with guns in hand. The intent was to fight this battle the human way, to use the weapons of mass destruction that seemed to be so accepted, it was no wonder the murder rate in this country was so high. It would have been easier to come in jaguar form fighting and ripping everyone in this place to pieces, but Rome refused to do that without provocation.

They were on the third floor of the row house walking down a narrow hallway, following Kalina's scent. Just a few steps from the door every part of Rome's calm, human plan fell apart as a scream ripped through the walls, traveling down his torso to settle in heated despair in his midsection.

Rome broke into a run and kicked in the door without hesitation. Never in a million years would he have been prepared for the scene that confronted him.

* * *

Kalina screamed in pain again and again.

Every part of her body hurt as heat engulfed her and pressure assailed her bones. Her clothes felt heavy and sticky, agitating her skin. Ripples ran beneath, pressing painfully against her limbs.

Her chest constricted and she struggled to breathe. Everything around her was changing. As she inhaled, scents became acutely stronger, one after the other pushing against each other in a tug of war for her attention. Her tongue felt thick, dry as her gums ached. Teeth seemed to fill every corner of her mouth.

She convulsed, feeling the chair shaking beneath her as the ropes that bound her stretched and popped. Her breasts tingled, hanging full and aching on her chest. In her ears she heard everything from dogs barking outside to hissing and cursing in this very room. At first it grew very dark; then she closed her eyes, opened them, and felt as if someone had dumped sand into them.

Just as quickly her vision cleared, the darkness becoming crystal-clear. She searched for him, needed him to be there, but didn't really understand why. Kalina saw Rome bust through the door, saw his cat's eyes in the face of his human form. Inhaling deeply, she latched on to his scent and clung for dear life.

Her heart hammered in her chest, arms extending before her and shaking almost uncontrollably. Something was happening, something big was happening, and Rome knew what it was. In his eyes she saw knowledge and understanding; in her mind she heard him comforting her, reaching out to her to let her know she would be okay. He was here to save her, again.

Then again, that other part of her, the one she'd

ignored for so long, stood inside and roared. She didn't need to be saved this time. This time it would be her who did the rescuing.

She felt the motion, the swaying of the room as she fell from the chair. Her jaw ached and her head pounded. With stinging fingertips she lifted her arms, looking down to see why her skin itched so badly. Waves of golden-yellow fur raced down her arm. She opened her mouth to scream but instead her jaw locked, teeth elongated, sharpened, extended. Her skull felt like it would explode as she heard cracking and felt her entire spine bend and contort. Rolling over she pulled herself up on fisted hands and wobbly knees. Her back arched and there was a series of cracks as her body contorted. More fur spread along her back and the pain in her head thumped to a sickening crescendo.

Screaming wasn't an option any longer. The sound coming from her opened mouth this time was guttural; it was primitive and rocked the entire room as it rumbled through her.

"Shoot that bitch!" she heard a male voice roar.

"No!" another sounded, but it was too late.

There was a gunshot and Rome lunged for the tall shifter who'd fired his gun. Flattening the guy with his body, Rome pulled back, pounding a fist into his face. The shifter attempted to fight back, tossing heavy blows of his own.

"Get her and let's go!" another voice yelled.

X moved quickly, crossing the room to where Kalina's cat form, still a bit wobbly, struggled to stand on four legs.

A female screech tore through the air as a redhead leapt from the shadows reaching for X but was quickly dispatched by Nick's blow to the side of her head. She crumpled to the floor just as Darel struck out at Nick.

Pulling his own gun from behind his back, Sabar turned and aimed at Rome. Kalina saw his intentions and pushed her now much larger and stronger cat's body past X. Jumping up on hind legs, she tackled Sabar, knocking him to the floor and sending his gun across the room.

The fear in his eyes as he turned to face her made her heart race. Baring her teeth she growled loudly in his face, heavy paws on his chest.

"My mate," he said, a sick smile spreading over his human lips even as his eyes shifted to cat.

Beneath her she felt his shift, the connection of his fur against hers causing an eerie warmth inside. She backed off. The man who'd come to her house and stared at her with orange eyes now stood in front of her in his full cat form, baring his teeth and heading straight for her.

In a blur of black, Rome pounced on Sabar, knocking the other cat into the wall. There were cats all over the room now, all growling and thrashing against one another. Kalina couldn't tell who was who. Instead she felt dizzy, heat still running through her body like a blazing fever.

Glass broke as cats rammed against the window. The scent of blood filled the air and Kalina choked. Backing into a corner she thought about Mrs. Gilbert's cat, the one that had scared her so badly for years. Her legs wobbled, and she felt herself going down.

Her head hurt like hell, images of cats blurring with humans. Confusion racked her mind as heat continued to tear through her body. She blinked and blinked, breathed in and out hoping to calm this wave of emotions and physical changes going through her, but there was no use. It was too much and she finally fell back, closing her eyes to it all.

When she opened her eyes again it was to see a blur of spots moving fast and ferocious in front of her. They were fighting, big cats that belonged in the jungle were fighting, breaking everything in this medium-size human room.

Instinctively the cop in her came to full alert. Kalina scrambled her human legs across the floor, reaching for the gun she saw lying there, and grabbed it with human fingers. She looked down at her hands holding the gun. They were normal again, four fingers and a thumb on each, creamy butter-toned skin wrapped around a cold black gun that she was now lifting and aiming.

How to tell who was who? She took a deep breath as she stood, her human legs not necessarily accepting the quick shift she'd apparently made, but cooperating just the same.

Rome was the black cat, his green eyes and dark rosettes like a beacon to her in this room full of felines. She would not shoot him. But the cat he was fighting, the lighter one with black rosettes set far apart, was the enemy. She remembered his eyes from the night at the party and she squeezed the trigger happily.

The bullet tore through the fat skull of the cat, and it fell back away from Rome's clutches. Next, she turned to a thinner yellow-gold cat that was swiping at a reddish brown cat with her heavy paws. Kalina knew this one, too.

The yellow-gold cat was Melanie, the lying back-stabbing so-called friend Kalina had believed like some naive schoolgirl. The woman had tricked her; she'd known all along who Kalina was and why she was there. She also knew something Kalina didn't. They'd mentioned it several times when they thought she was asleep. Kalina was Sabar's mate, whatever that meant.

Lifting her arm, Kalina aimed at the bitch and fired, cursing the cat and the one time she'd opened herself up to friendship. She fired again for good measure and felt waves of fury ripple through her.

Two other cats had pulled back. A huge one with heaving sides and jade-green eyes. That one kept watching her, its long tongue lolling from its mouth as its labored breathing continued. The one beside it, which was only smaller by a fraction, nudged its big head against the other's flanks.

"Shoot him," Kalina heard a male voice saying, but she couldn't tear her gaze from the one with the dark eyes.

His head lifted, his nose sniffing the air, and she took a step back. The gun was still in her hand but her fingers were shaking. She'd never shaken before, never hesitated to shoot. But at this moment, something held her back.

The other cat nudged again when the sound of sirens echoed in the air and the two took off.

"It's okay, baby," were the next words she heard. Strong arms encircled her, a hand going to her wrist, pushing at her fingers until the gun fell to the floor. "It's okay, I'm here."

Rome hugged her close, whispering all kinds of words into her ear as his hands rubbed up and down her back. She let her head drop to his shoulders, let the heat continue to swim inside, and wondered what the hell had just happened.

* * *

Dorian heard the vicious roaring and was out of his car heading for the house when out of nowhere something smacked him from behind. He was falling to the ground just as he managed to get off one shot.

JC ran from the house the moment he heard the gunshots. They were up there, those animals, fighting and whatnot. He didn't want to be a part of it. Hoped they all killed one another so he could get on with his life. He had money now; he could go anywhere and make any future he wanted. He just had to get out of here.

But his next steps were quickly halted by two huge look-alike goons. With shaking fingers he quickly reached into his pocket, pulling out his badge. "MPD," he said with authority.

The one guy laughed while the other landed a beefy fist against his jaw. Lights flashed before JC's eyes as he reached for his gun, determined not to go down without a fight. But go down he did, falling with a sickening *thump* against the concrete.

"Leave them here. Their people are coming," Baxter said, coming up behind Eli and Ezra.

The twins didn't even ask where the old man had come from or what he was doing here.

"Let's get Rome and the others. We've gotta move now!" Ezra said, leading the way up the steps.

Eli and Baxter were right behind him, taking the stairs until they found the room where the shifters were. In a far corner Rome was holding Kalina. Baxter immediately went to them, gathering up Rome's clothes as he did and trying to cover them both as much as possible.

Nick and X had already put on their pants and were looking out the back windows with deadly glares.

"What happened?"

"Sabar and his man got away," Nick said tightly.

"Kalina shot the other two," X added.

Eli looked to the floor at the two cat bodies with blood oozing from their wounds. "We need to get rid of them and get the hell out of here. Cops are on their way."

X nodded. "Get them out first."

"I'm working on that, Mr. Xavier." Baxter was trying to guide Rome and a still-dazed Kalina out of the room.

"Burn it to the ground," Rome said as he approached the door.

"Yes sir," Ezra said, already reaching for the can of lighter fluid he'd brought inside with him.

A shifter's body must never be found, so with each death the corpse was burned. There could be no evidence of their species, no reason for anyone to come looking for more of their kind. It might seem inhumane to some, but for the shadows it was a survival tactic, one they'd used for years. One they hoped would continue to protect them.

Chapter 28

Kalina rolled over to look at the clock. With a moan she deduced she'd been asleep for about twelve hours. Flopping onto her back, she let an arm fall over her eyes and waited until she was fully awake.

The room was dark, the blinds and curtains closed, but she knew exactly where she was.

He'd brought her here again, to his home, his bed.

They'd arrived here after the fight in the city. Every part of her body hurt, especially her head. She felt nauseous and wanted nothing more than to curl into a ball and just lie somewhere. Instead Rome had taken care of her.

He'd stripped his shirt from her otherwise naked body and lowered her into a tub of very hot water. Climbing inside with her he'd bathed her tenderly, even washing her hair. She'd been too tired to protest and let the lovely feel of his tender touch wash over her. After the bath he'd carried her to his bed, where he'd tucked her in tightly. A few minutes later she heard Baxter's voice; then Rome was at her side encouraging her to drink. It was hot and sweet and floated through her body like honey. She had no idea what kind of drink it was but knew that it made slipping into sleep a lot easier.

It had been a dreamless sleep, which was a welcome relief. If she'd thought her dreams of one cat were bad, just imagine what her subconscious would conjure up after seeing six of them.

But now she was alone. Her body was still sore, her mouth more than a little dry, but she was alone. The way it seemed she always ended up. With that thought she tried to roll out of the bed but came to a complete stop when she felt him.

Rome was there.

Had he stayed with her the entire time?

"Where are you going?" he asked in a gruff voice.

"I need to use the bathroom," she said swallowing at the realization that not only was he here, he was also awake.

Again with tender hands he helped her from the bed and walked her to the bathroom. He didn't join her, for which she was supremely grateful. But when she came out he was right there, ushering her back to the bed once more.

When she was lying beneath the covers again and he'd settled next to her but not close enough to touch, she cleared her throat.

"You knew, didn't you? What I was, you knew all along?"

He was silent for a minute, a routine she'd become accustomed to. Rome took his time giving his answers, thinking them completely through before speaking. Whereas she, on the other hand, tended to speak now, think later.

"I didn't know for sure. I knew there was something about you that kept calling to me. I didn't know it was your cat."

"My cat," she whispered, still astounded at the revelation. "I'm afraid of cats, or at least I used to be."

"A defense mechanism."

"Defense from what? Deadly house cats out to kill me because they sensed that I was bigger and badder than them?"

He chuckled, which made this really intense moment a little less intense.

"With the report X came up with, Elder Alamar traced your heritage back to two Elders within our tribe. They were joined before having you. Right after you were born they were brutally killed in the forest and you were taken. None of the tribes knew where you were. Somehow you ended up here at the orphanage. It's not clear who dropped you off or why."

His words moved around in her mind, filling a gaping hole that she'd fought to ignore all her life. In just a few sentences, he'd given her a past, a connection to people she'd thought lost to her forever.

"What were their names?" she asked, letting everything from being the child of Shadow Shifters to being kidnapped after their murders sink in.

"Natalia and Adao."

"What are Elders?"

"They are the most knowledgeable of our kind, selected from our tribe to represent us in the Assembly."

"We're from a tribe." It wasn't really a question; she'd just wanted to hear the sound of it from her own lips.

"The Topètenia of the Gungi rain forest. The jaguars."

His words seemed simple enough, but suddenly Kalina was hit with a realization. She wasn't human. She wasn't the woman who'd worked her way up in the ranks at the MPD. She wasn't the woman the DEA wanted on their squad. She was something . . . different.

Sitting up in the bed abruptly, she struggled to

breathe. Rome was there instantly, putting his arms around her. This time his tender touch wasn't going to be enough. She pulled away from him.

"What is it, baby?"

"Don't baby me! You did this to me," she yelled. "You made me like this. I didn't ask you to. I didn't!"

"Wait a minute, Kalina. Calm down."

"I won't calm down. And I'm sick of you telling me what to do all the time. I can do whatever the hell I want." She moved from the bed, leaning over the night-stand to switch on the lamp. Standing, she hugged her arms around herself, trying to absorb everything that had happened these last few days. It was so much, too much actually.

"I didn't ask to be different," she started. "I never wanted to be different. I just wanted what everybody else had. A family, a normal life. Was that too much to ask?"

He didn't come to her, but he was sitting up in the bed. "No. It wasn't."

"Then why couldn't I have it? Why couldn't I be like everyone else?"

"I used to ask myself that same thing," he admitted. "I used to want to be anything but who and what I was. Then I realized I didn't have a choice. Somebody once told me that you can't outrun your destiny."

His voice sounded different, and she turned to look at him. It had always been like this between them, this fine line they walked between fury and desire. Even with that she was drawn to him, even more so now.

"I can't be this. I mean, what you are. I don't know how."

He looked up at her seriously. "You are what you are, Kalina."

"I thought I knew who and what that was. Now I don't."

Rome remembered that feeling. He remembered the nights he sat alone in his bedroom as a teenager trying to figure out the very same things Kalina struggled with now. That's how he knew there was no one answer that would make everything click into place. Learning about the Shadow Shifters was a jolt to his young system, but he'd had years to get used to it. Kalina didn't. He'd only just told her about their species before she'd shifted. He should have told her everything at once, should have protected her. Seems he was always falling short in that area.

"When I was ten years old my parents were killed. Rogues broke into our house and killed them while I sat helplessly in a closet. I could hear their screams but I didn't go to them, didn't try to save them."

She sat on the side of the bed watching him closely. He knew he had to continue, he had to give her this part of himself so that maybe she would feel more comfortable with who she was, what she meant to him.

"I wanted to, but I didn't. For years I was angry and confused. I hated the shifters, hated what they'd done to my parents, my life. Then I began to think about my mother's words about fate and destiny and finding your own and living the life you were meant to live no matter what."

"Who killed them?"

The million-dollar question Rome had been trying for years to answer. Last night he'd received that answer. "The shifter that was there last night. The one you killed."

He looked at her, watching for some reaction. But

there was none. She'd killed before. In her line of work she'd had to draw her gun and shoot to kill to protect herself and others. As bad as it sounded, that was a good thing. Death didn't frazzle or surprise her. And he owed her deeply for the kill she'd made last night, no matter how gristly it may have appeared.

"I killed the man who took your parents."

He nodded. "Thank you."

"I didn't know."

"You were saving me for a change," he said with a half smile. "Look, Kalina, there's so much I want to tell you. So much you need to know. I'm not used to sharing myself with anyone, not used to caring what someone else thinks of me or what I do. But with you I do care, and I want to do the right thing by you."

She was already shaking her head. "I don't know how to do this, how to be this person. I don't know how to be with you."

He moved over to her, reaching out a hand to touch her cheek. "You don't have to be anybody but yourself with me."

"Who or whatever that is," she said, trying to make light of herself.

"You are a beautiful Shadow Shifter. You are my *companheiro*."

"You said that before. What does it mean?"

"My mate. For life you are mine and I am yours." He wanted to kiss her, to wrap his arms around her, pull her onto this bed and make love to her. But he waited.

"I thought I was falling in love with you. That made me both angry and a little scared. I didn't see how we could have a relationship after all we'd been through. And now—" She shrugged. "Now I don't know."

"Let me teach you, baby. Let me teach you about our ways and our traditions, about the lifestyle of a Shadow Shifter." He leaned forward then, kissed her lightly on her lips. "Let me love you," he whispered. "Please, my sweet *gato,* let me love you."

Two days later Kalina walked into a satellite office for the Drug Enforcement Agency. Agent Wilson had finally returned her call.

Eli drove her, as he usually did now. He was officially her guard. Rome had explained that as the mate of a Faction Leader, she was almost like shifter royalty; as such she had her own security detail, which consisted of the twins and a group of five other guards. Both Eli and Ezra had come to be like the brothers she'd never had. They joked with her and teased her and basically made her transition a little more comfortable. Not that she was 100 percent at ease with this new life of hers, but she was trying, even though she hadn't shifted since that night.

She walked into the building alone wearing a pale gray pantsuit and high-heeled sandals. Her hair was a little longer and fell in waves at the top of her head; the sides had grown out as well. As she walked through the halls she felt sexy and alluring, not like the old Kalina at all.

Knocking on the door, she waited to be admitted, then casually took a seat across from the agent.

"It's a pleasure seeing you again," he said.

Kalina smiled at the man she'd only met one other time. He was an attractive African American with close-cropped hair and a thin mustache. His eyes, which she always looked to now to tell her about a person, were completely guarded.

"Same here," she said not feeling nervous at all. She had no idea what he was going to say to her or what she was going to say in response, but realized it didn't matter. As Rome had stated before, she was who she was and she wasn't going to apologize for it. Neither was she going to sell out the species that she now belonged to.

"I'll cut to the chase, Kalina. We have a lot of questions," he said placing his elbows on the desk.

"So do I."

He nodded. "What did you find on Roman Reynolds?"

"Nothing," she answered immediately, confidently. "There was nothing in his records that supported the charge of facilitating a drug cartel."

"You're sure about that?"

"I'm positive that I found nothing to prove that allegation."

"What about Ferrell?"

"I was going to ask you the same thing. I found it odd the amount of pressure he put on me to speed the case up. That's why I was calling you—to find out what his deal was."

"Ferrell was dirty."

Why didn't that surprise her?

"He'd been working with some of the lower-level dealers for years."

"Then why did you put him on the case with me?"

"We were hoping his employers would take an interest in your investigation, maybe slip up somewhere along the line."

"Wait a minute, you sent me to investigate Roman in an effort to reveal another drug lord and to expose a dirty cop?"

Wilson shook his head. "We wanted to know what

Reynolds was doing, *and* we wanted Ferrell and his employers."

Sonofabitch, she thought to herself. They'd used her and lied to her. The very people she'd wanted so desperately to work for hadn't even had the decency to tell her what the real assignment was. Maybe being a cop wasn't her destiny. Maybe she'd had it all wrong. It certainly felt like she did.

"Did you get what you were after?" she asked finally.

"Not everything. Ferrell's in jail crying like a baby, but not really giving us much."

"That's strange. I figured a punk like him would be singing names and addresses right about now."

"He's giving names, but none that we know. He's also talking strange stuff."

Kalina felt a ruffle against her neck and sat up straighter. "Strange like what?"

"Like big cats killing and selling drugs in the city. You know anything about that?"

Kalina smiled, slow and full. "Why would I know about something so preposterous? I'm just a city cop trying to get a paycheck," she said. "Are we finished?"

"If that's your full report?"

"It is."

Wilson hesitated a second. "Then we're finished."

Kalina stood, going to the door before turning back to him. "And just in case you were thinking of offering, I decline the opportunity to work for the Drug Enforcement Agency. I like to face the lying and deceitful criminals head-on instead of working alongside them."

Wilson didn't say a word as she closed the door behind her and walked out of the building.

* * *

"Sabar's leading them, and now he's pissed that Rome has Kalina," X said, rubbing his knuckles as he sat at Rome's conference room table.

Elder Alamar nodded solemnly. "He was a problem years ago. We thought he was gone, that he had moved on to other things."

"Apparently he was simply laying low," Nick said. "He's making his comeback."

"Now he's hiding," Rome surmised, still not at all pleased that Sabar had been the one stalking Kalina all this time. The fact that Sabar thought she was his mate just made Rome hate the Rogue more.

The cheetah they had in custody had finally decided to talk, right about the time he realized that Sabar wasn't planning any daring rescue for him, and that one of his cohorts was already dead: Chi, the jaguar Kalina had killed, the one who'd killed Rome's parents years ago. Rome figured now that the hit had probably been ordered by Sabar, giving him yet another reason to hate the SOB.

Rubbing a hand over his chin, he tried valiantly to let the bitter feelings he still harbored inside go. He'd wanted his parents' killer and Kalina had gotten him. And now he had Kalina. All should be well in his world. The operative word being *should*. "It won't last," he surmised.

"You are correct," Alamar agreed. "He will return. It is power that drives him, and he will not stop until he attains it."

"Or until we dispatch him," X added.

"Kalina had some interesting information to share after her visit with the DEA," Rome offered. His mate had come home earlier today eyes burning with fury, and only after much coaxing did Rome manage to get the story from her.

"Melanie was the other shifter in the room that night, the other one Kalina shot."

"Melanie from work?" Nick questioned. "We've got to do better screening our employees, Rome."

Nick had been in an even testier mood since that night in the city. He'd stayed behind to help Ezra and Eli burn the house, and Rome suspected that the act had brought back memories for his friend.

"Ezra figured out Melanie was a shifter after he'd picked Kalina up from her house," Rome said.

"And nobody thought it was imperative to inform me?" Nick questioned, feeling like an ass since Melanie had come into his office acting strange and asking all kinds of questions about Kalina. Had he known what she was, he would have killed the bitch then. "Okay, so she was a shifter. We've already talked about having some sort of registry for the stateside shifters. When did she go Rogue? And why didn't we pick up her scent?"

"There are ways to mask a scent," Alamar offered.

Rome nodded. "All the more reason we need to implement that registry Nick just mentioned. Melanie's mated to Peter Keys, a low-level jaguar who mainly keeps to himself. But she was also sleeping with one of our good friends—Ralph Kensington."

"That's why Kensington stank of shifter back in LA," X added.

"Exactly. So by sleeping with a human and a shifter, the change in her scent wouldn't have been noticeable. We would never have known she'd gone Rogue."

"Dammit! So she was working with Sabar, too. And

they knew about Kalina even before we did." Nick wasn't liking what he was hearing.

"It seems that way," Rome admitted.

"What about the threat from their government?" Alamar asked, bringing more silence to the room.

X spoke up first. "They don't have any positive proof, just some reports from people who think they've seen things. If we go under the radar, it may die down." He looked pointedly at Rome. "But they are the government. They lie and cheat for a living. My guess is they're going to keep investigating until they find something tangible."

Rome had a sick feeling in his gut. "You mean until they actually find one of us."

X only nodded.

"One of our biggest fears is becoming a reality," Alamar said solemnly.

Baxter slipped into the room at that moment, coming to stand by the Elder, handing him a piece of paper.

The older shifter's usually restrained features changed, his lips drawing into a tight line.

X and Nick looked at Rome, who waited a few seconds before asking, "Is everything all right, Elder?"

Alamar shook his head solemnly. "There has been trouble in the forest. One of our cherished *curanderos* has been taken. No one has seen her for two days now. There is great concern from her family."

Curanderos were imperative to the tribes' survival in the Gungi. They were considered saviors to the shifters, providing remedies—be they medicinal or spiritual—to the infected. Without *curanderos* the tribes would almost certainly be near extinct. There were only one or two within each tribe, and they usually carried on from their parents' training, so losing a healer was not a good thing for Shadow Shifters.

But for the three shifter friends, this announcement held a different message—a much more personal one.

The air in the room crackled with tension as they each sat up just a little straighter, listening intently.

"Which one?" Nick asked, ignoring the fact that Rome should have been the one speaking first.

Rome and X were perfectly still as they waited for Alamar's answer.

"It is Aryiola."

"Nick," Rome said, immediately standing from his chair. But it was already too late. Nick was up, wrenching the door open and letting it slam against the wall.

"I'm on it," X said with a slight bow to the Elder before going after Nick.

Rome sighed. "She was his first love."

Elder Alamar only nodded. "She is his *companheiro*. I have known this for some time. Go to him," he told Rome. "This will not be easy for him or his cat. I will leave for the Gungi in the morning."

Rome bowed to the Elder and moved to the door himself, stopping to add, "We'll be going with you."

Chapter 29

The Gungi rain forest, Brazil

The scents hit her first. From the moment they stepped off the boat that carried them from the village where two jeeps had taken them after picking them up at the airport, Kalina had been inhaling deeply. It was the euphoric scent from her dreams, the one she'd sworn was heaven. It was here, in the rain forest.

A seemingly small boat had carried her, Rome, Nick, Elder Alamar, Eli, and Ezra and all their luggage smoothly down a river with gurgling water and jutting rocks. Everywhere she looked was green, fresh, and filled with vitality. It was such a contrast to the smog-filled city and the hustling and bustling of people.

Rome helped her out of the boat, his hands sliding from her hips the minute her feet hit the ground. She heard it then: birds, lots of them. She looked ahead, down a hill of grass, to trees as tall as her neck could stretch. Above, the sun beamed as humidity rose to an almost stifling rate. But she didn't feel hot, she felt exhilarated.

Her breath came in short quick pants, her eyes moving here and there trying to take in everything as quickly as she could. It was surreal, this feeling overwhelming her, this sense of immediate acceptance in a land that for all intents and purposes should feel foreign.

"She'll want to get loose, to run free. Stay with me for now. She'll have her chance later," Rome said, taking her hand and leading her down the hill.

He was talking about the cat within her—that's how he referred to it, as if it were another person inside her. He referred to his own cat the same way. Kalina wondered if she'd ever become that comfortable with the two parts of herself.

Anxiety swamped her the minute they entered the deep foliage of the forest. It was unlike anything she'd ever seen except in books or on documentaries on television. Vines and mosses roped through the terrain like some intricate road map that only the natives would understand. Eli and Ezra were in front of the group carrying packs on their backs and bags in their hands. They knew exactly where they were going. Beside her Rome's breathing seemed to change, his eyes drinking in the sights just as she did.

Elder Alamar walked with a regal air, his feet lightly touching the thick vegetated lining of the forest floor. X moved agilely, which was something of a mystery for a man built as he was. And Nick—Kalina's heart went out the man and the beast. He was a solemn form of anger, walking but not experiencing this lush forest.

He'd lived here for eight years of his life, so there was no doubt that he'd walked this same path before, had seen the wonders that Kalina was just experiencing. But there was pain here as well. It all but emanated from his body and was etched over his face. This woman, the *curandero* whose name was Aryiola—pronounced *ah-re-olah,* as Baxter had informed her—had once been very important to Nick. Baxter, who was quickly becoming a great reference guide for all things Topètenia- and rain-forest-related, had told her a little about Nick and his first love. Her heart had broken at the what sounded to her like the jungle version of Romeo and Juliet.

Now Aryiola was in danger. They believed she'd been kidnapped. Rome and X had even discussed Sabar's possible involvement last night. Kalina still wasn't clear on the Rogue's intentions. She knew the thirst for power and money well but was having a harder time digesting the rule-the-world mentality. Then again, she'd only known of her heritage for a matter of days. There was still so much she had to learn.

Her mind was so deep in thought Kalina hadn't been watching where she was going, and she tripped. The downward descent was halted when Rome grabbed her around the waist, lifting her up then setting her down again.

"Sorry," she said, feeling as foolish as she possibly could when she looked down to see she'd tripped over a tree root. But this wasn't any tree root, it was gigantic, as big as the entire trunk of a tree back in DC. The spidery-looking limb stretched upward beside others just like it, sprawling above to one mammoth tree that branched out hundreds of feet above.

It was then that she noticed how dark it had grown. She wondered where the sun had gone.

"It's okay, take a few minutes to get your bearings," Rome said, pulling a bottled water from the backpack he carried. "The jungle's a tricky place when you're here for the first time."

"Tell me about it," she said, taking the bottle he offered and drinking. "Where'd the sun go?"

Rome chuckled as he nodded to the others to keep moving ahead.

"The trees branch out at the very top, forming a canopy of sorts that allows a minimal amount of sunlight onto the forest floor. These are called buttress roots," he said, stomping his booted foot on the root she'd tripped over.

"Guess I should watch where I'm going, huh?" She smiled, handing him back his bottle.

"I'm not going to let anything happen to you," he said seriously. "I know you're worried about all this and still trying to figure out your place, but I need you to trust me."

Looking up into his eyes, she couldn't help but feel the love she had for this man swelling in her chest. "You've been telling me to trust you since the first time I met you."

"You'd think you'd get the hint by now." He smiled.

She loved his smile, loved the way it put a light in his dark brown eyes. She'd seen that light much more often in the days since the weight of finding his parents' killer had been lifted from his shoulders. He still had other worries, she knew, as a leader of his people; that was justified. But he definitely seemed happier now. Kalina liked to think she'd played a part in that.

"I trust you, Rome. I trust you with my life."

He kissed her hard and quick. "Good. Now let's go before they get to the Gungi ahead of us."

"We're not in the Gungi yet?" she asked holding his hand and trying to keep up with his gait.

"No, this is the rain forest, but it's not the Gungi. Our land is concealed deep within the recesses of the forest so that tourists and poachers can't easily find us."

She nodded. "It's hidden well. I have absolutely no idea where I'm going."

Rome chuckled. "Then I'll have to bring you here more often so you can get to know your homeland."

Her homeland. Kalina wasn't so sure about that.

That night with the sounds of the jungle echoing around her, Kalina lay on a cot next to Rome. They were in a hut, one of the larger ones in the village with as many of the modern amenities as one could expect in the middle of a rain forest.

Sheer netting covered the cot to keep away the mosquitoes and other insects that shared this living space. She'd had a full night of meeting various Elders and speaking with the women of the Topètenia tribe.

Elisa, one of the younger jaguar shifters, had come to the table where Rome and Kalina sat with the Elder Alamar for dinner. They'd eaten on the Elders' Grounds, which to Kalina's shock was not Elder Alamar's personal lodgings. The Elders' Grounds was a huge hut divided into two halves. On the one side was the temple where the Elders met and prayed for guidance; that side was sacred. The other half was a large space with heavy tables made of cut and sanded wood and benches designed for special occasions. Apparently, announcing the joining ceremony for a stateside Faction Leader was a pretty big deal.

Elisa was garbed in what Kalina'd learned was the traditional outfit for female shifters—a soft leather top with intricate and colorful beadwork that looked like an elaborately decorated bikini top, and a matching skirt that put Kalina in mind of a rap video dancer. She noticed that this was the attire for younger female shifters, while the older women opted for more flowing cotton sarong-type dresses. None of them wore pants—which for Kalina was a huge issue.

"The joining will be tomorrow night when there is a full moon," Elisa whispered as they made their way down the aisles of tables toward the front entrance.

"Can we see a full moon from here?" Kalina had asked and quickly felt like a colossal idiot for daring.

Elisa smiled, her skin the color of golden-brown leaves. Her eyes were an intricate mixture of orange and gold, which Kalina figured would transform easily to the eyes of a cat. Her dark hair had been cut viciously to her chin, but it worked for the female Kalina sensed might be just a bit unconventional, even by the forest standards.

"Full moons are beautiful in the Gungi. They are sacred times for commitment and renewal. That is why we have joinings at that time."

She held Kalina's hand and with her other hand pushed through the screened door of the hut so they both could walk through. Once outside Elisa led Kalina down a winding path to another hut. When she stepped inside, Kalina was greeted with a variety of different scents.

"It is purification," Elisa said. "Breathe deeply, let them move throughout your body. It will prepare you."

"Prepare me for what?" Kalina asked while inhaling once more.

"For taking your *companheiro*." This new voice was deeper, raspier, and came from Kalina's left.

Instantly she looked in that direction to see a wide woman with a long graying ponytail that stretched down her back. She was wrapped in dark red material from one shoulder down to her ankles. A thick dusky-tinted shoulder was bare, as well as beefy arms and fingers that folded in front of her generous midsection.

This was an older female, Kalina thought. Not because of her staunch build and webbed eyes, or even the graying hair. It was the look in her eyes, the knowledge stored there that gave her away. She was a woman learned in the ways of the Gungi, one of wisdom whom all females most likely went to for guidance. Kalina didn't know whether to be fearful or thankful to Elisa for bringing her here.

"This is Magdalena. She is a Seer of the Topètenia."

Kalina wanted to ask what a Seer was but something kept her from doing so. Maybe it was the stern way in which the lady, the Seer, was eyeing her. Instead she cleared her throat and said, "You have a lovely place."

Once again she looked around the interior of the hut, which was a filled with candles and incense. There were several tables, some high and some low, all crudely built but sturdy looking. On each was at least one candle along with clay pot burners filled with heating oil. In the far corner of the room there was a fireplace with wood that crackled beneath glowing flames. Along the walls slim sticks jutted from invisible openings, all burning at the tips, filling the space with a spicy aroma.

Alongside another wall hung a dress of flowing white material that was as see-through as a layer of gauze. Along the neckline was more of the intricate beadwork she'd seen on Elisa's top, except this was different. The beads, unlike Elisa's, were not multicolored but gold and frosty white. They bordered the neckline and slim sleeves that grew wider at the bottom. They also sparkled from beneath two layers of wavy solid white material at the very bottom.

Elisa whispered in her ear. "This is the dress you will wear to the joining. It is made by the older women when a joining is announced."

"But he just announced it," she spoke to Elisa, her eyes never leaving the dress, as if the material were somehow calling to her.

Elisa shook her head. "Elder Alamar knew before he left for the States this would be needed."

So he'd known a hell of a lot longer than Kalina had.

"You are Topètenia," Magdalena interrupted. "We believe in loyalty and commitment. Your parents believed and were forever joined."

At the mention of her parents Kalina's heart thumped louder. "Did you know them?" she asked, her voice sounding eager to her own ears. She didn't care. All her life she'd wondered about the people who'd had her and given her up. Wondered why she hadn't been good enough for them and continued to not be good enough for anybody to keep. If this woman and her scent-filled hut had an answer, Kalina wanted to know.

For a moment Magdalena looked as if she wouldn't speak, wouldn't dare tell her about the people who'd created her. Kalina was more than prepared to yell. They'd known about her all along, this tribe of people who'd left her out there alone all her life. They'd known she existed and that someday she'd come back. That's why they'd designed that dress. She'd bet her life savings the dress fit perfectly. It was beautiful and had almost brought tears to her eyes if she weren't still full of so much doubt about belonging here.

Magdalena continued, "They were good and honest. It was not their fault that you could not stay."

"Were they forced to give me up?"

"The choice was never their own. Their lives were soon ending. It was a sacrifice they make to save you, to keep you safe."

"Safe from who? From what?" Rome had told her the Rogue Sabar wanted her, but Kalina wanted to know why.

"You are of natural power, they knew this. They knew others would want that power. In the Gungi they cannot protect you, so you go away." She stood a little straighter, her gaze grabbing hold of Kalina's and refusing to waver. "Now you are back to claim your rightful place as a leader of our people. A leader to walk and fight beside her *companheiro* forevermore."

Something about those words, about the way she spoke them, created a shift inside Kalina. Not the weird kind of shift she'd felt when her cat had taken over, but a welcoming revelation. Words couldn't quite explain it, but her eyes felt brighter; what she could see through them clearer.

"This belonged to her," Magdalena said gruffly, reaching into one of the deep folds of her dress and pulling out a necklace.

She handed the necklace to Elisa, who quickly snapped it around Kalina's neck. Kalina's fingers went instantly to the shiny piece of onyx that hung from the corded string.

"It is the symbol of the Topètenia," Elisa informed her. "The mark of the jaguar."

Inside the circle it did look like the paw of an animal, but it wasn't just the look of it that struck Kalina. It was the feel of it against her fingers, a simmering heat that the cat inside her immediately responded to with a leap.

"I wish I could have known them," she said in a low voice.

Elisa smiled wanly. Magdalena cleared her throat loudly.

Elisa took a step back from Kalina and gave her a more serious look. "As part of the purification, she will cleanse you for the ceremony."

Kalina wasn't sure, but she didn't think she wanted to be cleansed by another woman. At that precise moment a smooth almond-like scent wafted through her nostrils and Kalina's shoulders relaxed.

"It will open your mind," Magdalena said. "You are a shadow but you do not know the Gungi. You do not know our ways or our thinking. I will show you," she finished, moving her body with an agility that shocked Kalina.

When she pulled out a stool and turned to grab one of those clay pots, Elisa came to Kalina's side and guided her to the chair.

Elisa's voice was soft as she spoke. "Do not be afraid, it is customary for the mother to cleanse and prepare her daughter. Your mother is not here, so Magdalena will do it."

When she was in the chair Magdalena pushed the thin straps of the tank top Kalina wore off her shoulders and down to her waist. Kalina's top half was naked, all but the necklace that connected her to these people, to this place. With both her hands Magdalena reached into the clay pot, cupping the liquid inside in her palms.

"Bow your head. Close your eyes," she instructed Kalina. "Think only of your *companheiro*."

Kalina did as she was told, a picture of Rome's face instantly filling her mind as she closed her eyes. The liquid that splashed against her back was hot, but it didn't scorch; it touched her skin and seeped into the pores, into her system.

As Magdalena worked she talked.

"You will hunger for him like no other male in your lifetime. Your body—human and cat—will need him always. This will not go away. He will become yours and you his. No other will ever compare and will most assuredly die for trying to come between you."

Kalina inhaled and exhaled deeply, letting the scents and the feel of Magdalena's hands rubbing up and down her back sink in. Never before had Kalina felt this relaxed, this at ease. And by the end of the session when she'd been stripped naked and completely marinated in the warm oil, she'd thought her languid body would never move again.

Yet now, as she lay in bed with Rome beside her, she was hot and unsettled.

She slipped out of the bed, bare feet padding across the matted ground that served as a floor. She went to a window and looked out into the dark night. Tiny beads of light showed here and there, and she assumed they were eyes of the natives, going about their normal lives. There were several nocturnal species here in the rain forest; Kalina didn't know all of them, but felt an eerie connection to just the same. There were some in the tribe who had homes high up in the trees, but since they were only visiting they'd taken the ground huts, which were guarded like the White House. She didn't see all the shifters that were guarding the circle of about six huts, but she knew they were there, felt their eyes deep in the foliage as she looked out into the night.

"Can't sleep?" Rome asked from behind.

"No. I feel like . . . like I need to do something," she tried to explain but words were failing her. "I want to move, to get out of here, to feel the breeze on my skin. I want . . ." She trailed off, her arms wrapping around her, hands moving up and down over skin that rippled with anticipation.

"She wants to run," he said, coming to stand beside her. "Your cat knows that she's home and she wants to run."

"But I haven't done that since that night. I thought maybe it was a onetime thing for me."

Rome shook his head, running his fingers through her hair then letting them slip down to the nape of her neck. "You're a jaguar shifter, Kalina. Now and forever. She was just giving you time to acquaint yourself with that fact. But now she wants to be free."

Kalina inhaled deeply, loving the smell of the damp air, the scents of the forest. Closing her eyes, she tried to accept Rome's words.

"Reach for her and she'll tell you what she wants," he said.

"How?"

"Just concentrate. She's a part of you, so you'll understand her better than anyone else. You have to learn to co-exist. You'll recognize her signals and she'll recognize yours."

Keeping her eyes closed, Kalina reached for that other entity she knew was there. And as if she'd opened a door the cat emerged with power and regality that simmered throughout Kalina's body. She was a sleek cat, long and lean, with a strong body, a rich golden coat, and vivid black rosettes. Her eyes were yellow-gold and shimmered at Kalina with recognition.

She gasped at the familiarity and reached out. They were one and the same, kindred spirits in different forms. Slinking into her mind, the cat stretched and yawned, and Kalina sensed her need. Her eyes opened and she stared at Rome. "She wants to run."

Chapter 30

Even the rain here in the forest was different. Its smell was refreshing, cleansing. The sound it made as it trickled through the canopy, sluicing over vegetation to puddle on the already sodden ground, was almost musical. She'd run as fast as she could, pawed feet clomping over the soaked foliage on the ground. Her claws had extended as she climbed the tree and walked along its branches. Over rock formations, through brush she ran, startling the inhabitants as she went. Monkeys screeched, their little mouths opening wide with surprise. Snakes hissed, vampire bats shrieked. And Kalina's cat ran as if she were free for the first time in her life. When she'd gone as far as she could with her heart pounding right through her flanks, she fell to the side on a large rock and just lay there. Her eyes opened and closed and opened and closed as the rain-blurred scenery wavered in front of her.

"Feels good doesn't it?"

She lifted her head, saw Rome through her golden cat's eyes, and growled low in her throat.

He only chuckled, his dark skin beaded with droplets of rain. He'd probably run behind her, his cat that is, since he still didn't think he could leave her alone for long periods of time. It was the *comapnheiro calor*—that's what Magdalena had called the deep hunger she was experiencing. It would subside only after the first birthing. Something Kalina wasn't so certain she was looking forward to. She'd barely just accepted Rome and his presence in her life before he'd thrust this shifting business on her. To be fair, he couldn't have thrust this on her even if he'd tried. Shifters weren't like vampires; they couldn't turn a human into one of them through a bite.

Shifters were born either pure or mixed breed. There had to be a coupling of male and female—either or both being a shifter—to birth a shifter. She knew that now, just as she knew her parents had been powerful joined shifters.

"I used to run through here as a cub. Nothing I've done in my life since then has matched the feeling."

Rome reached out and stroked the long length of her tail. She nipped at him, only to have him slap playfully at the top of her head.

"You're home now, Kalina. This is where you belong."

With a long stretch and her human half demanding her presence be known, the cat that lounged on the rock shifted to the now naked female with fire in her eyes.

"This is not my home." She tossed the words with the tightness she felt in her chest. "It's yours."

Kalina was still so confused. Although the time with Magdalena had opened her eyes to the people her parents were and what was expected of her, she still wasn't 100 percent sure. And for Kalina, being certain was important. For so long she'd waited to belong somewhere, to someone, to be a part of something special. All this had happened so fast, she was too jaded to simply believe.

"It is ours. We are both Shadow Shifters. You know that now" was Rome's serious reply.

"I know that I am not who or what I thought I was." And that was the honest truth. She was not Kalina Harper, the orphan who'd become a cop and lived a solitary life, not anymore.

"And that's a bad thing?"

She sighed, rubbing both hands over her wet hair. "It's just something I guess I'll have to get used to."

"Why won't you let me help you?"

"Because I don't need any help. I don't need anything."

He touched one finger to her chin, tilting her head up to face him. "But you do, *gato*. You need me. And I need you."

The truth to his words only heated her more. "I need to find me."

"You aren't lost. You're right here where you belong. You only need to let go of everything you thought you knew, you thought you were, and embrace what is. This is why you never belonged, Kalina, why you never fit in with anyone back in the States. Because you belonged here, to the Gungi. It's been running in your blood all these years, begging you to accept your heritage."

"I just can't believe this."

"You can because you know who they were," he said lifting the piece that hung from her necklace. "And you know it in here."

Rome tapped lightly on her chest with his fingertips, then let them slide down to feather over one turgid nipple. "In your heart you know where you belong."

She sighed, arching her back to welcome his touch.

"And you know now to whom you belong."

Without warning Kalina moved toward him, using her palms to push against his chest until he fell back on the rock she'd just been lying on.

What she knew right now was what she wanted. Under the dark cover of night she wanted her mate. Her pussy pulsated, swollen lips dripping with arousal. Her breasts were heavy, nipples painfully erect. What she wanted was right here and she planned to take every inch of it.

Rome watched her steadily, his hands reaching up to cup her face.

"My *gato inferno*," he whispered. She let the endearment roll over her body, let the hunger of the cat take over.

With long, slow strokes she licked at his chest, felt the ridge of his pectoral muscles, the tight bud of his nipple beneath her tongue. She moved along slowly over the ridges of his abs, determined to taste every inch of him. From above the rain tickled her back, provided a slight reprieve to the heat boiling inside her.

Moving down his torso, she licked at his muscled thighs, loved the light sprinkle of hair that tickled her lips as she did. His erection was thick, long, hard, and as she moved along she loved the feel of it on her cheek, over her face, whispering past her lips. Her fingers roamed, touching lightly the base of his dick then moving down to coddle the heavy sack of his balls. Dipping her head lower she put the sack into her mouth, moved each one over her tongue, suckled deep, then released and licked again.

Rome was groaning low, the sound mingling with that of the jungle and the light pitter-patter of the rain. Her tongue continued its assault until her thirst for more brought her mouth upward to his thick length. She licked him from the base to the tip like a fudge ice cream pop. Her tongue stroked over him hungrily, drinking in the scent of their union as she did. His hands were in her hair now, pulling the short strands, gripping her head, guiding her to take him deep. She didn't want that just yet, was content to lick him for a little longer.

When her tongue slid over the tip she paused, pressed into the tiny slit of his dick, loving the taste of his arousal as it slid smoothly over her tongue.

Rome's hips jutted forward at the sensations ripping through him. Moving his hands to her shoulders, he pulled her away from his dick before he exploded right then.

When she looked up at him in question he simply shook his head. "You little temptress. Now I've got to punish you for that stunt."

Kalina licked her lips slowly. "Punish me, huh? I'm so afraid."

"Oh, it's not fear you're going to feel, baby. Nothing but pleasure for you, I promise."

Lifting himself up off the rock, Rome turned Kalina so that her palms splayed along the smooth, wet surface. With his palm to her back, he pushed her forward. Spreading her legs, he sank his length into her with one deft stroke. She hissed then turned to cast him a satisfied glare over her shoulder.

His *gato inferno,* he thought as his thrusts began. She was tight and hot and sweet as hell as he fucked her here, in their home, in the Gungi. His palms smacked the wet cheeks of her bottom as she thrust back to meet his deep stroking. And just when Rome felt the first tremors of her thighs, knew she was about to come, he pulled out.

Falling to his knees, he moved his face between her legs to lick and stroke her plump folds, capturing her release into his mouth with a satisfied groan.

"My turn," she whispered once her release had racked through her body not once, but twice, and his mouth continued to feast on her.

Moving out of his grasp, she found his still-burgeoning arousal and took the length into her mouth, suckling hard and deep continuously until he was roaring in the air with the other night animals. His release came in thick hot spurts that she took wantonly, loving the essence of him moving through her body.

Lying on the damp floor of the forest, they caught their breaths and stared up into the night.

"I love you," Rome said, reaching for her hand.

Kalina would never know if it was his words, or the oils Magdalena had used to cleanse her, or her mother's necklace, or the scent of the Gungi itself. At this moment it didn't really matter what one thing had pushed her over the edge of indecision. None of it mattered anymore.

She let his fingers wrap around hers, relishing the feeling, the sense of belonging that filled her so completely. The Gungi was not only a place, it was the birthplace of her parents, it was where the man she loved originated. It was her home. And she was a Shadow Shifter; her cat lying languorously sated inside her proved that point.

"I love you, too," she admitted out loud for the first time.

Seconds later they both shifted, running through the forest, beneath the sheets of rain now dropping around them, finally free.

Epilogue

Nick heard the night sounds and cringed at the thought that Aryiola was out there somewhere. He had no doubt that Sabar had taken her, if not personally then by orchestrating the mission.

He wished to hell Kalina would have shot his ass that night in the row house. But she'd frozen, a mixture of fear and confusion at what had happened around her taking control. He understood but still wished Sabar were dead. Then he couldn't have taken Aryiola, he couldn't have touched the one thing in Nick's life that he couldn't control.

Getting up, he went outside, let his cat rip free, and charged into the depths of the jungle, roaring his displeasure as he went. He hoped Sabar was near and heard him, prayed that fucker knew he was coming for him. Because Nick vowed not to leave the jungle again without the woman he loved.

It was dark but at least it was clean. The last hut reeked of
filth, body odor, and other less appealing things. When
they'd stuffed that gag into her mouth, Ary had wanted to
vomit, and when she'd seen him, she'd wanted to kill.

Sabar Tavares, adopted son of Elder Julio and Maria
Sabien Tavares. A Topètenia shifter who should have
walked in his parents' footsteps, striving to enforce peace
and equality amongst their kind. Instead he was doing
this. Again.

And this time she was his target.

Ary had heard of him before; she'd seen him in the
village throughout the years before he left for good
about six years ago. After that she'd only heard of what

he was doing and even that was just whispers. Nobody wanted to be caught talking about the Shadow who'd gone Rogue.

Now he was back and he was holding her captive. Why, Ary had no idea, but she knew it couldn't be anything good.

This new location was an old building. She'd seen a little through the blindfold she'd managed to loosen by rubbing her head against the cab of the truck they transported her in. It was a dilapidated shack once used to mix the drugs that were eventually shipped out of the forest and sold. They were beyond the Gungi now, on the other side of the river through the thick brush that was good for hiding drug houses such as this one. The boards around her creaked and had slats missing from the walls. But it was covered with a huge, dark-colored tarp that kept the elements out and whatever unlawfulness that was going on inside in.

They'd dragged her through one large room, her legs slapping against table legs that wobbled and fell. The racket they'd created was deafening, but they were so far out there was no one to hear. They could do whatever they wanted to her out here and she could scream until her lungs dried of air, but nobody would hear her. Nobody would come to her rescue.

Ary inhaled deeply, exhaled slowly. Her chest hurt with the action because they'd kicked her when she fell to the ground. She'd done so hoping to roll out of their reach, but one grabbed her up, throwing her over his massive shoulder. The other had tied her ankles and hands, and when she'd screamed a string of obscenities at them, they'd gagged her. She suspected the bruise to her face came when they dropped her to the floor and she'd landed painfully on her cheek. But after Sabar's directive, they'd moved her a little more carefully this time around.

She was still tied up so escape wasn't going to be easy. The disgusting gag was thankfully gone, left on the floor in the first hut where Sabar had thrown it. And they'd taken the blindfold off, probably figuring she couldn't see much. But her cat could see everything. If she could just get outside, she could figure out her exact location, shift, and go home. Or she could just shift.

The idea had come to her many times since they'd taken her. Shift into a jaguar, kill her assailants, and call it a day. Then what? The bodies would be found; autopsies would prove a vicious predator had taken their lives. Humans would be outraged and pour into the forest looking to shoot anything on four legs. It would be like leading the lamb to slaughter, something she would never do to her people.

But she would escape, there was no way in hell Sabar Tavares would have the satisfaction of killing her. That's what she assumed this was all about. After all, killing was what Sabar was best known for.

Closing her eyes to that thought, Ary let her head fall back against the rickety wall, felt spears of loose wood sticking into her scalp but didn't care. She needed to think, needed to figure out what to do.

Only when her eyes closed, the one thing Ary saw, the single person appearing in her mind wasn't Sabar or her other two captors. It was Nick. The only man to hold her and her heart captive and live to tell about it.